Faerie Dust

by

Linda Ciletti

Edited by Gallagher Editorial Services
Cover by Ittelical Designs
Ittelical Press

Books by Linda Ciletti

Hearts of Faerie Series

Faerie Dust
Book One

Faerie Knights
Book Two

Faerie Dreams
Book Three

Other Romantic Adventures

Draegon's Lair
Medieval

KnightStalker
Contemporary Time Travel

Dream of the Archer
Medieval Time Travel

Lady Quest
Humorous Medieval

Dedicated to Cast in Bronze
Frank Della Penna

Whose beautiful carillon music inspired me to write
Faerie Dust and served as my muse.

Songs that inspired me:
Rotation
Lullaby of the Lost
Red Earth
Things Running From Me
Summer Guests
Pavane for an Angel
The Hunt

Thank You
Greensburg Writers Group
for your valuable critiques and support.

Prologue

Faerie, Galandore Palace

Tazia paced the expanse of her private solar, her bejeweled gown sweeping the floor behind her. She turned to face the two guards kneeling before her. "Where is my nephew this time?" she bellowed. "If no one else, surely Alasdair has told you two about his latest escapade?" She set a hard gaze on Alasdair's two closest friends. "Rise and tell me what I wish to know. Where is he?"

Lysander nudged Gideon and coughed. They both stood, adjusted their swords, and faced their Queen.

"Well?" Tazia prompted, her hands firmly on her hips.

Gideon lifted his chin and met her hard stare. "I cannot, My Queen. He said naught to us." He raked his fingers through his hair, pushing the dark waves back. "We are as concerned as you."

Tazia's glare narrowed.

"In truth, My Queen. He said naught," Lysander confirmed.

Tazia ran a measuring look from one guard to the other. When neither yielded, she spun away and began to pace. "Well, he had better return for my daughter's wedding, or I will—I will—" She sucked in a breath. A hot flush rose up her neck.

Lysander and Gideon held their breath.

"Oh!" Tazia huffed. "Never mind what I will do." She crossed the solar to stand before a tall and ornate gilded mirror. Her gaze fixed on her reflection and the multitude of gemstones dotting her hair. After patting her carefully coiffed locks into place, she turned to face the two guards once more. "Should you see him, remind him that the wedding is less than a sennight away and, as part of the royal family, he is expected …" She stepped closer to the guards, her cold gaze locked with theirs. "… nay, *required* to be there." She waved a dismissive hand. "Now go."

Lysander spoke. "Would you have us search for him?"

"Nay. The outer realms are far too treacherous. By the Creator, I did warn him about entering such dangerous territory. The dragons, the trolls, the sprites. Where gets he this passion to explore? One day, he will surely meet his end there." She closed her eyes and lifted the back of her hand to her forehead as though she would swoon. A spiral of dark chestnut hair fell over her fingers.

Lysander knew better than to believe she would actually faint. Her theatrics were well documented amongst the fae. She was far too strong to swoon and far too cold to care. But she lived by formality, and Alasdair needed to be at his cousin's wedding.

Tazia's hand dropped. Her eyes turned suddenly alert and hard. "Leave me!" she ordered. She turned her back on the two guards, the jewels on her cerulean gown catching the breaking sun as it slipped through the east windows, casting a rainbow of light on the walls. "I have much to do in preparation for the nuptials."

Both guards bowed, then quickly left the room. When they reached the outer walls, Gideon spoke. "Where think you he went?" he asked as they hurried down the stone palace stairs.

Lysander shook his head, his long blond hair, pulled back and secured at the nape, reflecting the golden light of dawn. "I know not, but I have a suspicion." He and Gideon exchanged a look.

"Oh, nay," Gideon refuted. "He knows 'tis strictly forbidden."

"Aye."

When they reached the lower garden, away from prying ears, Lysander stopped suddenly and turned to Gideon. "But ponder this. Is it not odd the bond Alasdair has formed with the human child?"

"Sachi?"

Lysander nodded.

"Aye, it perplexes me as well. All in the realm know not to bond with humans," Gideon said. "Especially one who is slated to be tithed."

Lysander chuckled. "'Haps someone should have deemed to tell Alasdair."

Gideon scoffed. His eyes narrowed in frustration. "Alasdair is quite aware of the law."

"'Haps he merely went to fulfill his curiosity regarding humans," Lysander offered. "Surely his relationship with Sachi has further whetted that."

A silence fell between them. Suddenly Gideon's eyes lit. "Think you he went in search of the changeling?"

Lysander's jaw dropped. "But—but—" he stammered. "'Tis treason."

"Think you his bond with this child is so strong that he would commit treason?"

Lysander thought a moment, then nodded. "I dare to wager 'tis that strong. Never in all these centuries have I seen him tutor a tithe or teach one to sing the songs of the fae. But I have seen Alasdair teach Sachi when he thought no one was looking. Doting on her as a father on a daughter."

"Foolish boy to become so involved," Gideon muttered.

"Boy? He is only slightly younger than you and I."

Again silence.

"But he is like a brother to me," Lysander finally said. "An impetuous younger brother. And a good friend. I cannot allow him to do something so foolish that it will reap punishment from Tazia." He smiled wryly. "Or at least to be caught at it." Gideon nodded. "Nor I. But I swear, if Tazia does not kill him, I just may."

Lysander laughed. "We must seek him out."

Gideon kicked hard at the dirt. "We cannot enter the human world without Tazia's permission. She would have our heads should we be caught." He sighed. "We are the law; we cannot act against it."

"But we *can* keep watch for him along the border of the realm, can we not? 'Tis not the same as seeking out." Lysander's visage fell. "But which border?"

Gideon cupped his chin in thought. "There are but two ways to return from the unknown world, the Trenalyn Gate and the Galandorian Gate. He will not attempt the Galandorian Gate. It sits in the central market, and he knows 'tis always guarded on this side. He would surely be caught and brought before the Queen."

"Which means he will return by the Trenalyn Gate and then through either the dark swamp or Sprite Wood." Lysander swallowed. "But the trolls?"

"They are lax in their watch over the gate, so confident they are that a fae would not dare attempt such a foolish act."

Lysander snorted. "They do not know Alasdair."

4

Chapter One

Human World

A cloud of shimmering dust wafted over him. Alasdair felt himself grow to human proportion, felt the distinct air of human existence fill his lungs. He released a ragged breath.

Human. It was the last thing he wanted to be, but what choice had he? Somewhere in this world was the one thing that could save Sachi, and if to find it, he had to transform himself, then that was what he would do.

It was why he'd risked leaving Faerie without the queen's consent. Why he'd not confided his plan with even his two closest friends, Lysander and Gideon. They were the queen's guards. If things went awry, he did not want them involved. The quicker and stealthier he carried out his plan, the better.

Alasdair pondered his furtive leave from Faerie. Slipping through the portal gate had not been easy. Always there stood guards at the gate betwixt Faerie and the human realm—two worlds once similar, now different as night and day, yet parallel. But he had outwitted the sentries, had timed the changing of the guards to the second—discovered a small measure of time when he could slip through unseen.

Returning to Galandore would be the challenge.

Alasdair drew a second handful of dust from his pouch. Another sprinkle and his gossamer wings fell away. His faerie garb transformed to that of a human—blue jeans, a white button-down shirt, and white leather travel shoes that laced up the front. The strange-cut cloth felt odd at first, but soon he grew accustomed to its feel, in part if not fully.

He had but a sennight to find the changeling and return to Faerie. Sachi would soon turn five summers—the age when she would be handed over to the trolls and tithed to Hell. Her life would be forfeit if he failed.

He could not fail.

His chest ached at the thought. He knew not why he felt compassion for the youngling. In truth, faeries had little empathy for humans. But he was unlike the others. He felt. He cared. Despite Sachi being human, he loved her as a father loves a daughter and, as a caring father, he would do all that he could to save her.

He ran his plan through his head. It was simple enough. All he need do is find and return the changeling to the world to which it belonged, set it in Sachi's place, then steal Sachi away to her own world where she would be free to live out her brief human life as the Creator had intended.

But to steal away a tithe was treason, and the cost of treason was high should he be caught.

He sighed. It mattered not. Whatever the cost, he would face it. What he could not face was Sachi's death.

Pain radiated in his temples. He was drowning in his thoughts. Drawing breath, he set them aside to commit the woodland to memory. One step at a time, he told himself. Firstly, he needed to find the changeling. Then he needed to find his way back to this exact location in the wood to return to Faerie.

The town of Oak Meadows sat just beyond the woodlands. It was where the child/changeling exchange had taken place four years past. It was where he would find what he was seeking.

He noted the pattern of the trees, the thickness of the foliage, the density of the undergrowth—so overgrown he could scarcely see the circle of mushrooms surrounding him. Leaves whispered on the wind. The twitter of birds carried through the overhead branches. He filled his lungs with the forest's scent. It smelled like home. Like Galandore—the capitol city of Faerie that sat nestled between lush forests, clear waterways, and mountains.

But this wasn't Faerie. This was the human world. A world he had visited only once before under the watchful eye of the elders and exalted royal guards. A world in some ways much like his, but different. He again drew breath, savoring the essence of the forest. It was a wonder to find such woodland perfection in this modern human realm. So little still existed.

Humans! He scoffed. What knew they of faeries? Only that which had been passed down through myth—slightly exaggerated or lacking truth. But he knew much about the human race. Humans and their wars, their hatred and crime. Humans who destroyed entire populations through ignorance, vanity, and greed. It was no wonder the faeries chose to live in secret. There was a time when humans and faeries lived side by side. But no longer was there a future alongside the human race. He often wondered if there was a future *for* them.

~*~

Leisa smiled up at her niece and ward who climbed excitedly on the playground monkey bars. This would be her's and Sybil's first full summer together since the car accident.

Her smile faded. Her sister, a single parent only three years older than her own twenty-five years, had left this world far too soon.

Tears fogged her vision. She shifted sideways on the wooden park bench to hide them. Sybil's pain of losing her mother was still too fresh. Leisa didn't want to open that wound again—not when Sybil's grief was finally on the mend.

Drawing a tissue from the oversized purse on her lap, Leisa dabbed her eyes dry. It had been a difficult year dealing with her grief as well as that of her niece. Sybil had been devastated at the loss of her mother, crying inconsolably far into the night. After six months, the weeping subsided. After eight months, they picked up the pieces and moved on as best they could. Twelve months had now passed and Sybil was finally behaving like a normal five-year-old.

"Aunt Leis!" Sybil called from her perch.

Leisa tucked the tissue back into her purse. She turned and faced Sybil who sat on top of the monkey bars, her pale blonde hair glimmering in the dappled afternoon sun as it filtered through the canopy of trees shading the play area. Her faltered smile lifted. She waved at her niece and blew her a kiss. Sybil would be starting kindergarten in the fall. Leisa had never seen a child more eager to go to school. Sybil was ready. More than ready.

Satisfied her niece was safe and happily playing, Leisa settled comfortably on the bench, pulled a slightly worn paperback out from her purse, and prepared to read. A wash of sun streamed over her. She closed her eyes and lifted her face to its warmth—a warmth that would surely gift her with a few more freckles. It was days like this that made her glad of her career choice. Being a teacher was the most rewarding profession she could imagine. But as much as she loved her job, she loved her three-month summer reprieve even more—loved the warm weather, the longer days, and the woodland park not far from her apartment.

She drew a deep breath, inhaling the woodsy scent of the surrounding trees. Then she tossed her long red hair back over her shoulders and began to read. An easy, fun summer read. During the school year, there hadn't been time for pleasure reading. Teaching and caring for her niece had consumed every spare moment. But now it was a week into June. She had three months to catch up on her to-be-read list.

As she began reading Chapter Three, a sense of unease crept over her. She paused. Something was wrong. She peered over the rumpled pages of her book to where her niece had been playing only moments before. Branches of several tall oaks stretched out over that corner of the lot, the resulting shadow and sunlight stippling the ground beneath the monkey bars. The monkey bars sat empty. Leisa lowered the book to her lap. Where was Sybil? She shot a concerned look over the playground sandboxes, pausing at each tow-headed child in search of Sybil's familiar face.

Nothing.

Leisa stood up from the bench, her anxious gaze fixed on the play area. After blindly shoving the book back into her purse, she swung the purse's long strap over her head and across her chest; then she ventured farther into the squealing fray of children. "Sibby!" she called. She scanned the swings, the slide, and again the monkey bars.

All came up empty.

Two heavy plastic playhouses rested in the corner of the lot next to the woods. Leisa frantically called out Sybil's name as she approached one. "Are you in here?" She poked her head through the first playhouse doorway. Three young girls sat inside. All three turned at Leisa's query with a look of affront that she dared to disturb their tea party. None was Sybil.

Her heart began to race. "Sibby, answer me," she called as she approached the second playhouse, the panic in her tone frightening her all the more. She had just checked on her niece not two paragraphs ago. How could Sybil have disappeared so quickly?

Leisa pulled open the creaky plastic door of the Victorian style playhouse and looked inside. Empty. As she drew back, a familiar object caught her eye. It was wedged under the ivory, fold-down plastic table, its soft cloth body limp on the floor, its yellow yarn hair mussed. Her breath caught as she dropped to her knees and gave the cloth object a sharp pull, crushing its wings. It was Sybil's favorite rag doll, a fairy doll she had pleaded for for months—a doll she would not have parted with willingly.

Hugging the doll to her chest, Leisa raced to the border of the woods. "Sibby!" she screamed into the dense woodland. Tears again welled in her eyes. She wiped them dry with her sleeve and headed into the trees, scanning the forest floor for clues as she ran. Few ventured into the heavily-forested area so there was no clear path, which made the trail of flattened grass look frighteningly suspicious. "Sibby, answer me!" she called again, then murmured, "Please."

She tucked the doll into her purse and listened. Children squawked and screeched in the play lot at her back. She struggled to hear past that for a familiar voice.

At first she heard only the soft rustle of leaves as the June breeze swept through the foliage; then a dim cry answered her call, achingly faint and in the distance. *Aunt Leis* was all it said, then fell to dreaded silence.

No! Leisa felt her heart near to bursting. *Not again.* She had lost one child. She would not lose another. "Sybil!" she screamed into the shadowed woodland, her hand deep in her purse as she rummaged through its contents for her cell phone. When she pulled it out, her heart sank. No service.

"Damn!"

She dug deeper still into the black hole of her handbag. Finally she located the small taser that she carried for protection. Wrapping her fingers about its grip, she drew it out and cupped it in the palm of her hand; then she raced farther into the trees, following the trail of trampled grass.

~*~

Alasdair stepped out from the ring of mushrooms. As he prepared to make his way to Oak Meadows, the woodland suddenly quieted. He paused and listened, his ears perked at a noise out of place in the heavy woodlands—not a bird, nor beast, nor rustling leaves.

A timid voice carried in the crisp forest air—a terrified cry, then frail weeping. A frightened child.

He could smell the fear.

Another voice followed—harsh, dark, oppressing. It muzzled the first; then all sound once again fell to dreaded silence. Suddenly the forest seemed a dark and foreboding place.

Alasdair pondered the wisdom of getting involved. He was here to retrieve the changeling. Naught else. Getting involved in human affairs was ill advised. But something about the terrified cry touched him and he could not walk away.

Instead he followed the scent of fear through the towering trees and twisted brush until he came to a trail of flattened grass. Alasdair paused to catch his breath. Again he listened. Heavy footsteps sounded in the distance. He spun to chase after them and stumbled. The transformation had left him weak. He needed time to adjust.

There was no time. The thudding steps began to fade.

Alasdair hissed a frustrated breath. The only way to help the youngling was to race ahead and block the man's escape. He could not do that staying on the path.

He studied the jagged curve of a miniscule trail, then sprinted back into the trees. The undergrowth was thick and he struggled to push his way through.

Too slow. Too slow.

Just when he thought he would never catch up, the undergrowth thinned and he hurried forward through a grassy copse of trees until he found himself ahead of his quarry. His cheek burned where pointed foliage had swiped his face. He brushed the pain aside and listened.

Footsteps approached.

Alasdair sucked in a breath and steeled himself for confrontation. Soon the air grew chokingly thick as an aura visible only to him rounded the path and filled the air with a muddied grey hopelessness—and in its center stood a burly man—one thick arm clamped about a small tow-headed child, his free hand covering her mouth.

"Hold!" Alasdair commanded.

The large human stopped and glowered. Alasdair knew the man would not easily concede.

"Release the child," Alasdair ordered in his most authoritative tone. He drew himself straight to belie how compromised the transformation had left him.

"Back off," the man warned. His hold tightened on the girl and she squealed.

"I said, release her," Alasdair repeated.

Faeries were often thought to be frail creatures of the wood. They were not. Faeries were wily and smart and carried in their souls the magic of the ages. No human, hulking or otherwise, could best a faerie.

But he was human now, and would be until the setting of the sun. In truth, in this post transformation state, he would be no match against this child-napping beast.

He paused at the realization and staggered back. Then his gaze fell to the child's pleading eyes, eyes that held the same innocence as Sachi's, and he knew he could not walk away. His only chance of besting the man was to take him by surprise.

Alasdair lunged forward and grabbed for the girl.

"Fool!" the man growled. He yanked the child out of Alasdair's reach and swung a solid fist into the side of his head.

Alasdair staggered back. Pain ripped through him and he doubled over, then sank to the path. The scent of dewy moss and composted earth filled his nose and lungs just before a booted foot struck his gut. Air burst from him with such force that he thought never again to breathe. Then instinct kicked in and he sucked in a painful breath. His thoughts flew to calling on the magic of the fae, but he was no longer one with the faerie world.

Again he heard a scream. He looked up and saw the human beast moving away, the girl secured in his grasp.

Alasdair clutched his side and forced himself to stand. "Release her!" he called as he stumbled after them.

The man turned to face Alasdair. "Ain't you had enough?" he growled.

"Never!" Alasdair watched the man fling the girl into the bole of a tree, saw her fall limp in the grass. Hatred filled his gut, and he knew then what it was to be human. Again he lunged, striking the man. Pain shot up his arm. A ferocious punch knocked him to the ground.

"This time you ain't following me. You ain't following nobody." The man drew a knife from his belt and raised it for a strike. Then he cried out, convulsed, and toppled over.

"You okay, baby?" Alasdair heard in the near distance. It was a woman's voice, soft and feminine, sweet like the songs of faerie nights—yet distorted with fear. He turned his head to look at her. Sunlight filtered through the trees, dappling the stark white cloth of her blouse and the autumn red hair that fell softly over slender shoulders. Her pleasingly heart-shaped face was smooth and lightly freckled and for a fleeting second he thought her a woodland sprite who had taken human form.

She knelt on one knee before the youngling, brushed the girl's tousled hair back from her face, then reached for her. He could see the woman trembling despite her calm façade.

The child moaned. "Uh-huh." Her small arms lifted to wrap about the woman's neck.

"And you? Are you okay?" Clutching the child to her, the woman approached him, her clear olive eyes watchful and worried—and glistening with unspent tears. Her voice sounded husky with concern. She cocked her head slightly, waiting for an answer. Despite the low forest light, the movement set her hair to gleam like flame.

"I deem so." He wasn't sure, but it seemed the correct answer. What was okay for a human anyway?

The woman nodded, forced a smile, then turned away. He watched as she pried the child's arms from around her neck and, after whispered words he could not discern, set the child down; then she slid off her belt. Though her hands shook, she managed to pull the unconscious man's arms behind his back where she wrapped the belt around his wrists. Bending one of his legs at the knee, she snaked the belt through the laces of his boot and tightly buckled it. "That should hold you until the police come," she said to the unconscious man.

She turned her attention back to the girl.

Alasdair sat up and rubbed his head. "The youngling. Is she hurt?" he asked.

The woman set a curious look on him. "Youngling?"

"Child."

"She's shaken, but okay," the woman answered. She tucked the girl's hair behind her ears to further study her. "She's got a nasty bruise on her temple. I'll have to get that checked."

Alasdair stood. He wiped a spattering of blood from his lip with his sleeve. "I am sorry. I tried—"

"Big as you are, you didn't stand a chance." She hefted the girl up in her arms.

"And you? How did you best him so easily?"

"Taser. A girl's gotta protect herself." She looked down at the bundle in her arms, her eyes watery and bright.

Alasdair knew she was more shaken than she let on.

"Or in this case, the one she loves," she continued. She took several steps, stumbling with the added weight on uneven terrain.

Alasdair held out his arms. "Please, allow me."

The woman gave him a wary look, then her gaze softened. "Are you sure? You seem a bit shaky on your feet."

Alasdair suppressed a laugh. It was she who was shaky on *her* feet. "I am fine," he replied.

She hesitated; then she whispered something in the young girl's ear and handed her over to him. "It's okay, Sibby," she assured the child. "I'm right here with you."

Alasdair secured the young girl against his shoulder. "How did he—"

"We were at the playground," the woman replied, anticipating his question. "I was reading and she was in the far corner on the monkey bars."

"Monkey bars?" Alasdair caught her disbelieving look. "I am sorry, I am not from this country."

The woman managed a faint, but honest smile. "It's a bunch of bars welded together for kids to climb on—like monkeys."

"Ah." Alasdair knew puzzlement still covered his face, but he allowed her to continue, holding questions back for another time.

"Anyway, I was reading a book while she played. One minute I looked up and she was there, and the next she was gone. Just like that. I ran to the border of the woods. That's when I heard her scream. The rest is—well, you know. I chased after her until I found you two fighting." She pointed to the still unconscious man.

"How did you know 'twas not *I* who took her?"

A faint smile touched her lips. "'You ain't following me. You ain't following nobody.' Had you taken her, you wouldn't be following anyone. You'd be running."

15

Alasdair smiled at her deduction, then looked down at the frightened bundle in his arms. Soft, golden hair veiled the youngling's face and rested on his shoulder. Small, warm hands clung about his neck. A sudden flash of Sachi's face entered his thoughts, her childish innocence, and the deadly fate Queen Tazia had in store for her. His throat clenched and he swallowed hard to gain his voice. "Is she your child?" he asked as they made their way down the trail of flattened grass toward the playground.

An unexpected sadness crossed the woman's face. "Yes and no. She's my niece. My sister passed away last year. She was a single parent. There was no one else." Her chin briefly quivered, then calmed. "By the way, I'm Leisa Vandermann. And the little girl you're carrying is Sybil."

She smiled, and he wondered how much more brilliant her smile would be had the shadow of a near crisis not hung over her. Perhaps, he thought, there was beauty in the human world after all. Perhaps there was love and kindness and joy.

When they reached the play area, Leisa held out her arms. "I'll carry her from here. I need to find a cop and turn that guy in, then take her to the hospital and have that bruise checked."

"Are you sure you can support her?" Alasdair asked.

Leisa nodded.

He handed Sybil over to her aunt.

"Thanks for all your help." She cradled Sybil against her shoulder. "If you hadn't slowed that guy down, I might never have caught up with him."

Alasdair smiled despite the pain of a cut lip. A genuine smile he thought never to share with humankind. "You are welcome."

Leisa began walking away. She had nearly cleared the play area when Alasdair realized that he hadn't given her *his* name.

"By the way," he called out, quoting her earlier introduction, "I am called Alasdair."

Leisa stopped and turned to face him. "Alas … what?"

"Alasdair. It means 'defender of mankind'."

Leisa smiled warmly. Then she turned away in search of a police officer. "Well," she called over her shoulder. "You certainly lived up to your name today."

Alasdair watched Leisa walk away, her long red hair bright in the full sun. He recalled the perfection of her lightly freckled skin when she'd fully faced him, and her eyes, a deep green like the mosses that surrounded Galandore's River of Tears. He wondered where she lived. If only he could transition back to his true form, he could follow her unseen. In fae form, faeries were small and winged in the unknown world, and rarely seen by the human eye. To those who did not believe, they were a flash in the vision and nothing more.

Stepping onto the main path of the park, he studied the humans around him. Most were plain at best, lacking the physical beauty of the fae. He wondered if his human form mirrored his fae appearance. As he passed a parked truck, he stole a glance in its tall, sideview mirror. A pleased grin crossed his face. He looked much the same as in the faerie realm, minus the luminosity that set the fae apart from humans. The magic of the fae blessed him with a comely shell as it blessed all faeries, resulting in vain creatures who saw themselves as the highest of all that lived. Despite this belief, apart from the twenty-year tithe, they never truly set out to harm anyone. And they knew love amongst themselves, which was why he never understood the changeling practices.

Changeling.

Once again his thoughts centered on his task. To find the changeling and free the human child before it was too late. Alasdair understood the importance of the human offering. It gained the trolls rich mines and the fae eternal life. Trolls and fae alike depended on the twenty-year tithe. However, the trolls could not cross over to the human realm as could faeries. When the fae passed a human child to the trolls, the tithe was paid on both counts and it kept safe the few children of Galandore. He knew his interference could upset the balance, but he could not leave Sachi to a deadly fate. He had to save her.

Alasdair stepped off the curb. A car whizzed by, nearly searing his flesh. Quickly, he jumped back to the walk. This was an unpredictable world, he thought. The sooner he fulfilled his mission, the sooner he could leave. There was nothing in this world that called to him.

Nothing but the smile of Leisa.

Chapter Two

Human World

"Sibby, did you put your pajamas on?" Leisa folded the last of the towels and placed them in the hall linen closet. As she shut the door, she saw Sybil racing down the hall, her long downy hair lifting with the breeze, her fairy rag doll clutched to her chest. Pale blue pajamas dotted with daisies covered her from neck to foot, snug at the ankles and wrists with a wide ribbed band of white.

"Uh-huh, see!" Sybil jumped up and down, setting her golden locks to flutter.

Leisa smiled. "I see. Did you pick out a bedtime story?"

"This one." Sybil held out a large, thin-spined book, its cover green with foliage. A rainbow bled off the outer rim. In the center two fairies hovered facing one another as if conversing.

"Didn't I read a story from that last night?" Leisa asked, wondering when or if Sybil would ever tire of it.

"Uh-huh. I love it!" Sybil handed the book to Leisa and padded toward the kitchen.

Leisa sighed. "I set a snack and milk on the table, Sibby," she called from the small living room. "Bring it in here and I'll read while you eat."

"Okay." Sybil entered the living room and carefully set her milk on the coffee table. Then she hopped onto the sofa next to Leisa and snuggled close, her cookie in hand, her doll nestled at her side.

Leisa spread the book open across her lap and began to read. When Sybil finished her snack and the story ended, Leisa tucked her into bed. She then got comfortable on the sofa to continue reading her own book. The chick-lit she'd started at the park.

The park.

Images of Sybil's abduction flashed in her mind. Again she felt a sinking in her chest. Thank God for the dark-haired stranger who, though unable to best the man, had slowed him down long enough for her to use her taser.

She had spent over two hours at the police station explaining what had happened and letting them know where they could find the man who'd kidnapped Sybil. He'd been brought in while she was still giving testimony and she was asked to identify him. They even asked about the dark-haired stranger who had aided her, intent on questioning him as well. But she had no clue as to who he was or where he could be found. She could only say he was tall, leanly muscled, and attractive in an ethereal kind of way. And that his name was different, something that started with an A. But she couldn't recall what it was.

They had cocked their brows at the ethereal statement.

Leisa smiled recalling their disbelieving expressions. She wasn't sure what it was about the helpful stranger, but being close to him had set her at a peculiar ease, like the ease you feel in the quiet moments with an old friend. But there was unease as well. There was something about him that made her feel off balance, made her want to know more. And it wasn't just that he was strangely attractive, or that his deep male cadence had calmed and soothed her frazzled nerves. It wasn't even his tempting smile or his light green eyes that pierced the dark and looked into your soul. There was something more. Something she couldn't quite figure out.

She frowned at her failure to get more information from him. She had no way to find or contact him, even if just to thank him properly. What were the chances of running into him again, she wondered. In the three years she'd lived in the town of Oak Meadows, Pennsylvania, this was the first she'd seen him. She sighed deeply. Most likely, he was long gone by now—a stranger from another country who was just passing through.

Again she sighed. Then she set her regrets aside, opened her book, and began to read. Something fun, something light, something to take away her disappointment.

Alasdair watched through a window four stories up from the ground. Once dusk had stolen the light and he'd returned to his small and winged fae form, tracking Leisa and the child had been easy. Faeries had a keen sense of smell. Having held the girl so close to him, he had not only picked up her young scent, but he carried it with him. Humans, like all living creatures, had their own unique scents. The girl's still clung to him just as it still hung in the air. Another hour or so, however, and it would have dissipated. Thank the Creator it had not.

He studied Leisa's interaction with the child. So motherly. A pink aura filled with bright flashes of silver surrounded her. An aura associated with a true mother. He wondered at it as he watched Leisa rise, pick up the sleeping child, and carry her down the hall out of view. He wished he could enter the dwelling and follow her. He wanted to watch their human bedtime ritual of caregiver and child.

After several minutes, Leisa re-appeared. This time she carried a small, thick book no larger than her hand. She sat on the sofa next to a tall spindly lamp, drew her legs beneath her, and began to read. Her hair, pulled back in a soft fabric tie, shone softly in the lamplight. Shorter feathery strands that had slipped from the tie fell across her cheek like wispy flames.

Alasdair watched so intently that the magic of the fae set him to glow.

Suddenly Leisa looked in his direction.

Alasdair started, then relaxed. He would appear little more than a firefly to her. The fact that she saw him at all was heartening. Perhaps she believed.

Still, he would do well to remember, though in Faerie his aura was invisible, in fae form, in the human world, it often cast a luminous and visible light—and the more he called on the magic of the fae, the brighter the glow. Alasdair drew a filling breath and released. A deep calm fell over him. The glow dimmed, then faded away.

Tiring, he settled onto the window ledge and leaned sleepily against the frame. When the lights went out and Leisa disappeared down the hall, he willed his gossamer wings to become the feathered wings of a dove, cocooned himself in their downy warmth, and slept.

Alasdair woke refreshed. He looked to the ground below. People milled about on the walks and over the crosswalks. The sound of congested traffic filled the air. Occasionally, the blast of a horn shattered the breeze and his wings undulated with the shockwave. He looked in the apartment window. There was no sign of Leisa or the youngling. But things had been moved and he knew they had already roused and gone. It surprised him that he'd slept so late. He usually wakened with the birds.

Rising, he stretched out the now translucent breadth of his wings. Then he flew off into the crisp morning air in search of a private place for his transformation.

Once again human, Alasdair pulled a sheet of parchment from his pocket. Records were kept on changeling/human switches and he had risked all to snatch what information he could. He skimmed the fine print with his finger, stopping at an address. 1027 Forrester Lane.

Spotting a nearby café, he chose a sidewalk table near a large split-pane window to further study his notes.

"Can I help you?"

Alasdair glanced up from his paper. A middle-aged woman looked down at him. She wore a simple white frock belted in black with a red apron. In one hand was a pen, in the other a pad. Her hair was the shade of fresh earth. It fell to below her chin and was partially pulled back in a clip.

"Pardon?"

"Would you like to order a drink or food?"

Alasdair pondered her request. In faerie, food was abundant and free for the taking. "I would like to, but I have no means to pay. May I have some water?"

A look of regret crossed the woman's face. "You have to order something if you intend to sit here."

His stomach rumbled. "I have nowhere else to go. I shall only be a few minutes." He turned the paper to face her. "Know you this address? Forrester Lane?"

The woman studied him intently. A strange look crossed her face that she quickly veiled. She shook her head. "Wait," she said and walked away. Several minutes later she returned with a steaming cup of coffee, a bagel with cream cheese, and a folded paper.

"What is this?" Alasdair asked as she set the food before him.

"It's on the house."

"On the what?"

"On the house. It's complimentary. Free."

Alasdair looked at the food. "My thanks," he replied. He reached for the coffee. "And this?" He pointed to the paper.

"It's a city map." The waitress unfolded it and spread it open. She skimmed the side bar with her finger, then ran it across the map. "Here."

Alasdair read. *Forrester Lane.* "And where am I now?"

"Here." The waitress pointed to a far corner of the map. "It's outside of town. About a forty-minute walk."

Or five as the faerie flies, Alasdair thought, then remembered he was again human. He nodded then took a bite of bagel, appeasing his stomach. "I hope you will not get in trouble for bringing me food for which I cannot pay."

The woman smiled. Her face lit, lifting ten years from her age. "Hardly. I own the place."

Alasdair's feet ached as he turned onto Forrester Lane. Had he thought sooner he could have waited until dark and flown, but he was anxious to find the changeling and return to Galandore.

1019, he read as he passed an older home.

1021. Another older home in need of some repair.

The next two houses were well maintained. Then came 1027.

The windows were dark voids, the grass slightly overgrown. It was obvious no one had lived there for some time. He stared at the parchment, then back at the house. It was the right place.

It was empty.

He frowned. Now what? Head in hand, he sank onto the porch stoop outside the front door giving his tired feet a much-needed rest.

"Hey, fella!" a man called out.

Alasdair looked up. A silver-haired man looked back at him from the front porch of the house next door. He wore loose khaki pants and a geometrically patterned sweater that stretched over his slightly protruding belly.

"They moved several years ago," the older man offered as he adjusted his glasses. He made his way down several wooden steps, crossed the side yard, and walked closer.

Alasdair stood as the man approached him. "Know you where they went?"

The man shook his head. "Nope. Sorry."

"Have you a name?"

"Fred. Fred MacElvay. Pleased to meet you."

"Nay. I mean—I mean, aye, pleased to meet you. I am Alasdair." He shook the man's outstretched hand. "Know you the name of those who lived here?"

"Ohh. Ah–" The man shook his head. "No, wait. I think the guy's name was Robert. Yeah. Robert Johnston. Can't recall the wife's name. Nice young couple."

Alasdair sighed. It was a name at least. How much good it would do him, he didn't know. "For what reason did they move?"

"I think, when their baby died, the marriage just fell apart," the man replied. His thin lips turned down. "Shame."

"Baby?"

"Yeah. A little girl. Named her Blaise. An odd name for a girl, don'tcha think? Probably why I remember it."

"How did she die?"

"Crib death. She was just short of a year old when they found her. Just passed away in her sleep." He shook his head. "Sad."

"Blaise," Alasdair murmured, realizing with so little information to go on, he may never find the changeling.

"What?"

"Nothing." Alasdair turned away. "I must return to town." He started down the long stone walkway of a house now empty and forlorn.

"I'm going into town if you'd like a lift," the man offered. He smiled and pointed to a midsize silver car. His tired eyes brightened. "Wouldn't mind the company either."

Alasdair looked over his shoulder at the elderly man. He thought of his two aching feet. "I would like that very much. My thanks."

25

Alasdair roamed town most of the day. Humans were interesting to observe. And so unpredictable. One human might be gracious and kind, another intolerant and rude. Many times, he noted, this changed within the same person. It all depended on circumstance. Faeries remained fairly constant in their natures. That was not to say they did not feel sadness or joy. But in day-to-day existence they behaved more steadily. Perhaps they had less to affect them so, or perhaps they were more advanced. Still, because of this constant shift of mood, humans were worth the watching. But observing them brought him no closer to his objective. If the changeling had taken the place of Blaise Johnston, deceased or nay, he needed to find it.

He sighed heavily. But how?

His stomach rumbled, eliciting a frown. He looked around. The sun was soon to set, and he was eager to return to his true form. It was one way to rid himself of the hunger pangs.

"Hey, mister!" a woman called to him from across the street.

Alasdair looked to a familiar face. It was the woman from the café, still dressed in her work frock. He crossed the busy intersection dodging more than one car.

"Oh, my God. Be careful, mister. You could have been killed."

Alasdair nodded agreement.

"Did you find what you were looking for?" she asked.

Alasdair saw alertness in her clear, blue eyes. He knew she sensed something about him, but he wasn't sure what. He smiled faintly. "Aye … and nay."

"What do you mean?"

"I found the house empty. Those who lived there moved on years ago."

"I'm sorry." The café owner lowered her eyes, then looked up at him. "Excuse me if I'm being personal, and you certainly don't have to answer, but what was the urgency to find these people?"

Alasdair hesitated. Certainly he couldn't divulge the truth. "Robert, the man who owned the house, was a friend from our youth. I heard he had married and had a child. I wanted to surprise him with a visit." He paused, feeling the twist in his gut at the lie. "But I have since been informed that their infant child died in her crib. After, Robert and his wife parted."

"That's so sad, but it happens a lot under those circumstances. Who told you this?"

"An elderly man who lived next door to them. He knows not where Robert moved, nor his wife."

"I'm sorry." The woman's eyes misted slightly and he knew she was sincere.

"'Tis no fault of yours. But I would like to visit the child's grave and pay my respects. 'Tis a shame I cannot."

"What do you mean you can't? Of course you can."

Alasdair felt a measure of hope. "How? I know not where to find it."

"Do you know the baby's name?"

"Blaise. Blaise Johnston."

"Come inside and I'll explain." She ushered him through the front door of the café to a nearby booth. "I'm Rita," she said, sliding into the booth. "Entrepreneur, waitress, sometimes cook. I wear many hats."

Alasdair slid onto the seat opposite her. He set a puzzled look on her head. Her brown, chin-length hair was lightly streaked in silver. She wore no hat.

Rita laughed. "It means I do many different things."

Alasdair smiled. "I am Alasdair."

"Alasdair. That's different."

"A family name."

"Well, have a seat, Alasdair."

"You may call me Ali if you wish."

Rita smiled. "Okay, Ali. Have you had dinner yet?"

"Nay, but—"

"No buts. I insist you join me in a meal. It's almost closing time anyway. The dinner rush is over and there's always leftover. I'd rather someone eat it than throw it away." She waved to a young man dressed in midnight blue pants and a white top. "Max!" she called out. "Bring us a couple of specials."

Alasdair had made his exit just in time. At the full setting of the sun, he changed back to his true form. Once again small and winged, he flew to the apartment building's fourth-story window. As before, Leisa sat with the little girl on a sofa. This time they watched an odd black box with moving pictures. Time and again they smiled, sometimes outright laughed. It was a pleasant sound even through the glass. He settled on the ledge, cushioned by his aura, and watched until, once again, Leisa read the girl something from the same book as the night previous, then escorted her down the hall.

With Leisa and the girl out of sight, he pondered his plans for the following day. Rita's instructions swirled in his head. "Visit the courthouse," she had said. "There you'll find documentation of the little girl's death. Get the exact date, then visit the library. It has archived newspapers, if not in print, then in the computer system. Look up her obituary and most likely the cemetery where she was buried will be named." Rita had offered to go along and help but he'd refused, graciously of course. This was *his* mission.

Alasdair closed his eyes. Before the sun completely set, he slept.

Morning came quickly. He felt the warmth of it on his lids. Opening his eyes, he saw Leisa and her ward breaking fast. Quickly, he flew to a nearby alley and sprinkled faerie dust over himself. No sooner had he turned human than his stomach rumbled. He swiftly set the complaint aside. Stepping out from the alley, he saw Leisa and the girl walking away from him, the contrasting red and blonde of their hair gleaming richly in the sun. His first inclination was to approach them. Fear held him back. Fear that she would not remember him. Fear that she *would* and wish him gone. He sighed heavily. Leisa was not his mission, and he should well remember that. Such a strange thing to be so drawn to her. It was a bodily feeling he did not understand. So human.

He sighed and set out in the opposite direction.

"Hi Alas—umm, Alas—"

Alasdair froze in his tracks, then spun to face Leisa. "Alasdair. You can call me Ali." Her sudden appearance startled him. Her almost remembrance of his name elated him.

"Ali. I like that." Leisa drew the little girl in front of her. "I saw you out of the corner of my eye and wanted to say hello. I never properly introduced you to my niece. This is Sybil. I call her Sibby mostly." She looked affectionately down at the girl. "Except when I'm mad at her, then it's Sybil Ann." She smiled. "Which is hardly ever."

Sybil giggled.

Alasdair hunched down to Sybil's level and gifted her with a smile. "Is this true?"

"Mostly," Sybil answered. "'Cept when I'm bad."

"When are you ever bad?" he asked.

"When I colored the walls with red crayons."

Alasdair nodded. "Ah, I do see the issue." He stroked Sybil's hair back from her face then stood. "Perhaps next time you should use yellow."

"Hey!" Leisa protested.

Alasdair shrugged.

"So where are you off to?" Leisa asked.

"I must visit the courthouse, then the library. Then I must visit the cemetery for a bit."

"Which one?"

Alasdair shrugged. "I know not. 'Tis why I visit the library." He watched confusion cross Leisa's face. "'Tis the grave of a friend's child. I have need to find the obituary to discover where she was interred."

Leisa nodded. "I have to visit a cemetery today, too. Laurel Hill Cemetery. We could meet there later, then after my visit, I could help you find whichever one you need to go to." Her gaze lowered, then shyly lifted. "That is, if you want."

Alasdair smiled. Had she actually blushed? "I would like that."

"Okay, how about I meet you at the Laurel Hill Cemetery gates at two-thirty. I have a few errands to run this morning, my usual Saturday thing. Then I'm dropping Sibby off at a friend's house for the night. You know, girls and their sleepovers."

Alasdair felt his brow crease.

"Well, maybe you don't know." Leisa smiled. "Two-thirty then?"

"Aye. I would be pleased to meet you." He looked at the sun. He knew straight overhead to be twelve noon. Two-thirty would be a little past. Currently, it was barely nine.

"See you later then." Leisa and Sybil turned and headed in the opposite direction.

"Later," Alasdair echoed to himself.

Chapter Three

Human World

The courthouse had been an ordeal. In retrospect, he wished he'd allowed Rita to accompany him after all. But after getting lost in the maze of halls, he'd finally found someone to direct him to the Recorder of Deeds' office. After he'd explained his recently concocted reason for needing to see the certificate, a kindly gentleman helped him find it.

Blaise had died at two forty-five a.m. on the fifth of April four years previous. He'd expected that, as the girl living with the fae was soon to be five—the usual age when children were handed over to the trolls.

Time was short.

He'd written the date on a slip of paper provided by the clerk and tucked it in his pocket. Now at the library, he pulled it free.

A young woman sorted books at the front check-in desk.

"Pardon," he said.

She looked up over her wire-rimmed glasses at him, her thick, brown hair pulled back at the nape, a cloth wrap holding it in place. Her skin was smooth and pale and he deducted that she didn't spend much time in the sun. "Yes?"

"Know you where I can find a newspaper with this date?" Alasdair showed her the slip of paper with the April 5 date.

She squinted behind her thick-lensed glasses. "That's over four years ago. It would be in our electronic archives now."

"How do I find it?"

31

She arched a brow. "Haven't you been to a library before?" she asked incredulously.

Alasdair felt the accusation in her tone. Obviously, to not frequent a library was a crime in her eyes. "Not recently." *Not in a hundred years.*

The librarian motioned for him to follow her. She led him to a computer and showed him how to look up newspaper articles, then promptly brought up the date he'd shown her. "Anything else I can do for you?"

Alasdair set on her an appreciative smile.

Her eyes widened, her lips lifted at the corners. He was sure he saw a blush color her cheeks.

"I am fine now," he said. "My thanks."

Her tone softened. "Okay. Let me know if you need more help." She walked to the main desk, picked up a stack of books, and began returning them to the shelves.

Alasdair scrolled through the e-newspaper as she'd shown him, until he came to the obituary page. He scanned all of the listings. Blaise's name wasn't among them. He brushed back his hair in exasperation.

Soft steps sounded behind him. The librarian peeked over his shoulder at the computer, her arms empty of books. "Look at April 6. That's probably when it was listed." She clicked off the April 5 newspaper for him and brought up the one from the following day.

Alasdair searched the April 6 obituaries. At the top was Blaise Marie Johnston, ten months old. Born on June 13. Date of death, April 5. She was buried at Laurel Hill Cemetery, the same location where he was to meet Leisa. That was convenient. He added the information to his paper and tucked it in his pocket.

"Anything else you need help with?" the librarian again asked, a hopeful look in her eyes.

"Nay. My thanks for all of your help. You know not how important it was for me."

Afternoon sun blinded him as he exited the library. He looked to the sky and groaned. The sun was past the noon position. He guessed it was nearing two-thirty, and he was unsure of the location of Laurel Hill Cemetery. Sprinting down the library's long stretch of steps, he made his way toward Rita's Café. Had he had wings, it would have taken mere minutes to fly. His legs, as long as they were, slowed him. Thankfully, his post transformation weakness had been temporary and was long gone.

When he reached the café, Rita was standing in the back conversing with a customer. He smiled at the sight of her. She was quite astute. One day her suspicion about him would be realized. By then, he would be long gone.

Her posture straightened and he knew she sensed his presence. She looked over her shoulder at him.

"Ali!" she called. She bade her customer goodbye and walked up to him. "How'd it go?"

"It went well, but very time consuming, and now I am late to meet someone." He pondered his next question, but knew he had to try. Surely Rita owned a vehicle like Fred. "Could I impose on you for a ride?" He looked around the room. It was busy, but a second server was on duty.

"Where do you need to go? If I can't take you, our delivery guy can."

"Laurel Hill Cemetery. Is it far?"

"Not at all. It's at the edge of town, about seven blocks west. She pointed down the road that ran past Leisa's apartment building.

"So close?" Alasdair breathed a sigh of relief. "I can easily run that distance. My thanks." He turned quickly and headed for the door.

"Are you sure, Ali?" Rita called after him.

"Aye," he replied. Thrusting the door open, he disappeared into the afternoon crowd. Moments later he arrived at the cemetery. Large wrought iron gates sat open to cemetery visitors. As he walked through, he saw Leisa waiting on the other side, her autumn-hued hair loose and brilliant in the mid-day sun. He felt unexplainably warm at the sight of her.

"I am sorry to be so late," he apologized, catching his breath.

Leisa glanced at her watch. Then she smiled up at him with straight white teeth and rosy lips. Alasdair felt a sudden urge to cover those lips with his own. He took an awkward step back.

"You're not late. In fact, you're six minutes early."

"In truth?" Alasdair looked down at his legs. 'Haps they weren't so slow after all.

"Really. I only just got here myself." Leisa hefted her purse strap more securely on her shoulder. In her other hand, she held a bouquet of daises. He could smell their fragrance wafting in the air.

"Did you find out which cemetery you need to go to?" she asked.

"Aye."

"Which one?"

"Ironically, or haps coincidentally, 'tis this one."

"Well, that's convenient. We'll kill two birds with one stone."

Alasdair tensed and frowned. "I'll not kill one bird with any stone, let alone two." His gaze narrowed, and he saw her in a different light.

Leisa set a puzzled look on him. "It's an expression, Ali. It means we'll accomplish two things with one action, not that we'll actually kill anything."

His expression softened. "'Tis a morbid play of words of which I am not so fond."

"I'm sorry. I'll try to be more careful of what I say."

Alasdair smiled. That she cared enough to do that heartened him.

"Do you want to visit your friend's daughter's grave first, or mine?"

"Your grave?"

"My daughter's grave."

Of course! A sudden veil lifted and he understood her aura. "You had a daughter?"

"Yes. She …"

He felt the grief in her pause. Heard a slight sniffle.

"She died several years ago."

Alasdair pondered her loss. Because her motherhood aura remained as brightly lit as if she had just given birth, he knew she hung onto her love fiercely. But why did she refuse to let go? "I am sorry. Let us visit your daughter's grave first."

Leisa nodded. "It's this way."

Alasdair assessed the grounds as he followed close behind her. Gravestones of various sizes, shapes, and colors dotted the field, each inscribed with a name and date, many with two names. Some resembled crosses, while others were mostly square or rectangular in shape. On several stood statues of humans rising from marble bases, while some lay lower than the surrounding grass, visible only if you stood in front of them.

The grass, though tall, was not exceedingly so. He saw the groundskeeper in the distance riding a vehicle that cut it low.

"It's not far now," Leisa assured him.

He followed her down a narrow path that led to a patch of graves separate from the rest. Most of them looked sadly neglected. The grass had been recently cropped, but no fresh flowers or trinkets adorned their sites. One stone stood out. It rested on the edge of the wood near a tree and was obviously well cared for. The grass was slightly taller there as the stone's location was not conducive to cutting grass by vehicle, but no stray twig littered it, and the wilted brown remnants of fresh flowers rested in a small urn on its base. Unlike the gray, black, and beige stones, this one glimmered soft pink like a summer's rose, with rivers of sparkling white marble running through it— a small but beautiful heart-shaped stone. White marble cherubs rested on top, glistening silver in the bright rays of afternoon sun that filtered through the overhead foliage.

When Alasdair drew near, a strange sensation fell over him and he stumbled back.

"Is something wrong?" Leisa asked.

He felt his eyes roll upward, his lungs go still. He pulled a sharp breath and choked on the dank stench that hung in the air.

"Ali?"

Again he drew breath. "I am fine," he lied.

"You don't look fine."

Skepticism lined her delicate face, but her olive eyes were warm with concern.

"Worry not. I am fine," he repeated. He cleared his throat and stepped warily forward. This time he was ready when the thick gray aura rose from the ground to encompass him, its pungent smell filling his lungs. Again he stepped back—a small imperceptible step. He glanced at Leisa who was unaffected. An uneasy sensation raced the length of his spine and down his arms as he read the inscription on the stone.

Blaise Marie Johnston.

Born June 13. Died April 5. She had been not quite ten months of age. His throat tightened as he watched Leisa replace the wilted flowers with a bouquet of fresh white daisies. She drew a small plastic container of water from her purse and poured some into the urn. Then she knelt next to the grave and traced the name with slender fingers. The afternoon sun brought fire to her hair. Alasdair had never seen a more beautiful, serene, and heart-wrenching sight in his life.

"She was not even ten months old," Leisa explained softly as though speaking to herself. "Why? Why did she die?" Leisa wiped at her cheeks. "She was perfectly healthy. We played on the grass that day in the park—watched the birds scavenging twigs for their nests. It was such a beautiful spring day. I was so glad winter was over and we could get out and enjoy the sun."

Leisa sniffled and he knew he should say something.

He didn't know what to say.

Tears slid down her face. She didn't bother to wipe them away. A strange sound issued from her throat. Without thought, he knelt beside her and drew her into his arms. She turned her head into his shoulder and wept.

Minutes passed. When her crying diminished, she pulled away.

"I'm so sorry." Leisa brushed disheveled hair back from her face and tucked it behind her ears. "This is the first time in a long time I've broken down like this. It's been four years. I should be over it by now. I don't know why I keep hanging on."

Alasdair listened. He knew why. Blaise wasn't dead. And to raise her sister's daughter of the same age in belief that her own daughter was dead had to be difficult. Such a daily reminder would tear at the strongest of hearts. Yet she showed Sybil nothing but love and caring, a daily display of the true depths of her compassion.

If only she knew the truth.

Leisa stifled a new bout of weeping. "She'd be five today." She sniffled lightly. "This fall she'd be starting kindergarten."

Alasdair wasn't sure what kindergarten was, but he let her talk.

"I just can't believe she's gone. I'm sitting here at her grave as I've done every week for four years and I still can't believe she's gone."

Alasdair stilled. Mixed with the pungent scent common to a changeling of wood, he detected a mild scent of the five-year-old girl held by the fae. He wasn't surprised. Most times the changeling carried the scent of the child it replaced mixed with its own. He had no doubt that the girl he had set out to save, the girl he knew as Sachi, was Blaise. Blaise Marie Johnston.

~*~

Leisa drew a tissue out of her pocket and dried her eyes. How foolish she felt breaking down in front of a near stranger. Really. What did she know about this guy besides that he sucked at street fighting? She cast Alasdair a side glance. To her relief, he seemed distracted by his own thoughts, giving her opportunity to assess him.

There was something different about him. Not his manners or speech, though they were certainly not the norm, and not the golden strands interspersed throughout his silky black hair, though that was certainly unique. Something more. Something inexplicable. But he was kind and beneath his raven hair were the most beautiful misty green eyes she'd ever seen. He seemed to ponder slightly before he spoke as if he wanted to get it right. At a quick glance, his clothes appeared the usual, blue jeans and a white button-down shirt, cuffs rolled. But at closer scrutiny, the threads of both garments had a slight iridescence that shimmered when he moved. It was barely visible, even up close. Leisa had noted the strangeness when her cheek had been pressed against his shoulder. She'd also noted the extreme softness of his shirt, softer than any cloth she'd ever felt.

Like down. Like a cloud. *Like breath.*

She shook the ridiculous thought from her head and brushed dried leaves from her jeans as she stood. "Let's go visit your friend's grave now."

"His daughter's grave, you mean?"

"Yes."

Leisa admired his leanly muscled body as he rose. She had never been fond of overly buff men. Alasdair was not. He had strength and great muscle tone without all the unsightly arm and chest bulges. He was perfect.

When he spoke, it was slow and calculated. "Perhaps another day."

Her brows knitted. "But this morning it was the most important thing."

"Things change."

"So quickly?" She looked Alasdair in the eye and knew he was holding something back.

He nodded.

If she'd known him better, she would have questioned him further. Now was not the time. However, she wouldn't mind knowing him better. She drew a deep breath. *Be bold, Leisa. Be bold. You may not get another chance.* "Alasdair?"

"Ali."

Leisa smiled. She spoke quickly before she lost her nerve. "Ali, would you join me for dinner tonight? Sibby is sleeping over at a friend's house, and I make a pretty good lasagna."

Alasdair smiled. A sincere, attractive smile Leisa knew she'd never grow tired of.

"I would like that very much," he replied.

Alasdair walked into Leisa's apartment. It was just as it appeared from the outside window ledge. Being in it, however, gave him a much warmer feeling, as if he were a part of something rather than merely observing. The eating and lounge areas were open to one another. The walls were pale green and the sofa warm beige. Honeyed oak floors gleamed under the soft overhead lights. In the eating area, a brass chandelier hung centered over a round white table with four mismatched chairs. Magazines lay scattered on a short-legged table in front of the sofa.

"Please. Have a seat." Leisa motioned toward the sofa. "I made the lasagna yesterday, so I just need to warm it up. It shouldn't take long." She grabbed a heavy pan from the refrigerator and set it on the counter.

Alasdair stood unsurely just inside the door. "May I help you?"

"Sure. Do you want to make a salad?"

"I can do that." He didn't move.

"You'll need to get stuff out of the fridge." Leisa pointed to a large white box.

Alasdair walked over and opened its door. Cold air spilled over him as he stared blankly inside.

"Here." Leisa pulled out a bunch of romaine lettuce, red and yellow peppers, a cucumber, carrot, and tomato. She set them on a cutting board next to the sink. Making her way to the cupboard, she grabbed a large glass bowl and a small bag of croutons from a shelf and set them beside the produce.

"Here's a knife. Rinse the veggies, cut everything up small and put them in the bowl. While you're doing that, I'll put the lasagna in the oven, then freshen up a bit."

In Leisa's absence, Alasdair began rinsing and cutting.

He couldn't get the cemetery out of his mind—the beautiful heart-shaped stone, its pink hue, the white cherubs, and the fragrant daisies Leisa had placed in the urn on its base. Moreso, he couldn't get Leisa's despondence out of his heart; unwarranted despondence, because her child was alive. But how could he tell her that without revealing his true self? How would she react? Would she even believe? And most of all, how could he give her hope when none might exist? Nay, everything rested on him. He had to dig up the grave, remove the changeling, and carry it back to Galandore. There he would steal back the child and return her to her own world.

To Leisa.

Digging up the grave, however, would be a problem. He could do so only in human form, which meant he had to dig during the day. Once night fell, he would revert back to his faerie self and would not have the size or strength to accomplish such a task.

It was good fortune, at least, that the grave stood so close to the wood and near the base of a tree. Foot traffic near the grave would be minimal, and the grass cutting vehicle would not be manageable there. The dirt would be less packed.

It was also good fortune that Leisa had just made her weekly visit and that the grave area had been recently tended to.

He'd had a week to complete his task. Four days remained. In four days he would run out of dust and would need to return to Galandore.

He pondered a plan. He would wake as the first ray of dawn broke through the clouds and work until he could no longer hold his human form. He would stop only to eat.

His thoughts stalled. Where would he get food?

Then he thought of Rita and the café. He was sure he could arrange something.

"Oh, my!" Leisa entered the kitchen, her gaze fixed on the salad. Quickly she stilled his hand before he massacred the croutons.

"Did I not do it right?" Alasdair asked. He looked at the minuscule colorful pieces in the bowl.

"It's fine," Leisa lied. "We may, however, have to eat it with a spoon."

After clearing the dishes, Leisa settled on the sofa. "Sit down." She patted the cushion next to her, then stilled her hand. "I'm sorry. You probably have somewhere to be. Someone to see?"

Alasdair smiled. "No. Nowhere until early morn." He sat on the sofa next to her.

Leisa jumped up. "Are you thirsty? I'll get us some lemonade."

"I shall help." Alasdair stood. He stepped in front of the wall cabinet next to the fridge and pulled out two glasses.

"No. You don't have—" Leisa paused.

At her sudden silence, Alasdair turned to face her. Her awed expression told him he'd made a mistake.

"How did you know where the glasses were?" she asked as she filled them.

Alasdair scrambled for an answer, then shrugged. "It seemed a logical place." His reason sounded absurd, even to himself, but she seemed to accept it. He handed her a glass and they sat on the sofa once more.

"Obviously, you're not from around here. Where are you from?"

Alasdair drew from his recently concocted story. "I am from the country of Galandore."

"Really? I've never heard of it."

"Most have not."

"Are you living here now or just visiting?"

"Merely visiting. I came to surprise an old friend, but it seems he moved."

"You came all the way from another country without letting him know in advance, without making sure he was still living in the same place?"

"It was to be a surprise. Had I told him, it would not have been so."

"I'm sorry you missed him."

"My thanks." He took a large sip of lemonade. His face puckered.

Leisa laughed. "Is it your first glass of lemonade?"

"Aye." He shook his head. "'Tis quite tart."

"Yes, it is. If you don't like it, I can get you something else."

Alasdair shook his head. "Nay. I like it a lot. I just was not prepared for such a culinary shock."

Again Leisa laughed. "What do you do in your country, Ali?"

"What mean you?"

"What kind of work do you do? You know, to earn a living."

Alasdair fidgeted under the inquisition. He drank slowly to buy some time. "I work in diplomacy."

"What do you m—"

"And you?" Alasdair quickly asked, turning the questions on her. "How do you earn a living?"

Leisa's eyes lit and he knew she was passionate about her career. "I teach grade school."

"Did you teach this day?"

"No. Teachers work from late August to early June. I just finished up, so I'm off work for about two and a half months."

"What will you do these two and one half months?"

"Relax."

"How so?"

"I'll spend time with Sybil. We'll go to the park, have picnics, visit the zoo, the beach. When Sibby is sleeping over at a friend's house, or just plain sleeping, I read."

"And this is how one relaxes?"

"It's how *I* relax."

Alasdair stilled. He'd not felt relaxed since he'd entered this human world. There was something about it that caused his every fiber to tense. Yet oddly enough, he embraced it. Such a contradiction. It was not a wonder he felt confused. He cast a quick glance at Leisa, who used a small rectangular device to turn on the black box. Immediately, moving pictures filled the screen, pictures depicting other humans. Leisa laughed and he assumed it was humorous. Though he did not understand human humor, he smiled.

After some time, he felt his eyes begin to droop. Glancing out the window, he saw the sun about to set. A tingling sensation coursed through his flesh.

He jumped up.

"I must go now," he quickly announced.

"So soon?" Leisa stood and brushed the wrinkles from her clothes. "It's only—" She looked at her watch. "Eight-thirty."

"I am sorry. I have much to do come morning."

"Like what?"

Like dig up your daughter's grave.

Alasdair hesitated to reply. He hadn't been prepared for such questions. "I cannot say."

"Is it top secret?" Leisa quipped.

"Aye. 'Tis top secret." He brushed a strand of hair from her face and set it behind her ear. Her shiver prompted him to step back.

"You're kidding, right?"

"Of course." Alasdair grinned. "But I really must go."

"Will I see you again?"

Alasdair pondered the question. It would be foolish to continue in Leisa's company. What he must do, he must do alone. To involve Leisa further would be foolhardy. He steadily moved toward the door. "Leisa—" he began.

He studied the hopeful glint in her dark mossy eyes, the light pinch of her brow, and the sprinkle of freckles across the bridge of her nose. Her naturally rose-hued lips pursed as she waited for an answer. He sighed inwardly. It would be a mistake to see her again. Already the attraction was too great. Nay. This was where it must end. For her sake, and for his own. He prepared to decline. His reply was silenced when she moved forward, slipped her arms around his neck and pressed her lips to his.

Her mouth felt warm and sweetly gentle and tasted mildly of lemons and Leisa's scent. A taste he knew he would crave long after the night ended.

When she stepped back, her eyes appeared wide and wild, her expression mortified.

"I'm so sorry," she apologized, her hand lightly covering those same lips that had set his heart to race. "I don't know why I did that." She laughed nervously. "I mean, I *do* know why, but I shouldn't have." She took another step back, putting distance between them.

Still, he could feel the draw.

"I'd just really like to see you again." Leisa smiled, her head pleasingly cocked to the side. "Will I?"

Alasdair felt a tightening in his chest. *Nay. Nay. Nay.* He grabbed the doorknob and turned it awkwardly. Pulling the door open, he stepped into the corridor. "Of course," he replied. Then he disappeared down the hall.

Chapter Four

Human World

Alasdair woke to the sound of birds celebrating the approaching day. Dawn was nearing the horizon as he flew from the fourth-story sill into a still dark sky to Blaise's grave. Leafy shadows danced across its pink-hued stone, giving the white marbled cherubs the illusion of life. He flew low to rest on the gravestone's wider base and again read the inscription.

Blaise Marie Johnston.

Father: Robert L. Johnston

Mother: Leisa Fae Vandermann Johnston

He still could not believe the child was Leisa's daughter. He hadn't put it together since Leisa had introduced herself as Leisa Vandermann.

His thoughts centered on the night before. Spending time with Leisa had been wonderful. They'd talked. They'd laughed. They'd even had quiet moments. And the quiet moments were the best of all. It was during those times that he'd felt closest to her, as if their auras had meshed as one. It was during those moments he'd wanted to hold her in the silence and drink her in.

Procreation for faeries was different than that for humans. The fae oft had sex for amusement or to expand the race. Fervent need of another was not the norm in the faerie realm. But it was for him. It was an imperfection he'd struggled with all his life. An imperfection he did not understand.

He set his thoughts of Leisa aside and studied the grave. He thought about the changeling buried just beneath. Before Sachi, he had never bonded with a human youngling stolen for the tithe. Always he had kept a distance, protecting himself from the pain of the child's demise.

He closed his eyes against the lie. In truth, he had tried to keep a distance, but always he had failed. Always he had felt grief, wept in secret as each child met his or her death. But not this time. After pulling Sachi, half drowned and afraid, from the garden fountain two years past, he had grown unusually close to her. Meeting her in the gardens to teach her songs of the fae was the highpoint of his day.

His eyes fixed on the name carved in marble, on the year her life had supposedly ended. His jaw tightened. He would not let her die.

He set his thoughts back on his task. He needed a shovel. Something he hadn't thought of. He looked around. A wooden shed sat in the distance. He guessed it was where the groundskeepers kept their supplies. Riding the crisp pre-morning breeze, he reached the shed quickly. When full dawn filled the eastern sky, he drew forth his pouch, scattered faerie dust over himself, and transformed. Now human, he tried the door.

Locked.

He cursed softly. "Now what?" he muttered.

Two voices sounded nearby. Alasdair rounded a corner of the building and slipped out of sight.

"You got some rope in there?" a gruff voice asked.

"Yeah," a more mellow-sounding man replied. He set his key in the lock. The door groaned as it opened fully and they slipped inside.

Alasdair listened.

"Good. I was afraid we'd have to take a road trip to the hardware. Got to get those holes roped off so no one falls in."

48

"Here it is," the first man replied. "Come on. Let's get that done so we can get to work on the lower level. I've got a lot of trimming to do down there."

They exited the building. The first man pulled out his key.

Alasdair felt a sinking hope as he peered around the corner of the shed.

"Leave it," the gruffer voice said. "We'll only be gone a few minutes."

The mellow man looked at the lock, the key, then the lock again. He stuffed the key in his pocket. "Ten minutes," he replied. "Let's rope that off, return the excess, and get back to trimming."

They trudged off, winding their way through the stones.

Alasdair's heart pounded through the luminous cloth of his black, fitted shirt. He released a long-held breath.

Sure that the two men were out of sight, he slid around the building and tried the door.

Unlatched.

He held his breath as he pushed it open, slowly to avoid creaking.

The dark shed smelled of soil and grass. He felt the wall until his hand met a light switch. When he flipped the switch up, no light came, so he waited for his eyes to adjust. Soon he was able to make out shapes. Ten minutes the man had said. Only seven remained.

He scanned the contents of the nearly full shed. Devices of every sort leaned against the walls or hung from hooks. Finally his gaze settled on a shovel that sat partially concealed in a far corner of the shed. Grabbing its long wooden handle, he made his way toward the door.

Suddenly the door swung inward. He slipped behind it, hugging the tool's long handle to his chest. A burst of sunlight lit the room.

"Told ya it wouldn't take long," the gruff voice said. "Six minutes. I think that's a record."

"You want a prize or something?" the mellow voice quipped.

The first man chuckled as the second tossed the remainder of rope onto a counter. They exited and he pulled the door shut behind him.

Relief washed over Alasdair and he dared to breathe in the new and quiet dark.

Then he heard the click.

His breath caught.

Nay! He stepped away from the wall and tried the door.

Locked.

The two voices faded. Alasdair sank to the floor.

Setting the shovel aside, he crossed his arms over his knees and waited for his eyes to adjust once more to the dark. When he could again make out shapes, he glanced around the shed. It was old but strongly built of timber. There were no windows and the floor was rock hard. There was no way out.

Alasdair stood. "Sweet Mother Earth," he groaned. Anguish pulled at his insides. His throat felt tight.

"Nay!" he shouted. He banged on the solid walls and door, expelled his energy until he slumped exhausted on the floor. He could feel the pounding of his heart against his chest. Dampness crossed his cheek. He wiped it with his sleeve. Time was too short to spend it locked away. He had to get the changeling. He had to save Sachi. He pondered Leisa and how happy she would be to discover that her daughter lived.

If he got to her in time.

He closed his eyes, fatigued.

A light scratching sounded in the corner.

Alasdair's eyes snapped open. He listened intently.

Again the scratching, more insistent. It seemed to come from behind wooden shelving in the far corner of the shed. It would start, then stop, then start again. At first it seemed muted and distant. Now it sounded clear and loud.

The patter of tiny, skittering steps wound with purpose through the maintenance supplies.

Alasdair backed up against the wall, watching and waiting.

A small rodent slunk out from beneath a large roll of black felt. His tiny, golden eyes glittered in the shadowed confines of the shed then rested on *him*. The creature lifted a sniffing nose in the air and rose up on his two back feet, exposing a furry chest and fleshy front paws. Though his whiskered mouth remained closed, Alasdair heard him speaking in his head.

I am Naois.

"Naois?" Alasdair repeated aloud.

Aye. I was passing by when I picked up a strange scent. Again the rodent twitched his nose.

Alasdair studied the creature with interest, sensing he was something more than he seemed. "Strange? How so?"

A scent of despair.

"You could smell that?"

A wolf has a very acute sense of smell.

Alasdair stared at the rodent. "You are no wolf."

Laughter sounded in Alasdair's head. *Not now. But I was moments ago.*

"What are you?"

I am a rat.

Alasdair sighed. "I mean *what* are you?"

Again the laughter. *I am a theriomorph.*

"A theriomorph? Never have I heard of such."

Perhaps not. We do not go about announcing ourselves. But I have heard of faeries.

Alasdair started. "You know what I am?"

I know much. As I said, very acute senses.

Alasdair raked his dark hair back from his brow. It parted in the center and fell to either side of his face. His forehead creased in question. "Tell me, for I am at a disadvantage. What is a theriomorph?"

A theriomorph is a shapeshifter. I can take on the form of any animal or human. It matters not.

"Why were you just outside? It seems a strange place for a wolf, so close to the city."

I travel far north to what the humans call Canada. A wolf's long strides make better time than those of a rat. And its acute senses keep it safe.

"Why do you not shift to a bird and fly?"

"I prefer the cover of trees to open air."

Alasdair nodded. "What is in Canada that you travel so far?"

A colony, so I hear, of shapeshifters: lycanthropes and theriomorphs alike. They reside in the deepest forest, so deep that humans have no sense they exist. Some foolishly mistake a sighting for a creature they call Bigfoot. Again the laughter. *Let them have their delusions. Existence is easier in their ignorance.*

Alasdair understood.

So why are you in despair? Naois asked.

"I must escape this shed and begin digging up a grave. And time is short."

You seek a changeling.

Alasdair gasped. "How know you this?"

For what other reason would a faerie wish to dig up a grave? Again laughter. *Also, I smelled the changeling as I skimmed the woodland's edge.*

Alasdair smiled weakly.

Why do you seek this changeling?

"I needs must return it to its rightful place to save a human child."

What matters one human child? In a short time of eighty or so years, it will die anyway.

Alasdair nodded. Seventy, eighty, ninety years was nothing in the faerie realm.

Besides, is it not common for the fae to steal human children without care? To send them to their deaths.

Alasdair nodded in shame. "*I* care. I know not why. And I will save this child if I can escape this prison."

Naois shook his head. *I know why and you have my sympathies. I care not for humans nor the human form, so very vulnerable. But I will help you before I continue on my way. All creatures of the known world must support one another, else we will cease to exist.*

At that, the rat Naois skittered under the felt. Alasdair heard him scratching in the corner—then silence. Alasdair crawled through the supplies far enough to see the small hole the creature had chewed in the wood, giving him entry. "Naois, wait!" he called out. There was no reply.

"Much help that was," he muttered to himself. He sat down and waited. Soon his lids began to droop. He shook his head, determined not to sleep.

A click sounded at the door. Alasdair jolted awake and jumped to his feet, his eyes full and wide. Quickly he hid behind the door just before it swung open.

There was a long pause, then a familiar voice sounded, this time aloud.

"Come out from behind the door, faerie."

"Naois?" Alasdair grabbed the shovel and stepped out into the sun. Blinded at first, he rubbed his eyes. When he could again see, his gaze fixed on a lean, muscled man with hair as black as night and golden eyes that nearly glowed. No cloth covered his naked form. "But how?"

Naois locked the door, then dropped the key just outside the building. "He will think he dropped it."

"How know you this?"

The theriomorph grinned. "Humans are forgetful and easily fooled."

"But how did you get the key?"

"As the day is getting hot, the two men had shed their outer shirts and tossed them in the grass. It was easy enough for a rat to slip the key from a pocket. It was equally easy for a human to unlock the door."

Alasdair laughed. "My thanks, Naois. I have lost several hours for sure, but I would have lost many more if not for your kindness."

Naois smiled a wolfish smile. "Be careful, faerie." He projected one last thought to Alasdair as he shifted back to a wolf and headed for the trees. *The path you follow will not be an easy one.*

Chapter Five

Human World

Leisa picked Sybil up from her friend's house. It was a beautiful June day, not too hot and not too cold. She wondered what Alasdair was doing on such a nice day. He said he was from another country, a country called Galandore. She had searched it on the internet, but nothing came up. His accent was strangely unique, not like that of another country, but like that of another time. Modern medieval, which struck her as an oxymoron. It gave her pause, but not enough to dismiss him. In fact, it piqued her curiousity.

Would she see him again, she wondered. He said she would, but had not asked for a phone number. How odd. Was it his way of blowing her off?

Determined to put him from her thoughts, she turned her attention back to Sybil. "Did you have a good time with Halley?" she asked as they walked home.

"Uh-huh."

"What did you two do?"

"We swimmed in the pool for a long time. Then we eated dinner."

"Was it a good dinner?"

"Uh-huh. Hambigers, fries, an' chocolate milk."

Good dinner? Hah! "Hamburgers, you mean."

Sybil nodded. "Then we played with her puppy, then watched a movie an' eated lots of popcorn. An' Halley's mommy said I can visit all the time."

"Well, we'll see about that."

Sybil tugged on Leisa's arm. "Aunt Leis?"

Leisa looked down at Sybil. Her niece's brilliant blue eyes sparkled with excitement and she knew something big was coming. "Yes?"

"Can we get a puppy? Cause puppies are lots of fun."

Leisa paused to reply. "I know, sweetie. But where we live doesn't allow pets."

Sybil hung her head. "But I have no one to play wif."

"You have Halley."

"Not at home. Not all the time," Sybil whined.

"I'm sorry." She gave Sybil's shoulders a squeeze. "But I'll take you to Halley's as often as possible so you can play with her puppy. How's that?"

Sybil gave a slow, pathetic nod.

"Come on. How about we go to lunch and then stop at the park. I'll bet the carousel is open today."

"Oh boy!" Sybil squealed, her mood brightening. She grabbed Leisa's hand, speeding her along.

"Where do you want to eat lunch?" Leisa asked.

"Rita's!" Sybil shouted.

Leisa smiled. She liked Rita a lot. After Rita's husband had passed away at forty-six years of age, she'd thought Rita would sell the café, but she hadn't. She'd held strong and turned it into an even more thriving business. People liked it for its warm European decor, atmosphere, and delicious cuisine. And why not? Rita's husband had been French-Italian, an excellent chef from the Alsace-Lorraine region. Evidently his cooking skills and mannerisms had rubbed off on his wife and staff. Whenever Leisa ate there, she imagined she was on the continent, a short but satisfying vacation.

"Rita's it is," Leisa replied.

The carousel provided an hour or so of fun. Then they moved on to the swings and slide. A crowd of people stood in line at the long slide, awaiting their turn. It was worth the wait. The pure adrenaline rush of racing full speed down a hillside was worth the few minutes in line spent talking to strangers. They exhausted themselves before heading home.

Leisa opened the apartment door, ushered Sybil through, then set the lock. "I'm going to run your bath water, Sibby. Pick out some pajamas and underwear."

"Okay." Sybil padded quickly down the hall. The heavy thud of slammed drawers sounded several times before she appeared in the bathroom, her arms full.

"Are you okay on your own?" Leisa asked.

"Uh-huh." Sybil shed her clothes and climbed in the tub. She grabbed a toy from the tub's slick porcelain edge and began splashing it through the suds.

"Okay. Don't be too long. I'll get a snack ready, then we'll read a little before bed."

"Can we read the fairy book?" Sybil asked.

"Again?"

"I like it."

Leisa sighed. "Okay. We'll read the fairy book." She reached into the tub and splashed water at Sybil's back.

Sybil giggled.

Having fed and tucked Sybil into bed, Leisa sat to read for her own amusement. It was her favorite time of the day. Not that she didn't love being with Sybil, she did. But this time was her special time, time alone to ponder or read or just do nothing at all. She loved this time.

Or at least she used to.

Suddenly her much cherished alone time felt … lonely.

She couldn't get Alasdair out of her head. Where was he? What was he doing? Would she really see him again?

He had said she would, but he had hesitated. Men weren't very good at being truthful when they thought it would create a scene. In her experience, they merely said what they thought the woman wanted to hear.

Leisa sighed. Having a child didn't help. Most guys saw that as responsibility. Those who knew she had a child didn't ask her out. Those who didn't know soon made the discovery and disappeared. All commitment phobic. Still, she wouldn't trade Sybil for the world. Sybil. Such a beautiful little girl, so much like her mother, Leisa thought. Brilliant blue eyes. Long silky blonde hair. Leisa wondered what *her* little girl would look like now had she lived. Would she have red hair like hers or dark brown like her father's? Would her eyes be deep green or warm caramel brown?

And what about Alasdair? If they had a child together, what would it look like? Most likely it would inherit his silky black hair, black being a dominant color. But would their child have the golden strands interspersed? Surely the child would have green eyes, but would they be pale misty green like his, or dark like hers?

Leisa shook her head. *What the–!* She barely knew the man and she already had him shackled to a wife and children. She really needed to arrange her priorities. She picked up her book and began reading. A faint light glowed outside her window, catching her attention. It fluttered low and faded. Sure that she'd imagined it, she turned back to her book and continued to read.

Exhausted, Alasdair settled on the sill. He'd made little progress at the grave. Tomorrow he'd do better. After hiding the shovel in the trees, he'd waited until dark, then flown back.

Getting locked in the shed had stolen precious time. Thanks be to Mother Earth that Naois had freed him.

He stretched out on the comfort of his aura and yawned. He'd been starving when the sun had finally set. Once a fairy, however, he no longer felt strong hunger pangs, just weariness. Now he needed sleep. He closed his eyes, keeping the image of Leisa close in his thoughts.

A truck horn blew. Alasdair jolted awake. Streaks of red still blazed across the morning sky, but mostly the sun had risen to a golden hue. He'd slept too long.

Three days, he thought, rubbing his eyes. Time was slipping away. He hoped three days were enough to reach the changeling.

He rose and peeked in the window. The apartment was dark and he knew they still slept. He wished he could change into a human and spend the day with Leisa and Sybil. He wished a lot of things. But in the end, he had a mission to fulfill.

Dropping from the ledge, he spread his gossamer wings and caught the wind. Quickly he made his way to the cemetery. It was empty and serene, almost prayerful. Birds chirped a cheerful greeting. Everything was in its place. Everything was neat and orderly—except the grave with the heart-shaped stone. There the ground was breeched. Dirt was strewn across the grass, the largest amount mounded a short distance into the trees. He landed beside the hole. Gathering dust from his pouch, he scattered it over himself. Immediately he grew to human proportions.

Immediately he sank to the ground.

"Sweet Creator!" he swore as he forced himself to stand. His legs felt afire, the thigh muscles burning as he had never experienced. His arms ached from wrist to shoulder and were difficult to lift. Every breath was forced against the pain. He drew air deep into his lungs. His stomach cramped. What was

59

wrong with him? He slid farther into the woods, leaned against a tree, and waited. Still it persisted. He waited longer. Still the pain. Finally, he slid to the ground and fell asleep, his only escape from it. When he woke it was well past the noon hour. Alasdair breathed deeply and forced himself to stand. Every movement was excruciating, but he was able to move. He grabbed the shovel and continued to dig, infinitely slower than he'd intended. After a foot he was unable to continue and set the shovel aside. His stomach twisted in pain such as he had never experienced. He knew if he waited until dark, he would turn back into his true form and the pain would subside. But when he once again became human, it would strike him two-fold.

He needed to eat.

Dirt-smeared and with a slow, painful pace, he walked the seven blocks to Rita's Café.

"Good God! What happened to you?" Rita met Alasdair as he entered the door and ushered him to an out-of-the-way booth. "You look like you just dug your way out of a grave," she quipped.

Alasdair winced. "I am sorry to be so in your fine café," he apologized as he sat. "I just need something to eat." A sharp cramp ripped at his insides and he leaned forward into it. When it passed, he reached into his pocket and placed a large gemstone on the table.

Rita picked up the gem and held it to the light. It gleamed deep, rich red. "Is this real?" she asked.

"Aye." Alasdair straightened in his seat. "Take it, please, in exchange for a meal."

Rita sighed. "I can't accept a ruby this size in place of a meal. It wouldn't be right."

"You have been most kind and helpful to me. It is the least I can give."

She turned the ruby over in her fingers and examined its beauty and brilliance. "Darn good fake if it isn't real," she muttered as she walked to the kitchen. Minutes later she emerged with a tray of food and drinks.

A tired smile lit Alasdair's face.

Rita placed the food before him and sat. "How long's it been?" she asked. She wrapped her hands around her coffee cup.

Alasdair shoved food into his mouth with as much decorum as a starving fae could. "What do you mean?" he asked as he continued to chew.

"I mean, how long has it been since you last ate?"

"The night prior to last. Leisa cooked a wonderful lasagna dinner."

"Leisa Vandermann?"

"Aye. You know her?"

"She's a friend of mine. Beautiful woman. And her little girl is so sweet. They come here often."

Alasdair slowed in his eating, his initial pain satisfied.

"In fact," Rita continued, "they ate here just yesterday. She said they had been to the park. There's a wonderful antique carousel there."

Alasdair downed his last bite. He nodded, though he had no thoughts as to what a carousel was.

"It's magical, you know," Rita continued.

"Magical?"

"Yes. With the joy and innocence of youth."

Alasdair smiled tiredly. He noted that Rita's frosted, brown hair looked different today, and the clip that held it back seemed new. He pondered her thoughts, then took a deep drink of coffee. The heat of it warmed him through, and he leaned back and relaxed.

"Feeling better?" Rita asked.

"Much." He smiled contentedly. "My thanks."

"You're looking better." Rita slid the stone across the table to him. "I can't take this. Even if it's a simulated stone, it's still too valuable for a single meal."

"'Tis a true gem. You can verify that if you wish."

Rita sighed.

"Please." Alasdair sat up straight and slid it back to her. "If not for this meal, then for all meals for the next two days at most. It is all the longer I shall be here."

"How many meals?" Rita asked.

"I would need a breakfast and lunch that I can carry with me in the morning. Something simple. And supper in the evening. Is it a fair trade?"

Rita examined the stone. "No."

Alasdair hung his head.

"It's still too valuable." She smiled. Her eyes lit, and Alasdair thought her quite striking for her human age. "But I accept on one condition."

Alasdair looked up. "And what is that?"

"That you bring Leisa and her little girl with you for dinner tomorrow." She smiled.

"Covered in dirt?"

"Oh, yeah. About the dirt. What exactly are you doing that's so dirty?"

Alasdair thought for a moment. "Planting flowers at the cemetery."

"Whoa! So my guess wasn't far off after all."

Alasdair grinned. *Not far indeed.*

"So you found the grave then?"

"Aye. Even though I knew her not, it was very saddening."

"But at least you got to pay your respects. I'm glad." Rita smiled. "I'm also glad to see your color returning. You looked positively ashen when you walked in here."

"Oh?" He stifled a yawn.

Rita nodded. Then she sipped her coffee. "Go get yourself some rest. You'll feel better in the morning."

Alasdair rose shakily from his seat. Somehow he doubted that.

Chapter Six

Human World

Alasdair knocked on Leisa's door. After leaving Rita's café the previous night, he'd explored the city park where he'd discovered a woodland stream to wash away the dirt on his face and hands. His clothing would be renewed on the morrow. Then he'd walked the streets, taking in the many aspects of human activity. He'd needed to wait for nightfall until he once again turned faerie. Once he'd reached the sill, he'd slept like never before.

This day he'd awakened with the birds, but he was holding off going to the cemetery until he talked to Leisa. In order to carry breakfast and lunch with him, he had to start working a bit later than he'd have liked and walk the seven blocks from the café to the cemetery as a human. It was a small concession to fend off starvation. The café opened at 6:00 a.m. to cover the morning commuters. It specialized in a variety of foods, from bagels and muffins to eggs and ham. He had no care what he ate as long as it was accompanied by coffee. The coffee Rita had served him the night before had relaxed and warmed him through. It was a drink he would sorely miss when he returned to Galandore.

Again he knocked.

Stumbling sounded on the other side of the door, followed by a mild curse. He stepped back. Soon the door creaked open several inches, still secured by a short chain.

"Alasdair?"

The door shut, a rattling of chain sounded, and then it opened fully. Leisa stood in a white terry bathrobe that tied at the waist and fell to just above her knees. Her bare legs looked as smooth as petals. Soft white slippers covered her feet. Her ruddy hair, disheveled from sleep, fell in soft unruly waves that framed her face and shoulders. She was beautiful.

Leisa rubbed her eyes. "Good god, what time do you get up?"

"With the birds."

Leisa yawned. Though she tried hiding it with her hand, she failed miserably. "Too early for me." Again she yawned. "Sorry. I didn't sleep well last night."

"Nay. 'Tis I who should apologize. I should not have come so early." Alasdair shifted his stance. "But I wanted to see you before going to the cemetery."

"To visit the grave?"

"Aye."

"So," Leisa said confusedly, "Are you here because you would like me to come with you?"

"Nay. I would like to pay my respects privately."

"I understand."

"Also I have several errands to do after." It was one of many lies, but he'd need a few hours to finish the job and remove the changeling.

"So then, why are you here at the crack of dawn?"

"To say I would be pleased if you and Sybil would join me for dinner at Rita's tonight."

Leisa's lips twitched and he knew she fought a smile.

"Really? I thought maybe I scared you off the other night."

"Not at all. I have just been very busy."

"Okay. Rita's. What time?"

"Three hours before dusk."

He caught the furrow of Leisa's brow.

"Three hours before dusk? What time is that?" Leisa asked.

66

Alasdair sighed. He wasn't sure. But he needed to allow himself enough time to eat, exchange pleasantries, walk Leisa and Sybil home, and depart before the dust wore off. It was complicated. "I deem a bit after six."

"Okay, six." As Leisa closed the door, a coy smile teased her lips. He liked it.

Reaching the cemetery, Alasdair noted more activity than usual. He wondered if it was perhaps a human holiday. People filed in and out most of the morning and afternoon. All strolled at a distance, but still he dared not chance being seen desecrating a grave. When the grounds finally cleared, it was well past noon before he had a chance to dig. He accomplished little, though by the looks of his dirt-encrusted clothes and flesh, one would think he had worked all day.

Looking to the sky, he guessed it was near to five. He brushed his hands on his pant legs. When he'd stopped at the café after leaving Leisa's apartment that morning, Rita had given him not only breakfast and lunch but clothing as well. Something called a mechanic's jumpsuit. It seemed her son had worked as an auto mechanic before going away to college and had several pairs still stuffed in his closet. Unfortunately, her son was a tad shorter than he, so the sleeve and leg hems rode high on him. He didn't care. All he cared about was reaching the changeling. It would not take much longer.

He ran a fast glance over the cemetery as he tucked the shovel into the trees. Empty. After making his way behind the storage building, he shed his jumpsuit. Then, as did the groundsmen, he unwound the hose on the shed's side and turned on the tap. "Sweet Mother!" he swore as frigid water slid over him. When the initial shock passed, he poured water through his hair and over every inch of his body, washing away the evidence of a day spent in a grave. The air was seasonably warm. By the time he reached the tree where he'd hung his clothes, though his hair was still damp, his flesh was dry. Tucking the shovel and jumpsuit under some brush, he began the seven-block walk to Rita's Café, a lightness in his step. He knew he would reach the changeling the next day.

As he approached Rita's Café, he slowed. Leisa and Sybil sat at a sidewalk table. Rita stood nearby talking with them. The late afternoon sun was brilliant gold and filtered through the awning, setting Leisa's hair to glow vibrant red. Sybil played with the silverware, her short legs dangling as she swung them to and fro, her pale hair shining like that of an angel. Alasdair frowned. He would not miss his frail human body or the unpredictable ways of this world, but he would sorely miss watching Leisa and Sybil. Sitting comfortably on the window ledge as he watched Leisa ready Sybil for sleep had become his favorite nighttime tradition.

When he picked up his gait, Rita caught sight of him.

"Hi, Ali!" She waved him over to the table.

Leisa and Sybil both turned to look at him.

"Rita," Alasdair smiled. "How go you this day?" There was something about Rita that put him at ease. He would miss her.

"I'm great. Here, have a seat." She pointed to the chair next to Leisa and winked. "I'll give you guys a few minutes to check out the menu." She turned to another table and began a conversation. Alasdair sat down.

"Did you wait long?" he asked.

"Not long," Leisa replied. "Rita and I were just catching up."

Alasdair breathed deeply, relieved that he had told them both the same story.

"How was your day?" she asked.

"Quite tiring. I shall sleep well this night."

Leisa picked up the menu then looked at Sybil. "What would you like to eat, sweetie?"

"Umm ..."

"How about your favorite, chicken strips and broccoli?"

"An' 'tato soup?" Sybil fiddled with her napkin.

"And *potato* soup."

"Yum." Sybil's face lit. Alasdair thought he'd never seen such joy in all of faeriedom.

"And to drink?" Leisa asked Sybil.

"Root beer!"

"Okay, a glass of milk."

"Aunt Leis!" Sybil pouted.

Leisa ruffled her niece's hair. "Soda will rot your teeth."

Sybil grinned, baring her pearly whites.

Alasdair laughed. It was the first time he'd truly felt levity since coming to the human world. "And you? What will you eat, Leisa?"

"I think I'll have a salad and sirloin tips with a sweet potato."

"And to drink?" Alasdair asked, his brow arched.

"Pep–" Leisa paused, looked at Sybil, and sighed. "A glass of milk."

Alasdair chuckled. "I shall have the same."

"Milk too?" Sybil asked incredulously.

"Of course. I'll not have your teeth stronger than mine."

Sybil covered her mouth and giggled.

The sun was near to setting as Alasdair walked Leisa and Sybil to their building. It had been a comfortably quiet dinner but for the time Sybil spilled her milk. He wondered if it hadn't been purposeful. If it had, it hadn't gained her the root beer she'd originally wanted, only a fresher glass of the same. He cast a side glance at Leisa. She was beautiful, like poppies in the field, like a vibrant autumn leaf. Her hair shone soft muted red in the dimming light, complementing the rich olive hue of her eyes.

She looked up at him and caught him off guard.

"Are you okay?" she asked.

"I am fine." Fighting the urge to touch her, he tucked his hands in his jeans pockets. "Why do you ask?"

"You're just so quiet."

"It is how I am."

"Ali?" Sybil asked.

Alasdair lowered his gaze to Sybil. "Aye, little one?"

"Are you a fairy?"

"Sybil Ann!" Leisa admonished. She turned a stunned look on Alasdair. "I'm so sorry. She's got this fixation on fairies." She turned to Sybil. "Sybil, say you're sorry."

"But–"

"Say you're sorry," Leisa repeated.

Sybil lowered her head, but her eyes rolled up to look at Alasdair. "I'm sorry," she murmured.

Though startled by the question, Alasdair remained calm. "For what reason need she be sorry?" he asked Leisa. "She merely asked a question."

Leisa spoke quietly to Alasdair. "Because fairies don't exist. They're fantasy. I don't know why she would ask you such a thing."

Sybil broke in. "I asked if he was a fairy 'cause—"

"We are here." Alasdair spoke over Sybil's comment and motioned to the entrance door of Leisa's apartment building.

"So we are." Leisa opened the door. "Would you care to come in?"

Alasdair glanced at the sky's fading light. "I cannot."

Leisa shifted uncomfortably. "Would you like to get together sometime tomorrow?"

Alasdair smiled. "I would like that. I should very much like to see the carousel in the park. Rita said it was magical."

"Sybil's going to Halley's again early tomorrow and coming home late, so I'm free most of the day and early evening. What time would you like to meet?"

"Three hours before dusk."

"Let me guess. Six o'clock?"

"Perhaps four hours before dusk."

"Five o'clock. Okay."

"Meet me at Rita's for dinner tomorrow eve. Then we shall go see this famous carousel."

Leisa arched a brow. "You really want to see the carousel?"

"Aye. Very much. Do you not like it?"

"When I was a kid, yes. But now ..."

Alasdair cocked his head. "But now?"

"Now I'm grown."

"And you have forgotten the magic?"

"Magic?"

"The joy and innocence that comes with being young."

"No, I—" Leisa bit her lip. "Well, maybe a little."

"Then we shall rediscover it." He stepped close as if to kiss her, then shuffled back. "Good night, Leisa." He hunched low and stroked Sybil's silky golden locks. "Sleep well, little one," he said. Then he whispered in her ear, "'Haps one day I will answer your question."

Again he let his gaze fall on Leisa. "Until tomorrow," he said as he walked off into the dusk and quickly rounded a corner of the building.

"Ali, wait!" Leisa hurried after him. Rounding the corner she abruptly stopped. "Where'd he go?" she muttered aloud. A single firefly glowed in the distance.

"Aunt Leis, can we go in now?"

Leisa sidled up to Sybil. "Yes," she replied, her focus still on the corner of the building as she ushered Sybil up the steps and in the front door of their apartment building.

As she prepared to read Sybil a bedtime story from a book of *her* choosing, Leisa asked, "Sibby?"

"Yes, Aunt Leis."

"Why did you ask Alasdair if he was a fairy? Please don't do that again."

"But, Aunt Leis."

"Sibs …" Leisa drawled reproachfully as she opened a book about a family of bears. "No buts, and I mean—"

"Didn't you see his wings?" Sybil asked. She sat straight up, her eyes lit with excitement.

"I said no but—" Leisa stilled. "His what?"

Sybil jumped up and raced down the hall. When she returned, the fairy book was clenched in her hands. "His wings, Aunt Leis. Didn't you see them?" She flipped the book open to an illustration of a fairy with barely visible gossamer wings. "They look kinda like this," she said as she poked at the picture. "Only more fuzzy and wavy."

Leisa pulled Sybil onto the sofa next to her. "Of course I didn't see his wings. There are no such things as fairies."

Sybil pouted and hugged her book.

Leisa sighed. She gestured to the book Sybil clutched. "I think maybe we've read that book too many times. Let's put it away for a while and read some others."

Alasdair regarded them from outside the window. That had been close. He needed to keep a better watch on the time. The magic had started to fade and Sybil, being a strong believer, had seen his wings as he began transforming. A moment longer and she would have seen him in his true form. Whether Leisa would have seen the same he didn't know. He was sure she had spotted him outside the window on occasion. He was equally sure she'd discounted him as something *believable*. A firefly. A moth. A dragonfly. Most humans did.

Stretched out across the sill, he breathed in the cool night air, cooler than any he'd yet encountered. Closing his eyes, he concentrated. Soon his transparent wings grew thick, dark and downy. Draping a warm feathered wing over himself, he settled in for sleep. Tomorrow would be his last full day in the human world before returning the child. Tomorrow he would exhume the changeling from its grave and hide it in the wood; then he would spend one last time with Leisa before saying goodbye and heading back to Faerie the following dawn. He released a ragged breath. He and Leisa would come together as friends, that was all. Human emotions were easily crushed. He did not wish to hurt her.

~*~

"Good day," Alasdair greeted.

"Good morning, Ali," Rita replied from across the counter. She handed him two brown bags full of food and a coffee.

Alasdair took the bags from Rita's outstretched hands; then he sat at the counter.

"You're not running off this morning?"

"I should like to stay a few moments, if you do not mind." He sat on the corner stool nearest the door. Peeling the snap-on lid from his coffee cup, he took a sip and sighed. "I do so love this drink."

Rita laughed. "You and a billion other people."

An awkward silence fell between them.

"What is it, Ali?"

Alasdair sighed. Rita always sensed his moods. He had no doubt she sensed his origins as well. "You know, I will be leaving early on the morrow."

Rita frowned.

Alasdair knew she'd had hopes of a match between Leisa and himself. Were he human he would have obliged. But some things were not possible. Surely Rita knew this. He took another drink.

"That's right. I'd forgotten."

Alasdair smiled warmly. "*I* did not."

"So what are you going to do your last night in town?"

"At four hours to dusk Leisa and I shall come here to dine. It will be our last dinner ere my departure."

"What about Sybil?"

"Regrettably, she is staying with a friend. I will not see her before I go."

Again silence.

"Rita?"

"Yes?"

"I would like tonight's dinner to be memorable, but I know not how to do that."

Rita grinned. Her chin and shoulders lifted slightly. "You just be here. I'll make sure it's a night she won't soon forget."

"My thanks." Alasdair stood. Grabbing his bags and coffee, he headed for the door. In mid-push he paused and looked back at Rita. "Four hours to dusk is five o'clock," he said then slipped outside.

Again there was a flurry of activity in the cemetery, too much to risk being seen digging. Thank the stars the disrupted grave was close to the border of the wood. No one seemed to take note of it. He was close. So close. But he knew he would get almost no digging done that day. Tonight he would spend time with Leisa. Tomorrow he would finish the job and return to Galandore.

Alasdair watched an elderly couple stand before a stone, their heads hung in silent sadness. He had witnessed this before but had never truly understood it. Whoever had passed on was no longer there. Their spirit had moved on to a better place. *They* were happy. If the living only understood this transition of the spirit, they would not mourn death, but rather celebrate it with song as did the fae.

Then again, he supposed it was not death itself that they mourned, but rather the loss of this person in their lives. A pained smile shadowed his face. Love. So abstract, yet felt to the core of the heart. He finally understood.

Chapter Seven

Human World

"You're leaving?" Leisa bolted up from her chair and backed away from Alasdair. She paced an agitated circle, then faced him once more, her hands planted firmly on her hips, her sensual black dress now a dark barrier between them. "So what was this dog-and-pony show all about?" she asked motioning to the table where they'd just shared a wonderful dinner. "When were you going to tell me? After I slept with you?" Her gently freckled face flamed nearly as red as her hair.

Alasdair frowned. "I am telling you now." He stood, but stayed his distance.

"Why?"

"Why am I leaving?"

"No. Why did you get close to me? To Sybil!" Leisa huffed. "You led her to believe you cared about her, and now you're just going to walk away without even saying goodbye?"

"I was kind to her. Aye. But I did not lead her to believe anything more."

"And me? Did you lead me to believe anything more?"

"Aye." Alasdair hung his head. "I am sorry."

"Sorry? A convenient word."

"Leisa, I must return to my home. 'Tis imperative that I—"

"I don't care." She turned from him, then snapped her attention back in his direction. "Why would you share a romantic dinner with me one minute, then tell me you're leaving the next?" She huffed in frustration. "Don't answer. I don't even want to know." She stormed to the door. "Goodbye, Alasdair!" she said, slamming it behind her.

Alasdair winced at the resounding echo. He sighed deeply as he shoved his hands in his jeans pockets and began to pace. It had been a wondrous evening. Rita had outdone herself in the preparation of food—a colorful salad of greens, peppers, mushrooms, cucumbers, tomatoes, and crisp squares of dried bread that absorbed the tart dressing. The meat was thick, red, tender, and moist. It melted in his mouth with each bite. In the faerie realm, excepting trolls, dragons, and woodland beasts, to kill an animal for consumption was forbidden. In this human world, he ate meat as did most humans, perhaps because it *was* forbidden.

He looked out the window of the second floor private dining room. He hadn't meant to deceive her, but the evening had intoxicated him. Leisa had arrived precisely on time. She'd worn a snug black dress that flared slightly at the hips and bared flesh beneath an open V collar that ran from her throat to several inches past the collarbone. Her pale arms were exposed, as were her long slender legs. A silver chain encircled her neck. On it hung a circular pendant. In the center of the pendant was a tree, its branches reaching out in all directions. The tree of life.

When Alasdair had inspected the tree, a summery scent of flowers and mist rose from her flesh. He'd tried to remain on the level of friend, but he had failed. Rita had decked the private dining room with flowers and rich delicate linens. She had arranged soft music to whisper in the background. But his undoing had been the wine. Fruity and rich, it passed the lips as smoothly as sun-warmed honey, fogging his brain and dimming his thoughts. Then it happened, a kiss beyond any he had ever experienced.

True, it was merely the touching of lips and mating of tongues as any other kiss. But what rose from within him set his human body aflame, an intense heat that filled his gut and spread to his every molecule of flesh. Had Rita not delivered dessert just then, he knew not where that kiss would have led. Rita's sudden appearance had brought him to his senses.

Unfortunately, dinner had stretched on much too long leaving no time to visit the carousel before dusk. When Leisa had suggested visiting it the next day with Sybil, he'd had no choice but to tell her he would be gone by the morrow.

Now Leisa was gone.

Alasdair shuddered. It was for the best. Tomorrow he would scrape away the final few inches of dirt from atop the coffin and remove the changeling. Then he would return to Galandore and steal back the child. Leisa's child.

A soft knocking on the door pulled him from his thoughts. "Enter," Alasdair answered.

Rita peeked in, then entered. "Ali. What happened? Leisa just stormed out of here like a bat out of hell. And I won't even begin to say what she was muttering aloud to herself about you, but it wasn't flattering."

Alasdair lowered his gaze, then lifted it to meet Rita's inquiring stare. "I told her I was leaving on the morrow."

Rita's eyes widened. "You told her tonight?"

"Aye. I had hoped a pleasant evening together would soften the blow. It seems not."

"I thought she already knew." Rita whistled through her teeth. "I wish you would have told me your plans for tonight. A pleasant evening together only made the blow harder."

Alasdair nodded. "It seems so."

Rita gave Alasdair a sympathetic look. "Can I get you anything?"

"Nay. The sun is near to setting. I must go now."

Rita raised a brow and quipped, "You're not a vampire, are you?"

A tired smile crossed Alasdair's face at her attempt at humor. "Nay. I am—spent."

77

Rita nodded. She approached Alasdair and gave him a hug. "I'm pleased to have met you, Alasdair. I hope everything goes the way you want it to." She paused. "I hope you didn't make a mistake pushing Leisa away."

An unfamiliar ache filled his chest. "'Twas no mistake. 'Twas necessary," he replied. "Though I shall regret it for all time." He turned and walked toward the door.

Rita gaped as she watched Alasdair leave. Behind him the air rippled strangely. She rubbed her eyes to clear her vision. Still it remained. Like the wavering of rising heat, it followed him and slowly took shape. The shape of wings.

Rita gasped. She opened her mouth to speak, but no words came.

Alasdair turned just outside the door to face her, a strange luminosity surrounding him. "Rita?"

"Y—yes?" she replied shakily.

"Many thanks for all that you have done for me. And for being a friend."

Unable to find words, Rita nodded.

Alasdair shut the door.

Again Rita rubbed her eyes. Had she seen what she thought she'd seen? Had the wings been real? Had his aura actually glowed? She shook her head. Impossible, and yet she had always sensed something different about Alasdair. Something almost otherworldly. Growing up Gaelic, she had heard tales of the fae. Some nice, some not so nice. But they were only tales.

Weren't they?

Again she shook her head. "Impossible," she muttered out loud. "No more wine with dinner for me."

Too tired to clear the table, Rita flicked off the light and headed downstairs to lock up. Then she made her way to her third floor apartment to sleep. Sleep, however, did not come easily. Behind closed lids she failed to see the dark that usually lulled her to slumber. Instead she saw Alasdair, a faint glow surrounding him, large luminous wings at his back.

Once again fae, Alasdair looked to the west. A brilliant band of light lit the horizon in vibrant shades of red and gold as the sun slowly sank from view—the Creator's flawless plan to renew each day with a nightly respite.

Unfortunately, his own plan had not gone as well.

The air around him felt dark and suffocating. When he spread his wings, they were leather thick and black like those of a bat. He glided downward to rest on the base of Blaise's gravestone. He would sleep here tonight. He couldn't face watching Leisa one last time. He knew her grief would be great. Or her anger. He wanted to witness neither. Rather, he chose to remember her as her true self. The radiant, smiling Leisa he had come to know. Also, he felt a strange comfort resting on the stone. He knew not why. Perhaps because he was so close to the end.

He smiled weakly. End, indeed. In truth, it was but the beginning. To procure the changeling was the simpler plan, or it would have been had he not experienced an emotion so rarely known to the fae. He still had to cross the known world that was not part of Galandore, and he could not enter the same way he had left. Upon leaving he had timed the changing of the guards in the marketplace and slipped through the Galandorian Gate unnoticed.

He had not that advantage in returning. To avoid being caught on his return, he must do so through the Trenalyn Gate—the portal of the trolls. Fortunately, the trolls were lax in their guard. Chances were great that there would not be attendance at the gate. Still, that was merely the beginning. Beyond that lay the Trenalyn Forest, the River of Doom, the Sprite Wood, and the River of Tears. That, or he must slip through the dark swamp. To travel by either means would place him in great danger. He'd known this when he'd left. His odds of success were slim.

But what mattered eternal life without a purpose? Now he had a purpose. To save the child, even if only to assure her a brief life of eighty or so years. If caught by the Galandorian guards, he would be banished, of course. And not to the human realm. He would be stripped of all good magic and cast into the swamp of the dark faeries to live in eternal shadow.

Alasdair shuddered. It was best not to think on such things. Soon enow he would face the consequences of his actions. In the meantime, he must conserve what little magic remained and rest. He would need the last of the dust to pass through the gate, especially with the changeling.

Alasdair closed his eyes but found no darkness there, only a swirl of thought that set his head to ache. A chill filled the crisp night air and his leathery wings morphed to feathers. Drawing a dark, downy wing over himself, he slept.

The morning sun pierced his eyelids, waking him. The night chill had burned away. He lifted his wings to open himself to the sun's warming rays. Though his last thoughts had been dismal, he had slept soundly. He presumed exhaustion and his dimming magic to be the reasons. He stood on the stone's foundation and stretched, then turned to face it. From where he stood, in wide etched letters exceeding his height was the word "Vandermann." He ran his hands over the rough lettering.

Leisa.

He felt a strange ache in his chest, but there was no time to wonder at it. It was early, too early for visitors. This hour he would complete his task and begin his dangerous trek home. He still had not conceived how he would escape back into the human realm with a child in tow. He would give thought to that later. Today there would be no sustenance from Rita. The sooner he unearthed the changeling and passed through the gate, the better.

Alasdair sprinkled a glittery cloud of dust over himself until he took on human form. Again he stood garbed in jeans and a silvery white shirt that buttoned in the front–buttons formed from mother of pearl that fit neatly through fine slits. He ran his fingers through the black and gold strands of his hair, then glanced into his pouch. There was just enough dust to make the final transition back through the Trenalyn Gate. Lowering himself into the grave, he picked up the shovel and began scraping away the last vestiges of dirt that hid the small pinewood coffin. His heart raced. The pungent smell of the changeling filled his head. He was nearly there.

~*~

Standing before the bathroom mirror, Leisa studied the puffiness under her eyes and the red-rimmed ovals surrounding them. She had cried away her frustration and hurt far into the night, had heard the beginnings of birdsong, seen the first struggling ray of dawn filter through her bedroom blinds, striping the walls. Finally she had slept. Briefly. She was glad Halley's mother had called and asked if Sybil could stay the night. She needed time alone.

She ached in a way she hadn't felt since the deaths of her baby daughter and then sister, an all-consuming ache fed by a new disappointment, a new loss. Her wrinkled cocktail dress rested high on her hips. She stripped it off and tossed it on the floor in a crumpled heap. She hadn't bothered to change before falling into bed. Fatigue, fueled by emotion, had stolen her ability to follow her usual nightly routine. She had not had the strength. Instead, she'd embraced her bed and wept in the comfort of its pillowed arms until exhaustion claimed her.

A pair of indigo jeans lay folded on top of her dresser. She slid into them, then pulled on a cream cotton sweater. Grabbing a pair of folded socks from her nightstand drawer, she pulled them apart, drew them over her feet, then slipped on leather sneakers that laced to the ankle. The morning air still held a chill, so she eased into a black leather blazer fashioned for spring or fall. She knew she'd be carrying it later. She didn't care. For now, her heart hurt so much that there was only one thing she could think to do—one thing to remind her of a love that would never forsake her—and it called to her. She had to visit her daughter's grave.

It was a short walk to the cemetery. The gates were open and the cool morning air filled her lungs. The sun blinded her and she knew a warm day lay ahead. Soon late morning rays would burn off the dew. For now the grass shimmered as each glistening blade reached for the light.

Leisa studied the many rows of gravestones. So many varied colors, sizes, and shapes, all glowing gold under the rise of morning. She walked swiftly, eager to reach her destination. When Blaise first passed away, each weekly trip to the grave site had been heart-wrenching. The first year she'd wept each time. The second year she had merely ached. By the third year she had set her pain behind her and found comfort in her visits.

Why? She didn't know. Perhaps because she had never truly accepted that Blaise was gone.

Topping the hillcrest, she headed down the far slope toward the tree line. She'd wanted Blaise buried in a natural way. No embalming. No funeral parlor visitations. No fancy coffin or vault. Just a green grave with a plain pine coffin lined in biodegradable pink fabric and a quick one-day burial. Natural. Because the ground tended to sink in such cases, green graves were placed near the tree line or beyond. She'd bought the plot next to Blaise for herself. They would spend eternity together.

Lifting her gaze, Leisa saw movement near Blaise's gravestone. She hurried her steps. As she got closer, she made out a familiar shape.

"Oh, my God." Leisa began to run. When she reached Alasdair, she grabbed his shirt and pulled frantically. "What are you doing!" she screamed. "Stop it!" He stood chest deep in the grave, a shovel in his hands. She grabbed the shovel handle and tried ripping it from his grasp.

Alasdair held tight. "Leisa. Why are you here?" He yanked the shovel back, breaking her grip on it.

"Why am *I* here!" Leisa bellowed. "Why are *you* here? And what the hell are you doing?" Again she tried to grab the shovel. When her sights fell on the wood coffin lid, she covered her mouth and turned away. Tears filled her eyes and she fell back. "You're insane!" she cried. "I'm getting the police." She broke into a run, cutting through the strip of woods that separated the cemetery from the road. A tall wrought iron fence prevented her escape, so she continued sprinting through the trees, following the fence line until she thought her lungs would burst. Tears fogged her vision, and she tripped on an exposed root.

"Leisa!" Alasdair called.

Picking herself up, she ran once more. She could see asphalt through the foliage and the long iron bars of the fence, could hear the passing of cars.

"Leisa," Alasdair called again. Closer.

"Go away!" Leisa shouted over her shoulder. A sharp stitch in her side slowed her and she doubled over. Hurried strides approached from behind. She could hear the crush of ground cover at each nearing step. Sucking in a breath, she straightened and prepared once more to run. A firm grip wound about her arm and yanked her back.

Leisa screamed.

Alasdair muffled it with his hand as he locked her between his arm and chest. "Leisa, let me explain," he pleaded.

Leisa struggled and shook her head.

"Please, Leisa. You must listen." Alasdair shifted his stance for balance. "I will loose my hand now."

At the drop of his hand, Leisa bit his arm. "Let go of me!" She shrugged out of his hold and again ran.

"Sweet Mother Earth!" Alasdair groused. His strides were swift and long. He quickly caught up with Leisa and grabbed her from behind. When she swung around, they both lost balance and fell to the ground. Sharp twigs bit into Leisa's back. Alasdair hurriedly straddled her and held her firmly down, his hands clamped about her wrists, pinning them to dirt, leaves, and rock.

Leisa tried screaming, but powerful sobs closed off her throat. She began gasping for air.

Alasdair swung off of Leisa. He lifted her to a sitting position and waited until she caught her breath.

"Why, Alasdair? Why would you do that?" Leisa rested her elbows on her knees and covered her face with her hands. A muffled groan sounded through her fingers.

"Leisa," Alasdair began. He knew he should not divulge the truth, but he had no choice. Leisa had seen him desecrating what she thought to be her daughter's grave. No lie could correct this. "Leisa," he repeated. "Your daughter is not in that grave." He felt her tense and he paused. When she looked up at him, eyes red and swollen, he declared, "Blaise is not dead."

"Yes, she is!" Leisa cried. "I saw her dead in her crib. I saw her in the coffin before it was sealed. Don't tell me she's not dead."

"Yet in your heart you cannot believe her gone."

"Wishful thinking. I don't want her to be dead. But she is, Alasdair. And you're digging up her grave. Oh, God!" Leisa covered her face and began sobbing hysterically.

Alasdair grabbed her by the shoulders. At her flinch, he lowered his hands. "Look at me." When Leisa turned to again face him, he said, "Blaise is alive and I have come here to save her. To bring her home. To you."

Leisa averted his gaze and plucked at the grass resting against her leg. Then she lifted her chin and glared at him. "You can't save her. She's dead!"

Alasdair shook his head. "Nay," he replied with steely affirmation. "She is not."

"Why are you doing this?"

"Leisa. I can prove she has not passed on."

"How?"

"Come back to the grave with me. When I lift the lid and remove the changeling, you will see."

Leisa gasped. "You want me to watch you remove her body?"

"Not her body. A changeling."

Leisa opened her mouth to speak, then grew quiet. Her eyes widened. "Changeling?"

"Aye. 'Tis a–"

"I know what a changeling is. Sybil's fairy book has a story about one."

"Then you know what I say is true."

Leisa shuffled back on her elbows. "What I know is that you're insane."

"Leisa. I am not insane." Alasdair paused, not wanting to reveal the truth, but knowing he had no choice. "I am fae." He watched Leisa's eyes widen, then narrow.

"You're telling me you're a fairy? And you expect me to believe that?"

"'Tis true."

"No. It can't be."

Alasdair groaned. He needed to convince her. But how?

Sybil.

"Do you not recall when Sybil asked you if I was a faerie?"

Leisa looked thoughtful. "Yes. The other night outside my building."

"Aye." Alasdair rested his arms on his knees. "Did she ever tell you why she had asked me such a question?"

"She said she saw your wings. But she was just a five-year-old being fanciful."

Alasdair smiled. "She saw the truth."

"No, it can't be."

"When I left, you ran after me. Called my name."

"Yes, but you were ... how do you know that? You were gone."

"I was there. You merely saw a firefly."

Leisa shook her head and rubbed her face. "I remember. I thought it was strange to see a single firefly so close to the building. Usually they hover en mass over grassy areas. And it was brighter than any I had ever seen."

"'Twas no firefly. 'Tis the true form of a fae in the unknown world."

"Unknown world?"

"Your world."

"You're telling me you're from another world?"

"Aye."

Leisa shook her head and scoffed. "No." A nervous laugh escaped her. "It can't be."

"You ushered Sybil up the stairs. You later set her on the sofa and read to her. She brought you the book on faeries, her favorite, but you refused to read from it and chose another."

"How do you know this?"

"I have watched you and Sybil many times this week past. I have slept on the ledge just outside your window."

Leisa laughed hysterically. "Oh, God. I'd rather you were crazy."

"Nay. Were I crazy, Blaise would be dead."

Leisa shot him an icy look.

"I am not crazy–and Blaise lives."

Leisa pulled air deep into her lungs and let it out slowly. "I wish I could believe you. I wish that were true. God, more than anything, I wish that were true. But I buried Blaise." Her eyes watered.

"You buried a changeling." Alasdair stood. He brushed off his jeans, then held his hand out to her. "Please, come back with me to the grave and I will prove all that I say."

Leisa bit her lip. "I—I don't know if I can. If you open that grave and I see my dead baby ..." She drew a shaky breath and shuddered. "I couldn't face that."

Alasdair dropped his hand. "You will see only a length of wood."

"Wood?"

"Aye. There are several types of changelings. In the distant past sickly faerie babes were put in place of a healthy human. Now with sickness easily cured by the dust, lengths of wood are used."

"Lengths of wood?" Leisa scoffed. "How could I mistake a hunk of wood for my baby?"

"Faerie magic is strong." Alasdair watched Leisa ponder the possibility of magic so strong that a mother could not differentiate wood from her child.

"If what you say is true, how do you know I won't see a baby now?"

"Four years have passed. The magic has faded. You will not see a baby. You will see only the truth of what was put in that coffin." He again held his hand out to her. "Wood."

Alasdair took Leisa's lifted hand and pulled her up from the ground. "Come."

"How do you know that it's wood? It could be the body of a sickly fairy baby."

"Nay. When I say distant past I mean thousands of years. Also, I can smell it, Leisa"

"The coffin is wood. You're probably smelling that."

Alasdair grinned. "Nay, Leisa. I know the scent of a changeling from that of rotting pine."

Leisa worried her lip as Alasdair led her back to the grave site. She could feel his fingers tighten about her own. A part of her wanted to break free and run like the wind. Another part wanted desperately to believe him.

A fairy. Could such a thing exist? Sybil had said she'd seen his wings. Leisa cast a stealthy glance at Alasdair's back.

"They are not there."

Leisa jolted. "What?"

"Wings. 'Tis what you seek, is it not?"

"I–umm–no." She sighed. "Yes."

"They are not there because of the magic."

"But Sybil said she saw them."

"At sundown the magic fades and I become what I was born to be."

"Sundown?"

"Aye."

Leisa laughed nervously. "Like a vampire?"

Alasdair stopped suddenly. He turned to face her, his look hard. Leisa would have stepped back had he not been holding her hand. "Vampires suck the blood of the innocent. Pure evil feeding off what good is left in the world. Do not compare me to the likes of them."

"Vampires are real, too? I thought they were a myth."

"All myths are birthed from truth," Alasdair replied. He turned and continued toward the grave.

Upon reaching the site, Leisa dared to fix a look on Alasdair. His face was hard yet weary, his eyes clouded.

"I'm sorry," she said.

"Sorry?"

"For comparing you to a vampire. I didn't know."

Alasdair nodded. He grabbed the shovel and slowly slid down into the hole he'd dug, his head and shoulders still visible above ground. With the pointed end of the shovel, he scraped away the last vestiges of dirt from atop the coffin and began prying the lid free.

Leisa stumbled back, her fingers splayed over her mouth.

After several minutes of Alasdair prying in different spots, the lid began to creak and lift.

"Oh, my God." Leisa buried her face in her hands, each creak of the wood raking her heart. She peeked through her fingers. Her chest began to burn and she realized she was holding her breath. Her throat constricted so that she could barely swallow. "Alasdair?" she squeaked.

Alasdair gave the shovel handle a hard push and the lid fell to the side.

Leisa jumped. She turned away, composed herself, then looked down past Alasdair's shoulders into the hole. Cramped inside the child-sized grave, his body blocked her view. When he shifted position, a painfully familiar flash of pink cotton lining caught her eye.

Leisa slammed her eyes shut, afraid of what more she might see. When she dared to again open them, Alasdair was bending forward into the coffin.

Her first impulse was to flee. Instead she inched closer to the grave. She needed to believe him. She wanted to believe him. She had to believe him—had to believe Blaise lived.

She sucked in a breath and again peered past his shoulder. As he turned to face her, she caught sight of the once white christening gown she had buried Blaise in, now slightly yellowed and wrinkled. A baby's face stared out at her.

"Oh, my God." She spun away and fought the urge to retch. Her heart pounded with such force that she thought her chest would burst.

"Leisa," Alasdair said as he climbed out of the grave to stand behind her.

"I can't," Leisa replied. "I—I can't look."

He touched her shoulder. "'Tis as I said." He nudged her, urging her to turn and look.

Leisa shook her head. "I saw the gown. I saw a face."

"Aye. A gown wrapped about a length of carved wood."

"Promise me! Promise me, it's not my baby."

"Leisa!"

Leisa sniffled and shot a wary look over her shoulder. Her body shook. "W—wood?"

"Aye. Look, Leisa."

Leisa turned. Again the gown met her gaze, a small log free of bark and loosely carved into the shape of a baby wrapped in its folds. She caught her breath, then released it in short, spastic spurts. "I-it's wood!" she cried. "It's a frickin' piece of wood." She began to laugh and cry at once.

"I did say that, did I not?"

Her crying turned to relieved laughter. "You did. You said that." She gasped. "Blaise is alive."

Again she laughed, unable to contain her joy. Then she turned suddenly somber. "But—" she said, then paused. "Where is she? H—how do we get her? When can we get—"

"Hold." Alasdair held up a hand. "'Tis not as simple as you would like. Aye, Blaise lives. But I must take this wooden babe to the faerie realm and exchange it for the true child. It is the only way to free her. It is why I am here. Why I have been watching you all week."

Leisa set her hands on her hips. A stance that made him swallow. "You mean why you've been peeping in my windows and stalking me all week."

"I would not call it that."

"What would you call it?"

Alasdair made no reply. Instead he grasped the changeling tighter in his fists, turned, and began walking away.

"Whoa." Leisa ran in front of him. "Where are you going?"

"Home to Faerie."

"Not without me."

"You?" He shook his head. "Leisa, you do not understand. 'Tis not so simple as to walk into the realm and make an exchange. The fae will not be willing to give her up. I needs must cross treacherous territory even to get to Galandore. The way in which I came to this world is closed. The way of return is fraught with danger."

Leisa gulped. "I don't care. I'm going with you."

"Nay!" Alasdair clung to the wood as though it might flee. "You will stay here with Sybil. I will do all that I can to free your daughter."

"And what if that's not enough? What if something happens to you? I'll never know. I'll be waiting here—forever. And I'll never know that you're not coming back. That Blaise isn't coming back."

"Leisa—"

"No! I can't wait here and not know. I'm going with you."

Alasdair held her pleading look. "You may not be able to return," he warned.

"Then I'll die trying. Blaise is my baby, and I'm damn well going to do what I can to get her back."

Leisa kept a close watch on Alasdair the entire morning. There was no way he was going to Faerie without her.

Back at the apartment, she made a private call to Rita, then grabbed a knapsack from the hall closet and handed it to him. "The changeling will fit in this nicely and you can carry it on your back, leaving your hands free."

Alasdair slipped the length of wood into the knapsack and zippered it closed. He shrugged into the straps and smiled. "This will work," he replied.

Leisa moved to the kitchen cabinet and began packing food into another sack.

Alasdair watched in amusement, then shook his head. "You cannot take that."

"Sure I can. I'll just carry it on my back like you—"

"The food will change in constitution as it passes through the gate—becoming toxic."

Leisa stilled in her packing. "Seriously? But what will we eat?"

"We must find food as we travel."

Leisa caught her breath. *Find food?* "What kind of food?"

"Acorns, nuts, mushrooms, berries, apples, cherries. Shall I go on?"

Leisa shook her head.

"'Tis better that we eat well before we leave." Alasdair stepped before Leisa. He smiled dryly. "We shan't starve, but we may hunger for a time." He took her hands in his. His smile faded. "Leisa, 'tis not too late to change your mind. Stay here where 'tis safe. Should I not return, 'twill be because I have failed and for no other reason."

Leisa's heart lurched at his suggestion. "No. I can't just wait and wait and wait. I have to go. I'm not afraid."

Alasdair arched a brow. Leisa knew he saw through her façade.

"Okay. I *am* afraid. But I'm still going." She pulled her hands free, breaking the bond that would weaken her resolve. "Blaise is my child. I'll do all that I can to save her. I have to."

"What of Sybil?" Alasdair asked. "Is she not also your child?"

Leisa sighed. "Yes. And I love her very much. But a mother's bond to a child she birthed is the strongest of all loves, and I can't just do nothing."

Alasdair exhaled the last of his objections and nodded. "Who will care for Sybil while you are gone?"

A sudden calm filled Leisa. Alasdair had acquiesced. "I talked to Rita. She said she'd be happy to take care of her."

"You told Rita where you are going?"

Leisa rolled her eyes. "Of course not. I told her a teachers' training conference came up and asked if she could babysit for a few days. She's watched Sibby other times when I've had to do training."

"You are very confident about returning."

Leisa looked up at him. "I have to be."

"Why?"

"Because if I let myself think I won't return, it scares the hell out of me."

"Better out of you than into you."

Leisa gave him a stunned look.

"'Twas a bad jest."

Leisa forced a smile.

"Did Rita believe it was a training trip?" Alasdair asked.

Leisa tugged her full bottom lip with her teeth. "Well, she did get strangely quiet when I said you were coming with me."

"How so?"

"Almost like she didn't believe me, but understood why I couldn't tell her the truth."

Alasdair nodded. "She knows where you are headed."

"What makes you think so?"

"I have felt her emotions heighten when I've stood near to her. She senses something about me, but either she is not sure what, or she doesn't believe what she is sure of."

Leisa walked a few steps in silence. "She knows I'm going to Faerie with you?"

"I deem so."

"And that it could be more than a few days?"

"Aye."

"And that there is the possibility I won't be able to return?"

Alasdair nodded.

"Yet she didn't try to stop me and agreed to keep Sybil?"

"I deem she believes your going to Faerie is of grave importance. And she loves Sybil. She will care for her until you return."

Leisa unpacked the food and stuffed it back into the cupboard. "Can I at least carry the empty knapsack through the gate?"

"For what reason?"

"Well, if we find food, we can load it up to carry with us."

"A wise idea. Aye, bring it."

Leisa stuffed several small plastic food containers into the pack, then looked at her attire. "What should I wear?"

"It matters not."

"What do you mean, it matters not?"

"I mean, it does not matter."

Leisa rolled her eyes. "I know *that*. *Why* doesn't it matter?"

"For reason that upon passing through the gate to Faerie, you will—" Alasdair paused. "Change."

Leisa stilled. She stared at Alasdair. "What do you mean, *change*?"

"Just as I change to be more suited to your world, so shall you change to be more suited to mine."

"But you said you use faerie dust to change here."

"Aye. Because there is little faerie magic in this world, I bring it with me. But in my world, magic floats upon the breeze, rides upon the waters. 'Tis in all the earthly elements. You will be changed automatically."

94

Leisa brightened. "Will I have wings?"

"Aye and nay. In the faerie realm wings are visible only should a fae will them. A human has not that capability. You shall have them only should we touch and *I* will them for you."

"I don't understand. When you come to this world, you take a fully human form."

"Nay, not fully."

"Your wings are gone."

"When I become human, the aura of energy that surrounds me as a fae is gone, so I have not the means to will my wings."

"So, if your body turns human here, will mine turn fairy there?"

"To some degree. You will appear fae, but you will still be human. You will not possess the magic of the realm within you, and you will not be able to will wings to fly."

Leisa sighed. "Shame." She slipped the empty pack onto her back. "Okay, I'm ready."

Alasdair took her hand. "Come."

Leisa purchased a couple of hot dogs from a vendor as they made their way through the park. Alasdair was glad of it. It would stay their hunger. The playground sat deserted as he led her past the swings, jungle gym, and plastic play houses, then into the trees. The flattened trail of grass was no longer flat. He was glad he'd memorized the way.

"Hey, this is where we first met. Remember, that guy was beating the hell out of you and—"

Alasdair tightened his grip on her hand. "Aye, I remember."

"Ouch. Okay. Sorry." Leisa pulled her hand away and shook it. "How much farther?"

"A bit."

He led her onward through dense brush and tall grass. When he stopped suddenly, Leisa sidled up beside him.

A wide circle of mushrooms, low to the ground and hidden in the thick undergrowth, rested near a small grouping of trees. Alasdair took several steps until he stood in the center of them. He could already feel the draw of Faerie. "Here," he said. He pointed to the ground beside him. "Stand next to me."

Grabbing his pouch, he pulled out the last handful of dust. He drew Leisa close. "Wrap your arms about me and hold tight."

"What!"

"'Tis the only way. I have not enough dust for two passages. We must pass through as one."

Leisa did as he said. "But won't this be like the transport machine in the movie *The Fly*? Won't we become fused as one entity?"

Alasdair laughed. "We will be fine."

"Are you sure?"

"Our constitutions are very different. It will recognize that and keep like with like."

"It?"

"The magic."

Leisa shuddered. "Ali? I really am scared."

"Hold tight to me and close your eyes. Do not let go."

"No chance of that," Leisa muttered.

Clutching the last of the dust, he showered it over them. Immediately his energies began to shift. The transformation from human to fae had begun.

Chapter Eight

Faerie

A burst of light blinded Leisa through her lids. A mild charge skimmed her flesh. "Can I open my eyes now?" she asked.

"I would not advise–"

Leisa screamed.

"–it."

"W-where are we?" she stammered. The heavy black void that surrounded them was palpable. Quickly she snapped her eyes shut. "Oh, God. Oh, God. Oh, God," she muttered.

"Stay calm, Leisa. You will feel a breeze of sorts, see another flash, and it will be done."

As Alasdair said, a breeze came out from the darkness and swirled about their ankles. Slowly it rose over their calves, their waists, their shoulders, until they were completely encompassed. A flash possessing every conceivable color passed through her lids. Then all went eerily still.

Alasdair's heat warmed her as she clung to him. Something whispery light brushed her fingers. Then she felt Alasdair peeling her arms from his waist. Leisa opened her eyes as he turned away. A tall arched doorway gleamed brightly behind them.

"We're there?" she asked.

"Aye. We are here." Before she could react, Alasdair grabbed her hand and pulled her quickly out from the open and into the deep shadows of a thick swath of woodland trees.

Faerie Dust / Linda Ciletti

Leisa stumbled after him, struggling to keep up. When he stopped a safe distance from the open meadow, she caught her breath. "What was that glowing doorway?" She shot a look back over her shoulder, but it was now out of view.

"The Trenalyn Gate," Alasdair said. "We have just passed through. He stood with his back to her scanning the forest.

Leisa gaped. Fitted through the knapsack straps, his wings rested low against his back—translucent and gossamer, long and weightless. An intricate webbing ran through them like that of a spider's design, each individual strand glimmering. Then they disappeared.

"Trenalyn Gate?" she echoed.

"Aye. 'Tis the portal gate guarded by trolls."

"Trolls!" Leisa straightened. "You didn't mention trolls."

"Rarely do they guard the gate. They are overly confident that no one would dare cross their land to leave or return by it."

"You really didn't mention trolls." Leisa gulped. "Now what?"

"Now we begin our journey." Alasdair turned to face her.

He had changed. Not dramatically, but in a magical sense that she did not understand. His face was the same but different. There was strength there, solid warrior strength. His light-green eyes nearly glowed and his raven hair gleamed like polished ebony. The golden strands interwoven throughout looked like soft metallic threads. His lean muscled body retained its height, but his flesh seemed luminous and perfect. Like his clothing in her world, each garment had a slight luminescence. Dark-brown pants fitted closely to his muscled legs. His ivory tunic, belted at the waist, hugged his chest, its full gathered sleeves billowing in the breeze. A leather strap wound several times about his hips, supporting a scabbard that ran from waist to knee.

Leisa glanced down at her hands. Her skin appeared smooth and luminous as well, devoid of freckles or beauty marks. She lifted a shock of hair that had fallen forward over her shoulder.

Though they stood in shadow, it gleamed as if she stood in brilliant sun. She wore a pale-green chemise that felt lighter than silk and soft as down against her skin. It shimmered in the dim forest light. Wrapped several times about her waist was a rope of gold weave. On her feet were matching slippers. Curious, she cast a look over her shoulder.

"You will not find wings at your back," Alasdair said. "Take my hand." He held out an open palm to her.

Leisa eyed him warily.

"Please."

She rested her hand in his and noted the luminosity begin to fade to normal skin. When his fingers closed over hers, his wings reappeared, filmy and large and green like the foliage of the trees. At the same instant, she felt a sudden surge of energy course through her fingers. It rose up her arm and flowed through her completely.

"Now look."

Leisa looked over her shoulder and gasped. Behind her were beautiful wings similar to his.

"As long as we have contact, and I will my wings to appear, so shall yours. Should I loose you, they will fade to nothing." He released her hand and her wings fell flat, faded, then disappeared.

"So I *can* fly?"

"Only with me." He grabbed her hand and began pulling her along with him.

"Wait." Leisa stopped. "Why don't we fly? Wouldn't it be faster?"

"'Tis too dangerous."

"Dangerous?"

"Leisa, all is not as children's books portray. 'Tis not safe to fly outside the faerie realm." He commenced walking along the mildly rutted path.

Leisa studied the forest closing in on them. The scattered dirt of the path appeared as any other dirt, but the heavy foliage on either side of the path hung over them in a rich, lush green that paled any forest greenery in the human world. Most trees looked similar in shape to those of her world, but some took on sinister shapes, their trunks twisted and warped and dark as coal.

"We're not in the faerie realm?" she asked.

"Aye and nay. Faerie magic carries on the breeze, so I can access it here, but we are on the lower path of Trenalyn, land of trolls."

"There you go with the trolls again," Leisa said tightly as she struggled to keep stride.

"They are not to be taken lightly."

"So wouldn't it make more sense to get out of here as fast as we can?"

"Aye. But not to fly."

"Why is it too dangerous to fly?" Leisa asked.

Alasdair explained as he led her farther into the forest. "Think of the fae as birds in the human realm."

"Birds fly."

"Aye, they do. But when you look out over the woodlands, home to thousands of birds, how many do you see flitting through the air without concern?"

Leisa pictured the woodlands near her home. "A few, here and there."

"Aye. For reason that there are predators who would pluck them from the open air."

"What are the dangers here?"

"Firstly, trolls. Troll guards have mastered the bow. They would shoot us down as trespassers as easily as a hunter shoots a dove."

Leisa shuddered.

"Also, to fly across the river is to welcome certain death. The Red Dragon guards the rivers by night."

"And by day?"

"The White Dragon."

"You failed to mention them as well."

Alasdair stopped to look at her, his green eyes sparking. "I did say the way was fraught with danger. Did you not believe me?" He turned and continued walking.

"Yes. I believed you," Leisa said as she hurried in his steps. "I just didn't know what *kinds* of danger. That might have been useful information."

Once again Alasdair stilled. He turned to face her. "Would it have made a difference in your decision?"

Leisa paused. She shook her head.

"There is more."

"More?" She gulped.

"Aye. You must be aware."

"What else?"

"Should we have need to pass through the dark swamp, we may well cross paths with the dark faeries."

"Dark fairies?"

"Faeries who were cast out from the realm."

"You mean it's a prison?"

"Similar."

"Why would they be cast out?"

"Why are humans put in prison?"

"For committing crimes. Or for breaking societal rules that are considered crimes."

"'Tis the same." He looked back at her over his shoulder. "Leisa, there is nothing to be gained by worrying. Let us merely continue on our way and pray for the best."

"Right," Leisa muttered as she timed her steps to his.

Alasdair felt the weight of his knapsack resting low on his back. As they walked, he considered the choices of their paths. There were only two ways to reach Galandore. Either they followed the border of Trenalyn into the swamp or they crossed the Trenalyn Forest and forded the River of Doom to the Sprite Wood, then crossed the River of Tears to the borders of the fae kingdom. Each way held its own dangers. Dark faeries inhabited the swamp, a place of gloom. They were prisoners of sorts, but not. Though no physical wall held them captive, should they cross the swamp's borders, the band on their wrists would detonate and they would be no more. Inside the swamp they ran their designated area as they saw fit. No rules, no laws, no forgiveness. Who you crossed paths with as you passed through determined whether or not you exited the other side. Once they entered the swamp, his magic would diminish. He may be able to will wings, but he would not be able to take flight.

Crossing the Trenalyn Forest held a different kind of danger. It was dark and thick and full of gloom as well. Flames from hell shot up from the earth should you step unwisely. Troll sentries traveled the paths. Wild beasts foraged for fresh prey. On occasion the earth would sink beneath your feet, swallowing you. When the night winds blew, the trees seemed to come alive, murmuring one to the other. It was a dark and evil place Alasdair would rather avoid, for even should they make their way through unscathed, to cross either river without a dragon spotting them would be miraculous. Dragons had hated the fae since as long as he could remember. He gave his head a mental shake, wishing he could remember why.

Then there was the Sprite Wood. Sprites were not purposefully dangerous, but they had even less empathy and compassion than faeries. Sprites were careless beings who flittered through the wood with only one objective, amusement. Sprite fun usually meant someone else's misfortune. His faerie magic could protect them some, but he feared it would not be enough. Sprites were quite magical themselves.

"Why are you stopping?" Leisa asked.

"We are at a crossroads." Alasdair pushed back his hair. He looked down one path, then the other.

"Crossroads of what?"

"'Tis here we must decide which way to go."

Leisa looked at the split pebbled path, then eyed the heavily treed darkness that stretched in either direction. Branches hung low and partially over the path. Twisted vines ran from tree to tree, connecting them as one living unit. The forest flora grew tall and dense, its deep green shading the landscape with shadows that wavered with a life of their own. She shot Alasdair a look of weakly suppressed fear. "Does it matter?"

"Oh, aye. It matters." Alasdair studied each path, weighing his options. He wished Leisa had stayed at home with Sybil. Now it was not just his life he had to consider, but hers as well. Both paths were dark and full of gloom, both filled with hidden and not-so-hidden dangers. He should have thought this quest through more fully before embarking on it. At the time, however, all he could think of was saving the child.

He nodded to the narrow path on his right where the tree limbs hung like those of weeping willows and the ground was littered with dark pools of water that rippled in the breeze.

Leisa gulped. "We're headed to the swamp, aren't we?" she asked, grabbing his hand.

Alasdair set a finger to her lips. "Aye," he whispered.

Chapter Nine

Faerie

Alasdair grabbed Leisa's elbow and yanked her aside.

"What?" Leisa asked, rubbing her arm.

"Do not step in the water."

Leisa studied the harmless looking puddle. "Why not?"

"They are as deep as the depths of hell. You would sink into cold emptiness and then into flame."

Leisa's eyes grew wide. "Flame?" she muttered. She picked up her gait, not wanting to allow distance between her and the fairy who understood this world. Tree branches drooped ominously low, their gnarly vines sweeping against her clothes. More than once she thought she felt the brush of fingers on her back or thigh. When she turned to look behind her, the path lay empty. Alasdair strode on, skirting the puddles and whipping his short sword through reaches of brush that blocked the way.

Where did that come from? Leisa eyed the glistening sword Alasdair wielded, then recalled the sheath she'd seen hanging at his side when they'd transitioned. Her gaze fixed on the gleaming metal of the sharp-edged blade. Jewels beyond human imagination covered its grip. A gleaming stone of pure white light crowned the hilt, a stone more brilliant than any diamond she had ever seen. It cast off sparks of vibrant color even in the dimness of the forest. A fairy with a sword. This was a far cry from the stories she'd read to Sybil, where fairies were happy, frolicking little beings who used magic, not weapons.

Then there was Alasdair himself. Following behind him had its rewards. She could appreciate the sinewy muscles of his arms and back as they strained beneath the damp and clingy fabric of his tunic. She could admire the lengthy strides of his impossibly long, sculpted legs. She wondered why she hadn't noted their lean strength before. But then, she'd never truly studied him from this vantage point.

The perfect view became less and less appreciated, however, as the long trek wore on. For every stride he took, she took two. She was beginning to feel that if she didn't soon sit, she would collapse.

"Can we stop soon?" she asked. "I'm exhausted and my feet need a rest. Too bad that magic change didn't give me boots." She lifted one foot and massaged its ball through the thin fabric of her slippers.

Alasdair glanced up the narrow path. "A clearing lies ahead. We shall rest there."

Leisa tried to look over Alasdair's shoulder at the clearing. Finally she stepped slightly off the path to peek past him. A length of vine brushed lightly over her slipper, then wrapped about her ankle, stilling her. She tugged and it wound tighter still. "Ali?" she said as his long strides carried him farther away. She tugged again and the vine twisted up her calf. It pulled at her as it wound higher still, knocking her off balance and sending her sprawling in the dirt across the path. "Ali!" she screamed as it began dragging her into the brush.

Alasdair spun at her call.

"Leisa!" He sprinted toward her, his sword raised high above his shoulder. When he reached her, he thrust it down, slicing the vine in two. Leisa screamed. A faint and eerie cry sounded in the wind, then faded.

"Kick," he ordered as he grasped her under the arms.

Leisa kicked feverishly against the vines as Alasdair pulled her safely onto the path. She drew her knees up against her chest, struggling to catch her breath. "What was *that*?"

Alasdair settled on one knee next to her. He brushed a fiery cascade of tousled hair back from her face. "Naemis vines."

She looked up at him. "Naemis vines?"

Alasdair nodded. "They drag unsuspecting travelers who stray from the path into the brush and continue wrapping about them until they become part of the wood."

Leisa's gaze shifted nervously from one side of the path to the other, then back to Alasdair. "And then?"

"Nothing. You remain there for all time."

"D-do you become a plant?" Leisa asked shakily.

"You look like a plant, yet your eyes still see, your ears still hear, and your thoughts still pass. But you have no voice to speak, to scream, or to cry out in warning."

Leisa shivered. "So these plants ... people ... things could be watching us right now? Listening to us?"

"Aye." Alasdair stood. He reached down to Leisa and offered his hand. As he pulled her to her feet, he said, "Fear not, they cannot harm you. Nor do they wish to."

"Not harm me! They nearly turned me into one of them."

"Nay, those who are dragged into the wood are not naemis vines. They are victims as well. Their hearts break to see an innocent stray from the path. They wish to call out in warning but cannot."

"They have hearts?"

"Like you and me." Alasdair tried releasing her hand, but she refused to let go. "I need both hands to clear the path, Leisa."

"Sorry." Not wanting to be separated again, she grabbed the back of his tunic.

Alasdair grinned. "Do not stray from the path and you will be fine."

"Do not stray from the path," Leisa muttered to herself. "Do not step in the puddles." Her fist tightened on the hem of his tunic. "Do not. Do not. Do not." She wondered how many more 'do nots' she had to suffer on this journey. Her independence felt wounded. But she'd rather that than the alternative. She skirted another puddle. The water was dark and still and deceivingly deadly.

Reaching the clearing, Alasdair motioned for Leisa to stay back while he walked the perimeter. She watched as he studied the plant life surrounding it, then motioned toward a fallen log. "Sit and rest. 'Tis safe here."

Leisa tested the spongy grass with the toe of one slippered foot.

Alasdair laughed. "Truly, 'tis safe."

"Are you sure?"

"Aye."

She set a second foot on the grass. "I'm not so sure I like this swamp."

"Swamp?" Alasdair cast her a questioning look. "We have not yet entered the swamp."

"We haven't?" Her brow creased. "You mean it gets worse?"

Alasdair sat next to her on the log. "'Twould be best if you refrained from screaming." He smiled roguishly.

Leisa gaped at him. "Refrain from screaming! That plant nearly turned me into ground cover."

"And what an exquisite flower you would have made." He twisted a fiery lock of her hair around his finger.

Leisa narrowed her eyes. "That's not funny."

Alasdair suppressed his smile. "'Haps not." He brushed the back of his hand across her cheek—met her gaze with the heady warmth of his own. Suddenly Leisa didn't mind the *do nots*.

"Ali," Leisa whispered. "I don't think …" Her voice trailed off as he leaned forward. She closed her eyes just before his lips brushed lightly over hers.

A howling sounded in the trees.

Leisa jumped up from the log. "W–what was that?" She looked around nervously.

Alasdair stood, his eyes aglow as he scanned the forest around them. "A wolflych," he replied. Grabbing Leisa's hand, he led her to the path. "Come."

"But we hardly rested."

"We must move now."

His sudden urgency for speed set Leisa's skin to prickle. "What's a wolflych?" she asked as she quickened her gait to keep stride.

"A faerie who shapeshifts to a wolf. Usually upon the rising of the moon."

"A shapeshifter?"

"Aye, of sorts."

"What do you mean 'of sorts'?"

"They can shift only to the form of a wolf."

Leisa swallowed. "Like a werewolf?"

"Aye. Though the moon need not be full to shift. And should they hold the form overly long they cannot shift back. Also, though equally fierce, a wolflych does not kill out of bloodlust."

Leisa relaxed slightly.

"Hurry. Night approaches."

Leisa looked around at the surrounding darkness. "How can you tell? It's so dark under these trees."

"That the wolflych howls is sign enough. We must reach the swamp before night falls completely." Drawing his sword from its sheath, he guided her around a puddle and continued on. "Stay close," he warned.

"Why before nightfall?" Leisa asked. She looked warily behind her. "I thought you said they weren't dangerous."

"I did not say they weren't dangerous. I said they do not kill out of bloodlust."

"But?" Leisa prompted.

"They guard the night path that leads to the swamp and kill those who trespass upon it."

Leisa looked at the rocky trail beneath her feet and tensed. "Like us?"

Alasdair cast a fleeting look over his shoulder at her. "Stay close."

The howling faded into the distance. That would have been a relief had the trees not grown eerily twisted and the ground soft beneath her feet. Soon her slippers felt damp clear through. She shivered. Still she continued walking, keeping silent so Alasdair could concentrate. When he spoke at all, he spoke in hushed tones. Suddenly he came to a halt.

"What is it?" Leisa whispered. She peeked around Alasdair. The path disappeared into endless dark waters. Large trunked trees speared up from its depths, while heavy moss-laden branches rained down like a deep green veil to another world. "I'm guessing we reached the swamp."

Alasdair nodded.

"Do we have to walk in that?"

"'Tis the only way."

Leisa caught her breath.

Alasdair led, his weapon in one hand, Leisa's clenched fist in the other. After several strides, he stopped, pried open her hand, and intertwined their fingers. He looked at her before continuing on. "Glide smoothly through the water," he instructed. "Do not splash."

Leisa nodded. The water felt oddly warm against her legs. A mossy film dotted its surface and undulated on a bed of ripples as they strode through. With each step, the swamp water's ominous opacity rose higher and higher. Leisa let out a sigh of relief when it leveled off at her waist. "Why glide?" she asked as the drag of her dress caused her steps to slow. She could feel Alasdair tugging her along.

"I would not alert the dark faeries of our presence, and I do not wish to stir any life that rests beneath the surface."

Leisa swallowed. "Like crocodiles or snakes?" she asked. She worried her lip as she ran a quick scan over the gently rolling waves.

"In truth, I know not what lies beneath, but I am certain something lurks there. He glanced at her over his shoulder, not breaking stride. "'Tis best not to discover what."

Leisa gripped his hand tighter.

"Leisa," Alasdair admonished. "Do not splash!"

Leisa swallowed. "I'm not splashing."

Alasdair stilled.

Leisa stilled.

The splash of water continued.

"Hurry." Alasdair pulled Leisa with him, fighting the water's resistance with each hampered stride.

"Do you think they know we're here?" Leisa asked between labored breaths.

A whistling sounded and Alasdair flung an arm across Leisa's back, thrusting them both underwater. Leisa broke the surface sputtering.

Alasdair shook the water from his hair and grabbed her hand. "This way." He led her to a large tree that rose from the swamp. They leaned against the far side of its craggy bole.

Leisa tried muffling her water-choked cough.

"I am sorry." Alasdair apologized softly.

"Try to warn me next time you plan on drowning me," Leisa whispered.

"There was no time."

"What was that whistling sound?"

"An arrow."

"Arrow!"

"Aye. And to answer your question, Aye, I think they know we're here."

Leisa rolled her eyes. As the splashing grew louder, she peeked around the tree and saw several dark forms approaching.

"Quickly!" Alasdair pulled Leisa against him. Then he knelt in the water until it reached their throats. Leaning close to the tree, he lifted his wings and covered them. His green gaze brightened until it nearly glowed; sparks of light glinted in his eyes. His lids fluttered as he rested on his knees as though caught in a trance. When Leisa dared to speak, he set a finger to her lips.

Leisa looked up through the cover of his wings. From beneath them, they were nearly clear but for a light-grey haze. She could see the swamp beyond them and the five dark figures approaching. She swallowed her gasp as they stood tall and foreboding not three feet away. Their straggly hair brushed past their shoulders. Three had black hair like Alasdair, though without the golden strands. The fourth's hair was fiery red, and the fifth's milky locks transitioned to green at the ends. All wore hard expressions, their faces drawn and pinched and scarred. Having seen Alasdair and her own transitions, Leisa had surmised that faerie flesh was flawless. But these dark fairies wore the jagged scars of street fighters, signs that to survive the swamp and what lurked within was an ongoing battle. Their common clothes were spun of dark cloth. No shine glimmered in the threads, and the edges of the cloth were shredded. Their ears were slightly elongated and their noses flared with anger. They looked straight at her but saw nothing. Leisa looked at Alasdair. His pale green eyes glowed in the shadow beneath his wings. When the dark troop wandered out of sight, Alasdair released a breath, closed his eyes, and hung his head.

"Are you all right?"

"I am spent. I know not that I can do that again. The darkness of this place drains my magic."

"Why couldn't they see us? We could see *them*."

"They saw a reflection of the tree we rest against."

"So your wings act like a chameleon," Leisa murmured.

"Only in nature. A tree, a leaf, feathers. Had we made a sound, they would have torn my wings back and we would have been at their mercy." Alasdair raised his head and looked at Leisa, his green eyes now dull with exhaustion. "And they have no mercy."

Leisa rested her head on Alasdair's shoulder, feeling his warmth. "You live in a scary world, Alasdair."

Alasdair forced a smile. "Much like yours." Sure that the danger had passed, he drew back his wings and stood, lifting Leisa with him. "This way," he said as his wings faded and disappeared.

"Have you traveled through here before?" Leisa asked.

"As a youth."

"And how long ago was that?"

Alasdair began counting by hundreds.

"Never mind."

"A long time ago."

~*~

Time passed in silence. Only the soft sloshing of water broke the quiet air. Thick hanging branches covered in moss, vines, and long drooping leaves blocked out the sun. The shadows of the trees weighed on them. A ghostly mist spiraled off the water and hung in the air. Fortunately, nothing emerged from the water's depths, but a heavy knot hung in Leisa's chest as Alasdair's eyes remained dull. She knew his magic was depleting.

Her stomach rumbled. "Will it be much longer?" she asked.

"Nay."

Leisa sighed in relief. She'd been afraid they would have to spend the night in this dark, dank place. Or maybe they already had. She felt certain they would never find food here. Again her feet began to ache, but she held back complaining. The sooner they left this place the better.

Alasdair stopped. "Shh," he hushed.

Leisa stilled.

Alasdair nodded to a clump of trees.

Something moved in the shadows, then disappeared. "What is it?" she whispered.

"It seems we are being watched," he murmured so low that Leisa had to lean into him to hear.

"A—a wolflych?" Leisa asked.

"'Tis not a wolflych. We are too far into the swamp for them. They disdain the water and stay on dry, solid ground."

"The troop of faeries that passed earlier?" Leisa shivered.

"Nay. They would have attacked by now." Alasdair brushed back his hair. "'Tis an observer."

"Why would someone follow us just to observe?"

"I know not. Let us just keep moving. He, or she, seems not to be a threat."

Leisa followed behind Alasdair. In her world she would have walked beside him, but Alasdair understood this world far better than she. He would sense danger before she walked into it.

Though she would have thought it impossible, the trees grew denser still. Leisa and Alasdair wove through them, brushing low-hanging vines aside as they silently waded through the dark waterways. Occasionally she heard a distant splash so minute that she wondered if it were her imagination. Then louder splashes sounded dangerously close. Leisa felt Alasdair tense. He released the tenuous entwinement of their fingers, wrapped a tight grip about her wrist, and pulled.

"Hurry," he called.

"It's them, isn't it?" Leisa asked.

"Aye."

"Can you hide us?"

"Nay."

Leisa fought to keep stride. Snagging a root with her foot, she stumbled face first into the water.

Alasdair yanked a sputtering Leisa to her feet.

"Wait!" Leisa cried. "My foot is stuck."

"Stuck?"

"Under a root. It's wrapped around my ankle."

Alasdair dove under the water. When Leisa felt him pry the root open, she pulled free. Several seconds passed.

"Ali!" she screamed.

As the red-haired faerie caught up with them, Alasdair broke the water's crest. He shot Leisa a quick glance and lifted his sword. "Go!" he ordered. He pushed her away from the battle, then raised his sword over his shoulder and drove it down to block his opponent's forward thrust. Metal clashed. Again Alasdair swung. Again their weapons clashed.

Leisa froze.

"Go, Leisa!" Alasdair again ordered as he parried another blow.

The chilling slide of metal pierced her ears and she cried out against it. Reaching into the rippling waters, she grappled at the uneven terrain until she found a smooth, round rock that fit in her palm like a baseball. Quickly she stood. Then she heard a solid hit and saw Alasdair fall to his knees, the dark fairy looming over him. The fae's hair suddenly brightened as flame in the dim-lit swamp as he lifted his sword for a killing blow.

"No!" she screamed. She whipped the stone at him, striking his head.

Alasdair rolled and vanished beneath the water.

The faerie shook his fiery head. Having lost his prey, he set his sights on Leisa, his hard eyes gleaming with a fierceness that shook her through. He took a step toward her. She stumbled back.

A splashing sounded and Alasdair rose from the water, his sword in hand. With a forward thrust, he pierced the faerie

115

through. Leisa had never heard such a scream. It rent the air like a banshee's cry as the faerie staggered back, fell, then sank beneath into the water's dark depths.

Alasdair stood in a moment of stunned silence; then he turned to face Leisa, his sword held firmly in his grasp. He swished it in the water, cleaning the blade.

Leisa's gut wrenched. She was sure she was going to be sick. Even Alasdair looked frighteningly pale. She wanted to embrace him. Instead her gaze fell beyond his shoulder to the cluster of dark faeries approaching them.

"Ali!" She pointed behind him.

Alasdair glanced over his shoulder. He sped toward Leisa and grabbed her hand.

"Hurry, this way."

Leisa followed as he led her into a maze of trees. They wove through the watery copse, striving to put distance between them and their pursuers. The waist-deep water hampered their efforts, pushing against their every frantic stride. She saw Alasdair stumble more than once. He'd been injured. She listened intently. The splashing grew closer.

Alasdair paused to catch his breath.

"This way," a male voice sounded from the trees.

Leisa and Alasdair exchanged glances.

Again the voice. "This way. Hurry."

The faeries closed in on them. Alasdair had no choice. Grabbing Leisa's hand, he followed the voice. It led to a perfect circle of trees. In the middle of the circle stood a figure cloaked in black.

"Follow me." The figure pressed his palms to an especially large bole. An opening appeared. Quickly, he strode into the darkness.

Alasdair hesitated and glanced over his shoulder. Seeing four dark faeries advancing on them, he passed through as well, dragging a reluctant Leisa with him.

The open doorway morphed to solid wood and they stood silent in the dark. Suddenly torchlight splashed across the room and they shielded their eyes. When they opened them, two cloaked figures stood directly across from them. The figures raised their hands and slid back their hoods. On the left stood a fae with darkest brown hair. It framed his face in loose waves that tapered back to the nape of his neck. His violet eyes glimmered in the torchlight. Beside him stood a fair-haired fae, his smooth, long blond locks pulled back in a tie, his golden eyes fixed on Alasdair. Both wore curious smiles.

"Sweet Mother Earth!" Alasdair cried out. "Gideon! Lysander!" He rushed forward and gave each a crushing embrace. "I cannot believe my eyes." He stepped back for a full view. A wide smile crossed his face. "You are a most welcome sight. Another moment or two and—"

Gideon silenced him with a look. "Nay. 'Tis we who are pleased to see you. We thought you dead."

"Dead?"

"Aye. When we heard you had slipped through the gate, we knew your least dangerous way back was through this swamp. We've been watching for you."

"I could have passed through the Trenalyn Forest."

"You would not have done so," Gideon refuted with confidence. "The dangers are much greater there."

"Forgive me for causing you worry. How did you know I had crossed over to the human realm?"

"We surmised it to be so based on your relationship with Sachi," Lysander replied. "After much questioning, we discovered that the kitchen maid saw you leave. You were very fast, but not fast enough to evade her gaze."

"She was there?"

"Aye, at the market choosing food for the upcoming celebration."

"Celebration?"

Gideon clapped Alasdair's shoulder and gave him a slight shake. "Do you not remember? Elgar and Edeline marry this very eve. A noble match if ever there was one."

Lysander quietly scoffed but said nothing.

Alasdair smiled. "I did forget."

"She is daughter to the queen. How could you forget?" Lysander asked. "Tazia will have your head if you are not there."

Gideon looked Alasdair up and down and laughed. "She will have his head if she catches him soaked to the bone and covered in mud and swamp weed ... and on the day of the wedding."

Alasdair brushed at his clothes and grimaced.

Leisa moved behind Alasdair and grabbed his hand.

"This is Leisa," Alasdair said. He stepped aside so she could be seen.

Both friends bowed courteously.

"Leisa, these are Gideon and Lysander, my two closest friends."

Unsure of fairy protocol, Leisa curtsied.

Both fae exchanged glances.

"You need not curtsy, Leisa. They are not royalty."

Leisa looked chagrined. "Well, neither am I," she whispered. "But they bowed to me."

Alasdair leaned close to her ear and spoke softly. "I am royalty, so they assumed you were as well."

"You're what!"

"Is something wrong?" Lysander asked.

Alasdair shook his head.

Leisa's stomach rumbled.

"Do you hunger?" Gideon asked. "He motioned to a table and benches forged from fallen timber. "Sit awhile. Rest." After casting off his cloak, he set a spread of fresh bread, cheese, strawberries and wine across the linen table cover. Grabbing silver goblets from a shelf, he put one at each setting and then poured the wine.

As Alasdair and Leisa made for the table, Gideon asked, "Do I detect a limp, Ali?"

"'Tis fine."

Gideon persisted. "Nay, you are limping. Are you wounded?"

"'Twas not a piercing blow. I deem I'll have a few bruises, but they will heal quickly enough."

Gideon nodded. "So tell us," he said as he popped a ripe strawberry into his mouth, "why did you cross over? And how?"

Alasdair swallowed a cube of cheese and took a long draught of wine. "How was easy. I merely studied the changing of the guards. There is a five-count lapse when the gate is unobserved."

Lysander laughed. "Five counts!" He raised his goblet and took a drink. "That is a blessed fraction of time in which to get through."

Alasdair nodded. "I know this."

"But why?" Gideon asked. "Why go to the unknown world at all? Surely you knew you could not return through the Galandorian Gate without serious consequence."

Alasdair heard Leisa pull breath and gave his head a small shake. "I knew this."

"And I deem you also know 'tis forbidden to cross over without permission from the Queen and council."

"I do."

Leisa caught her lip in her teeth. She'd been about to tell all, but she didn't know how deeply in trouble it would get Alasdair. It seemed he was fairly deep in it already. She cast him a furtive glance.

Gideon drummed the table with his fingers. "And the why?"

Lysander sniffed the air. "What is that smell?" he asked. He stood up from the bench and set about the room, sniffing.

"I deem you already know." Alasdair pulled off his knapsack and set it on the table.

Gideon sniffed. "A wooden changeling?" he asked.

"Aye."

"You brought a changeling back from the unknown world?"

"I did."

"Why?" Gideon paused. "Surely you do not intend to exchange it for Sachi." He set on Alasdair a firm look.

Leisa leaned into Alasdair. "Who's Sachi?"

"Blaise," he whispered back.

Leisa could hold her tongue no longer. "Her name is Blaise, and she's my daughter!"

The room grew eerily quiet.

"Have you lost your senses!" Gideon exclaimed. "You intend to steal Tazia's prize and leave naught but rotted wood in its place?"

Leisa erupted. "First of all, she's a she, not an it. Second, she's nobody's prize. And we aren't stealing anything. We're reclaiming what was stolen from *me*!"

"And!" Gideon continued slamming his fist on the table. "You dare to bring a human back with you. Surely you have suffered a head wound, Alasdair. You know how Tazia feels about humans."

Alasdair remained silent, letting Gideon finish his rant.

"Well?" Gideon prompted.

Alasdair set a firm gaze on Gideon. "She is Tazia's prize only until Tazia tires of her, which is traditionally about the fifth year." He glanced at the ceiling in thought, then lowered his sights onto Gideon once more. "That would be now." He cast a quick look at Leisa and swallowed what he was about to say. His focus back on Gideon, he continued. "And you know what follows. Secondly, *you* did not detect that Leisa was human."

"Aye." Gideon assessed Leisa. "'Tis an excellent transition, but beneath the magic she is human all the same."

"Should the magic fade," Lysander added, "she will be found out. I'm surprised it held out this long."

Alasdair stood. "Then pray that the magic does not fade."

"As soon as you step back into the swamp it shall fade," Gideon warned. "I saw the dimness of your eyes when you bested your opponent."

Alasdair opened his mouth to speak.

"You know it to be true. You could not hide from the dark faeries the second pass. You nearly depleted yourself the first time."

"You have been observing us for some time, it seems."

"I have."

"Why did you not speak up sooner? Why did you not help?"

"I deemed you possessed enough magic to avoid confrontation."

"Which I did."

"Aye. The first pass. But it depleted you."

Alasdair nodded. "Once I am through the swamp and back in Galandore, my aura will be fully restored."

"Ali. You know it is our duty to arrest you," Lysander said sadly.

"Surely you will not do so."

An uncomfortable silence filled the room.

Gideon sighed. "Nay." He shot Lysander a glance, then took a long swallow of wine. "We shall think of something." He turned to Leisa, the first time he'd actually acknowledged her. "So, you are Leisa?"

"Yes."

"And you are the mother of Sachi?"

"Blaise. Yes."

"Blaise?"

Alasdair interjected. "Sachi's birth name."

Gideon nodded. "How long has it been since last you saw your child?'

"Four years, two months."

"And all this time you believed her dead?"

"I never believed it."

Gideon looked at Alasdair.

Alasdair shrugged.

"She will not know you," Lysander informed Leisa.

"I don't care. She belongs with me."

Gideon's face softened. "She will not wish to go. The fae are all she knows."

Leisa shot Alasdair a look. "Ali?"

Alasdair tried to soften the reality of their situation. "'Tis true, she will not remember you. She was but ten months old when you two ... separated."

"Separated?" Leisa clenched her teeth. "You mean when she was stolen from me."

Alasdair let the comment pass. "It will be a true test to tear her away. She will not understand."

Leisa felt tears roll down her cheeks. "I never thought of that."

"Sachi knows *you*, Ali," Lysander reminded him.

"Aye, she does."

Leisa looked hopeful. "She does?"

Alasdair found Leisa's hand with his. "Aye. I have tutored her a bit and played some in the gardens with her."

"*You*? Played?"

"Is it so inconceivable?"

Leisa arched a brow. "So she would trust you." It was a statement and question at once.

"I deem so," Alasdair paced the width of the small room. "But I know not if she trusts me enough to willingly leave the queen."

Gideon looked at Alasdair. "Have you a plan?"

"A plan?"

"Aye," Gideon expounded. "A plan of return to the unknown world with two humans at your side."

Alasdair broke eye contact. "Nay."

Lysander laughed.

"No plan!" Gideon snorted. "By the stars! Twill take more than five counts for three of you to pass through the gate without detection, I can tell you that."

"Truly, Gideon, I am not the strategist you are. But I will find a way."

"Oh, aye. I strategize. And you ... you have too much empathy. Where does this flaw come from?"

"I know not. Perhaps I am not flawed at all. Perhaps it is all of faeriedom that is flawed by lack of empathy."

Gideon laughed. "Perhaps." He took a bite of bread and swallowed. "What will you do once Leisa and her child are back in the human realm?"

"I will return here, to Galandore. What else is there to do?"

"You will be charged with treason upon your return and—" Gideon cast a look at Leisa and fell silent.

"And what?" Leisa prompted.

Gideon shook his head and turned away. Alasdair said nothing.

Leisa felt her heart drop. She hadn't thought about what would happen once they returned home. *Her home.* She hadn't considered that Alasdair would have to make a choice. Naturally his choice would be to return to his own people. She lowered her head and stared at the tabletop.

"Leisa?" Alasdair gave her a concerned look.

"Yes?" She forced a smile, then lifted her wine glass to her lips, hiding her ensuing frown.

"Nothing." Alasdair turned back to his two friends.

"Alasdair, you dream," Lysander said. "Speak the truth and let it be known. If you return after stealing back the child, you will be cast into this swamp for eternity. A short eternity because as nephew to the Queen, you shan't find many friends here."

"Will you visit me, my friend?" Alasdair quipped.

Leisa shot Alasdair a frantic look.

Gideon shook his head. "This is not a time to jest, Ali."

"If I jest not, the darkness will consume me." He looked at Leisa. "I will deal with whatever consequences come of this." Then he cast his two friends one last pleading look. "Will you not help us?"

Gideon scratched his chin. "Let's see. Stealing the queen's prize and leaving her naught but rotted wood. Risking a conviction for treason and being cast into the dark swamp for all eternity? Aye, we will help."

"Speak for yourself, Gideon."

Alasdair and Gideon turned to Lysander.

Leisa caught her breath.

Lysander looked chagrined. "I did not say I would not help. I merely wish to speak for myself."

Alasdair smiled. "Then you will help?"

"Aye. To a point."

"To a point," Gideon agreed. "We are limited to what we can do without detection. But if it falls within our ability, we are there for you."

Alasdair rounded the table and clapped a hand on a shoulder of each friend. "I can ask no more."

Leisa brightened. There was hope. She followed Alasdair and stood beside his friends.

A strange sound sent vibrations through the tree.

"What is that?" Lysander asked.

Everyone stilled and listened.

Gideon leaned against the wall. "It sounds like chipping ... chopping."

"They're cutting down the tree!" Alasdair's hand flew to the sword at his side.

Gideon and Lysander donned their cloaks. "Stand here," Lysander advised. When all were in position, he waved his hand and the room emptied of all its contents. When he waved his hand in a circle above the floor, a trap door appeared.

Gideon opened it. "Quickly. Through here."

Lysander was the last to leave. After lowering himself through the trap door, he sealed it.

Leisa's eyes grew wide. A long, dark tunnel stretched out before them, so black that she could see only a foot or two in front of them. "Is it safe?" she whispered, afraid that to speak too loudly would bring down the tenuous dirt walls. Scattered roots poked out from the crumbling dirt, and she moved closer to the center of the path.

Gideon grinned. "Would you prefer to be up there?" he asked.

Leisa shook her head.

Alasdair grabbed her hand and gave it a squeeze. "'Tis safe enough. There are no two fae in all of the realm whom I would trust with my life more than these two rogues."

Lysander blustered. "Rogues! Did you hear that, Gideon? He called us rogues."

"Hah!" Gideon replied as he lit a torch. "You had best thank your stars for that," he said over his shoulder. "Were we not rogues, you would be lying dead in the swamp."

Leisa watched the play of light on the walls—bouncing and dancing with each of Gideon's steps. She knew he was right. Had these two loyal friends not set out to find Alasdair and helped them escape the dark faeries, she and Ali would undoubtedly be dead. When Alasdair had told her the way was fraught with danger, she could not have imagined how much. She wondered if they would ever escape this world. Would she ever get back home? *Home.* Her thoughts flew to Sybil. The poor girl had already lost one mother. Leisa bit her lip. She prayed Sybil would not lose another.

Chapter Ten

Human World

Rita bade the cook and waitress goodbye, then locked the front door of the café. She slipped the key into her pocket. It had been a busy day with the summer festival in full swing. Tourists abounded. Bad for peace and quiet, but good for business. She watched Sybil, who sat contentedly in a back corner booth with a stack of paper and a large box of crayons. Leisa had told her that she'd be gone a few days and left her a cell phone number, even though she already had it. Rita had babysat Sybil before when Leisa had to do training. But this trip had come up too suddenly. Rita worried her lip. And this time, Leisa had not said *where* she was going. She'd merely said a training trip.

Rita wasn't fooled.

There had been a catch in Leisa's voice that spoke of more. Fear. Trepidation. But most of all, hope. Hope for what, Rita didn't know. She had not pried even though she'd have liked to. She knew that Leisa would not have asked her to babysit had it not been important. And that was enough. She looked at Sybil once more.

As if feeling Rita's gaze, Sybil looked up and smiled fully. "Look what I drawed!" she squealed.

Rita strode to the booth. "Let's see." She picked up the paper. On it were two stick figures. On the left, a man with bright green dots for eyes, black spiky hair, and wings. On the right, a woman with dark green dot eyes, her long red lines of hair crowned with a flower. She, too, had wings and was wearing a flowing white dress that ran off the page. They hovered above the ground facing one another, their stick arms held out in front of them, hands touching. There was no doubt in Rita's mind who the couple was.

"That's beautiful," Rita gushed. "Is this Alasdair?" She pointed to the tall, winged stick man.

"Uh-huh."

"Why does he have wings?"

"'Cause he's a fairy."

"And this is your Aunt Leisa?" Rita asked, pointing to the stick woman.

"She's a fairy, too."

"Really?"

Sybil tucked her chin into her chest. "Well, not 'xactly. But they have to be the same so they can get married."

Rita started. Married! Was that why they'd asked her to babysit? They were running off to get married? Surely Leisa wasn't that irresponsible. They just met. And even if they were getting married, surely they would have told her. At the least, they would have taken Sybil with them. Rita sat next to Sybil, who had begun another drawing.

"Why do you think they're getting married? Did they tell you that?"

Sybil shook her head. "Oh, no. I just wished it. And if you draw your wish, and put it under your pillow when you sleep, it comes true."

Rita's brows rose. "I never heard that before."

"My mommy told me and she never lies."

Never lied, Rita thought, but did not correct the child.

Sybil's eyes looked suddenly sad. Her hand stilled. When her bottom lip protruded in a pout, Rita spoke. "Of course not." She kissed Sybil's golden head then looked at her watch. "Come on," she said, urging Sybil up. "It's getting late. Let's go upstairs to my apartment. We'll get a bath, read a story, and tuck that wish under your pillow—and we'll keep it there until your Aunt Leisa comes back."

Sybil hopped out from the booth, her expression brighter. "Do you think it will work?" she asked. Her eyes glittered with excitement.

Rita took Sybil's hand and escorted her to the steps that led upstairs. "I think there's an excellent chance of it."

~*~

Faerie

The tunnel was dank and narrow, so narrow that they walked single file. In the lead, Gideon lit the way by torch. Lysander took up the rear. Following behind Alasdair, Leisa asked, "What happens when they cut down the tree? Will they find the tunnel?" She looked back over her shoulder, but it was too dark to see anything clearly.

"'Twill take them the better part of a day to fell the tree," Alasdair replied. "By then, we shall be long gone and the tunnel filled."

"But the tree was hollow."

"Was." Alasdair glanced back at her. "Once the trap door was sealed, the tree became solid again."

Leisa gasped. "That's amazing." She reached for Alasdair's hand and wound her fingers in his.

Alasdair squeezed her hold without breaking stride.

"But don't the dark fairies know this? I mean, why bother if it's futile?"

"They do not know. They have forgotten."

"Forgotten?"

Alasdair slowed so that she stood next to him. It was a tight fit in the narrow passage, but he wound his arm about her waist to take up as little room as possible. "Leisa," he said. "Do you recall how my magic depleted in the swamp?"

"Yes."

"'Twas but a small part of a day. Imagine many days, weeks, years. In time the magic falls to naught. As time passes, the memory of it dies as well. The dark faeries have no recollection of the power of the fae. They have no magic. It has long since fallen away. The swamp is our equivalent of hell. To forever live in a world of darkness and gloom with no sun or moon, no crisp bouquet of spring foliage or perfume of flowers breaking through the ground is the worst imagining any faerie can know."

"What about Lysander and Gideon? They had magic in the swamp."

"Aye. But Lysander and Gideon are exalted royal guards."

"Exalted royal guards?"

"An elite segment of guardsmen. Bestowed upon them is magic greater than that of the normal fae to ensure the safety of our borders."

"Who bestows this greater magic?"

"Tazia, our queen."

"The one who has Blaise?"

"Aye."

Leisa grew troubled. "Do you think we'll be able to get her back?"

"'Twas always my intention."

Leisa nodded. "I know. But do you think it can be done?"

Alasdair quieted for several long strides then sighed. "I hope it."

Hope? It was too feeble an answer. Hope was for dreamers. Hope rarely won in a game of chance. She wanted hard cold facts and a definite *yes*. Leisa worried her lip, not sure how to respond. She lowered her gaze to their hurried strides and noted the caked mud on her slippers and his booted feet.

Her heart thumped faster as she anticipated seeing Blaise. She wondered what her daughter looked like after all these years. Was she a happy smiling child as she had been as a baby? Were her silky locks still red or had they changed in time? Were her eyes still the dark blue of babydom or had they morphed to green or brown? She hadn't seen Blaise since she was ten months old. Blaise wouldn't remember her. But Blaise knew Alasdair. At least that was in their favor.

She looked at their entwined fingers—Alasdair's long and lean and warm. So incredibly warm. His large grip covered her hand in a firm but gentle hold and clung as though he feared she would somehow slip away.

Suddenly the tunnel grew brighter. When she again looked over her shoulder, she saw that Lysander had lit a torch. Behind Lysander, what had been open tunnel was now solid dirt and rock. As they made their way through, the walls closed in behind them. She caught her breath, hoping the closing wouldn't overtake them.

"We're nearly there," Gideon called back.

Leisa strained her eyes to see ahead. The path led to a barrier wall of rose quartz. Upon reaching it, Gideon murmured a few words and ran his hand in a circular motion. Suddenly a crack appeared in the quartz and a door opened.

"By the stars!" Alasdair exclaimed as he passed through. He squinted at the bright light. "We are in the forgotten gardens of the palace."

"Aye. No one comes to this corner of the garden. 'Tis old and grown over, a perfect place for comings and goings." Gideon grinned.

"Right under the queen's nose." Alasdair laughed. "Only you, Gideon, could devise such a plan."

"And I!" Lysander called out. "Do not forget me."

"And you, Lysander." Alasdair added.

Leisa wanted to ask if their activity was dangerous, but she was sure it was. She didn't know much about the faerie world, but surely it would be highly frowned upon for two of the queen's most elite guards to sneak into the dark swamp to find an AWOL Alasdair. "Now what?" she whispered to Alasdair.

Gideon answered. "Now you go to the palace and clean up, then report to the formal garden for gaiety and dance. The wedding commences shortly. I deem Tazia, Edeline, and Elgar will be more than pleased to see Alasdair there."

"Aye," Lysander added. "Come, Gideon. We must clean up as well before we are missed."

"Why is it so important for you to be there?" Leisa asked.

Alasdair looked down at Leisa. "Edeline is my cousin. Tazia, my aunt."

"So you're nephew to the queen. A—a prince!"

"Aye."

"The queen whose prize we intend to steal?"

"The same."

"She'll kill you!"

"Most likely."

Leisa laughed at the jest. When she looked up, there was no humor in Alasdair's eyes. "Ali—"

Alasdair led her toward an overgrown garden path.

"We shall see you at the feast," Lysander called out as he and Gideon headed in the opposite direction.

"Aye. Do not be long," Gideon added.

"We shan't." Alasdair turned to Leisa. "Come," he said. "There is a back way in, a way I discovered as a young lad. The palace will be empty but for a few servants, since all are at the feast. We'll wash hastily in my upper chamber and make our way there."

"Your upper chamber? You live in the palace?"

Alasdair looked amused. "Of course. I am nephew to the queen."

Leisa walked beside Alasdair, soaking it all in. "Are you next in line for the throne?" She swallowed hard.

Alasdair grinned. "Nay. Edeline is. It passes through the female line."

"Oh! A matrilineal society." She nodded approvingly.

Alasdair gave her a sharp tug.

"Hey!" Leisa cried.

"Do you imply that I would not make a great king?" he quipped.

"Not at all. I imply that I would make a greater queen."

Alasdair laughed. Upon reaching the back wall to the palace, he opened a cleverly hidden door. "'Tis a secret exit should ever the need arise to escape unseen," he explained.

"Has that need come up often?"

"Not often. More times than not, 'tis used for discreet liaisons."

"Yours?"

He didn't answer. Either he hadn't heard her question or he chose to ignore it. Ducking inside, Alasdair and Leisa traveled a dark and narrow corridor. They slipped through the empty kitchens. Ahead lay the servants' spiral staircase. As they reached the top stair, a wide hallway stretched out before them. Torches, held in place by leafy sconces covered in gilt, hung on the walls, their flickering golden flames setting the beige stone to glitter. When he led her through a chamber door, she gasped.

Sunlight poured through a tall arched window, casting its brilliance on the polished stone floor and gleaming walls. A large bed rested to their left, round and scalloped, like a clam shell. Soft white linens with threads of gold, sage, and silver running through them covered the bed. Sheer sage curtains hung from a canopy of gold that encircled the bed for quasi-privacy. An enormous armoire sat against one wall, its gleaming mahogany glowing as the brilliant sun bathed it in light. An exquisite tapestry hung from the far side of a wooden rod that crossed above the window, ready to be pulled closed when the need arose. Sculpted carpets in similar colors were splashed about the floor—one on either side of the bed, one at its foot and one by the window seat. Another carpet rested before a gilt-framed mirror that easily stood ten feet high and five feet wide.

Leisa stared in awe.

Alasdair released her hand and made his way to the armoire. He whipped open its door and began tossing clothing onto a settee. "Choose one," he said. He pointed to a door directly across from him. "'Tis where you can wash and take care of any needs."

"What about you?"

"I shall change in my room."

"This isn't your room?"

Alasdair looked at her. "'Twas a noblewoman's room, but she married and moved to another barony."

"Won't she be angry with you for sharing her apartment and her things?"

"Nay. I deem she has more than enough being married to a noble of high standing. I doubt she will return for a few meager belongings." He slammed the armoire door shut. "Hurry and dress," he said. "I shall do the same."

Leisa waited for Alasdair to disappear through the door; then she turned to examine gowns fit for a princess. She lifted each one, felt its exquisite texture and admired its sheen. These were courtly gowns of highest quality. She held each of the three in front of her before the mirror. Regal red. Glistening gold. Resplendent ivory embroidered in shimmering vines that twisted up the form-fitted sleeves and around the scooping neckline in a darker ivory thread. The gown's semi-sheer gathered skirt fell to the ground in multiple layers, giving its translucency the illusion of opacity. She quickly forgot the gold and red gowns.

She'd expected the bathing to be primitive. Instead, it rivaled any modern convenience of her world. She stood in a warm shower of water that sprayed out from a crevice in the stone for several long minutes before washing. The shampoo and soap resting on a shelf of shale smelled like wildflowers and refreshing rain.

When she'd entered the shower, its door had automatically locked behind her. The only way out was to walk through a passage of warm swirling air. When she exited, she was completely dry. Once more, standing before the mirror, she noted the smooth skin of her face and the clean shine of her hair. Silken waves fell like a river of red over her shoulders, the brilliant sun as it speared through the window and splashed across the room, setting it to glow. She tried pulling it up, but it would not give in to such constraint and slid from its pins. Finally she gave up and let it flow where it would. When she slipped the ivory gown on and gazed into the mirror, she gasped. The gown transformed her all the more. Her face took on an even greater glow. Her cheeks appeared sun-kissed and rosy. The weariness of their travels through the swamp had disappeared. She tried to reach the tiny rosette buttons that ran up the back of her gown. She could not.

"Are you ready?" Alasdair asked as he entered the room.

She turned and his face lit. She had never seen him smile so fully.

She glanced over her shoulder toward the back of her gown. "I can't button it," she said.

Alasdair stepped behind her and began slipping the rosettes through satin loops. She felt his breath caress her hair and noticed he was breathing heavier than normal. Finishing the task, he lifted his head to look at her in the mirror. His hands rested at her shoulders. "You are beautiful," he said.

She felt his gentle pull, felt his cheek rest against her temple. In the mirror she watched him ponder, then shake himself free.

"But there is something wanting," he declared.

Leisa looked over her attire. She lifted the skirt of the gown. "Shoes!"

Alasdair drew a pair of satin slippers from the armoire. When she slipped them on, he said, "Nay. 'Tis something more."

He feigned a quizzical look, then reached into his pouch and pulled forth a wispy gold chain. Hanging from the chain was a lavaliere—a twisted gold leaf bathed in diamond dust that glistened in the light. Simple, but rich beyond measure.

"Oh, no, I couldn't!" Leisa exclaimed as he moved behind her and slipped it around her neck.

"The queen will expect no less."

"It's hers?" Leisa tensed.

"Of course not. It belonged to my mother. Now I gift it to you." He smiled at her reflection.

Leisa fingered the pendant and looked in the mirror. It was the perfect touch, almost as though he had known she'd choose the ivory gown. She licked her lips nervously, then turned. When she did, she felt his arms slip around her back. His embrace drew her close and he lowered his head. His lips touched hers, gentle and searching as though savoring forbidden fruit. Then his grip tightened and his mouth opened for a deeper taste.

Leisa parted her lips and accepted him, relishing the feel of his mouth and the warmth of his body pressed against her. She pulled him closer still, unable to get close enough. The heat of his hands explored her back and caught on the tiny rosettes. They settled on her waist and slid upward, his thumbs touching the outer curve of her breasts.

Leisa caught her breath.

Alasdair stilled, then pulled back from her. "We must go now," he informed her. He took her by the hand and headed for the door. He was jolted back.

Leisa's feet were planted firmly on the floor, her eyes wide. "I'm scared."

Alasdair turned and took her other hand. "Do not be so. I will speak with Tazia and explain your presence."

"You'll tell her the truth?"

Alasdair shook his head. "There are many baronies, Leisa. You could hail from any one of them."

"What if she asks questions?"

He grinned. "I deem she will be too elated to see me with a beautiful woman to do so. Also, forget not, this is her daughter's wedding feast which will last throughout the night and into the dawn. She will not have time to question us. We are safe enough, for now."

"What about Blaise? Will we see her?"

"I deem so. I shall keep my eyes and ears open for her. Perhaps 'twill be the perfect time to take her, when others are caught up in the frivolity and the gate is weakly guarded."

Leisa's eyes lit.

"Do not put all your hopes on that. 'Twould be the best scenario to be sure. But Sachi may not be at the wedding. The children may be set apart in a play area."

"We'll hunt them down!"

"Leisa, we must first follow protocol; speak to the queen, congratulate the couple, eat, dance, do what normal wedding guests do. Then, when all are besotted with drink and merriment, we will break away and seek out Blaise. I am back after an unexpected absence. Many eyes will be upon me, *and you*. We must be patient."

Leisa nodded. "I understand."

"Good. Now let us go. We've a long day and night ahead of us."

Faerie Dust / Linda Ciletti

Chapter Eleven

Faerie

Leisa watched from a distance as Alasdair conversed easily with his fellow fae. The bride and groom, Edeline and Elgar, stood to one side of him, dressed in pale blue silks trimmed in silver thread. Queen Tazia stood to his other side, her red bejeweled gown sweeping the floor behind her. He had bowed briefly to Tazia, then risen with a whisper of a grin on his face. He had introduced her to Tazia as a friend of a friend he'd been visiting in an outer barony. Tazia had seemed to believe him. Leisa was relieved it had gone so smoothly. Now she sat alone on a garden bench while Alasdair caught up with old friends. She didn't mind. It gave her time to think and to admire him from a distance.

Alasdair stood in noble elegance. He was not the vulnerable human she had met in her world, nor the warrior who had led her through the swamp. This was another side to him, a side she could admire in a very different way. His black brocade tunic matched the gleam of his hair and the polish of his boots; his close-fitted pants were silver gray. Around his waist was a twisted strap of metallic silver that reflected the light. She noted the softness in his gaze as he watched his friends, the flashing of his light-green eyes, now subdued to misty sage.

She ran her fingers over her lips. On the path she'd not had time to reflect on his kiss, but watching him now, studying the movement of his mouth as he spoke, she remembered that moment in the clearing before they'd reached the swamp. The moment before the wolflych howled. It was just a kiss. No more. A butterfly kiss, like a gentle sweep of a summer breeze. It had been sweet, sweeter than any confection she'd ever tasted.

The kiss in the upper chamber had been so much more. Desperate, passionate, hungry. She could still feel the weight of it on her mouth, could still taste him. She glanced over the multitude of guests, all elegantly dressed and coiffed. She thought of her own hair hanging down loose and unstyled. Perhaps that was how all ladies wore their hair in her barony, she mused. She closed her eyes and envisioned a hall of courtly noblewomen, their hair hanging silkily over their shoulders. She smiled at the thought.

"I like you smiling," Alasdair said.

Leisa jumped. She looked up and her smile widened. "I didn't hear you approach."

"I was especially quiet so as not to wake you."

"Wake me?"

"From your dream."

Leisa laughed, then turned serious. "Have you seen Blaise?" she whispered.

Alasdair lowered his voice. "Nay. I have seen no children. I deem they are set apart in the play area." He took her hand. "'Tis too soon to seek it out. Too many eyes are yet upon us. We must wait until all are besotted with drink and gaiety."

"So what do we do in the meantime?"

Music rose from the orchestra, a symphony of strings and horns and gentle bells.

"We dance." Alasdair pulled Leisa up from the bench.

"Dance?" Leisa yanked her hands free from his. "I don't know any of your dances." Fear tensed her face to the very lids of her eyes.

"'Tis no matter."

"Yes, it is." Leisa stepped back. "If you think all eyes are on you now, just wait until I make a fool of you on the dance floor."

She saw a smile in Alasdair's eyes. "Do you recall how your wings work?" he asked.

"Yes."

"'Tis the same with dance."

Leisa blinked.

"As long as we touch, you will know what steps to take."

Leisa bit her lip. Her gaze darted over the crowd. "Are you sure?"

"I am more than sure."

Leisa eyed the couples wistfully, so beautifully graceful in their silken attire and sweeping gowns.

Alasdair held out his hand.

Leisa sighed. "I don't know if I can."

Alasdair listened to the song being played. "This dance requires constant touch. This one you can do." His eyes sparked with wonderment and magic, and something deeper.

"Ali?"

"Trust me." He took her hand and led her to the center of the floor.

Leisa stepped close to Alasdair. "I don't know what to do," she whispered. She glanced around and saw all eyes focus on the two of them. "Ali?"

Alasdair smiled warmly. "Your body will know. Just relax and follow my lead." He bowed gently, moving in time to the music. Leisa curtsied. Then he held up his right hand, palm out. Leisa did the same.

When their fingertips touched, they stepped forward and to opposite sides so that their palms pressed fully together and they stood side by side. Then they stepped back and repeated with the left hand. When they again stepped back, Alasdair took her hands in his and drew her close once more, then spun her so that she stood at his side yet remained in his embrace. The music changed and he turned her so that their arms intertwined but they faced opposite directions. They spun a full circle, then repeated, going the opposite way.

Leisa was amazed at how easily she followed his lead, as though her feet had a mind of their own. Upon a side step, Alasdair twirled her about, then back stepped and spun again. She swung slowly out from him and their hands parted.

Leisa gasped.

Quickly, Alasdair regained contact. Then they fell back into a repetitive pattern. At times they danced so close she could hear the beat of his heart, feel the warmth of his skin. Then their bodies would part and she would admire his stance, his movements, his grace. He moved fluidly, as though he had executed this dance a million times. And though their flawless performance baffled her, she had no time to wonder at it. The beauty of the music filled her completely, an intoxicating mix of medieval, renaissance, and a soft play of bells that titillated the senses as a lover's hands titillate the flesh.

When the music faded, Alasdair led her off the floor to a lone bench that rested at the edge of the garden.

Leisa caught her breath. "How was that possible?" she asked. She sat on the marble bench.

Alasdair settled next to her. "As long as we touch, my knowledge is passed on to you."

"Really?"

Alasdair cocked his head. "Perhaps not so much knowledge. Rather you feel the steps through me. It is why, when we broke contact, you were confused."

"I was, wasn't I?" She pondered a moment. "So it's like flying? As long as we touch, I'll react through you?"

"As I did say."

"So you can make me do whatever you want as long as we're touching?"

Alasdair grinned. His brows rose. "Nay, Leisa. I cannot *make* you do anything. It was your wish to dance, I merely gave you the steps."

"But I said I didn't want to."

"Those were your words. Your heart spoke differently."

Leisa smiled. "You can read my heart?"

"'Tis not so difficult."

"Could you accidentally pass government secrets to me?" she teased.

"Not even if I knew them." Alasdair grinned. "And even then, it would be too depleting. To pass knowledge requires much magic and deep concentration."

"But dancing doesn't?"

Alasdair explained, "Think of magic as money. You can give a little or a lot, depending on the value of the purchase. You give what is required for the action. That is all. Dancing requires little magic. It is merely passing on an intuitive physical action, not deep thought."

Leisa scanned the celebration and the many fae still dancing. "The fae are so blessed to have such magic. Humans have nothing like that."

"You are wrong, Leisa. Humans possess great magic as well."

"Yeah, right," Leisa scoffed.

"Truly. For example, have ever you looked upon someone and known what they were thinking?"

"Well, yes, but—"

"Intuition is a powerful thing. Most humans barely touch the edge of their possibilities. A very few have honed this gift, but most fail miserably at it because of either disbelief or fear." Alasdair took Leisa's hands in his. "Think of Telekinesis, to move objects by thought. Energy, to heal. Premonition, to foresee. All of these and more have been gifted to humans. It is their magic. They just fail to see it. Think of the possibilities if all humans used their gifts for the better. We have learned to embrace our gifts. We know how to use our magic."

Leisa sat dumbfounded. He was right. "But humans will never fly."

Alasdair grinned. "Not without wings."

A new song sounded from the orchestra. Alasdair and Leisa rose for the second set.

"Wait, Ali!" Edeline called, stopping them before they joined the crowd. "I wanted to talk to you without Mother hovering over us." She gave Alasdair a sisterly hug.

Alasdair laughed and hugged her back. "How goes you, cousin?" he asked.

"I am well as you can see." She gestured to herself with open arms.

Leisa watched the casual interplay. If Edeline weren't Alasdair's cousin, she'd have been jealous. Edeline was beautiful and appeared no more than nineteen years of age. Her silky blonde hair coiffed high on her head glistened with tiny gemstones. Long wispy tendrils spiraled down around her shoulders. Her skin was alabaster flawless, and her pale blue eyes rimmed in black seemed to glitter with excitement at seeing Alasdair. Her long flowing gown was a crystalline blue silk that glimmered in the torch lights.

"How goes *you*?" Edeline asked. "You have been gone for some time."

"Aye. As I said, I visited a friend in an outer barony. 'Tis where I met Leisa." He held his hand out to Leisa.

Leisa took his hand, rose, and smiled at Edeline.

Edeline's eyes lit. A small grin curled her lips. "Oh?" She turned to Leisa. "I am much pleased to meet you." She shifted a quick glance at Alasdair. Leisa was sure she saw her wink. "I hope you will be very happy here, Leisa," Edeline said.

Alasdair coughed.

Leisa stifled a laugh. "Thank you. I'm sure I will."

Edeline turned back to Alasdair. "We must get together soon. I wish to hear all about your travels. I so long to travel myself. Haps Elgar and I will plan a trip when he returns."

Alasdair looked over Edeline's shoulder to the dais where Elgar stood. "Returns? He is right there."

"Aye, but he will leave on the morrow to the unknown world." Edeline pouted. "A sudden secret mission that Mother has come up with."

Alasdair grinned. "Speak softly or it shall no longer be secret," he jested.

Edeline laughed.

"Edeline!" Tazia called authoritatively from the dais.

Edeline rolled her eyes. "I must go. Enjoy the feast, Ali." She turned and walked away.

Leisa smiled. "She seems very sweet."

"That she is," Alasdair replied as he slid an arm about Leisa's waist. "So sweet, that I oft forget her to be fae." He grinned.

Leisa smacked his arm.

"Ow." Alasdair rubbed his arm feigning a wound. "You did strike the queen's nephew. A crime punishable by much dancing." He smiled. "Come, let us enjoy the feast while we can."

Gideon descended the courtyard steps, Lysander close behind him.

"When did you receive this news?" Lysander asked, keeping stride.

"Mere moments ago."

"When will you tell him?"

Gideon shook his head as his gaze fell on the dancing couple. He noted the joy and passion in their eyes and the blissful rainbow aura surrounding them.

145

"Not yet," Gideon replied. "Let them enjoy the festivities. There is time enough for sorrow."

Lysander followed his gaze. "Can naught be done?"

"Nay. Sachi was delivered to the trolls whilst we were in the swamp. I fear she is lost to them now."

Lysander wiped at his eyes. "I do not envy you the task of telling him."

Gideon turned to face Lysander. "What is this?" he questioned. "Tears for a human?"

Lysander shook his head. "For Alasdair. No greater friend have I than you and he."

"I do not understand why he cares so for these human creatures. They are fleeting, with a promised life of seven or eight decades should naught else take them first."

Lysander whistled through his teeth. "'Tis barely a first breath."

"Aye. Take Leisa, for example." Gideon nodded at Alasdair's dance partner. "If she be twenty and five, she has a mere sixty years before her, more or less. Sixty years." He shook his head. "'Tis nothing compared to the lifespan of the fae. Nothing." He set his sights on Alasdair again. "Would he stay at her side whilst she grows old and withered?"

Lysander studied the dancing couple. "Perhaps when he learns the child is gone, he will return the human to her own world and all will be as it was—with Tazia none the wiser."

Gideon watched the couple end the dance with a bow and a curtsy. He saw their mutual passion. "We can only hope it, Lysander."

Chapter Twelve

Faerie

Alasdair surveyed the situation. Queen Tazia sat at the high table chatting with her daughter and new son-in-law. Several guests hung about them, partaking of the usual wedding banter. Their wine glasses rested half-empty in their hands—for the fifth time, more or less. The guests had gotten over Alasdair and Leisa's sudden appearance. No one was keeping watch on them now. It was the perfect time to search for Sachi. If they waited much longer, the children would be put to bed. He didn't want to drag Sachi from her slumber. It would be much simpler to lead her out from the youngling play area and then through the gate, which he was sure was being guarded feebly due to the grand celebration. This opportunity would not present itself again.

He grabbed Leisa's hand. "Come. 'Tis time."

"Time?" Leisa said, then straightened. "Oh, time!"

He led Leisa toward a garden path that morphed into a maze. It was a path that lovers took for privacy. No one would be suspicious of such a move.

Leisa eyed the maze entrance skeptically. "In there?" she asked.

"Aye."

"What if we get lost?"

"We will not get lost," he said, leading her along a path flanked by tall hedgerows. "I oft played in this maze as a child."

"So you've lived here all your life?"

"Most of it. My parents died when I was little more than a babe. I have lived here ever since."

"So you didn't always live here at the palace?"

"'Tis all that I remember. I did hear tell in later years that there was a discord betwixt Tazia and my parents. I know not what it was. Never was it revealed to me."

"Since you've become an adult, have you asked?"

"Aye, but Tazia refused to speak of it. I did not ask again. Life here was comfortable. I did not wish to incur her wrath." Alasdair made several turns in the maze. He exited at an outbuilding with a play yard in the back. A group of children sat at a table, engaged in some sort of game. Alasdair glanced at them. His brows arched quizzically. "Wait here," he said to Leisa. He released her hand and approached the group. "Good eve, little ones," he greeted. "Have any here seen Sachi?"

The children looked up at him. "Good eve," one answered. "Nay, we have not seen her all this day."

Alasdair frowned. "My thanks," he replied. He quickly made his way to Leisa. "We needs must check Sachi's room now," he said tightly.

"You mean Blaise."

Alasdair's jaw tightened. "Sachi ... Blaise ... what matters a name!" he whispered fiercely. Heat consumed every ounce of his flesh. His head felt thick with worry, his thoughts disoriented. He drew a deep breath, let it out slowly, then turned to Leisa. His voice softened. "I am sorry."

Leisa had never seen Alasdair so angry. Something must be very wrong. She followed quietly behind him as they made their way to the tall palace doors. She could hear merriment and music in the background, a contrast to the biting fear inside her. She wanted to ask Alasdair what troubled him. Suddenly she knew. By checking Blaise's room, he was merely confirming it.

As they skirted past the revelers and raced up the courtyard stairs, a familiar voice halted them. "There is no need to check, Alasdair. She is gone."

Alasdair spun to face Gideon. "How long have you known?" he demanded.

"Shortly after returning from the swamp."

"And you did not tell me!"

"What could you have done? She was out of our reach."

Alasdair ground his jaw. His eyes flamed. "Nay!" he shouted, slamming his fist against the air.

Several guests seated on the outskirts of the merriment turned to look at him. Alasdair lowered his voice. "I will reach her, whatever it takes."

Gideon moved closer. "Speak not so loudly that Tazia will hear."

"Tazia be damned," Alasdair swore.

Gideon gasped and Leisa realized that even he had never seen Alasdair in such a mood. She felt a twinge of empathy for Gideon. Neither knew how to deal with this new development. She was about to speak when Gideon spoke first.

"Ali," Gideon said calmly. "By this time she is in the hands of the trolls. To reach her you must cross the River of Tears into the Sprite Wood, then make your way through Trenalyn Forest to snatch her from them." He paused a moment. "Or," he continued, "you must cross the river into the Sprite Wood, traverse the mountain past the white dragon's lair, traverse more mountain past the red dragon's lair, and once again snatch her from the trolls."

"Or," Alasdair replied, "I could go back the way we came, through the dark swamp and past the Trenalyn Gate to the mountains."

"Nay. The dark faeries will be on watch now. You would not get far." Gideon set a caring hand on Alasdair's shoulder. "Do you see the impossibility of it now?"

Leisa's heart weighed heavy in her chest. All hope of getting Blaise could not be gone when they had traveled so far to save her! She watched Alasdair deflate, saw anger fade from his face as he struggled to bring it under control. No, not anger. Frustration and worry. His stance softened and he led Gideon into the shadows of a column flanked with plants. When he spoke, his words were calm and soft, but firm.

"I know what odds I face, Gideon." He fixed his friend with an intense stare. "When we were in the birth of adulthood, when our hearts were stout and brave beyond reason, what was our motto?" Alasdair asked.

Gideon set on Alasdair a knowing look but said nothing.

"Naught is impossible if we but believe," Alasdair answered for him.

Gideon nodded. "We were foolish youths at the time."

"Aye. Foolish, but with convictions. Now ..." Alasdair left it hanging. "You need not involve yourself in this, Gideon," he continued. "I understand the risk and would not put you in such danger. I ask only that you not inform Tazia of my intention."

"So you will place yourself in danger for a human?" Gideon shook his head. "How many other humans has Tazia sent off, and you did naught? Why this particular one? Why now?"

Alasdair shook his head sadly. "I died each time a child was sent to the trolls—forty deaths at the least since my birth. Hundreds since Tazia's reign. 'Haps more. I know not. I merely feigned indifference." Alasdair began to pace. "So many!" he cried hoarsely. He pressed his palms to his temples, then thrust them down and glowered at Gideon. "I cannot pretend anymore. I cannot do this again, Gideon."

Leisa stepped beside Alasdair. "Wh—what happens once a child is turned over to the trolls?"

Alasdair briefly closed his eyes. "Naught that is good," he said as he opened them to look at her.

Leisa swallowed. "How much time do we have?"

"I know not."

"'Tis already too late," Gideon added.

Alasdair's head shot up. He glared at Gideon. "We cannot know that unless we try," he spat. "We have to try. *I* have to try. Leisa can stay here. Will you keep her safe?"

"I ... uh ..." Gideon stammered.

"Like hell. I'm going with you."

"'Tis dangerous, Leisa. Even should I make it to Trenalyn, I must enter the trolls' lair to steal her back, then return."

"But if we go together, you won't need to return to get me," Leisa replied. "We could leave through the Trenalyn Gate."

"I know not if that will be possible. 'Twill depend on whether the rescue is stealthy enough. If I—we—are discovered, the gate will most definitely fall under guard, doubly I daresay, and our only option will be to return by the same path that took us there."

Gideon spoke. "You will never make it, Alasdair. No one ever has."

"No one has ever tried."

"You are wrong. Hundreds of years ago such an attempt was made. A group of young nobles seeking adventure packed a trunk of supplies and clothing and set across the River of Tears. They never returned."

Footsteps approached and they fell silent until Lysander rounded the corner of the building.

Alasdair sighed in relief. "'Tis only Lysander."

Lysander looked from Alasdair to Gideon. "You told him?" he asked Gideon.

"Aye," Gideon snarled.

"And?"

Alasdair stepped forward. "And I will go after her."

Lysander gasped. "Surely you jest!" He shot Gideon a look. "He jests, does he not?"

"Nay," Gideon muttered.

"But—"

"Save your efforts, Lysander. He has made up his mind."

Lysander stared at Alasdair, then Leisa. "Know you the chances of surviving such a quest? Minuscule at best."

Leisa mimicked back. "Know *you* the chances of Blaise surviving if we don't go?" She narrowed her eyes. "*None.*"

Lysander grimaced. "Blaise? Who is Blaise?"

"Sachi!" the remaining three said at once.

"Ahhh, yes, of course. Blaise was her birth name."

Leisa rolled her eyes. She looked at Lysander, then at Gideon. "I know you think humans are inferior to the fae and that their short lives aren't worth fighting for. But we humans love deeply. At first I thought that was what made us different, that the fae didn't feel or understand love. But then I saw how Alasdair cares not only for Blaise, but for me, for Edeline, and for you, and I see how much you care for him, enough to risk the dark swamp looking for him. So I know now that fairies can love one another. Imagine my love for my child and understand my willingness to risk my life to save her, just as you risked your lives in the dark swamp looking for Alasdair."

Lysander swallowed and nodded. "She makes a valid point."

Gideon glared at Lysander, then shot Leisa a hard look. "Do not deceive yourself, *human*. Fae love, to be sure, but I know not one who would risk life and limb for another."

"What about you and Lysander in the dark swamp?" Leisa reminded him.

"We were in no danger. Our magic protected us."

"But you loved enough to look for Alasdair."

Lysander lifted a brow at Gideon.

"Aye ... well ..."

"Aye." Lysander clapped Gideon's shoulder. "And I blame this entirely on Alasdair." Lysander smiled. "He has always been a bad influence on us."

Leisa smiled back. Somehow she believed him.

"Take this, Alasdair." Lysander pulled a jewel-studded band from his wrist.

Alasdair quickly stepped back. "Nay. What are you doing?"

"It will bring you greater magic." Lysander shook his head. "'Tis all I can do for you."

"'Tis too much. I cannot accept it."

"Ali, my powers are made great through the band. The stones draw the magic from the air and concentrate it. The band transfers it to the flesh. You will need all the magic you can summon."

"Lysander, nay!" Gideon grabbed for the band. Lysander yanked it back. "Are you mad? That band belongs to the exalted royal guards. It is not yours to give. If Tazia finds out, your life will be forfeit."

"Then it shall be forfeit. We are not at war, nor do we expect to be. The power of the band will serve a much more noble purpose for Alasdair."

Alasdair balked. "Nay. I will not take it."

Lysander's face hardened. He stepped before Alasdair. "Take it, Ali," he commanded, "or I do swear I shall turn you in to Tazia myself."

Leisa studied the usually gentle Lysander. She had never seen such a stern expression on his face, not even when they'd been pursued by the dark fairies. He meant what he said. She turned to Alasdair and knew he saw it too.

Gideon groaned. "Take it, Alasdair. Lysander and I will share my band until you return. 'Haps Tazia will not take note that one is missing."

"And should we not return?" Alasdair asked.

Silence hung in the immediate air. Only the faint sounds of wedding revelry could be heard in the distance.

"Just take it," Gideon ordered.

Alasdair held out a shaky hand.

Lysander dropped the band into his palm.

"Never have I worn such a band," Alasdair said. "Never did I have need for so great a magic."

"Keep it hidden beneath your sleeve, Alasdair."

Alasdair nodded.

"Have you a plan?" Gideon asked.

"Nay. I did not expect to need one. I expected Sachi to be here at the palace."

Gideon shook his head. "You are the worst strategist ever." He looked around the corner of the building to be sure no one listened. "Fortunately for you, I am the best."

Alasdair laughed. "Aye. You are."

Gideon forced a smile. "Come," he said, motioning to the others. He led them around the corner of the palace wall to the servants' entrance door. "I am sure the library will have some maps. 'Haps we can establish the least dangerous route. Beyond that, you are in the hands of a higher power. May she favor you this day."

Leisa's head was whirling as she watched the three discuss a strategy. She'd not said much, only what was important. It seemed to have done the trick. Lysander's jeweled band would greatly improve their chances. She would be sure to thank him before they left. She wondered where Blaise was now. Was she frightened? Was she even alive? Then her thoughts fell to Sybil. Did Sybil miss her? Was she comfortable staying with Rita? Leisa prayed the quest would be successful—and quick. All she wanted was to be home with her two little girls and live a normal life.

Her thoughts moved to Gideon and Lysander. Though the two of them had given Alasdair a hard time, they were both willing to help. Gideon's offer of his skills was greatly welcomed. Not that she didn't trust Alasdair's abilities, but even *he* admitted to Gideon's greater knowledge of strategy and of the land itself. Leisa thought about the dynamics of the three fae—so different, yet so close. Their closeness didn't make sense when she thought of them separately. But when she thought of them as a single unit, it made all the sense in the world. Gideon was the head, Lysander the hands, and Alasdair—Alasdair was the heart.

Chapter Thirteen

Faerie

Leisa opened her eyes to a near dark room. The side of the mattress where Alasdair had lain was still warm. As they'd not slept in nearly forty-eight hours, he'd insisted that they get at least two hours' rest before embarking on their journey. She had not refuted him. In fact, two hours was not enough. Night had fallen and the wall tapestry had been drawn across the window. Only a single wall torch lit the chamber. She could see Alasdair rummaging through the armoire. He tossed an outfit on the foot of the bed.

Leisa's gown had twisted about her legs and she struggled to right it before crawling out from under the covers. "What's that?" she asked, rubbing her eyes. She moved to the foot of the bed and picked up the thick material.

"'Twill be more functional than a gown," Alasdair said.

Leisa noted that he had changed as well. He wore heavy black pants and a coarse gray tunic sans embellishment, simple and functional. Across the neckline of his tunic was draped a black woolen cowl. From his shoulders hung a long black cloak that was clasped with a silver leaf. But for the flashing green of his eyes and bronzed hue of his skin, he was devoid of color. She looked at what he'd given her. Dark green leggings, a tan knee-length tunic that belted at the waist with a rope of twisted gold, and a cloak that matched the leggings. All heavy fabrics. Even the slippers were thick and brown, with heavy soles to protect her feet. She glanced at Alasdair's footgear, calf-hugging boots that skimmed the knees. She sighed deeply. "Why such heavy and dark fabrics?" she asked.

"We will be traversing the mountains. 'Tis cooler in the higher reaches. The dark earthy colors will help us blend with our surroundings. They will also help us slip from the grounds unnoticed."

Leisa approached Alasdair. The sounds of merriment and music wafted in past the tapestry, the wedding party went on. She turned her back to him and lifted her hair from her shoulders. "Can you, please?"

Alasdair gave her a puzzled look. Then, his expression turned to one of realization and he began drawing the tiny rosettes out from their loops. When he released the last rosette, he slipped his hands inside the gown and encircled her waist. He drew her back against him. Leisa warmed to the heat of him, felt his breath on her hair.

"Leisa," he said, "Please reconsider." He kissed her below the ear and nuzzled her neck. "I would that you not be harmed."

Leisa turned and cradled his face with her hands. "I'm going with you, Alasdair."

Alasdair drew her hands down from his face, leaned forward, and kissed her.

Leisa felt his urgency, his need, his fear. She was afraid, too. Afraid they would not reach Blaise in time. Afraid for their lives. Afraid she was falling in love.

An impossible love. A fairy and a human? She would live another fifty or sixty years, he hundreds, if not thousands. She belonged to the human world, he to the world of the fae. She looked forward to a simple life with Sybil and Blaise. He was royalty. Yet for all of their differences, his kiss was warm and passionate. There was love in it. She could feel it clear through to the bones, or rather, to the heart. Impossible, impossible love.

She pressed against him, eager to feel his body meld with hers. Eager to be one.

Suddenly Alasdair stepped back, his voice strained. "There is no time to linger. We must go before the wedding party breaks, while the borders are passable without notice." He pointed to her traveling garb. "Hurry and change. I will pack a few supplies and we shall be on our way."

Alasdair left the room. When he returned, he carried a large satchel. Leisa, garbed in the clothing he'd set out for her, tied the gold weave belt about her waist. Then she swung the cloak over her shoulders and clasped it with a brooch of gold—three twisted and flowering vines. Her embroidered ivory gown and slippers were discarded on the bed.

They slipped through a side door and wound through the maze. When they reached the river, Lysander was waiting. "Had you any trouble?" he asked.

"Nay. The guard was besotted with drink." Alasdair looked around. "Where is Gideon?"

"Tazia called him away just as we were about to leave. He sends his regrets—and this map. He said it might be of value. On the back are some notes as to our discussion."

"My thanks."

Lysander clasped Alasdair's shoulder. "Good luck, Alasdair." He looked at Leisa. "You also. I pray that your journey be swift and without incident." Lysander turned to leave. "I must go now ere Tazia misses me."

"Did she question *our* absence?" Alasdair asked.

"Aye. She wondered why you and your lady were no longer at the celebration."

"What said you?"

Lysander grinned. "I did not lie."

Leisa felt herself grow cold and saw Alasdair's face pale.

Lysander clapped his shoulder. "I told Tazia that you and Leisa took a short respite after such a long journey."

Alasdair released his breath. His color returned. "Do not tease me so, friend." He tucked the map into his satchel.

Lysander frowned. "Ali, have we not always done so? I merely sought to do so one last time."

Alasdair's head shot up.

"One last time until your return," Lysander quickly added. He shot his friend a troubled gaze.

"I understand," Alasdair replied.

"I must go now." Lysander hugged Alasdair. "May all the magic of the fae travel with you."

Alasdair nodded and swallowed hard. "My thanks." He watched Lysander disappear from view, then turned to Leisa. "Remove your clothing."

"What!" Leisa hugged her cloak tighter about her as she watched Alasdair strip.

"Remove your clothing," Alasdair repeated.

"I just got dressed."

"And now you must undress."

"No."

Alasdair turned in unclothed perfection. "We must cross the river unnoticed. There is but one way, and we cannot have soaked clothing upon reaching the other side." He pulled a square of cloth from the satchel and began unfolding it.

"What's that?" Leisa asked, looking anywhere but at him.

"A watertight sack for our clothing and supplies." He withdrew a dagger from the sack and began packing his clothes into it.

Leisa stared at him. *Undress? Here? Now?* She wasn't ready for that.

"Leisa!"

Leisa jumped, drew a resigned breath, then commenced removing her clothes. She tried not to stare at Alasdair, but he was too flawless to ignore. Tall, lean, muscled in all the right places. Not a follicle of hair dusted his chest. Glancing lower, she had no doubt as to his prowess as a lover. Her throat tightened. She gave herself a mental slap, turned her back to him and removed her slippers. She then peeled her leggings down her legs and kicked them free. Her fingers fumbled at her belt. Finally she worked it free and let it drop to the ground. She paused to peer over her shoulder at him. He waited patiently, his neutral gaze set on her. She swallowed, then lifted her tunic over her head.

Alasdair tried to avert his eyes, an impossible feat. As he packed Leisa's clothing into the sack, he couldn't help but notice her petal-soft skin, long lean legs, and high rounded breasts—breasts that would fit perfectly into his hands. Her vibrant red hair cascaded gently over her shoulders, falling to just above their rosy tips. Shorter wisps of hair framed her eyes, eyes as deeply green as a summer leaf. She put on a brave front disrobing in front of him, but he could see bashfulness in her stance. He supposed he should have given her advance warning so she would have been prepared, but he had forgotten. He wanted to approach her, to caress her shoulders, sweep back her hair, and assure her that his motives were pure, but he did not trust himself to stand so close. Instead, he finished packing the clothes. Then he stuffed the satchel into the waterproof sack, squeezed out as much air as he could, sealed it shut, and flung its long strap over his head and across his chest. When he looked back at Leisa, he saw her push aside her modesty and straighten her shoulders. She lifted her chin.

"Now what?" she asked.

Alasdair could think of several things. He gave her an appreciative look, then stepped into the water. A wide log half floated close to shore, a gift from Lysander and Gideon. Alasdair pushed it fully into the water, then he motioned to Leisa to stand on its opposite side.

Leisa slid into the cold, rushing water and shrieked.

Alasdair fought a grin. "I did mean to warn you, the water is cold."

Leisa readied to splash him.

Alasdair shook his head. "Do not. Even from a distance, a dragon's eyes are extremely sharp. We do not wish to draw its attention." He motioned to the log. "Feel beneath the log. There is a strap. Put your hand through the strap and hold tight as we float to the other side. The red dragon can be seen from a distance. Always there is flame spouting from his nose. When the flame draws near, duck beneath the water and under the log and count to twenty. He does not linger, merely passes by. On the count of twenty, resurface until the next pass."

"Are you serious?"

"If he sees us, he will pluck us from the water with talons as sharp as blades. If you live through that, it will not be for long. Once in his lair, you will make a tasty meal."

Leisa caught her breath. "How did they get Blaise across the river and to the trolls?"

Alasdair shoved the log from shore and began propelling it with his legs, careful to cause only a gentle ripple. "That I do not know. Only the queen and her successor know this."

"Why don't we just fly across?"

"We would be like a dove to the hawk. We would not get far." The log began to shift in line with the river flow. "Move your legs to keep the log on course. We must reach the other side without traveling too far downstream. I wish to come ashore close to the mountain base and not downstream of the Sprite Wood."

Leisa kicked her legs. The log turned. When she looked up, a plume of fire lit the night sky. "Ali," she cried as she nodded toward the flame.

Alasdair watched the dragon approach, waited for the right moment. "Now, Leisa." He ducked under the water. Leisa took a breath and followed. Beneath the surface, Alasdair grabbed Leisa about the waist and drew them together beneath the log.

Leisa felt his leanly muscled body press against her, his steely arm clamp about her waist. She held her breath until she thought her lungs would burst. When his arm released, they came up for air.

Leisa gasped.

"Are you all right?" Alasdair asked.

"Yes. That was the longest twenty seconds I've ever known." Leisa glanced over the log to see Alasdair smile.

"I did think it not long enough."

Leisa flicked water at him. "You would."

The dragon passed several more times. Each time they sank beneath the water out of view. Suddenly panic crossed Alasdair's face. Leisa looked up and saw that the dragon's body had shifted in position for the coming pass. "What's he doing?" she asked.

"He suspects the log. Release the strap and dive deep!" Alasdair quickly disappeared beneath the rushing water.

Leisa held her breath and followed. When she tried to slip her hand out of the strap, she could not. She yanked frantically at the twisted leather wrapped tightly about her wrist. When she looked up through the water's crest, she saw the dragon nearly upon her. A small burst of air escaped her lungs. She tightly pressed her lips.

Alasdair swam up beneath the log, his dagger in hand. Quickly he sliced the strap. As the log lifted from the water, he shoved Leisa's head down, pushing her deeper still. When the danger passed, he grabbed her beneath the arms and dragged her to the surface. Leisa broke water gasping and choking. Alasdair's arms kept her buoyant, and she thanked God for that.

Without the weight of the log, the current swept them down river. Reaching shore, Alasdair pressed her to the grassy bank and flung his wings over them.

Leisa looked up through his wings to see the dragon pass once more, the log crushed in its talons. When it was at a safe distance, Alasdair stood, pulled Leisa to her feet, and quickly headed for the trees. Once sheltered from view, he divvied out their clothes.

"Dress swiftly," he advised as his wings faded away.

Leisa struggled to pull dry clothes over a wet body. "Will he come back?" she asked. She tugged her tunic down over her head and shoulders. It twisted oddly and she yanked it straight. Pulling soaked hair out from beneath it, she squeezed out as much water from her hair as she could. Still it wetted the back of the tunic through. Her gaze darted along the riverbank, then to the sky.

"Aye. But he guards only the rivers and their banks. We are safe from him beneath the trees." Alasdair clasped his cloak. When he looked up, Leisa was wrapping her belt about her waist.

"What next?" Leisa asked as she tied the belt off. "Monstrous snakes, poisonous lizards, rabid unicorns?"

Alasdair laughed.

Leisa had rarely heard him truly laugh, and it calmed her.

"Leisa," he said. He stood before her. "I wish you had not come." He fitted his arms about her and drew her into an embrace, then released a breath. "I wish you safe. But it is too late for such wishes now." He set her back and she saw his eyes blazing with need. Reaching up, she caressed his cheek.

"I was so scared," she admitted. "I still am. But this is where I want to be—with you, saving Blaise."

Alasdair cupped her face in his hands, and she knew he was going to kiss her. She closed her eyes and wound her fingers into the dark hair at his nape. She was not disappointed. His lips touched hers, softly, then firmly. Warm and insistent, his mouth claimed hers with such fervor that she thought they would combust. Then his body tensed. She opened her eyes and saw him looking over her shoulder. He pulled away and grabbed the sack and satchel.

"We must go."

Leisa grabbed his hand. She looked around and saw nothing but the soft blinking lights of fireflies. She remembered Alasdair's earlier conversation. *I was there. You merely saw a firefly.* Her heart quickened. *Sprites?*

"Loose your hold, Leisa," Alasdair said.

Leisa hadn't realized she'd been holding Alasdair's hand in a crushing grip. "I'm sorry." She let go. As they made their way along the border of the wood, she kept a lookout into the trees. "The lights—they're sprites, aren't they?"

"Aye. They are. We are farther down the river than I had planned. If we pass by quietly, however, haps they will not take note of us."

"And if they do?" Leisa asked. "Will they hurt us?"

"It depends upon their mood. Sprites are not purposefully harmful creatures, but they do have their mischievous side."

"Meaning?"

"Meaning they could initiate a prank that could cause us harm, though harm be not their intent."

Leisa nodded quietly, hoping to not meet up with any sprites. An hour passed and they still had not reached the mountain base. Suddenly she tripped. Alasdair grabbed her before she could fall.

Leisa stopped and caught her breath. "Sorry. I'm just so tired. Two hours was not enough sleep."

Alasdair nodded. "I, as well." He ushered her into the trees to a hollow in the brush. "Here." He pulled a thin blanket and what looked like unleavened bread from the satchel. After spreading out the blanket, he rested on it.

Leisa sighed then sat beside him. It felt like heaven to be off her feet. He handed her some bread and a flask of water. As Leisa made short work of the bread, she looked up and saw him watching her. "What?" she muttered past a bite.

"You were quite starved." Alasdair smiled and took a bite of bread, chewing it with far too much decorum in Leisa's estimation.

"Starved and exhausted," Leisa replied.

Alasdair lay back on the blanket, his breathing slow and even. When Leisa finished eating, she lay next to him. Turning on her side, she rested her hand on his chest and nestled against him. "Can we sleep now?" she asked drowsily.

Alasdair pillowed her head with his arm. "Aye. Sleep, Leisa." He closed his eyes and stroked her hair. Willing his wings, he covered them.

Leisa raised her drooping eyelids and looked through them. She knew they weren't there merely for warmth. She knew he hid them. "What do they look like?" she mumbled sleepily.

"What?"

"Your wings."

"Like twisted brush." Again he stroked her hair.

"It will deplete you," Leisa replied, remembering the swamp. Her eyes drifted closed.

Alasdair settled his arm beneath her shoulder and held her close. "Nay. I do not use my own magic. I use that of the band."

"Oh," Leisa mumbled, then fell into a deep sleep.

Chapter Fourteen

Faerie

Leisa opened her eyes and gasped.

Alasdair set a finger to her lips. "Shh," he mouthed. "Do not move."

Flashing lights hovered above and around them, searching. Seven at the least.

"Sprites?" Leisa mouthed back as she watched the lights through the inner gray shadow of his wings.

Alasdair gave a nod.

She bit down on her lip and waited for him to declare when it was safe to talk.

When the lights disappeared into the trees, he spoke. "They are gone."

"Do they know we're here?"

"I think not. They merely sensed something was different. Happily, their sense of smell is dim."

Leisa slapped Alasdair playfully on the arm. "What are you saying?"

He laughed quietly. "All things living have their own scent. 'Tis a blessing the sprites cannot so easily detect that." He withdrew his wings and sat up. "Did you sleep well?" he asked as his wings faded, then disappeared.

Leisa stretched. "I think so." She looked at the circles under Alasdair's eyes. They were nearly as dark as his hair. She stroked his cheek. "Did you lie awake all night?" she asked as she raised herself up on her elbows.

Alasdair stood and began folding the empty sack. "Not all."

Following his lead, Leisa rose. She grabbed two corners of the blanket and gave it a snap, then folded it.

Alasdair shoved it into the satchel with the sack.

"Alasdair?" Leisa said.

"Aye."

"I'm curious about crossing the river. Why didn't you use your wings for camouflage in the water?"

"My wings can replicate only stationary objects, not water."

"Why not?"

"Because of its constant motion. The dragon would see a patch of water with no movement and know it was a ruse." He pulled a clear bag full of bread and various dried fruits from the satchel.

Leisa gasped. "Fruit!"

"I pilfered it from the wedding feast." Alasdair smiled.

"You're quite the stealthy one, aren't you?"

Alasdair laughed. "At times." He shoved a chunk of dried sugary pineapple in her mouth and a handful of raisins in his own. Closing his eyes, he savored their sweetness.

"Mmm, this is heaven." Leisa ate a handful of cranberries, followed by more pineapple.

"Eat heartily." Alasdair broke off a chunk of bread and handed it to her. "We have a long day ahead of us."

Alasdair led Leisa toward the mountain, staying just inside the woods. Gideon's notes had warned him not to venture too far into the forest lest they never get out. However, Gideon had also warned him to not walk along the river's edge. The dragons guarded not only the river but its shores as well. By traveling just inside the trees, they would be hidden from view from the air and would most likely avoid confrontation with the sprites. *That*, he could not guarantee.

Also, they were not to fly for any reason. In the air there would be no cover from the dragons. Gideon's strategy was to avoid air travel at any cost and hike the mountain trail just below the dragons' lairs. Gideon had warned that the higher the climb, the more narrow and treacherous the ledges. He'd begged them to be careful.

Alasdair reread the notes and studied the map, then tucked it in his tunic. He walked a few feet in front of Leisa, surveying the area. He had seen several sprites hovering deeper in the trees, but none had ventured close. He deemed they were waiting for him and Leisa to travel farther into the wood, never believing that they would choose to climb the dangerous mountain path instead—so close to the dragons' lairs.

When Leisa cried out, Alasdair turned.

"What is it?" he asked.

"I tripped on a root." Leisa grumbled, examining her foot.

"Is it all right?"

Leisa nodded. "I think so." She rubbed her ankle.

"I meant the root."

Leisa's head shot up. "What!"

Alasdair grinned. "A jest, Leisa."

Leisa sighed. "Funny, Alasdair." She continued rubbing her ankle. "I just need to sit a minute."

Alasdair waited sixty seconds. "Are you ready?"

Leisa shot him a look of disbelief. "A minute doesn't mean sixty seconds."

"In human terms, a minute is exactly sixty seconds," Alasdair refuted.

Leisa rolled her eyes and groaned. "When someone says 'I need a minute', it's merely a figure of speech. It means I need a little time, which could be thirty seconds, one minute, three minutes ... or more."

Alasdair crossed his arms over his chest. He cocked his head at her, causing a strand of ebony hair to fall across his eyes.

"Rather confusing, think you not?" he said, pushing it back. "How then would I know how long to wait?"

Leisa sighed. "Oh, for God's sake." She stood to test her foot. "Never mind. I'm ready."

Alasdair turned away to hide his grin, then continued along the path. Soon the trees thinned and the ground took a sharp upward turn. He stopped and looked up the steeply angled slope.

Leisa continued on. She stopped several yards ahead of him. Shielding her eyes, she looked straight up. Her jaw dropped. "Up there?" she asked, pointing to the rocky trail and narrow ledge.

'Tis the only way."

Suddenly rock broke loose from the mountain's jutting ridge, sending an avalanche of stone raining down the hillside.

"Run!" Alasdair yelled. He raced toward the shelter of the trees.

Leisa sprinted behind him. A boulder rumbled down on them and she spun away, running as fast as her legs could carry her. Brush tore at her clothes, and she stumbled more than once as she made her way deep into the woods. The path twisted and turned and disappeared at times. When she tripped and fell, she realized the danger had long since passed. She closed her eyes, lay back, and caught her breath. When she opened them, she saw a thick canopy of foliage above her. Glints of sunlight turned the upper leaves a vibrant translucent green. Leaves closer to the ground remained dark and greatly numbered, obscuring her vision.

"Uh-oh." Her heart thudded painfully and she slowly sat up. Trees and brush surrounded her. Verdant, dark, and heavily overgrown. The steep, mountainous hillside was nowhere in sight, hidden by the thick canopy above her. "Ali!" she called. Silence. "Ali!" she called again.

Nothing.

She swallowed hard and stood. Her breath had returned to normal, but her heart still pounded alarmingly fast. "Alasdair, where are you?" she muttered. Again she surveyed the woods. This area of the forest was thick with trees, their craggy boles nearly touching. The dense foliage hung low, and the vibrant green of the woodland brush glistened like new-fallen snow beneath a brilliant full moon. There was no path where she stood. She had no idea which way to go. A flickering light floated in the distance.

Leisa quit calling for Alasdair, afraid the sprite would hear her. What harmful mischief might it be up to? She hunkered low so it wouldn't see her. When it drifted off, she rose again.

Loose grass clung to the thick fabric of her tunic and leggings. She brushed at them futilely. What had happened? She recalled the rock falling from the cliffside, but she hadn't felt the ground tremble or heard the rumbling roll of stone. She'd only seen the tumbling boulders descending on them. She concentrated deeply. Why hadn't she heard or felt anything?

Then she understood. Her breath caught. It had been an illusion to panic them. To drive them into the forest.

It had worked.

Alasdair stopped not far into the trees. His first thought had been for their safety and he'd panicked. But he'd soon realized the landslide was an illusion, a sprite trick to force them deep into the forest. Alasdair turned. "Leisa, 'tis all right. 'Twas but a ruse—" His words stilled. He ran back to the border of the wood and spun in several directions. "Leisa!" he called.

Silence.

He replayed the rockslide in his head. She had to have veered to the right. To go left would have taken her to the river. He looked at the foliage. It was thick and overgrown. Vines hung from the branches, brush stood tall, some taller than he. If she had fled into the deep wood, she was surely lost. He felt his heartbeat quicken. The sprites were the least of their worries. Other dangers lurked within the forest, dangers he had only heard tale of. Also within the Sprite Wood were the spirits of those fae who had met a tragic end within its borders. These spirits had nowhere else to go; their immortality had been stolen from them. The thought of entering their domain gave him a moment's pause. Then the moment passed. His heart pounded. He had to go in.

Chapter Fifteen

Human World

Rita drew a thick white comforter over Sybil. Two days had passed and she'd not heard a word from Leisa. She had called her cell phone numerous times. It went directly to voicemail. She was beginning to worry. Still, she kept a positive attitude for Sybil's sake. Lifting Sybil's arms over the comforter, Rita tucked the cover to just below her chin.

"Can you read me a story?" Sybil asked. She pointed to the fairy book that she'd packed with her clothing.

Rita picked it up. When she opened the book, she felt none of the whimsy that Sybil so loved. Instead she felt strangely uneasy. She shook it off. *Ridiculous*. "Of course, Sibby. Which story?" she asked.

Sybil flipped the pages to a well-worn section. "This one."

The story looked innocent enough, Rita thought. Too innocent. Coming from Scottish stock and pagan parents, she had read tales of the fae in her youth, and they were nothing like these. These were watered-down versions with none of the violence and trickery of the tales of old. And though it had been many years since she'd even considered the possibility that the fae actually existed, a part of her still believed. She recalled Sybil telling her of Alasdair's wings. Recalled the drawing now safely tucked under Sybil's pillow. Rita knew that the little girl before her was not prone to lying. She shuddered. Perhaps Sybil was merely being imaginative. But still, had she herself not sensed something different about Alasdair? Was the wavering air that followed him on that last day his wings?

A pang of guilt stuck in her throat that she did not even attempt to warn Leisa, afraid Leisa would think her insane.

"Are you okay?" Sybil asked at Rita's hesitation.

Rita jumped. She forced a smile. "Yes. Of course." She took a breath and began to read. Soon Sybil slept. Closing the book, Rita tucked it under her arm. She kissed Sybil's forehead. After flicking on the nightlight and turning off the overhead light, she quietly left, shutting the door behind her. Making her way to the kitchen, she brewed a cup of tea. Then she settled on her bed to drink it while she flipped through Sybil's book. Without intention, she found herself at the same story she had just read aloud. This time she paid attention to the pictures, not the words. At first they seemed innocent enough. Hovering faeries caught up in gaiety and dance, a queen with her royal court and guards, scattered lights in the far-off forest.

Then she saw something she hadn't before. She drew her glasses off the nightstand for a closer look. Deep in the trees where the sun failed to reach were eyes hidden in the darkness. Watchful, glowing eyes. A shudder ran through her. She slammed the book closed and set it on her nightstand, vowing to misplace it until Leisa returned.

She drew another book from the nightstand, something safe. Sipping her tea, she read several chapters. Soon her eyes felt heavy and she fell asleep.

A crash jolted Rita awake, her book still open in her lap, her spectacles askew on her face. She straightened her glasses and shot her alarm clock a quick glance. Three a.m. When she heard Sybil cry out, she bounded from her bed, grabbed her cell phone from the nightstand should she need to call 911, and quickly made her way to the bedroom door. Grasping the round, brass doorknob, she pulled hard. The door was jammed. "Sybil!" she yelled. Again Sybil cried out, then silence. Rita shook the knob violently. "Sybil!"

She closed her fists and pounded on the heavy oak door. Again she tried the knob. It turned without resistance. A chill ran through her as she shoved her feet into open-back slippers, grabbed a baseball bat from the hall closet, and edged her way towards Sybil's room. The bedroom door was closed, but Rita could feel cool night air on her legs as it slipped under the door and into the hall. She slowly turned the knob and inched open the door. The nightlight was out. "Sibby?" she said as she peeked into the dark room. Feeling the wall, she found the light switch and flipped it up. Incandescent light flooded the room. Sybil's bed lay empty. Rita looked up at the broken window, its filmy curtains riding the incoming breeze. She ran through the shattered glass on the floor. At three stories up, there was no possible way of entry or exit. Not by normal means.

She looked out the window. The streets were deserted, the silence taunting. Her chest felt tight. Tears welled in her eyes. "Oh, my God!" she cried. Rita lifted her cell phone to dial 911. Then she spied the fairy book lying on Sybil's bed—the book that had been in *her* room. Next to it lay Sybil's carefully drawn wish, a jagged rip separating the two dancing faeries.

Rita dropped the phone and screamed.

Faerie

Gideon paused on the steps that led from the formal gardens to the palace doors. He jabbed Lysander's side with his elbow. "What is that?" he asked.

"What is what?" Lysander looked back over his shoulder.

"There." Gideon pointed to Elgar escorting a small blonde child from the maze. Gideon knew three things. The maze eventually came out at the market square near the Galandorian

Gate. The girl being escorted into the palace was four or five years of age. And she was human.

"I know not. Did we miss a council?" Lysander asked.

"Nay. No council was scheduled ... that I know of." Gideon pushed dark wavy strands of hair from his forehead and quickened his stride. He stepped in front of Elgar and the girl, stopping them. "What is this?" he asked. He looked down at the girl. She was small and frail, her pale blonde hair tousled, her blue eyes wet with tears. Her wrists were bound in velvet rope.

"Orders from the queen," Elgar replied.

"For what reason? She did already pay the tithe."

"I do not question her reasons, Gideon." Elgar's brow narrowed. "Nor should you."

Lysander made his way to them, his long, blond hair loose and gleaming in the morning light. He hunched before the girl. The corners of her mouth turned down and her chin puckered. "Do not be afraid. I am Lysander. Pray, what is your name?"

The girl sniffled.

"Leave us," Elgar said. "I must deliver her at once." He tugged on the rope and led her through the palace doors.

Lysander pulled his hair back and secured it at the nape as he followed their steps, stopping just outside the entrance. Whimpering could be heard through the door. He turned to Gideon. "Why has Tazia stolen another child? And so far in years?"

"I know not," Gideon answered as he made his way to his friend. Together they slipped into the palace.

"Listen," Lysander said. "Did you hear that?"

"I hear naught but wailing."

"The child cried out a name."

"They all cry out names." Gideon felt his chest constrict at the admission.

"She cried out Leis ... Aunt Leis."

Their gazes locked. "Leisa," they said at once.

Gideon cursed. "Did Leisa have a child other than Sachi?"

Lysander shrugged. "I know not. None was mentioned."

Gideon growled his frustration. "'Tis the only thing that makes sense." He cursed as he slammed a fist into his hand. "Alasdair was a fool to think he could pass Leisa off as fae. Tazia sensed what Leisa was from the start. She will use the child as bait." Again, he growled. "It just gets worse and worse."

"What do we do?" Lysander asked.

"We must find Alasdair."

When they turned to leave, Tazia called to them from an adjoining corridor. "Gideon. Lysander. I would meet with you," she said.

"Now, my Queen?" Gideon asked.

"Now."

They turned to follow her to the room of council. When they entered the stately room, the door was shut behind them from the outside—leaving them alone with Tazia.

"I daresay you saw my newest acquisition," Tazia said. She cocked her head in a haughty manner and smirked.

Gideon met her gaze. "Aye. But I do not understand. Already the tithe has been paid. Why steal another? And of so many years."

The queen tsked. "You do not know?" She paced the room, keeping her gaze fixed on him.

Gideon shuffled uncomfortably. He was sure he *did* know, but he wasn't going to admit it. "Nay, my Queen. Did I miss council?"

"Oh, aye. You did."

"I do not know how I could have—"

"I did not invite you," the queen informed him.

"For what reason?" Gideon asked. "Are we not two of your most trusted guards?"

"You are."

177

"Then why did you not send Lysander or me on this mission?" Gideon asked.

"You are too close to Alasdair."

"What has he—" Lysander abruptly silenced himself at Gideon's nudge.

The queen smiled wryly. "He will not succeed, you know. No one ever has."

Gideon hoped she merely fished for information with no real proof. "Succeed? Who?"

"Alasdair," the queen spat as she studied the two guards' neutral expressions. "You truly do not know?"

"Know what, my Queen?" Lysander asked with such innocence that Gideon almost believed him guiltless himself.

Gideon could see uncertainty on the queen's face. "Is Alasdair in trouble?" he asked.

"Aye, he is."

"Is that why you did not include us in your plans? You do not trust us?"

The queen looked at Gideon, to Lysander, and back. "I trust you well enough. But I know your bond to Alasdair. I dared not take a chance that he could sway you. Still, you know the penalty for insubordination all too well, and I deem you would have done the job to my satisfaction. But I need you here. As I said, you are close to Alasdair. Should he by some miracle survive crossing the river and seizing the child from the trolls, he may yet attempt to contact you for aid. I would know when he does."

Gideon and Lysander exchanged stealthy glances. She was using them to trap their friend.

Lysander shifted nervously. "What will happen to Alasdair when he is brought back?"

Tazia met his gaze. "What think you?" she taunted with authority. "He will be tried like any other." She cast him a stern look. "And found guilty." She paced the room in slow, regal strides, her bejeweled gown trailing behind her. "He will then be cast into the dark swamp with his human pet."

"But he is your nephew," Lysander said.

"It matters not. It is the law, and I am the queen. I must uphold the law."

Gideon stormed up to her. "They would not last a day in the dark swamp!" he growled. "You know this."

Tazia leveled a warning at him. "You cross the line, Gideon."

Gideon clenched his jaw and stepped back. "Forgive me, *my Queen*."

Tazia eyed him a moment, then continued. "Is it not treason to steal from the queen?" she asked.

"Aye. But he has not stolen from you. You gave the child to the trolls. Is it treason to steal from *them*?"

"Until the child is tithed, she is property of the fae and essential to our immortality. She must be tithed."

"And the other girl? What is her purpose?" Gideon asked.

"You do not know?"

"Nay," Gideon replied honestly, though he had his suspicions.

"She is the niece of Alasdair's pet. More than a niece. Her mother is dead and she is now the human's ward."

"She is not a pet. Her name is Leisa."

Tazia glared at Lysander.

Gideon cleared his throat drawing her attention back to him. "Once Alasdair and the woman are captured, what shall become of your new acquisition?"

"I cannot tithe two human children. It would be expected every time if I did. Much too bothersome. So I fear she must be cast into the swamp as well. She is beyond the age of amusement and will be well past the age of innocence in twenty years when the next tithe is due."

"My Queen, I beg you, reconsider," Lysander pled.

"I cannot. Our immortality hangs by a thread. Should our tithe go unpaid, who knows how many of us will fall to age. Nay, it must be done."

"But—"

Tazia clapped her hands and the doors swung open, a guard on either side. "My decision is final."

"When would you have us leave to find him?" Gideon asked.

"You!" The queen laughed. "I would not have *you* leave at all."

"But you said you trusted us implicitly."

"In all matters save this. I forbid either of you to cross the river. I will send another."

"And if Alasdair refuses to return?" Lysander asked.

"They will come." Tazia smirked. "I have something precious to them." She turned away. "Leave me now."

Gideon straightened his shoulders, his back rigid, his expression barely controlled. He seethed with an anger he dared not express. Instead, he stepped back and bowed. "Aye, my Queen. As you wish." His throat burned so that he could scarcely breathe and his feet cried out to leave as swiftly as possible.

"Wait," the queen commanded. She turned to face them. "Give me your bands."

Lysander stilled. "What?"

"Hand them over. I would take temptation out of your hands."

Gideon and Lysander exchanged glances. Slowly Lysander lifted his sleeve and removed Gideon's band from his wrist. He handed it to the queen.

"And yours?" Tazia commanded.

Gideon fought hard to hide his deception. "I lost it last eve during the festivities, my Queen. I am sorry."

"Lost!"

"Perhaps merely misplaced. Fear not, I shall find it anon."

Tazia's eyes narrowed on him. "You have two turns of the sun to do so, Gideon. Should you not find it, you will pay the price for such carelessness."

Again he bowed. He turned to leave.

Lysander followed. When the door closed behind them, Elgar entered the room of council from a side door.

"Heard you that?" Tazia asked.

"Aye, my Queen," he replied. "When all is done, they will stand with Alasdair. You know this."

Tazia spun to face Elgar, her eyes blazing. "I know no such thing. That they are loyal friends to him, I do not dispute. But they will do what is right for the welfare of us all." She pursed her lips and strode to the window to look out over the palace steps. Gideon and Lysander were just exiting the building. "Still," she muttered.

Elgar stood behind the queen. "What would you have me do?" he asked.

Tazia watched the two friends converse far below. She could not hear their words, but she knew from their expressions that it was a serious discussion. She trusted them implicitly as exalted royal guards, but she wondered if their loyalty to the crown would hold up against their devotion to Alasdair. She hoped it would, for they were two of her finest, and she had no taste to destroy them. But she had her doubts. Tazia breathed deeply, calming herself. Then she turned to Elgar, her expression callous, her words tight and controlled. "Order them followed," she commanded.

"Sweet Mother Earth!" Gideon swore as they made their way swiftly down the palace steps toward the rear gardens. "Can you believe what she has done? It is unprecedented. To steal a child for something other than the tithe is ... is ..."

"Unconscionable," Lysander finished.

"Aye. Exactly."

"But what can we do?" Lysander asked.

"We must find Alasdair and warn him. If not, he will return to the unknown world, leaving the second child behind."

Lysander stopped suddenly. "What of our immortality?" he asked. "What if the queen is right?" He kicked a stone that had come loose from the pathway. "Are you not afraid of death?"

Gideon paused. He turned to face Lysander. "Truly I have dallied with Alasdair far too long. I fear his conscience has awakened mine." He quieted then spoke again. "I do not wish to die, Lysander. But I dare say I wish my life not to be contingent upon the death of another, human or otherwise. Not any more."

Lysander nodded. "Then we have both been equally influenced."

Gideon smiled at his friend then turned serious. "I wonder where he is now."

"Do you dare to believe he has safely crossed the river?" Lysander asked. "I did not stay to watch for fear of being missed."

"Aye. Despite his lack of strategic skills, Alasdair is quite capable, and he has sharp instincts. I deem he traverses the mountains as we speak."

"What about the Sprite Wood?"

"Nay, he would not enter there. He was duly warned." Gideon cast a stealthy glance over Lysander's shoulder. "Lysander?"

"I know. We are being followed."

"Damn that Tazia!" Gideon quietly swore. "How can we warn Alasdair when we are being followed?" He stood in a moment of silence before addressing Lysander, a gleam in his eye. "I have a plan," he said.

"Of course you do." Lysander grinned. "I would be highly disappointed had you not."

Gideon fought a smile. "Whatever I say, contest it. He will follow me, giving you leave to find Alasdair."

"Alone?"

"Aye. If we do not divide loyalties, he will dog our every step."

Lysander shook his head. "I do not like it, Gideon. Without a band, 'tis too risky."

"'Tis the only way," Gideon hissed. "Is it that you fear the dragons? If so, I will speak so that the guard follows you."

Lysander shuddered. "Not as much as I fear Tazia."

Gideon chuckled. "Then let us begin."

"Pray, tell me what to do."

"Contest all that I say. We must divide our loyalties so he will follow only one of us. I will take Alasdair's side. You take Tazia's. When he follows me, go—and may the magic of the fae travel with you."

"Why do *you* take Alasdair's side?"

"'Twill be more believable for me to side with Alasdair since 'twas *my* band that was missing."

"Lysander lowered his head. "I am sorry. It is I who should be in trouble for a missing band."

"Worry not, it is done. We must now think of Alasdair." He grinned at his friend. "Are you ready?"

Lysander nodded.

Gideon cleared his throat. He thought a moment before speaking loud enough for the guard to hear. "You would listen to Tazia when Alasdair needs us? What manner of friend are you?" He gave Lysander's shoulder a sharp shove.

Lysander's brows drew in question. Then his face lit in understanding. He shoved Gideon back. "I am the best of friends, but she is our queen. I would not disobey her. Not for all the jewels in Faerie."

"Well, *I* will not be dissuaded. And if you can so easily discount Alasdair, then discount me as well. I will not have a friend who cannot be trusted." Gideon pushed Lysander aside.

"Be gone from me," he said. He cast Lysander a stealthy wink. "I must warn Alasdair." Gideon took off running.

The guard followed.

Lysander headed for the river.

Chapter Sixteen

Faerie

Leisa stumbled, her traveling shoes catching on roots that had lifted from the earth. She pushed aside branches hanging low over a faint and narrow path. She'd been hiking the Sprite Wood for some time and had seen nothing but dark foliage, thick forest, and glistening ferns. She was hopelessly lost.

A couple of small glowing forms hovered in the distance, following her. Her heart raced each time she caught sight of them. Alasdair had said they would not harm with intent, but he had also said that their trickery could prove fatal. She now understood what he'd meant. The falling boulders were merely an illusion, harmless in itself, but her and Alasdair's reactions could have caused them serious injury. In fact, she could not be certain they had not.

Where was Alasdair?

She looked around, wanting nothing more than to call out to him. She dared not. Only two sprites followed her. She didn't want to attract any more. So far, they amused themselves by merely observing.

The path serpentined so much that Leisa had no idea which way she was going. When she'd started out, she'd been sure she headed toward the mountain. Now her confidence waned. With the overhead canopy blocking the sun and sky, she could not tell the time of day, let alone direction.

A rustling sounded in the brush. Leisa's heart leapt.

"Ali?"

No answer.

Again rustling.

Sure that Alasdair would have answered, she hurried in the opposite direction. When a low growl sounded behind her, she began to run. Jagged branches swiped her face as she pushed her way through thick, wild brush. Her breath rasped. Her side ached. Exhausted, she tripped and fell to the path. Quickly she rose. The path was gone.

She turned in a circle, unsure which way to go. Again the growl. Louder. Nearer. Leisa spun away from the sound and sprinted deeper into the wood. Suddenly she came to a jolting halt. Thick wet sand gripped her feet, rising higher on her legs as she struggled to free herself. *Quicksand.* Leisa stilled. To struggle would only cause her to sink faster, or so she'd read. She looked around for something to grasp. A twisted root lay within arm's reach. When she grabbed for it, a large creature jumped between her and her goal. She yanked her hand back and gaped in horror. Though similar to a wolf, the creature's strangely mutated body was larger and fiercer than any wolf she'd ever seen. It paced in stalking strides, watching her with eyes that glowed vibrant orange. Its lips curled, exposing sharp and pointed teeth. Drool fell from the corners of its mouth.

Leisa gulped. *A wolflych?*

It continued circling the puddle of sand, daring her to try to escape.

Leisa felt herself sink farther still, felt the cool sand press against her thighs. Again she reached for the root. Again the wolflych prevented her from grabbing it.

"Alasdair!" Leisa screamed. The risk that more sprites would discover her seemed the least of her troubles. She was sinking fast. She weighed her options. She had none. If she escaped the bog, the wolflych would get her. If she did nothing, she would drown in murky sand. Neither appealed to her. Her heart pounded against her chest, and though she kept as still as possible, her weight pulled her down and the sand continued to rise. Tears welled in her eyes. She wiped them away. She needed a clear head. Closing her eyes, she breathed deeply.

A figure of light swirled beneath her lids. She tried to open her eyes, but their lids were strangely heavy and unresponsive.

Be calm, the form said as it took on the ethereal shape of a woman. Long black hair with golden strands floated about a beautiful face. An oddly familiar face. *Struggle no more. All is not as it* seems, the voice sounded in her head.

"W—who are you?" Leisa asked as the sand engulfed her waist. Panic took hold and she struggled once more. "Alasdair!" she cried out.

Be calm, the voice repeated.

Leisa's breathing quickened. "Who are you?" She again tried to open her eyes. Again she failed.

I am a spirit of the slain. A soul lost between the worlds of fae immortality and spiritual freedom.

A cry escaped Leisa's throat.

Why are you here, human? the voice asked.

Leisa started at the spirit's keen perception. "T—to save my little girl," she answered.

Who aids you?

Leisa pressed her lips firmly together.

The voice turned strangely surreal. *Aaaaalasdair*, it drawled in a whispery hiss.

"No. I didn't say—"

You called out his name.

"I ..."

He whom you seek is far in the distance. He cannot hear your call.

Leisa sighed. She was sinking to her death and a spirit wanted to chat?

Breathe deeply, human. All is not as it seems.

Leisa drew several long breaths. She felt her body relax and stabilize in the sand. She tried to think clearly. Why would this spirit pick now to speak to her? "Can you help me?" she asked.

Beneath her lids she watched the spirit swirl about her and assess her situation. Finally it stilled and hovered over her.

I am but a spirit. I have no power in the physical world.

Leisa felt herself deflate.

But all is not as it seems in this wood, the spirit repeated.

"I—I don't understand," Leisa cried. "What do you mean?"

The apparition grew dim and the voice began to fade. Leisa felt panic well in her chest. "Please, don't leave," she pleaded.

Use your senses, human, the spirit said in a dimming voice. *They will not fail you.*

The light disappeared and Leisa opened her eyes. The wolflych continued to circle her. Again she reached for the root; again it jumped in her path. The movement caused her to sink farther still. She felt the sand just below her breasts. *Use your senses*, the voice had said. Leisa watched the wolflych intently. It was then she realized that, since seeing it, she hadn't heard it growl. She hadn't heard a sound issue from its throat, hadn't heard a footfall or even a breath. It was unrealistically silent. Like the boulders.

Leisa gasped. It wasn't real! She slowly reached out to the root. Immediately the wolflych jumped in front of it, its thin lips curled in a silent snarl. Her heart pounded as she instinctively pulled her hand back. What if she were wrong? Her thoughts fell to the rustling of brush she'd heard, then to the growling. Though she'd heard both sounds, she had not heard them simultaneously. Either the brush moved or the snarling sounded. Then it hit her. Sprites could deceive only one sense at a time.

Leisa watched the wolflych. Its vibrant orange eyes taunted her, daring her to try again.

She broke eye contact. "You're not real," she whispered. She lifted her gaze and met the beast's vicious stare. "You're not real!" she screamed. She grabbed for the root. The wolflych lunged at her, then vanished. A nervous cry escaped her as she took hold of the root with both hands and dragged herself free. Soon she lay on solid ground, half covered in sandy mud—but alive.

Sniggering sounded in the distance. She turned her head to see two small, winged humanoids bouncing happily in the air. Their glowing bodies twisted and turned in a merry dance, obviously pleased with themselves. Anger welled in her gut. Blood surged through her veins. She gritted her jaw until it ached. "You bastards!" she shouted. She sprang to her feet. "You cowardly little bastards!"

Fear turned to rage and she raced after the sprites, tearing through the low-hanging branches that grabbed at her clothes. She felt the sharp sting of twigs on her flesh, felt them pull at her hair. Then the sniggering stopped and the lights stilled for a moment before racing into the brush and disappearing from view. Leisa stopped suddenly. She fisted her hands and screamed her frustration, then sank to the ground. Bending her legs, she set her arms across her knees and pillowed her forehead on them. Tears dripped onto her lap. *Be calm,* the spirit had said.

Leisa inhaled sharply. Somehow she knew the voice referred to more than just the quicksand. It was a warning to keep a clear head. The sprites were toying with her perceptions. It was up to her to separate reality from trickery. The voice had also said, *He whom you seek is far in the distance. He cannot hear your call.* Leisa sighed. At least Alasdair was alive.

Alasdair pushed his way through the brush, following a tenuous path. Gideon had warned him not to enter the Sprite Wood. Sprite magic was full of mischief. Once one was lost in the forest, it was nearly impossible to find a way out.

And he was lost.

He'd seen several sprites in the distance. Each time, he had hidden beneath his wings until they disappeared. Each time, he'd thanked Lysander most ardently for his band. Beneath the trees, night was pitch and day near dusk. Little sun found its way through the heavy blanket of leaves above. What *did* manage to filter through cast a faint green glow over the path. Without the power of the band, his own magic would have long since faded. Still, the band could protect him only as long as he stayed aware. He needed to keep a keen eye out for approaching lights—to see them before they saw him. Otherwise, he would not have time to successfully camouflage himself and would be at the mercy of the sprites' amusements.

According to Gideon, the sprites were cowardly beings who kept their distance, wreaking their havoc from far enough away to be safe but close enough to enjoy the show. As an exalted royal guard, Gideon had gone on numerous missions outside the safety of Galandore. He knew more about the known world than Alasdair ever would. He had to.

In his peripheral vision, Alasdair caught a movement of light. Quickly, he hunched low and covered himself. Several more lights joined the first. They circled around him, hovered a moment, then flitted off. Alasdair rose. He spun around. The path was gone. He cursed under his breath. Pulling out Gideon's map, he studied it. There was no reference to pathways through the wood. Now he understood why. Paths changed at the whim of the sprites. He sighed heavily and began folding the map. Then a small notation caught his eye. He unfolded it again. Near the corner of the Sprite Wood was a note written in Gideon's hand. Alasdair squinted at the small print. A smile lit his face and he spread his wings. Lights suddenly flickered in the distance, then stilled.

With a sharp downward thrust, Alasdair's wings lifted him high into the trees, higher and higher until he could no longer see the curious sprites. Branches slapped his face and he lifted his arms to protect it. Then he crashed through the canopy of leaves into the brilliance of an evening sun. His eyes instantly closed against the light. When he opened them, he saw a familiar world, hills and trees and water all bathed in beautiful, golden light. Having climbed too dangerously high, he swooped to just above the trees, his heart racing with the thrill that he had outsmarted the sprites.

Or had he?

He looked down at the wood.

Despair crushed the breath from his lungs as an endless sea of lush green foliage met his eye. It spread in every direction, its glowing emerald waves undulating in the breeze. It was a shield against the elements, against the sun, and against ever spotting Leisa. Alasdair hovered a moment contemplating. Then he heard the scream.

Leisa snapped to attention at the sound of breaking branches. She jumped to her feet at the call of her name. "Alasdair?" she cried out. When no reply came, she shouted, "Alasdair!" Her hand flew to cover her mouth and she stilled. What if it was another trick of the sprites? But how would they know her name? She listened closely. The sound of snapping twigs drew near, accompanied by Alasdair's call. Two sounds combined. "Alasdair!" she again shouted. When he broke through the brush, she flung her arms about his neck and held tight.

"Where have you been?" she cried into his shoulder. "I was so afraid. The sprites and the wolflych. And the path kept changing. And the quagmire. Oh, my God, the quagmire." Alasdair tightened his embrace and stroked her hair. Then she felt his head turn.

"We must leave this place now," he said.

Leisa nodded. She lifted her head and wiped at her cheeks. "How?" she asked. "Sprites play tricks with your mind. The paths change. I nearly drowned in quicksand." She brushed at the half-dried mud on her clothes. When she looked up, she saw a circle of distant lights surrounding them. Her breath caught.

Alasdair wrapped an arm about her waist and spread his wings. It was the first time she'd seen them open for flight, and her eyes grew wide in awe of their opalescent beauty and breadth. When her own wings lifted, Alasdair clamped his free arm over them, holding them down. "Hold tight," he warned. Driving down his wings, Alasdair cut through the air, pulling Leisa up with him. Nearing the heavy canopy, he tucked Leisa's head under his chin, covered her face with his arm, and lowered his own face to her hair. Branches snapped as they broke through the foliage and into the fading sun, where he spread his wings to their full glory.

Freed from the forest, Alasdair set her back from him, and released his hold on her wings. Immediately, they spread like his. "Are you all right?" he asked.

Leisa gasped as they floated just above the trees. "I think so."

Alasdair sighed in relief. They had survived the Sprite Wood. Holding both her hands, he hovered a moment, meeting Leisa's stare of disbelief. She began laughing and crying at once. Alasdair smiled.

"How did you find me?" she asked. "You were so far away." She pulled one hand free to wipe at her cheeks. When she nearly did the same with the other hand, Alasdair squeezed tightly. "We must keep touch in flight. Remember?"

Leisa nodded. "How did you avoid the sprites?"

"Forget not, I have the band and the use of magic. More amazing is how *you* escaped them."

"I didn't." Leisa sniffled. "Not on my own."

"What do you mean?"

"When I was sinking in the quicksand, a vision appeared in my head."

Alasdair frowned. "What manner of vision?"

"A woman."

"Fae or human?"

"Definitely fae. Her skin was alabaster and nearly glowed. And her hair floated about her as though in water. It was black with gold strands like yours."

"Did she give a name?" Alasdair asked.

"No. She merely said that things were not as they seemed and told me to use my senses." Leisa quieted then added, "She also said you were far in the distance and couldn't hear my call."

"She knew me by name?" Alasdair asked.

"Well, I'd called for you several times. Maybe she just assumed it was your name."

Alasdair's frown lifted. "Perhaps." Turning, he guided Leisa closer to the trees. Though her wings beat with his, she suddenly seemed heavy and he felt himself being dragged down with her. "Are you weary?" he asked.

"Exhausted."

Scanning the foliage, Alasdair chose a nearby tree to rest on. Its leaves were darker than those of the surrounding trees, its heavily padded foliage thicker. He clasped Leisa's wings against her back and lowered into the wood. Then he noted the tree's unusually craggy bark and gnarled and twisted branches. This tree was ancient. It had been standing since the beginning of time. Beneath its highest branch sat an abandoned nest fashioned from twisted vines and twigs. Large, thick leaves padded it. It was there he landed.

"Night is nearly upon us. Let us rest here until daybreak." Alasdair lay back on the windswept leaves and stared into the darkening sky.

"How did you escape the sprites?" Leisa asked.

"I found a notation on Gideon's map. It said that sprites cannot fly at great heights and hover close to the ground."

Leisa smiled and released a long, slow breath. Her body relaxed and she lay next to him.

Alasdair wrapped an arm about her shoulders and pulled her close. He lifted his wings and sheltered her and himself from the cool evening wind. Then they closed their eyes and slept.

When Alasdair woke, he saw the sun high in the sky. He looked at Leisa and saw her eyes still closed in sleep. Alasdair shifted slightly. His chest pained at the sight of her and the thought of the danger he had placed her in. His loins ached in a way foreign to the fae. He wanted to kiss her, hold her, mate with her. He caught his breath. *Mate?* No. More than mate. Faeries loved to some degree, but they mated in frivolous fun. Human mating went far beyond frivolity, or so he had heard. It involved passion and need, suffering and ultimate joy.

Traces of such feelings wavered through him—there one moment, gone the next. They were his agony and his joy. They were what made him different from the rest, including Gideon and Lysander.

But his friends accepted him despite his flaws, protected him when his impulsive nature led him to risk banishment. He sighed heavily. Until now. They had not seen how far his empathy had taken him and had failed to draw him back from his quest. Still, they'd protected him as best they could without signing their own warrants of death.

Again he looked at Leisa peacefully lying beside him. If by some miracle he succeeded in this quest, what would become of the two of them? He brushed her hair back from her face. She stirred, then quieted again. He could not stay in the human world. He had no dust to maintain a human form and, in time, his fae body would weaken as the magic of the fae slowly ebbed away. He would not have the strength and fortitude of a human man—the persistence to survive against all odds. Nay. The fae relied fully on the magic of the known world. Without it they would die. His throat tightened. He would have to return to Faerie and face whatever consequences arose. Perhaps Tazia would have mercy on him. After all, he *was* her sister's son.

Alasdair closed his eyes and concentrated on the golden wash of morning sun on his face. He saw its brilliance through the thin cover of his lids, felt its heat seep into his flesh. He licked his lips and tasted the air, crisp and fragrant with new forest growth.

Again Leisa stirred. Waking, she reached up and stroked his face. When he looked down at her, he caught the warmth of her mossy gaze. Savored it. Then a stirring rose in his gut and his body gravitated toward her. He lowered his head and brushed her mouth with his. When her body rose to meet him, he rolled to his side and drew her tightly to him.

"Ali," Leisa murmured. When her lips parted, he tasted her fully. Warm and sweet and—

The ache in his loins fell suddenly away, the fleeting trace of feeling now lost. He pulled back and growled his frustration. Pressing his fists to his temples, he cried, "What is this? Why am I so torn?"

Leisa licked her lips, tasting the remnants of a kiss that lingered still. "It's okay," she assured him.

Alasdair sat up. "Nay, 'tis not okay. One moment I feel great passion, the next I do not. One moment I feel magic, the next it is gone." He shook his head. "I am not whole, Leisa." He hung his head and covered his face. "I am not whole."

Leisa sat up next to him. She drew his hands down from his face and held them in her own. "You're stressed," she said. "You'll be fine. I promise you."

Alasdair caught her gaze, then pulled her to him. Her warmth was intoxicating and comforting at once. "Are you sure, Leisa? Are you so sure this will end happily?"

Leisa's hesitation caused him concern. Then her chin lifted and she met his gaze.

"Yes," she replied

Alasdair camouflaged their wings to match the leaves of the trees. Flying just above the treetops, they could see the mountain and its base and still stay off the dragons' radar. At least he hoped so.

"There." Alasdair pointed. "We shall land there."

"Why can't we just fly up the mountain?" Leisa asked.

"'Tis too dangerous to fly out into open air. The dragons guard the rivers, aye. But they scour the mountain as well. It is their home."

"Won't they see us climbing it?"

"If we stay vigilant, we can hide when they come into view."

"Like in the water?" Leisa muttered.

"Aye."

"That wasn't exactly successful."

"Nothing is guaranteed, Leisa. We can only do our best."

Leisa nodded. "I know. I'm sorry. I'm just so frustrated ... and scared." She swallowed hard. "Really scared."

"I as well."

Leisa's eyes widened. "You? Scared?"

"Aye. To the dragons I am naught but a tasty snack. Is that not enough to evoke fear?"

"More than enough."

Alasdair lowered them to where the rockslide had sent them running. His satchel still rested on the ground. They had come full circle.

Chapter Seventeen

Faerie

Leisa stared at the climb ahead of them, at the slow fading away of the Sprite Wood from lush green forest to the weathered tan and gray of rock. Morning cast its bright golden light over the incline, setting the stony mountainside to glow warmly. They had waited just inside the treeline until the white dragon had left his lair to follow the river.

"Come," Alasdair said. "We must reach shelter ere the dragon returns. In the shadows, we cannot be seen from the air."

"Then what?" Leisa asked.

"When we reach the ledge, we follow it." Alasdair pointed to a dip that fell between two jagged peaks. "Once past the valley of the peaks, we will be in red dragon territory. I wish to pass through before he awakens."

"If the white dragon sleeps at night, why don't we just wait until dark to climb the hill?"

"We have lost too much time already. I know not how much time Sachi has left. If any."

Leisa swallowed. The correction of Blaise's name teetered on her lips. She held it back. As Alasdair had once said, *what matters a name.* Sharp rock bit into her shoes as she followed Alasdair through the thinning treeline, and she was glad they had worn traveling clothes and heavier-soled footwear. Suddenly Alasdair stopped and walked back into the trees.

"Where are you going?" Leisa called after him. She watched him melt into the surroundings, then disappear. "Ali?" she called out nervously. Several loud cracks rent the air. Alasdair stepped out from the trees with two long and twisted staves in his hands.

"Hold these," he said as he handed them to Leisa. He drew his dagger from its sheath and cut off all the spindly branches, slicing at the juncture of staff and branch until each walking stick rested smoothly in the palm. "These will help with the climb."

Re-sheathing his knife, he took the longer staff. "There," he said, pointing to a cluster of rocks and boulders at the foot of the mountain. He picked up his pace. "The dragon will soon return. Beneath the header stone is a place we can hide from view until he passes and swings around for another loop." Alasdair grabbed Leisa's hand and pulled her in his wake, his longer strides forcing her to quicken her steps.

With every other step, Leisa slammed her staff onto the ground, using it to propel herself forward. Her breath came in short, shallow gulps. "Are we almost there?" She chastised herself for sounding like a petulant child in the back seat of the family car. Though she had gotten a good night's rest, her legs still felt weak and unsteady. She made a mental note to work out more. As they neared the rocks, Alasdair ushered her to a massive boulder. It sat atop several large rocks, creating a shadowed hollow. Leisa crouched to fit beneath it, then sat on the hard ground. The sun shone brightly and grew warmer by the minute. She was happy for the shade. "Tell me again why we're waiting here?"

Alasdair crouched beside her, his body far from relaxed. "We wait for the white dragon to turn about and again head down the river."

"And why are we waiting for him to do that?"

Alasdair turned his vibrant green eyes on her. "Leisa, I did already say ..."

Leisa shook her head. "I'm sorry. My brain isn't functioning well today."

"We wait so that when he again leaves, we will have ample time to make it to the ledge before his next return." Alasdair pointed high on the mountain.

Leisa swallowed as she looked at the narrow ledge that lay in shadow. "I'm really not liking this."

Alasdair turned to Leisa. "Then let us turn back and avoid the pain of the climb and the fear of the unknown. There is still time."

Leisa cuffed his shoulder with the heel of her hand. "Avoid the pain? Fear of the unknown?" She hit him again. "Are you kidding me? I gave birth to Blaise. You want to talk about pain! And any woman who goes into labor for the first time dives head first into the unknown."

Alasdair's lips twitched as he fought a smile.

Leisa cuffed him again. "Why do you bait me so!"

Alasdair cocked his head. He slowly brushed the back of his hand up her cheek and slid his fingers through her hair. "For reason that such goading reddens your cheeks and sets them to glow. Most becoming."

Leisa huffed. "How can I get mad at you when you say things like that?"

Alasdair leaned into her, his verdant eyes fixed and hooded. Leisa felt his fingers spread over the back of her head, felt him pull her to him. Then a shadow passed over. Quickly, Alasdair shielded her.

"What was that?" Leisa asked.

"The dragon." Alasdair held them still. When the shadow passed a second time, he crawled out from the rocks and stood. Grabbing Leisa's hands, he drew her out and pulled her to her feet. "We must move with haste. He will soon pass again. We must reach the ledge before that happens. There is no other cover."

The climb was tricky, but they reached the ledge before the dragon returned. From below, it had looked treacherous to follow. Up close and personal, it was even worse. As Alasdair had said, the overhang shadowed the ledge, hiding them from view, but the ledge itself was barely two feet wide. Granted, she used to walk curbs as a child, balancing so as not to fall into the imaginary river far below. But those curbs weren't hundreds of feet up.

They followed the ledge for over an hour as it wound up the mountainside, higher and higher. Her eyes drifted downward and she wavered at the dizzying height.

Alasdair turned. He pressed up on her chin, lifting her gaze. "Do not look down. Doing so will cause you to lose balance."

"I'm really not too fond of heights," Leisa replied. She felt the blood drain from her face.

"I see that." Alasdair took her hand. "Why then were you not afraid when we hovered above the treetops?" he asked as they continued on.

"I don't know. I suppose because I couldn't see the ground through the trees."

Alasdair squeezed her hand. "Come. The ledge widens just ahead. We can rest there."

"I don't need rest. I need to get off this damn led—"

Leisa teetered as rock crumbled beneath her feet. She dropped, pulling Alasdair with her. Her breath caught, squelching her scream. She looked past her dangling feet to the rocks far below, then up at Alasdair who lay flat on the ledge, gripping the rough stone with one hand, clutching her wrist with the other.

"Don't let go," Leisa pleaded. She felt his hold slipping, felt the warmth of it grow slick with sweat as he tried to pull her up one-handed.

"Leisa."

Leisa heard the desperation in his tone and felt her hand slide in his grasp. "Ali, please don't let go." She swung toward the cliff face, trying to grab it with her free hand. Again she felt his fingers slip.

"Leisa, I shall roll from the ledge. Once clear of the wall, I can spread my wings—and yours. Just hold onto me."

As Alasdair shifted for the roll, her wrist slid from his grasp. Leisa screamed.

"Nay!" Alasdair cried. He jumped to his feet and dove from the ledge. With his wings tight against his back, he sliced the air, the wind stinging his face as he raced to reach her before she hit ground. Gaining on her, he reached out. Their eyes met.

Suddenly the air was knocked from his lungs. His body jolted, and he gasped hoarsely. Thick claws wound about his chest, crushing his lungs. Anguish clutched his throat. *Leisa.* Grief rose from his core. Again he tried to breathe, but the crushing hold of the dragon's claw refused him air. His eyes fluttered. Then all went black.

Sharp pebbles bit into his back. He opened his eyes to a gray haze and blinked several times to clear his vision. Above him was a ceiling of jagged gray rock. The walls were smoother rock of the same. His body felt as though it had been beaten and left for dead. But he could breathe. Thank the stars, he could breathe. He pulled a deep breath and winced at the pain. Then he remembered.

Leisa.

He choked on the grief and the horror. He had nearly had her! He wished he had died as well. He closed his eyes and saw her terrified face. *So close.*

Alasdair released a long-held breath and turned his head. Water spilled from his eyes. Then he heard a breath that was not his own. He rolled onto his stomach. Leisa lay face down in the distance, recovering as well.

"Leisa," he called out to her, his voice raspy and foreign sounding. He pulled himself up to his knees and elbows and began to crawl.

A cage of talons fell over him.

Leisa lifted her head. "Ali?"

The dragon lowered his other claw over Leisa. She pounded on a tall arched talon. "Ali!" she screamed.

The dragon lowered his head and peered between his talons at her. Though cramped, Leisa shuffled back as best she could. Had the dragon not been dangerous, she would have thought him a beautiful beast with his pearlescent scales and large glittering gold eyes. Even his talons were magnificent—a reflective silver, like chrome. But the beauty of the dragon did not change the fact that he considered her food. Fear clenched her throat.

The dragon moved to peer through the other side of his talons, prompting Leisa to quickly shift sides. His thin, forked tongue flicked out, tasting the air above her. His eyes widened, then hooded. With a final sniff, he drew back. "Human!" he said, his deep and throaty voice rumbling the cave. "Bah! I do not care for human flesh." He lifted his talons, releasing her. "But you," he said, turning to Alasdair. "You are fae." He opened his mouth to reveal a row of long, sharp teeth. Whatever beauty he possessed on the outside was quickly lost to the thought of his bite.

"No!" Leisa screamed. She slid to her knees beside the talons that held Alasdair captive. "Please don't."

The dragon's head lifted high and tilted. "Why do you defend him, human? He who over the course of thousands of years, has stolen countless human children as tithes to hell."

The dragon lowered his head so that they were face to face. Leisa shuffled back.

"Tell me, human, why do you defend such a loathsome creature?"

"Ali?" Leisa turned to look at him.

"Never have I stolen a child!" Alasdair replied. He sighed heavily. "But 'tis true that the fae have stolen human babes since the beginning of time. Paid them to hell in exchange for immortality."

"The beginning of time?" The dragon lifted his head and laughed loudly.

Leisa felt the ground shake beneath her knees.

"Pitiful fae. How long have you believed this lie?" The dragon snorted, releasing a plume of flame.

"'Tis no lie."

"Then you are deceived by either your own kind or the sentinels of hell itself. Most likely the former. The tithing of children is but three thousand years in the making."

"What say you?"

"I say that the tithing of children started with the reign of Tazia and that no sacrificed child has gained the fae even a day of life, let alone immortality. Hell has found a way to steal the souls of the innocent by deceiving the fae." Again he laughed. "Quite industrious, think you not?"

"How know you this?"

"I have lived more years than all the fae combined. I grow old." His gaze leveled on Alasdair. "There is no immortality. Everything that lives, dies. It is but a matter of when. My magic is great. Greater than that of the fae. Greater than that of the sprites. But I will die, and hell cannot promise me extra years. 'Tis not within its power. It is in only the Creator's power to promise life. And the Creator's decision as to my years was made before my birth."

"Then it has all been for naught? All those lives?"

Leisa heard the despair in Alasdair's voice.

"Aye, foolish fae."

"And this is why you despise the fae?" Leisa asked.

"Oh, aye. Such vanity it is to take a life for your own gain."

"Do you not kill?" Alasdair asked.

"For food, that is all."

Alasdair groaned. "Why did you not tell us? Why did you allow this to go on for so long?"

"What the fae do or do not is of no concern to me. They will pay for their sins in the end. My job is to guard the rivers by day and stop those such as you from crossing them." The dragon's tongue flicked out between his teeth. Saliva wetted his scaly lips. His talons slowly closed on Alasdair.

Leisa heard Alasdair choke. "Wait!" she cried.

The dragon snorted a short burst of flame and snarled at her. "What is it now, human? You are becoming quite bothersome. I may need to eat you after all just to silence you."

"True, Ali is fae, but he's on a quest to *save* a human child, not harm one."

"Explain."

Leisa recounted their story. "Please spare him. If you don't, my daughter will die."

The dragon closed his eyes in thought. When they opened, Leisa saw decision in their suddenly dark-gold depths, and she didn't like what she saw.

"I tire of woodland beast. I have not had a tasty fae in quite some time. What is one more life foolishly spent to a sumptuous meal?" He lifted his free talons and shoved Leisa back from Alasdair. Mouth open, he lowered his head.

Alasdair covered his head with his arms.

Suddenly the dragon drew back. He closed his eyes and sniffed, then lowered his head to just above Alasdair and licked the air. His eyes widened. Again he drew back.

"You are he!" the dragon exclaimed.

"What?" Alasdair lowered his arms in relief and confusion.

"He. The prophecy. You are the one." The dragon released Alasdair.

Alasdair slid back on his elbows, then pulled himself up on his knees. "What one?"

The dragon sniffed again. "Aye. My senses do not fail me. I know that smell."

Leisa hurried to Alasdair and sank to her knees beside him. "What's he talking about?" she whispered in his ear.

"I know not," Alasdair replied.

"He!" the dragon insisted. "The defender of mankind."

Alasdair gasped. It was the meaning of his name. "You are wrong. I have no such power. I merely seek to save one child."

"One child! And what of all the children of the future?"

"I have heard tale of this prophecy. It is not I."

"Why not?" the dragon asked. "Why not you?"

"Because the defender is prophesied to be born half fae and half human. I am fae."

The dragon laughed. The cave shook. Small pebbles rained down from the ceiling. Leisa and Alasdair covered their heads. When the dragon finished, he lowered his head so that his gaze locked with Alasdair's. He spoke each word with forced clarity. "You are human!"

"Human!" Alasdair jumped to his feet. Leisa followed. She grabbed his hand and stepped close to his side. "You are mistaken, great one."

The dragon looked down his long, scaly snout at Alasdair. "Mistaken? Nay. If anyone is mistaken, 'tis you. I grow old, aye. But I know what I smell."

"'Tis Leisa you smell. She is human."

"She is a female of the species. I smell also a male."

"It cannot be. I am fae."

"You are half fae."

Alasdair gasped. His hand tightened around Leisa's.

"Do not begrudge it, fae. 'Tis what spares you now," the dragon warned.

"My name is Alasdair."

"I know."

"How know you this?"

"It is the fae name meaning defender of mankind, is it not?" The dragon shook his head. "Do not answer. I do already know."

"Nay!" Alasdair cried out. "It cannot be."

"It was given to you by he who begat you and she who gave you birth. A human father and a faerie mother. They knew the prophecy. They knew their child was the one."

Alasdair fell to his knees and covered his face. "It cannot be," he muttered into his hands. Leisa knelt behind him and embraced his shoulders.

"Do not fret, fae ... er ... Alasdair," said the dragon. "It is a great honor to be the one. I knew your father."

Alasdair's head shot up. "That is not possible. My parents died in an accident when I was but a youngling."

The dragon snorted and shook his head. "Where heard you this lie?"

"Lie? 'Tis no lie. The queen herself told me."

Again the dragon snorted. "I wonder," he said, "what other lies she would have you believe."

"Nay!" Alasdair bellowed. "'Tis you I do not believe."

"'Tis your decision to believe or to not believe. I can only say what truth I know—and I knew your father," the dragon repeated. "I was quite impressed with him," he continued. "Comely, as humans go. Witty, intelligent, and full of compassion. His only flaw was loving a faerie." The dragon sniffed. "You smell of him."

"That is not proof he was my father."

"He married a faerie named Taelena, sister to Queen Tazia."

Alasdair gasped. "My mother."

"Aye." The dragon shook his head. "Tazia, too, is deceived, as are all the fae. Hell has a way of getting what it wants."

Faerie Dust / Linda Ciletti

Chapter Eighteen

Faerie

Alasdair sat in a shadowy corner of the cave, his arms resting on his knees, his forehead pressed against them.

Leisa sat near the dragon's claw, her arms wrapped around her knees. "What can I do?" she whispered to the dragon. Her gaze shifted to Alasdair. He'd been eerily quiet for some time, and she worried about him.

"You can do nothing," the dragon replied. "It is his decision to make. Either way, he is free to go. As I said, human flesh is not to my taste. And I would not eat he who is prophesied to defend humankind, whatever his decision. He can save one child or he can save future generations."

"You said your magic is greater than all else. Why can't you do it?"

The dragon's pearlescent scales gleamed soft pink in sunset's fading light as he dragged a glittery gold gaze from Leisa to Alasdair and back. "It is not my burden. And magic will not win this battle. Not the greatest magic in all of the realm can save the future generations of humankind."

Leisa pulled a sharp breath. "I don't understand. Then what can Alasdair do? What does he have that's greater than any magic here?"

The dragon's gaze softened to liquid gold. His mouth lifted in a watery smile. "Love," he said.

Alasdair lifted his head and opened his eyes—eyes red with fatigue and fretfulness. He walked closer to where Leisa sat and looked up at the dragon. "What must I do?" he asked.

The dragon sat taller. "You must convince Tazia that the law of tithe for immortality is false. That there is no immortality, however many humans she sends for sacrifice."

"How can I ask her to cast aside what has been upheld for thousands of years? What has passed through generations of fae? Fae who are still alive."

"For reason that they have not yet spent their allotted time."

"If this be true and no fae has died a natural death in several thousand years, how can I convince her of the truth of what you say?"

"That is your challenge. I am but a messenger." The dragon turned away. He circled twice and curled into himself for sleep. "Now I may die at peace."

Leisa gasped. "Now?"

The dragon chuckled. "Not now." He snorted then settled his head onto his front forelegs. "Now I merely rest. I am getting old and soft. See how I have let two humans live? In my youth, I would have eaten first and worried about taste later." The dragon smiled.

Leisa returned his smile. "I'm Leisa. What's your name?"

"I am *he*, the great one. I am the messenger of truth. Now I have delivered my message."

"But when I tell of your greatness, what shall I call you?"

The dragon closed his eyes for sleep. "Armadeous," he murmured. "I am Armadeous."

Alasdair straightened his shoulders and looked up at Armadeous. "I accept my lot on one condition."

Armadeous inched open one glittery eye. "I do not bargain," he warned. "It is not in me to do so."

"'Tis not a bargain I seek, only your kindness."

Armadeous opened both eyes, lifted his head, and stared down at Alasdair. "What do you ask of me?" He lowered his head to Alasdair's level.

Alasdair shifted uncomfortably. "Before I fulfill my destiny, I wish to save the child who is already taken. Will you help us?"

Armadeous shook his head. "I cannot. She is already in the cave of the trolls. I am too large to travel there."

"But *we* are not. I beg you, is there not a way I can find this cave and bring her back?"

The dragon licked the air. "There is one way. Most likely she still lives and is being held in waiting."

"Waiting?" Leisa asked. "Waiting for what?"

Armadeous pondered a moment. "Hell's vassal will rise from the flames in two days' time. There is a tunnel deep within this cave that leads to the troll lair. The trolls will not enter it. They fear me—as they should. Though they are vastly horrid to look upon, they are even tastier than the fae."

"So," Alasdair said, "we could follow this tunnel into the lair, find the child, and bring her back here."

"Aye. But know this, 'tis dangerous. I doubt not that the trolls guard the child, for they believe that when they deliver the tithe of the fae, hell blesses their mines with a multitude of jewels. Yet another deception. They will not give her up easily." Armadeous shifted, then straightened. "Also, I know not where they hold their prisoners. It may take some time for you to find her."

"Then I should not waste another minute," Alasdair answered.

Armadeous's eyes widened then relaxed. "'Tis your decision. I will not stand in your way. But I advise a night's rest before embarking on this journey. You will need your wits about you. And your strength. Another night will make no matter one way or another."

"How know you this?" Alasdair asked. "How know you 'tis not already too late?"

"The tithe takes place on the full moon following the fifth anniversary of the child's birth."

"And you know this how?"

"Your father told me all he knew about the fae that I did not already know."

"Her fifth birthday was last week," Leisa said. "The day we went to the cemetery to visit her grave."

"When is the next full moon?" Alasdair asked.

Armadeous spoke. "In two days' time."

Relief washed over Alasdair. Sachi lived. Three days of stress suddenly lifted from him, leaving him with a body that was weary and sore. A good night's sleep would do him wonders.

The dragon reached into a crevice and dragged out a trunk. "Open it," he said.

Alasdair lifted its lid. In it was clothing, both simple daily wear and wear fit for nobility, as well as thick, warm blankets.

"Take what you need. I have no use for it. I found it floating in the river many years past. I deem that those who owned it were quite a treat for Deliterous."

"Deliterous?" Leisa asked.

"The red dragon. A young, impetuous dragon who eats first and asks questions later, if at all."

Leisa swallowed.

Alasdair foraged through the trunk. "Hold these, please." He handed Leisa a long chemise, braies and tunic, then pulled out several thick downy covers. Finding an obscure corner of the cave shielded by a large rock, he piled the covers into a soft cushion behind it.

The dragon watched with interest. "There is a heated pool deeper in the cave should you wish to bathe," he informed them. "Molten lava from within the mountain keeps it always warm. 'Twill heal your sore muscles as well."

Alasdair caught Leisa's hopeful gaze. *A bath!* He grabbed the tunic and braies. Then he held his hand out to her. "Come."

Leisa eyed him skeptically.

"Truly, Leisa, I am too tired for naught but washing and sleep. I merely long to be clean."

Leisa smiled. "Me, too," she said, brushing at the dried dirt on her leggings. She grabbed the chemise, took his hand, and followed him.

When they reached the pool, it was as Armadeous said. The water was warm and effervescent, like a glass of tepid champagne. Their bodies relaxed and their eyelids felt comfortably heavy. After washing and dressing in clean raiment, they made their way to the makeshift bed and slipped beneath the covers.

"Ali?" Leisa said.

"Shh."

Leisa felt the breadth of Alasdair's chest at her back, felt the heat of him through her thin chemise. His arms tightened around her. "Ali, I'm worried," she said. "You can't go to Tazia and demand she stop the tithes. She'll have you killed."

Alasdair stroked Leisa's hair. "Worry not. I have the band to protect me."

Leisa heard the lie in Alasdair's tone. The band had enhanced his magic and protected him from the sprites, but she doubted it could protect him from the queen. "But Ali—"

"Shh. All will end as it should."

Leisa wished she could turn and face him, but his arm held her securely in place. She tried to look over her shoulder. "As it should?" she asked. "What does that mean?"

"Sleep, Leisa. We can talk on the morrow." Alasdair kissed the back of her head.

Leisa sighed. Utter exhaustion had dimmed Alasdair's voice to little more than a whisper. She felt his arms fall lax. "On the morrow," Leisa whispered. Then she, too, gave in to sleep.

Armadeous stood over the sleeping couple. He lowered his huge head to just above them and sniffed. Human and fae, this would not do. He knew all too well the trouble that came with such a union. He knew also that only pure love could fulfill the prophecy. The fae did not possess such self-sacrificing love, and the prophecy stated the "one" would be *born* half fae and half human. Alasdair was the one. Armadeous was sure of it. But Alasdair would not succeed in his torn state. He needed to experience a far deeper love to call upon its power. He needed to feel it to the very depths of his soul, to be willing to die for it. True, the troubled fae had accepted his fate, but he had done so out of duty to fae prophecy. It was not enough. It would not give him the inner strength he needed to fulfill his task.

Decision crossed Armadeous's face. He spread his talons wide and caged the sleeping couple beneath them. Then he summoned all the magic he possessed. Soon his foot began to glow with pure white light. Heat emanated from the soft underpads of his toes, swirling between the pointed talons and pouring over and through the entangled pair. Armadeous grinned contentedly. *Now*, he thought as he made his way deeper into the cave and curled into himself for sleep. *Now they are the same.*

Alasdair woke, his arms still wrapped about Leisa beneath the soft covers. The dragon was nowhere in sight and the first hint of dawn peeked through the cave entrance, a faint pink light mixed with gold. The cave still sat in darkness. "Leisa," he whispered as he brushed a strand of hair from her face.

Leisa mumbled something indiscernible and continued sleeping.

"Leisa ..." Alasdair stilled. He felt strangely different. There was a pull deep in his gut when he looked at Leisa, a pull stronger than any he had ever felt. His body reacted to her beyond the need to kiss, to touch. More than his body—his spirit, his soul, his heart. It ached in his chest, ached for an intimacy far deeper than any he had ever known. He tried drawing back from her, but the more he tried, the harder his body fought him. It wanted her. He wanted her. Alasdair rubbed his face. What was wrong with him? Aye, he had always felt attracted to Leisa, but not with such unimaginable desire. Not with such paralyzing need that he could not pull away. He rose up on one arm and looked down at her.

Leisa turned in her sleep. She breathed several long breaths then opened her eyes. "Ali—"

Alasdair touched his mouth to hers and felt the soft pillow of her lips, warm and moist against his own. He had kissed her before, but never had he been so acutely aware of her scent, her taste, the utter softness of her flesh. The part of him he'd always had control over rose on its own—hot and thick and painfully aching for release. He groaned, the discomfort both pain and pleasure at once.

When Leisa ran her hands up the soft material of his braies and touched him, he gasped. His body thrust against her with a will of its own. His kiss deepened, harder, firmer, demanding more. His tongue parted her lips and he tasted all that she was. Sweet, warm, and delicious. When her tongue met his, he pressed against her with an aching need to be one.

He lifted the thin fabric of her chemise and explored her body with his hands. He'd been right. Her breasts filled his palms perfectly as their rosy tips lifted to his touch. He tore his mouth from hers and tasted his way down her neck, then pulled her chemise up and over her head, dropping it on the blankets.

Their eyes met and he kissed her once again, full and hard. He felt her arms cling to his back, her fingers twine in his hair.

Her skin was flawlessly smooth, like the velvet petals of a rose. It tasted lightly of salt, a taste that had him craving more. He shuddered violently, fought to control it and lost. His hunger for her grew as he slid his mouth along the perfect line of her jaw and neck, tasting his way down to the soft mound of flesh still cupped in his hand. He squeezed it firmly, raising its tip, then drew it deeply into his mouth. His tongue lapped her sensitive flesh. When he caught the fleshy bud between his teeth and lip and pulled, Leisa moaned and arched to meet him. The softness between her legs brushed against him and he sought it out. He slipped his fingers inside her, thrusting again and again until she cried out his name.

Alasdair felt the air expel from his lungs. His heart hammered against his chest. His breaths fell heavily. Sex with faeries had never been like this. It was merely coupling for fun. This was passion, heat, love.

Love.

That was what made this coupling grander than any he had ever known. Love. He kicked free from his braies. Then he ran his hand through Leisa's hair, wound it tight in his fingers, and kissed her fully as his free hand slid between her thighs, then higher still. She rose to meet his touch. When he felt her wetness on his hand, he positioned his aching shaft.

Leisa parted her lips and opened to his hungry exploration. She wrapped her legs around his back and begged him enter. As if sensing her need, Alasdair grasped her waist, arched her back, and drove into her as deeply as her human body allowed. Leisa cried out against his shoulder. His breath released on a groan. She felt him suddenly still; then his body moved in a rhythmic dance that stole her breath. Leisa met that rhythm and rose to meet his every forceful thrust. Her body trembled and begged for release. Her hands slid across the damp skin of his back, pulling him close. "Now, Ali. Now," she cried. She heard his breath expel, felt his body freeze as the part of him that made them one pulsed within her. Then he pulled her tight against him and shuddered in her arms.

She felt the quickened beat of his heart, heard his labored breaths as he lowered himself beside her, sparing her his weight. Then silence. Finally he spoke. "Did I harm you?"

Leisa smiled. "No, Alasdair." She cuddled against him.

Alasdair raised his arms to cover his face. "I know not what came over me. 'Twas as though I had no control." He turned to Leisa, worry etching his face. "I am sorry."

Leisa rose up on one elbow. Their eyes met. "Don't faeries have sex?" she asked.

Alasdair looked at her, puzzled. "Aye. But with control." He shook his head. "Not with so little restraint. Never have I felt such a feeling. Such a lack of will. Not in all my life."

Leisa stroked his silky black hair, separated a golden strand out from the black and twirled it in her fingers. "Was it a good feeling or a bad one?" she asked.

"A frightening feeling. Good, aye. Bad, aye. 'Twas both."

Leisa worried her lip. "Is it a feeling you would want to feel again?" she asked.

"'Tis a feeling I cannot imagine never feeling again."

Leisa smiled. She kissed Alasdair softly on the lips; then she snuggled against him. "We'll go slower next time," she muttered sleepily. Her lids drooped with exhaustion. Soon she slept.

Alasdair lay awake, his eyes wide, his head reeling. He had changed. Somehow he had changed. He could feel it in the flow of his blood and in the beat of his heart. He could feel it in every sense he possessed. He rolled his shoulders and willed his wings. None came. He groaned.

He was human.

Chapter Nineteen

Faerie

Alasdair heard the heavy flapping of Armadeous's wings as the dragon hit the cave entrance, something clenched in his talons. Skidding to a stop, the dragon dropped the load on the floor. Quickly Alasdair secured his braies and left his and Leisa's makeshift bed. When he stepped into the open, he saw what looked to be a fae crumpled on the floor. His stomach lurched.

Armadeous lifted a talon to pierce his meal through.

"Hold!" Alasdair shouted.

Armadeous stilled. "What is it, *human*?" His hard lips lifted in a wry and knowing smile.

"You?" Alasdair asked, gesturing to himself. "*You* did this to me?"

Armadeous grinned. "You cannot complete your task unless you know love at its fullest. A fae will never know such things. Only a human feels with passion and depth.

"So you made me human!" Alasdair cried. "How?"

"I could not have done so were you fully fae. But for reason you were already half human, 'twas easy enough."

Alasdair cried a sound of anguish, grief, and loss. "How shall I save Sachi now! I have no power. I have no magic. I am stripped of all that would give me strength."

The dragon slammed his foot, just missing his prey who knelt folded into himself, his arms covering his head. "Be not so foolish! You are not without magic; it has merely changed. Call on the magic that is human and fulfill your destiny."

Leisa shifted beneath the blankets. Awakened by the noise, she pulled her chemise over her head and joined the others.

"What's going on?" Her eyes widened. "Lysander?"

Alasdair's gaze shot to Armadeous's prey. "Lysander?"

Armadeous clamped his talons over Lysander, pinning him down. "Be gone from here. I will speak with you after I eat." He opened his jaws revealing, sharp teeth.

"Stop!" Alasdair cried out. "I beg you, do not eat him."

"He is fae. I will eat him if I wish."

"He is my brother."

Armadeous lowered his head and sniffed. "You lie. There is no human in him."

Leisa's head shot up.

"He is my brother ... here." Alasdair slammed a fist to his heart. "You wished me to love, and I do. Now I pray you, spare him ... please."

"Bah!" Armadeous lifted his foot and shoved Lysander aside. "Is there nothing I can eat?" he bellowed. He turned away.

Leisa ran to Lysander. "Are you all right?" she asked. Alasdair was seconds behind her.

Lysander stood and brushed off his clothes. "I am." He studied Alasdair, his eyes squinting in question. After a moment of silence he said, "Thank you, Alasdair. I know not what hold you have on a dragon, but you saved my life."

Alasdair gave Lysander a hug. "Lysander! By the stars, I have missed you. How goes Gideon?"

"Gideon is well enough. He is why I am here. He has sent me." Lysander looked chagrined. "Well, not why I am *here*. I knew not that you were in the dragon's lair. But I was searching for you. When I dared to cross the river, I was snatched up." He smiled. "And now here I stand."

"Why did you seek me out?"

Lysander glanced at Leisa, then whispered to Alasdair, "I have grave news."

Alasdair sighed. "I know not that I can bear more grave news."

"'Tis important, Alasdair." Lysander led Alasdair away from Leisa and spoke softly. "The queen has stolen another child."

Alasdair groaned. "So soon?"

Again Lysander shot Leisa a look. "A child who cries out for Leisa," he said low, for Alasdair's ears only.

Alasdair led Lysander farther from Leisa. "Sybil?" he whispered.

"I know not the child's name, but if Sybil be near five human years of age and of golden countenance, then it be her."

Alasdair cursed. "How did Tazia find out?"

Lysander's hands shot up defensively. "Not from Gideon or me, to be sure. Haps she had you followed?"

"Surely I would have known."

"Would you?" Lysander asked. "With all her stealth and minions, could you in truth swear you would have known?"

Alasdair shook his head. "Nay."

"Saw you nothing that raised suspicion whilst in the unknown world?"

"Nay, truly I saw naught."

"Then 'haps she read the runes, or merely saw it on your face. In truth, never have you mastered the craft of hiding your feelings." Lysander sighed. "'Tis a trap, Alasdair. You know this."

Alasdair nodded. He forced a tired smile. "It matters not."

Lysander grabbed Alasdair's shoulders and gave him a shake. "Matters not! Have you lost your senses? Aye, it matters. It matters much. I will not see you cast into the dark swamp. Already Tazia has confiscated Gideon's band, and she has sent out her guard to bring you back." Lysander paced a small circle.

"Leave the faerie realm. Gideon and I will do what we can to help the child. I pray you, do not go back." Lysander jumped back suddenly as a hulking shadow fell over them.

"Hmmm. Another human child." Armadeous set a hard stare on Alasdair, then turned toward the open mouth of the cave. "I leave you now to find a tasty troll. Worry not. I shall not return with him for fear he, too, may be a brother." Stepping from the cave, he flew off.

Alasdair turned his attention back to Lysander. "I must go back."

"Be damned, Alasdair. What is wrong with you?" Lysander bellowed. "What—" Lysander's tirade caught in his throat. He stared at his friend. "You have changed," he said with a dead calm. "Alasdair, what has happened to you?"

Alasdair gathered his thoughts, and his courage. He removed the band from his wrist. "Take this."

Lysander reached for the band then drew back. "Nay. I will not take it. You need it."

"No longer, my friend. It holds no power for me now. I am on my own in this quest."

"Quest? What quest? To save the human child?"

"To save all human children from this day forth."

"*All* human children?" Lysander pushed his damp, blond hair back from his brow and paced. "Alasdair, you aim too high. What of the tithe? What of our immortality?"

"There is no immortality. We have been deceived."

"Who told you this? The dragon?" Lysander shook his head. "'He lies!"

"For what purpose?" Alasdair drew a deep breath. "The lie is that of the fae. I know not why, but I will uncover it and spare the lives of children to come."

"Oh, Ali, listen to what you say. 'Tis not possible, my friend. 'Tis ..." Lysander froze. He turned to face Alasdair. "The prophecy? But you are not—"

"I was always half so, though I did never know it until now."

Lysander fell back against the stone wall of the cave and sank to his haunches. "How know you this now?" he asked, looking up at his friend.

"Armadeous."

"Armadeous?"

"The white dragon. He knew my father." Alasdair held out the band. "Take it, Lysander."

Lysander stood. He shook his head. "Nay. You are still half fae. The magic is still in you."

"Nay, my friend." Alasdair sighed. "I have been altered."

"Altered?"

"I am fully human now."

"Nay! 'Tis not possible. How?"

"Armadeous." Again Alasdair held out the band.

Leisa gave Lysander and Alasdair their space. By their facial expressions, and body languages, she was sure their conversation was grave. She wished she could hear it. Something was being kept from her. But what? And why?

At some point, Alasdair had dragged the trunk of clothing close to their bedding. Feeling exposed in her thin chemise, she dug through the trunk for an overdress and slipped it on. Then she edged closer to where Alasdair and Lysander talked. Alasdair looked somehow different. She wasn't sure what had changed, but something had. Her gaze moved back and forth between the two friends. Suddenly she knew. Alasdair's skin had lost the luminosity of the fae. He looked human.

But how could that be? When could it have happened?

She recalled their making love the night before, and his inability to control his emotions. Now she knew why. The change had to have taken place before that ... while they slept. Her gaze fell to the cave entrance. *Armadeous.*

"Oh, my God," she whispered. The dragon had claimed great magic. Magic more powerful than all the fae and sprites combined. Leisa closed her eyes against an oncoming headache. But why do this? Why now, when their biggest challenge lay ahead? What did Armadeous have to gain by it? Tears filled her eyes. Alasdair was human. A part of her was elated. A larger part of her mourned his loss.

Lysander took the band and clasped it about his wrist. "Alasdair, haps Gideon and I can gain charge of dispatching the child. We can then take her through the swamp and smuggle her into the unknown world by the Trenalyn Gate."

Alasdair shook his head. "Firstly, Tazia would not trust either of you to do so. Secondly, did you not hear what I have said? 'Tis not about one child now. Or two. 'Tis about *all* children. About the safety of all future generations of humankind."

"They are but human children."

Alasdair cast his friend a weak smile. "*I* am human."

The dragon returned empty-clawed but sated, blood staining his lips. Alasdair and Lysander shot him a look.

"'Twas a troll, I swear!" Armadeous said. He licked his lips and smiled. "This time."

Alasdair turned to Armadeous. "Should I complete this quest a victor, you must swear to me that never will you eat another fae."

"Never?" the dragon bellowed. "You ask too much."

Alasdair grinned. "As do you."

Armadeous snorted, releasing a small flame. "I will agree. However, I cannot speak for Deliterous."

"I would not expect you to."

"What now?" Lysander asked.

Alasdair turned to his friend. "Go back to Galandore. You can do no more."

"I can help you, Alasdair."

"Nay!" Alasdair clapped Lysander's shoulder. "I am now human. I must leave this world. But you, my good friend, are fae. You must stay, and you cannot do so with Tazia as your enemy." Alasdair paused in thought. "I beg you, stay well clear of me when I return to the city. Gideon as well. I would not see either of you harmed for my sake."

"But—"

"Swear it."

Lysander sighed and nodded.

"Good. Now get you back before Tazia misses you."

"Back? There is no way down from here but a straight fall."

Alasdair laughed. "I am the human. Can you not fly?"

Lysander shook his head. "My aura has been damaged." He cast a cautious look at Armadeous. "Even with the magic of the dust, I fear 'twill take a day or two for it to heal."

Alasdair walked to the cave opening and looked down the mountain. He cast Armadeous a look.

Lysander caught the look. "Oh, nay. I'll not trust a dragon to carry me hence."

Again Alasdair looked at Armadeous. "Have I your word you will not eat my friend?"

"His word!" Lysander coughed.

Armadeous grinned. "I am full with meaty troll and have no room for skinny fae. You have my word."

"Skinny?" demanded Lysander.

"Good," said Alasdair.

Lysander gave Alasdair's arm a slight shake. "But Ali—"

"On your next pass, I pray you, take him to the far side of the river to spare him the crossing. Pray, do so stealthily."

Armadeous nudged Lysander with his snout. "Come, fae. And be sure to write this in your journal. You are the only pure fae ever to cross paths with a dragon and live." The dragon laughed. "Haps you should write it as fiction, as no one will believe it to be true."

Lysander cast a final look at Alasdair.

"Farewell, good friend,"Alasdair said. He struck a closed fist to his heart, then held out his hand, palm forward.

Lysander swallowed. He returned the gesture before disappearing with Armadeous.

Leisa watched the two friends say goodbye, saw the pain in Alasdair's eyes. When Alasdair turned to Leisa, she wrapped her arms about his waist and drew him to her. She felt his arms cross her back—strong human arms—and she hugged him tightly. She didn't beg him not to go back. He was resigned to his destiny. But something niggled at her deep within. Something more than stopping the tithes beckoned him to Galandore—though she knew, even if there weren't, he would still return. She felt his head rest on her shoulder, his breath on her neck.

Kiss me.

Her thought had barely passed when Alasdair lifted his head and touched his lips to the soft flesh behind her ear. Slowly they began to sway to a music that could not be heard, a music that came from somewhere inside of them. The warmth of his mouth sent a shiver through her and she clung tighter still, tilting her head in a plea for more.

Suddenly he set her from him and she missed his heat. Grabbing her outer dress, he drew it over her head and cast it aside, leaving her in the thin chemise. He ran a heated gaze over the length of her and she felt exposed despite her cover. He cupped her face in his hands and traced his thumbs up the length of her cheekbones until his fingers burrowed deep into the soft silk of fiery hair. He cradled her head.

Slowly. Slowly.

Alasdair pulled her close. When she closed her eyes and lifted her face, he claimed her with a languorous kiss that soon intensified. Her body tightened deep and low. Heat rose in her belly. His mouth moved to her throat. She gasped and pressed against him.

Though he seemed to know her every need, he focused solely on the taste of her. She felt its effect, felt the hardness of him against her belly. She reached for him. He pulled her hand away. Again he took her mouth, stepping forward and pressing her back until they reached the mound of blankets. Grabbing her waist, he lifted her. Leisa wrapped her legs about his hips and felt the head of his shaft press against her through the thin fabric of her chemise. Alasdair dropped to his knees and lowered her onto the blankets. They were soft and warm against her flesh. Again she silently begged for his kiss.

His mouth pressed to her throat, tasting the rapid beat of her heart. She wanted more.

Flesh to flesh.

Leisa felt a slight tug as her chemise lifted over her head.

Alasdair's gaze locked on her neck.

Leisa reached up and touched the wispy gold chain and twisted leaf lavalier. "I'll never take it off," she promised. She looked up and caught Alasdair's smile. Then he slid out of his tunic and braies.

Free of clothes, he looked down at her, his verdant eyes fixed and smoldering as he took in her nakedness.

Leisa gripped the blanket to cover herself.

"Nay." Alasdair grabbed her hand, stilling it. He lowered his head to her breasts and covered a rosy tip with his mouth. His tongue was hot and firm, his hunger, palpable. He lapped and toyed until she squirmed beneath him. She felt him smile as he continued tormenting her. "You are too beautiful to hide," he said as he moved to her other breast. He pressed himself to her and she felt the length of him between her thighs. Leisa grabbed his hair in her hands and urged his mouth to hers once more. Their lips parted. Tongues met, moist and hot. Hunger twisted deep in her gut.

Fill me.

Alasdair whispered in her ear, "Not yet." He slid a finger into her and she gasped, leaned back, and let him do what he would.

His thrusts were deep and searching. His thumb toyed with the sensitive nub that would bring her pleasure. Leisa held her breath and focused on the sensation. A delicious tightening formed in the pit of her stomach. A hunger. An aching. A need that demanded release.

Don't stop.

Panting breaths filled her ears. They were her own. She felt Alasdair hesitate. Then he plunged long fingers deep inside her once more.

Taste me.

She opened her eyes and saw him smile. He slid down her body, parted her thighs, and slipped his tongue between her lower lips. Leisa caught her breath. Again his fingers entered her as his teeth toyed with the tender nub hidden in the folds of her flesh. He caught the nub firmly between his lips.

Leisa gasped. Her insides lurched. Tremors rose from the core of her, closer and closer until they peaked as one all-consuming ache. Her body went suddenly still and she lost her breath. Then came the waves.

Quickly Alasdair entered her, catching her waves of ecstacy as they flowed through her body. Pulsing, hot vibrations gripped his sex. He moved inside her.

"Oh, God," Leisa cried as the waves started anew. She cried out, her body squirming for escape but wanting more. Alasdair thrust deep, then clutched her tightly to him. The sweat from their bodies ran as one. Her body trembled uncontrollably and she cried out her release. He drove deep and met her release with his own.

Leisa clutched his back and buried her face in his shoulder as she rode the last delectable wave. Then she fell back against the blankets.

Alasdair collapsed on top of her, his raven hair damp against her cheek. Catching his breath, he rolled to his side, pulled her close, and closed his eyes.

Leisa stared at a face both beautiful and torn. She listened to his heavy breaths. In a few minutes, she knew they would have to rise to face their destiny—whatever that was. She already knew Alasdair's, but she wasn't too clear on her own. Perhaps her destiny was to be at his side to help him through it. If not, some higher power was going to be highly annoyed, because that was what she intended to do.

She studied Alasdair's long black lashes as they rested against his cheeks. She knew he wasn't sleeping; he was merely recouping his strength for what lay ahead. A shiver ran through her and his embrace tightened about her. Leisa smiled. She closed her eyes, once again. She would need strength as well.

Alasdair felt her gaze on him. His body was spent, but he knew he had pleased her. He had managed to keep control and take it slow. Somehow he had known exactly what she wanted. A smile tugged at his lips. He would savor these few moments of peace, contentment, and absolute fulfillment as if they were his last. His smile faded. They very well could be.

Chapter Twenty

Faerie

Armadeous flew into the cave and skidded to a stop. His scaly lips twisted in a grin as he watched Alasdair and Leisa return from the passage of the heated pool, scrubbed and cleaned and wearing clothing that fell closer to travel garb than courtly wear. He sniffed. They could scrub all they wanted; the scent of their union still hung in the air. An unhurried union. Alasdair had experienced deep human passion and learned to control it. He was where he needed to be now.

"You have not eaten Lysander, have you?" Alasdair asked, half joking.

Armadeous shook his massive head. "Nay, all the pity for it. Such a tasty treat, now lost."

"But did you not say you were full with sumptuous troll?"

"Aye. But I would have saved the fae for later." His scaly lips curled in a grin. "Dessert, if you will."

Alasdair's throat went tight. "Forget not that you made a vow."

"I have not forgotten. But you have not fulfilled your part as yet."

Alasdair nodded. He opened the trunk and rummaged through it. Finding leather mail and arm guards, he proceeded to put them on. The mail laced up the front. The arm guards were more difficult to tie. He held his arm out to Leisa. "Tie this, please." He watched her wary expression as she laced the first one and tied it off.

"You are ready, then?" Armadeous asked.

Alasdair looked up at Armadeous and caught his gaze. "As ready as I shall ever be."

Leisa stilled Alasdair with a frigid look. "I? What's this *I* stuff?" She finished off the second arm guard with a sharp tug.

"Ow!" Alasdair shot her a look as he loosened the tie. "Leisa, 'tis dangerous."

"And being nearly mauled by a wolflych, stabbed by a dark fairy, drowned in quicksand, and attacked by a dragon aren't?"

"Leisa—"

"I'm going. Either you take me with you or I'll follow close behind."

Alasdair frowned. He turned to Armadeous. "Tell her."

Armadeous stepped back. "I can do only what prophecy dictates I do. This is not within my realm of choice. You two must decide." He turned away and stepped to the back chamber.

Leisa stared at Alasdair. "Blaise is my daughter. I'm going."

Alasdair clasped Leisa's shoulders. Her deep green eyes met with his. "Have ever you seen a troll?"

"Just in Sybil's books."

"They are much worse off the page. Leisa, I beg you, stay behind with Armadeous."

Leisa shook her head. "I'm sorry. I—I can't."

"Leisa, I have no weapon. I cannot protect you."

"Where's your sword?"

"It ripped from my waist and fell when Armadeous struck me. As did the satchel."

"Oh, my God. The changeling! We need that."

"I am sorry. We will worry of that once Sachi is safe from the trolls."

Armadeous sauntered in from the back chamber. He flicked a sheathed sword across the floor with a large talon. It slid to a stop at Alasdair's feet. "When I learned you were the chosen one, I sought it out. You will need it."

Alasdair retrieved the sword and drew it from its scabbard. He set a long reflective gaze on it, weighed it in his hands, and sighed with relief. "I feared I had lost it." He looked at the waiting dragon. "I was told 'twas my father's sword."

"Aye. It looks to be. Armadeous shook his head sadly. "But never was he proficient in using it. Though he did well enough when purpose called for it, he was more a scholar than a warrior."

Alasdair smiled. He swung the sword in several circular motions before resheathing it.

"But for the raven hair laced in gold, you look much like him."

Alasdair looked up at the dragon. "Truly?"

Armadeous nodded.

"What color hair had he?"

"The shade of ripened wheat."

Alasdair reflected on the dragon's reply, stood in a moment of silence, then asked, "Think you we have a chance?"

The dragon shrugged. "A chance as any other."

"And should we fail?"

"The world will be lacking two more humans, but it will go on as always, I assure you."

"'Tis what frightens me."

Leisa clasped Alasdair's arm. "We won't fail."

"I am not so sure."

Armadeous slammed his taloned foot on the ground, vibrating the rock surrounding them. "Speak not so defeatedly, defender. You have the prowess to succeed. Aye, you are much like your father, I see that clearly. But you are fae, or were, and as nephew to the queen, you were taught to fight. Within you is great courage. I have seen it. Do not doubt that courage now when you so sorely need it."

Alasdair drew a deep breath. He pulled himself straight and nodded. "Where is the tunnel?"

"Wait." Leisa turned to Armadeous. "When you retrieved the sword, did you find a satchel?"

"I did see one, but saw no significance to it. I left it."

Leisa laid her hand on his talon. "Please. We need that."

Armadeous cocked his massive head. His golden eyes darkened in question, his pearly scales glimmered in the light. "For what purpose?"

"The changeling is in the satchel. We need it to rescue my little girl. She can't leave Faerie unless it's put in her place."

Armadeous looked at Alasdair.

Alasdair nodded.

Armadeous exhaled sharply. He lifted a foot and scratched his jaw with a long talon. "It lies at the foot of the mountain." He turned to exit the cave. "I shall return," he said. Then he flew off into the morning.

Moments later he landed with a thud, the satchel hanging from a talon by its strap.

Tears streamed down Leisa's face. "Thank you." She ran up to the dragon and hugged his leg.

Alasdair retrieved the satchel. He pulled out the knapsack with the changeling in it, their sack of food, and a small dagger. After securing the dagger to his boot, he swung the knapsack over his shoulder and slipped his arms through its straps. Then he handed the food sack to Leisa. "Now," he said standing tall. "The tunnel." He fixed a determined gaze on Armadeous.

Armadeous grinned. "Come." He led them to the chamber with the pool. On its far side was an opening hidden by an outcropping of rock. He snorted a fiery breath to light a torch mounted on the wall.

Leisa opened the food sack. She tore off a chunk of bread for Alasdair and herself, then resealed the sack.

"Carry the torch with you until you near the end of the tunnel," Armadeous instructed. "You will know you are close by the sharp jutting of rock and the torch mount on the wall.

Take the torch no farther. When you get close to the trolls' lair, its light will too easily mark your presence. 'Twill be dark, but not for long. Your eyes will adjust. Leave the torch lit, however. You will need it for your return trip."

"How long is this tunnel?" Leisa asked as she peered into the dark hole.

"Near half day's journey," Armadeous replied. "And 'tis dark as pitch. You will need the light."

"Why did *you* need the light?" Leisa asked.

"It takes great energy to emit constant flame. I would not waste my energy stores for mere lighting." He smiled. "It has better uses."

Alasdair stared into the blue-orange flame. "How long will it burn?" he asked.

"'Twill burn from moon to moon, that is all."

"A full day," Leisa mumbled.

"Aye. Should you not return within that time, you will need to find your way back blindly. Be forewarned, there are smaller tunnels that run off from the main one. In the dark, you could well lose your way."

"Where do the smaller tunnels lead?" Alasdair asked.

"To certain death. They are an endless labyrinth, a maze that leads nowhere but back into itself."

Leisa swallowed. "We'll be careful."

"Armadeous, friend." Alasdair turned to face the dragon. "How well knew you my parents?"

"You wish to discuss this now, when it is time for action?"

Alasdair nodded. "I know not that I shall return." He heard Leisa gasp but kept his gaze fixed on the dragon.

Armadeous sat. He snorted a thin stream of fire and smoke. "I know they were cast out from the realm and lived for a time amongst the sprites."

Leisa's head snapped up. "The sprites? But they're evil and dangerous."

Armadeous laughed. "They are harmless enough once you know their ways. But aye, to one who does not, they can cause great harm."

"And my parents knew their ways?" Alasdair asked.

"There was a time of learning to be sure." Armadeous snorted. "But they were tenacious, those two. They had to be. Soon they learned the ways of the sprites. When the sprites could no longer cause them fear, living amongst them was easy enough."

Leisa shivered.

"How did you come to know them?" Alasdair asked.

"The sprites?"

Alasdair glared at the dragon.

Armadeous snickered. "Your father was an adventurous sort as humans go. And curious as well. He climbed the mountain much like you, when the rock was steadier."

"My father's name, do you know it?" Alasdair asked.

Armadeous snorted. "It surprises me not that Tazia never told you." He set his golden gaze on Alasdair. "His name was Alexander. I called him Alex."

Alexander, Alasdair mouthed to himself.

"What happened to Alasdair's parents?" Leisa asked.

"For many years they lived at peace with the sprites. Ofttimes your father would climb the mountain for amusement and to feel alive."

"To feel alive?" Alasdair asked.

"Aye. 'Tis nothing like danger to make one feel truly alive."

"Danger from what?" Leisa asked.

"From me."

Alasdair caught his breath and steeled himself to ask, "Why did you not eat them?"

A slow smile crossed the dragon's face. "At first they did amuse me. Oh, I oft thought of it, but there was food a plenty to keep me full. Had I devoured them as well, I would have lost

Faerie Dust / Linda Ciletti

my entertainment. I deemed fending off the boredom of the watch well worth the price of a meal."

"How knew you my father so personally?" Alasdair asked.

Armadeous quieted as though he would not answer. "I was sickly once," he finally replied. "Had eaten a bad troll, I deem. When Tazia noted I had not kept watch for two turns of the sun, she guessed I was vulnerable and sent several of her guards to finish me off."

"For what reason would Tazia want you dead?" Alasdair asked.

"Tazia hungers for power. She would do anything to gain access to the troll mines. Had she power over the mines, gems would be free and unlimited. She would no longer have need to barter for them. Tis only the fear of being eaten that keeps her at bay." Armadeous arched a thick dragon brow.

"Why care you if the fae war with the trolls over possession of the mines?"

"Why care I?" Armadeous snorted.

Leisa jumped back at the flame.

"Were she to destroy the trolls, so would she destroy my food source. They are a lumbrous feeble-brained lot, to be sure, but they are quite tasty once you get past the wiry tufts of hair."

Leisa scrunched her nose.

"And my father? What did he to deserve your respect?"

"He engaged the sprites to frighten the fae back across the river."

Alasdair stared disbelievingly. "Why would he do that?"

Armadeous snorted. "He had much for which to hate the fae."

"But why would he help *you?*"

Armadeous grinned. "I did not eat them."

Alasdair nodded. Sadness fell over him. "Know you how my father died?"

237

Armadeous shook his head. "I know not. After deceiving and driving off the fae who'd been sent to kill me, your father found his way to my lair. I had not the strength to fight him. Nor the will."

"But it's a straight drop down the mountain from here!" Leisa exclaimed. "How did he get in?"

"'Twas not always so. Remember, the lifespan of a fae far exceeds that of a human. This was hundreds of years ago. The landscape changes."

Leisa nodded, feeling a touch of guilt at Alasdair's lost years.

"Your father had on him a flask of cool spring water. 'Twas not much for a dragon such as I, but still he poured it in my mouth and thanked me for not devouring him and his mate." Armadeous sighed. "'Twas then I knew beyond a doubt that humans possessed a greater love than any fae. After he risked his life to comfort and thank me, never did I kill a human again. Not that there were many about."

"I thought you didn't like the taste?" Leisa asked.

"That, too." Armadeous continued. "Following, he and I met on occasion to talk and spar with wits. Then one day he came, sadness pulling down his visage, and I knew he had lost his mate. I saw it in the dullness of his eyes. When he parted, he could not bring himself to say goodbye. But I knew he would come no more. Never did I see him again."

"Know you how my mother died?"

"Never did I meet your mother. She was fae, as you know."

"So, you would have eaten her?" Leisa asked incredulously.

"Nay. She was mate to the human." Armadeous looked at Alasdair. "'Twas her choice to know me not. As a fae, she could not rid herself of her fear of me. I understood."

Alasdair nodded.

"Now go," Armadeous ordered. "Time runs short."

Alasdair stood silent for a moment, then asked, "Armadeous?"

"Aye."

"Why did my parents not flee to the unknown world and live amongst the humans?"

"Do you not know this, Alasdair?"

Alasdair thought a moment. His eyes lit. "Oh, aye. I did forget."

Leisa moved to face Alasdair. "Why didn't they?"

Alasdair looked to Leisa. "My mother would have died within a year. 'Haps less."

"Why?"

"Should any fae be gone overly long, their magic fades. They weaken, and die. She would not have survived in the human world for long."

"And forget not the other reason," Armadeous prompted.

"Other reason? I know not another reason."

Armadeous snorted a short burst of flame. "You know this reason more intimately than anyone."

Alasdair thought, then swallowed. "Me?"

"Aye. I know not the full story, only what your father told me. They lived in Galandore for some time. Tazia was sure her sister would tire of him, but she did not. Furious that a half-blood had been born to the royal line, Tazia sent orders to have your father cast into the dark swamp lest other half-bloods be born. News of her orders reached him before the guards and he fled to the Sprite Wood. Shortly after, your mother followed."

"Without me? Why?"

"She and Tazia argued. Angered, Tazia cast her out to live with her human lover, but without her child. That was her punishment."

Alasdair shook his head. "Nay. This cannot be true."

"These are the very words spoken to me by your father. That they are truth, I cannot know. But I deem he had no reason to lie."

"So she punished her sister by depriving me of a mother?" Alasdair's eyes grew dark, his voice hard. "How did my mother die?" he repeated. "You evaded answering me."

"Are you certain you wish to know this?"

"Tell me."

Armadeous settled on his haunches. "Tazia did not become queen for her fair ways and trusting nature, nor for her patience. I deem she feared your parents would attempt to steal you back."

Alasdair snorted. "What cared she for a half-blood?"

Armadeous sighed a plume of smoke. "Little, I deem. Regardless, you were still blood to the royal line. And that is sacred and should not be harmed by anyone—including the queen.

"Did she have a hand in the death of my mother?"

Armadeous's head lifted. "She did not. Or I should say it was not her intent. I deem she hoped your father would fall to harm in the Sprite Wood and your mother would then return of her own will, humbled and agreeable. That was not to be. Upon your father's last visit, he told me he had found a scrap of bloodied kirtle hanging from a thorny vine near a pool of soft, sandy earth. He said no more. He had no need. Though I cannot be certain, my guess is that Tazia tired of waiting and sent soldiers to slay the human to speed things along, and to drag your mother back to Galandore. When Taelena resisted, she was accidently slain. Rather than face Tazia with the truth of their crime, I deem the soldiers hid her body in the quicksand of the wood and devised a tale of how she met her end by your father's hand."

Alasdair's voice cracked. "Crime?"

"To outright kill a member of the royal family is a crime punishable by death, regardless of why."

Alasdair nodded. "Of course."

"Even Tazia would not dare to do so which is why you still live. Your mother was as a sister to her. I deem they would have mended their rift had Tazia just let Taelena be and allowed Alex to live out his promised human years. Such a small portion of your mother's life that would have been."

Alasdair formed his hands into fists, threw back his head, and cried, "Why have you done this, Tazia!"

Leisa slid her arms about his waist and hugged him. "Oh, Ali."

He lowered his forehead to her shoulder and pulled her close. After a moment of quiet thought, he turned to Armadeous. "How were my parents so easily able to cross the river into the Sprite Wood?"

"At that time, we dragons had no need to guard the rivers. But Tazia's sickness ever grew. When the human and fae fled to the sprite wood, we took it upon ourselves to protect them and all who dwelled beyond the faerie kingdom from her wrath and greed."

"Why did my father not help my mother when she was attacked?"

"Your father did not know. I deem he was here with me when it all came to pass. He was no coward."

Alasdair lifted his head, his eyes watery but hard. "Where think you my father went when he left here that last time?"

Armadeous's lips pulled firmly. "I have no doubt he went in search of you."

Alasdair drew a deep breath, held it, then released. "He went to save a child," he murmured. He shook his head, straightened, then slid the torch from its mount on the wall. "As must I." He turned to Leisa. "Come."

~*~

Alasdair led Leisa down the dark and narrow tunnel. The flickering light of his torch cast a soft glow on the dark walls, then faded behind them. Time dragged. All that was visible was a short distance before them. Beyond that stretched the black unknown. They walked for hours, taking as few breaks as possible and saying little, each lost in thought.

Finally Alasdair spotted the jutted rock and torch mount Armadeous had spoken of. "Here!" Alasdair pointed, then slipped the torch inside the empty mount. "The end is not far now." He took Leisa's hand, leading her away from the light and into the looming dark.

"I can't see a thing!" Leisa exclaimed.

"Nor I. Stand close and hold tight to my belt." Alasdair ran his hands along the wall as he continued on. "Soon your eyes will adjust to the darkness."

Leisa slowed her steps. "Ali?"

"Aye?" Alasdair answered over his shoulder.

"I'm so very sorry."

"About what?"

"All that Armadeous said."

Alasdair turned to face her. He reached into the darkness and cupped her face with his hands. "It was long ago, Leisa. I was naught but a babe."

"Still, what he said had to be hard to hear."

Alasdair nodded. "Aye." He tilted Leisa's face up and kissed her. Then he turned and continued on. As the tunnel rounded a bend, a faint light spilled inside. "There." Alasdair motioned to an opening that led into a feebly lit cavernous area. "'Tis the end of the tunnel, Leisa." He turned to face her. "Are you sure you will not wait here for me? Armadeous did say the trolls will not follow through the tunnel, they so fear him."

Leisa shook her head. "I'm going with you, Alasdair."

"Then stay close. I do not yet know my strengths and weaknesses as a human. Remember that first day in the park."

Leisa took his hand and squeezed. It was warm and moist with fear. So very human. She slipped in front of him and edged toward the opening.

"Wait!" Alasdair grabbed her arm and yanked her back. Two jagged rocks fell from the ceiling and landed several feet in front of them.

Leisa caught her breath. "H—how did you know they were going to fall?"

"I know not." He cupped his head in his hands and closed his eyes. When he opened them, Leisa was staring at him. "Truly, I know not. I but saw it in my head and it raised such fear that I pulled you back. That is all."

Leisa eyed him skeptically. "Are we okay to go now?" she asked.

"Aye."

As she began traversing the rocks, Alasdair grabbed her hand and again pulled her back into the tunnel until they were hidden in shadow.

"What—"

Alasdair set a finger to his lips and pointed. Just as Leisa turned to look, several trolls passed by the opening. Each stood as tall as two men and was slightly hunched. Their huge thick bodies lumbered rather than walked. Their leathery flesh, a green/brown mix, was flecked with wiry tufts of hair that jutted out helter skelter. They glanced in the tunnel for a second, their glowing red eyes perusing the narrow passage; then they went on their way.

"Ali?" Leisa whispered. "How did you know they were coming? I didn't hear a thing."

Alasdair breathed a ragged breath and shrugged. "I but started to walk and felt their presence." He set his fist against his chest. "Here."

Leisa grabbed his hand and pulled him farther into the tunnel where they could not be heard. "Ali!" she exclaimed. "You have them all!"

"All what?"

"All the gifts."

Alasdair shook his head.

"Remember at the wedding, you told me that the fae had harnessed their magic and knew how to use it?"

"Aye. But I am no longer fae, Leisa. I no longer have fae magic."

"No, you don't."

"Then what gifts do you speak of?"

"After telling me of the fae's magic, you told me that humans have magic as well. Do you remember? You said that sadly we were merely on the edge of understanding it."

Alasdair stared at Leisa, his thoughts turned inward.

"Intuition, premonition, telekinesis ..."

Alasdair's eyes widened.

"You have these gifts, Alasdair. Because you learned as a fae to use the magic given you, now you can fully use human magic."

"You are wrong, Leisa."

"I am right. How did you know the rocks were going to fall?"

"I did already tell you."

"You saw them falling before it happened." She paused. "Premonition, Alasdair."

Alasdair shook his head. "Coincidence."

"Premonition," Leisa insisted. "And how did you know the trolls were going to pass by the opening at that very moment?"

Alasdair shrugged.

"Intuition. You felt it in your gut."

Alasdair rubbed his forehead. "I cannot believe this."

"Believe it, Ali. You just saved our lives twice using human gifts, whether you meant to or not." Leisa smiled. "You preach about how humans don't use their gifts to their full potential, but when it's your turn to use them, you refuse to believe just as we do." Leisa set a light kiss on his lips. "Listen to your inner voice. We may need your gifts to get through this. *You* are not on the edge of understanding."

Alasdair drew a deep breath. He released it slowly, then took Leisa's hand. After a moment of silence, he spoke. "Let us go, then."

Moving out from the shadows of the passageway, they approached the opening. Alasdair waited a moment, then nodded. Carefully they edged around the rocks and slipped into the dim, musty cavern.

Chapter Twenty-One

Faerie

The cave stood several stories high, its dark center a huge rounded hollow with a deadly drop. Each level consisted of a narrow walkway and various tunnel openings. Fires burned far below, the pulse of rising orange flame setting light and shadow to dance on the craggy cavernous walls.

"Wait." Leisa stopped just outside the dragon's narrow tunnel. She grabbed three small rocks and piled them like a pyramid.

Alasdair watched, his forehead quizzically furrowed, one brow arched.

Leisa looked up at him. "It's for on the way back. With so many tunnels, I want to be sure we pick the right one."

"Clever, Leisa." He gave her a fatigued but sincere smile and reclaimed her hand. "As much as I wish you safe, I am glad you are with me."

Leisa gave him a friendly push. "Let's go."

Alasdair used his new found intuition as they made their way past each dark tunnel entrance. Occasionally a troll would approach and they would duck into the shadows.

Safely out of view, Leisa whispered, "It's so vast in here and there are so many tunnels leading to who knows where. How will we ever find her?"

Alasdair shook his head, closed his eyes, and leaned back against the wall. "I know not." He breathed deeply, held it a moment, then sighed.

Suddenly his eyes flew open. His breath caught. "Leisa!" He shot Leisa a shocked look and straightened. "I saw her!"

"Where?"

"Beneath my lids."

Leisa sighed. "I mean, where in the cave?"

"A level below us. There is a large hollow barred by two iron gates, a heavy lock securing them."

"Like a jail?"

"Aye, a human jail."

"Is she okay? Is she hurt? Is she alive?"

"They would not harm her, Leisa. She must be well and intact for the tithe."

"Tomorrow."

"Aye. But she will not be here tomorrow."

Leisa gave Alasdair a hopeful smile.

Again he closed his eyes and concentrated. When he opened them, his expression turned from elated to serious. "Two trolls guard either side of a split gate," he supplied. "They are much larger than the man at the park. Have you your taser?"

Leisa shot him a stunned look.

Alasdair smiled. He squeezed her hand and winked. "No matter," Alasdair continued. "We have our wits."

Leisa smiled weakly. "Will our wits be enough?"

"I know not." He led her further along the ledge. "Look!" He pointed to a spiraled stairwell. "There," he said. "'Tis the way down." He drew his sword from its sheath and began edging down the curved stone stairs. Leisa followed close behind, so close she felt his warmth fill the space between them. Her heart raced at the thought of seeing Blaise. What would she look like after four years? Her baby. Her daughter.

Her eyes filled with tears. She blinked them back. She needed to keep a clear head, to stay alert.

She descended several more steps, then slammed into Alasdair's back.

"What is it?" she asked at his sudden stop.

Alasdair motioned Leisa up the steps to where the curve hid them from view.

"What is it, Ali?" Leisa repeated. She stood on her toes to peer over his shoulder. A massive troll stomped into sight, snorting sharply with each lumbering step. Its thick, leathery body passed the stairwell entrance, then faded from sight, leaving a foul scent behind.

Alasdair motioned to go back down, then froze. He stumbled back as the troll filled the entrance, its beady eyes narrowed and fixed on him.

He shoved Leisa back and lifted his sword.

The narrow stairwell left little room to maneuver. Alasdair waited for the troll to make the first move. The wait was brief.

Though the limited space denied the troll a full and forceful strike, still his large wooden club descended with a killing blow. Alasdair flattened himself against the wall. The club fell short, missing him by inches. Bracing his hands on either side of the stairwell, he kicked up at the troll, striking its chin and knocking it on its back. Alasdair was sure he'd heard the troll's head crack on the stone; still, he readied his blade for a killing plunge.

As he approached the fallen troll, it jumped up and swung again. Alasdair recoiled, stumbled, and fell to the stair. The sharp-edged stone bit into his spine. He scrambled backward up several steps, then leapt to his feet, ducking when the troll again swung its club. Alasdair felt the breeze of it riffle his hair, felt the hot breath of the troll as it closed in on him. When the troll lunged at him, Alasdair slid on his back down several stairs, slipping between the troll's bowed legs. Sword in hand, he rose swiftly to his feet, turned, and plunged it into the troll's back. A fierce bellow ripped up the stairwell. Then silence.

~*~

Leisa stood frozen. A large shadow fell across the wall. She covered her mouth, stifling a scream. Alasdair rounded the curve and she sighed in relief.

"Step carefully," he said breathlessly. He slipped his blade into its sheath and held his hand out to her. Sweat shimmered on his brow. A single drop trickled down his face.

Leisa took his hand and followed him around the curve of the wall. She saw the troll sprawled on the stairs—large and ashen, with unruly tufts of wiry hair on its head, arms, and legs. Its face was strangely elongated, its wide snout flat and eerily still. Her throat felt achingly tight, and for a moment she thought she would be sick.

"Worry not, it is dead," Alasdair assured her. "Step around it."

Leisa gulped air into her lungs and did as Alasdair said, careful not to touch the gruesome beast. Again Alasdair paused at the exit. Then they slipped from the stairwell into the lower cavern.

No trolls patrolled the area as they made their way swiftly to within sight of the cell. Alasdair set a finger to his lips, signaling silence. Leisa nodded. They stood sheltered by an outcropping of rock, keeping out of view of the two trolls guarding the gate. Like the troll on the stairs, they were muscled and large with thick ashen skin and wiry tufts of hair. Dark ragged cloth hung down from their shoulders and draped their loins. Their nostrils flared with each weighty breath. Their eyes glowed vibrant red.

Alasdair leaned back against the rock and flinched. He released a ragged breath and cast a look at Leisa.

Leisa's gaze fell to the blood seeping through his tunic. "You're injured!" she whispered.

Alasdair set a finger to his lips. He spoke quietly. "'Tis naught but a scratch. But Leisa—"

"I know." Her attention rested on the two guard trolls. There was no way he could battle and defeat two of them. He'd tired himself fighting the one in the stairwell. Two would be impossible. Leisa felt tears well in her eyes. They'd come so far. The child she had thought dead was alive and almost within reach. Then Alasdair stirred and drew his blade. Her breath caught. She grabbed his arm and pulled him back.

Alasdair glared at her. He shrugged free from her hold, then turned to face the trolls. Again she grabbed him. *Wait*, she mouthed. She lifted her hands before her, palms facing in, fingertips touching. Closing her eyes, she feigned concentration, then flung her hands open.

Alasdair stared in confusion.

Leisa did it again. When his face lit, she knew he understood. *Telekinesis*.

Alasdair nodded. He leaned back against the stone wall and closed his eyes. Drawing breath deep into his lungs, he concentrated on the lock.

Leisa peered around the outcropping of rock. A troll stood at attention on either side of the double gate, tall and gruff, each wielding a club. She turned to Alasdair. His shuttered eyes flickered. His mouth was tight. Heat emanated from him. She could see his deep concentration in the absolute stillness of his body.

Then she heard a click.

She shot a look back at the trolls. They had heard it too. Each turned toward the center lock on the gate, their clubs at the ready. Suddenly the gate halves burst open, striking both trolls and crushing them against the walls on either side. They fell with a sickening thud. A small cry sounded from inside the cell.

Alasdair released his breath and opened his eyes. He looked to Leisa.

"You did it," Leisa whispered.

Despite his exhaustion, Alasdair smiled. He pulled himself away from the wall and grabbed Leisa's hand. "Hurry," he said. "We have not much time."

They rounded the outcropping and ran to the gate. Both trolls lay unconscious—or dead. Alasdair released Leisa's hand and sprinted inside the hollow. "Sachi," he called in a frantic whisper. Sniffling sounded from a hidden back corner of the cell. Alasdair followed the sound until he saw a small form huddled beside an ornate, gilded mirror that rested against the back wall—a twin to the tall mirror that stood in Tazia's private solar. "Tazia," he growled under his breath. He stared into the beautiful mirror at the horrified expression on his face. Nausea churned in his gut and he could not turn away from Tazia's doorway to death. Tentatively, he reached out to touch the wavering glass. Then a tiny sob broke his trance and stilled his hand.

Alasdair looked down at the small human child huddled into herself—her knees drawn up tightly to her chest, her face hidden in the fold of her arms. Long hair veiled her face, hair the same autumn shade as that of Leisa. "Sachi." He spoke quietly so as not to frighten her more. "'Tis I, Alasdair."

Sachi peeked up, her chin trembling. "Ali?" she mumbled.

"Aye, Ali." He held his arms out to her. "Come, hurry." He beckoned her forward.

Sachi scrambled to her feet and rushed at him. Her arms flung out and wrapped about his waist.

"Hush, little one," Alasdair comforted. He reached down and stroked her hair. "I will take you far from here. Just be very quiet."

He looked over his shoulder for Leisa.

She walked up behind him, her mouth agape. "Leisa," he whispered.

She stood unmoving, her eyes fixed on the little girl clinging to him.

"Leisa!" he called louder.

Leisa jumped at his call. "I'm sorry." She looked down at Sachi, then back at Alasdair. "I just—"

"The changeling," he whispered. "Set it in her place."

Leisa gave her head a mental shake. "Of course." She zipped open the knapsack on Alasdair's back and pulled out the wooden child.

"There," Alasdair said, pointing to where he'd seen Sachi cowering.

Leisa set the wood against the back wall of the cell as Alasdair pulled Sachi's arms from around his waist and crouched low. "Sachi," he said, facing her. "There is something I must do before we can go. Be not afraid." He drew the small dagger from his boot.

Sachi whimpered at the sight of it.

Alasdair gave her a fatherly hug, then set her back. "Be not afraid," he repeated. Taking a lock of her hair between his fingers, he carefully cut it free. Grabbing the hem of his tunic, he sliced the coarse material and peeled a long thread from its cloth.

"What are you doing?" Leisa asked. "We have to get out of here."

"I must attach her hair to the changeling so we can pass her through the gate." He tied the thread around the lock of Sachi's hair and then around the wood. After sliding the knife back in his boot, he picked Sachi up and held her against his chest.

Sachi buried her face in his shoulder. "Let us go," he said. He nodded to Leisa to lead the way back.

The cushion of the trolls' bodies between the gates and the walls had muffled the crash. No alert was sounded. Quietly, they made their way back up the stairwell. As Alasdair comforted Sachi, Leisa checked the opening of each tunnel until she found the one with the pyramid of stones. "Here," she whispered.

They slipped inside.

Farther up the tunnel, they stopped to rest. Alasdair sat on the dirt floor and tried to peel Sachi from him. She clung tighter. "'Tis all right, Sachi. The trolls are gone now."

Her hands gripped him in a desperate hold, but her head lifted, revealing a dark spot on his tunic.

Alasdair stroked her hair—beautiful fiery hair like her mother's. "They are gone, Sachi. Be calm."

Sachi sniffled. "Queen Tazia sent me away," she cried. She rubbed her face on his shoulder, wiping more tears on his shirt. "Why did she send me away, Ali?"

Alasdair sighed. He didn't know how to answer her.

Sachi looked up at him, her dark green eyes wide in question. "Does she not love me?" Sachi asked.

Alasdair felt an unfamiliar ache deep in his core. His throat clenched. "Sweet Mother Earth," he swore under his breath. His chest felt tight and he knew his heart had been wounded. Again a faint sniffle, this one his own. He hugged Sachi tightly. His head lowered to rest on her shoulder. "I am sorry," was all he could say.

Leisa slid across the tunnel next to the two. She stared at the beautiful little girl she'd not seen in over four years. Her daughter. Tears spilled down her cheeks. She wanted to grab Blaise and hold her, to tell her everything would be fine, that she was her mother and that she loved her very much.

She could not. It would frighten the girl all the more. Instead, she wiped away the dampness on her face with her sleeve.

Winning Blaise's trust would take time. Leisa knew that. It was too soon to tell her that she was her mother. She had to win her love first. She leaned against Alasdair and stroked Blasie's hair. Blaise—no, Sachi now—peered up at her.

"Tazia loved you the best she could." Leisa said. She smoothed her hand down the dark length of Alasdair's hair to rest on his back. "But Alasdair loves you so much more."

Alasdair lifted his head and gifted Leisa with a grateful smile. A smile she would never forget.

The dark, winding tunnel slanted uphill. They were nearing where they'd left the torch. Leisa felt her legs grow weak with the strain and silently vowed to use the treadmill that was stored away in her bedroom. "Where's the torch?" she asked when she saw no light.

Alasdair ran a hand along the wall. Sachi's small arms clung to his neck, her petite frame pressed against his side as he balanced her on his hip and braced her with his arm. Leisa held firmly to his shirt so as not to lose him in the dark. "It should be just around the bend," Alasdair replied. "But I do not see its glow."

"Wasn't it supposed to last a full day?" Leisa asked. "We haven't been gone nearly that long."

"'Haps it weakened with age." Alasdair set Sachi down next to him and felt along the wall for the torch.

"Ali, it doesn't matter. We have no way to light it anyway."

Alasdair stopped his search. "You are right." He reached for Sachi and met empty air. "Sachi?" he called. His chest clenched. "Sachi!" he called again.

The sound of shuffling feet could be heard in the near distance. A small voice sounded in the dark. "I am here." The steps quickened.

"Where?" Alasdair spun on his heels, straining to see through the inky darkness. "Where, Sachi?" Suddenly he no longer felt Leisa. "Leisa!" he called frantically.

"I'm right here," Leisa replied from behind him.

Alasdair spun and nearly knocked her over. He sighed heavily. "Do not release my shirt, Leisa. 'Tis the ony way I know you are with me."

Leisa gripped his shirt and gave it a tug. "Where's Sachi?" she asked.

"I know not. I set her down for but a moment."

"Oh, my God! Blaise ... Sachi!" Leisa called.

"Here," came the small voice from farther away. "I cannot see you."

Alasdair tensed. The dimming of her voice told him she was moving away from them. "Sachi, do not move." He quieted and listened. Her footsteps stopped. "Talk to us, little one, so we may find you."

Quiet.

"Sachi?"

"What should I say?"

Alasdair thought briefly. "Sing a song."

"What song?"

"Recall you the song we sang in the garden?"

"Aye."

"Sing it."

"Will you sing with me?" she asked timidly.

"Nay. This time you need sing alone. I must hear your voice to find you."

The cave grew strangely silent, and he feared she was afraid to sing alone. Then a sweet voice lifted and danced softly in the dank and heavy air.

Within this wood the faeries rise
to breaking dawn and golden skies.

Their wondrous magic gently flows
where fauna dwells and flora grows.
Beauty abounds at every turn,
majestic tree and lacey fern.
Bird, squirrel—duck and hare,
rabbit, unicorn and bear.
Faeries working side by side
serve this land with wondrous pride.
And all within this woodland thrives
when faeries rise to golden skies.

Leisa listened intently. "I think she's this way." She tugged on Alasdair's shirt, pulling him.

"Nay." Alasdair stayed grounded to the spot. "'Tis the echo you hear." Alasdair concentrated. "She is across the way in one of the side tunnels."

"Oh, God."

Alasdair felt along the wall until he found an opening. He listened. "Not this one." He continued listening to her song as he moved further up the tunnel until he felt another opening. Her singing was louder. "Sachi!" he called into the tunnel.

"Here, Ali. Here!"

"Walk toward my voice," Alasdair said. He began to sing the same garden verse, stopping only when he felt Sachi's arms wrap about his thigh. He fell to his knees and grabbed her in a hug. "By the stars, I thought I had lost you." He stood and removed the gird strap about his waist. Making a loop, he slipped it over Sachi's wrist. The other end he looped about his own. Then he backtracked into the main tunnel and walked in silence.

After what seemed forever, Leisa asked, "Are we nearly there?"

"I know not. I can see nothing. But I deem us to be close."

Leisa held tight to Sachi's tunic.

"I tire," Sachi cried. "And I am afraid."

"It's okay," Leisa assured her. "I'm sure we're almost there."

Alasdair knelt before Sachi. "Be not afraid, little one." He lifted her in his arms and cradled her against him. "We are near to the end." He stumbled on a rock, caught his balance, and continued on.

"Armadeous!" he called out. He stared into the darkness, fear clawing at his confidence. Had he taken a wrong turn? Were they lost in the labyrinth of tunnels? He concentrated, picturing the main tunnel, and was sure they were on the right path. Again he called into the darkness. When no answer came, he turned to Leisa. "Leisa—"

"Look! There!" Leisa cried, spinning him around. "Up ahead."

Alasdair looked up the tunnel. A faint light shone into the passageway. He laughed, releasing his tension. Leisa's laughter followed. "Armadeous!" he shouted. The light grew brighter. He lifted Sachi in his arms and picked up his pace. He could feel Leisa's grip on his shirt. "We made it!" he called to her as he quickened his steps. He pulled Leisa's hand from his shirt and gripped it tightly. Their fingers intertwined. "We are back."

Chapter Twenty-Two

Faerie

When they exited the tunnel, they saw Armadeous waiting. "By the stars, you succeeded!" Armadeous exclaimed. His golden eyes glittered brightly in the dimly lit cavern.

"Thought you we would fail?" Alasdair asked.

Sachi looked up at the dragon and gasped. Eyes wide, she buried her face into Alasdair's shoulder.

"Fear not," he whispered in her ear. "He will not harm you."

Armadeous shook his head. "I but knew the odds." He sniffed the air. Then his golden gaze fell to Sachi. "Another human." He snorted. "Is there nothing good to eat around here?" He winked a giant eye at Leisa but spoke to Alasdair. "Could you not have brought me back a sumptuous troll?"

Sachi tensed and clung tighter.

"Be calm, little one. He merely jests." Alasdair looked at Armadeous. "I have another task. You know this."

Armadeous nodded.

"What task?" Leisa looked at Armadeous, then back at Alasdair. Neither spoke. "What task?" she insisted.

Alasdair looked at her. Though he dreaded not telling Leisa about the queen taking Sybil, he knew if he did she would insist on going with him. He needed to keep her and Sachi safe. "Have you so soon forgotten? I must convince Tazia that the human tithe does not grant immortality. It is the only way to end the stealing of human babes."

Leisa grabbed his arm. "No! You have a choice. You don't have to do that." Tears filled her eyes.

"And if I do not?" Alasdair paused, giving Leisa time for thought. "If I do not, many more lives will be lost. Lives not yet even conceived."

"But Ali ..." With the heel of her hand, she wiped at her eyes. "If you go back, she'll kill you."

"A death well met should it happen." Alasdair forced a smile. "Though I shall do my best to prevent it."

Leisa worried her lip. "Is there no other way?"

"Nay. I must go back." Alasdair turned to face Armadeous. "I need ask a favor of you. I know I am unworthy, but—"

"Unworthy?" Armadeous lifted his lips, revealing two long rows of sharp pearly teeth. "You risked your life to steal back a human child from the trolls. You have committed treason to do this. You risk death to secure the future of humankind. And you say you are unworthy?" He shook his head. "You are more worthy than any fae I have ever known." Armadeous smiled. "Or eaten."

Alasdair would have laughed had he been able, but the gravity of what he had to do weighed on him. "My thanks."

"So what is this favor?"

Alasdair handed Sachi to Leisa. She went willingly. Then he stepped up close to Armadeous. "Keep them safe."

"No!" Leisa cried out. "I'm going with you."

Alasdair turned to face her. "Nay. I will not risk Sachi's life in this task. She needs you. You must stay with her."

"But Ali—"

"Please."

Leisa bit her lip.

"Please don't go," Sachi begged. She reached out for him and he took her. "Please." She hugged his neck until he couldn't breathe.

Alasdair loosened her grip and drew a breath. "I must, little one." He brushed back Sachi's vibrant, red hair and kissed her forehead. "Stay with Leisa and Armadeous. You will be safe here."

"I wish to be with *you*," Sachi insisted.

"And you shall be. After I complete my task."

Armadeous shook his massive head and turned away.

Again Alasdair handed Sachi to Leisa. "I must speak to Armadeous away from ..." He nodded at Sachi; then he and Armadeous walked farther into the cave.

"Armadeous," Alasdair began.

"Before you go on," Armadeous interrupted. "There is something I would like to give you."

"Oh?"

"Follow me."

Alasdair followed Armadeous deeper into the cave until light no longer lit the path. They traversed a short tunnel and entered another chamber. The room brightened when Armadeous shot fire from his nostrils and lit several torches high on the wall.

Alasdair's eyes grew wide. In the large inner room were mountains of jewels of every imaginable shape and size, some exceedingly small, some large, all piled in scattered mounds of every conceivable hue. The bright light from the torches reflected off of them, setting the chamber ablaze with color.

"What is this?" Alasdair asked.

"Have you not heard of a dragon's treasure horde?"

"Aye. But I thought it only myth."

Armadeous tsked.

Alasdair picked up a large green gem and held it up to the torchlight. "Where found you all of these?"

"They are a collection of my youth. When I was small enough to fit through the tunnels, I would often raid the treasury of the trolls, grabbing a tasty snack in the process. When the trolls realized they could not defeat me, they began leaving jewels at the mouth of the tunnel in hopes it would appease me enough to not enter their domain."

"And did it?"

"Sometimes." Armadeous snorted flame. "As the centuries passed, I grew too large for the tunnels and could no longer invade their lair." He nodded at the mountain of jewels. "But I have amassed quite a collection, think you not?"

"Aye. But why do you show me this?"

"There are jewels, and there are talismans. I give you both."

Alasdair arched a brow. "I do not understand."

Armadeous chuckled. He searched through the heap of stones and pulled forth a brilliant gem. It looked exceedingly small pinched between his talons, but in Alasdair's hand, it was large.

Alasdair held it to the light. It shone with the brilliance of a star, its radiant white light glimmering in a multitude of facets. Alasdair had seen many diamonds, but this was no diamond. This was a stone he did not recognize, a rare stone of beauty beyond any he had ever imagined. "Why do you give me this?" he asked. "Its worth is surely beyond measure."

Armadeous turned away. He began searching in another smaller pile. "Know you that dragons mate for life?" he asked. He used a long talon to dig deeper still.

"Nay."

"Well, they do. I am old now, but there was a time when I had a mate. A beautiful silver dragon called Ciel." He cast Alasdair a quick glance over his shoulder. "It means *from the heavens,* you know."

Alasdair nodded.

"Wolves mate for life, too," Armadeous went on as he continued searching through the pile. "As do humans."

"Some humans divorce," Alasdair corrected.

Armadeous whipped his head around to look at Alasdair, then once again concentrated on the mound of gems. "That is their folly," he snapped. "Humans who truly love one another mate for life."

"Why do you tell me this?"

"'Tis human custom for the male of the species to gift the female with a jewel ere they take a vow of marriage." When Alasdair didn't respond, Armadeous continued. "That jewel is for Leisa. It is the Meridian Star of Wisdom and Light, and it blesses any who wears it."

Alasdair stared at the jewel resting in his palm. "I cannot take it. It is too precious. Give another. A diamond. A ruby. An emerald."

"So you do not dispute that you will mate with her." Armadeous smiled then laughed. "Forgive me, you already did."

Alasdair felt a flush rise up his neck.

"I have a keen sense of smell." Armadeous eyed Alasdair. "But will you mate for life? Will you marry her?"

Alasdair closed his eyes in thought. When he opened them, Armadeous was staring at him, his golden gaze glittering with anticipation. "If I survive this quest," Alasdair replied. "And if she will have me."

Armadeous snorted. "Then conceal that jewel safely in a pouch." He nodded at a trunk. When Alasdair lifted the lid, he saw that it, too, was filled with jewels and a multitude of pouches, many of them glistening gold and silver. "Choose a pouch," Armadeous said.

Alasdair sensed Armadeous watching him and chose a simple brown leather pouch with a drawstring. He dropped the jewel inside.

Armadeous nodded his approval. "Excellent choice. No one would suspect the value of its contents."

"Aye. But this precious jewel is beyond all conceivable value. 'Tis too rare to waste on me. I am not worthy of it."

Armadeous lowered his head to face Alasdair, his pearlescent scales glowing gold under the torch lights. "Is Leisa worthy of it?" he asked.

Alasdair sucked in a breath. "She is worth far more than any mere stone."

Armadeous grinned. "You called it a stone."

"Only by comparison. Leisa is the jewel."

Armadeous smiled. "Now choose one and twenty gems and place them in the pouch as well. It matters not the color, size, or shape."

"For what reason will I need one and twenty gems?" Alasdair asked.

"I know not. But *you* will know when the time comes."

Alasdair faced a mountain of stones and carefully choose a handful of jewels—twenty-one in all. Small ones that fit neatly into his pouch without adding too much weight. When he faced Armadeous, he noticed the dragon had turned away and was fishing through the tallest mound of gemstones.

Armadeous turned, a small box caught between his teeth. He dropped it at Alasdair's feet.

Alasdair picked it up. He lifted the lid. Inside was a platinum chain. On the chain hung a large rainbow jewel of such brilliance that he shielded his eyes with his hand. "What manner of gem is *this*?" he asked.

"'Tis no gem. 'Tis a talisman."

Alasdair tried examining it, but it hurt to look directly at it. When he turned it away from him, the mountain of jewels it faced began to glow, dimly at first, then ever increasing. Soon the room filled with blinding light.

Quickly Armadeous covered it with his nail. "Do not stare into it. Its power could blind you."

"Power?"

"Aye. Magic hangs in the air to be sure, but magic's strongest form is of the earth. All gems of the earth contain the magic of the ages. Abundant magic. This gem, however, goes beyond magic. This gem is power. Should it be turned toward lesser gems, it absorbs their energy, concentrates it, and sends it back a thousand fold. Thus the blinding glow. Wear it concealed at all times, Alasdair. It will protect you from spells and cast brilliance upon your darkest hour."

Alasdair placed the chain around his neck. He tucked the talisman under his shirt. "I do not understand. Why have *you* not used its power? Or the fae?"

Armadeous grinned. "I have no need for such power," he replied. "And had the fae acquired it, they would have abused the power."

Alasdair thought to argue the point, then realized Armadeous was right.

"This talisman was meant for you, Alasdair. It has been waiting. Do not discount its importance by using it frivolously."

"But—but how will I know when to use it?"

"You will know," Armadeous assured Alasdair. "But be warned, it will not protect you from physical danger. A spear. An arrow. A wolflych. All these are still a threat. But no fae magic can touch you as long as you wear it."

Alasdair bowed to Armadeous. "You truly are a great one," he said. "I know not how to thank you."

Armadeous snorted. "Do not bow to me, Alasdair. 'Tis I who should bow to you." He grinned. "But I will not do so. I am old, and it is a privilege of age to forgo such formality."

Alasdair smiled, then turned serious. "There is more to my favor than merely keeping Leisa and Sachi safe."

"I thought as much. What is it that you dared not say in front of them?"

"Tazia learned of my treason and stole Leisa's ward. A ward who is like a daughter to her. Tazia will use the child as a weapon against me."

Armadeous nodded. "Aye, she will."

"I must steal her back."

"What would you have me do?"

"I merely ask you to meet me just inside the wood north of the Galandorian Gate in two days time. Bring Leisa and Sachi. Should all go well, I will meet you there with Sybil in tow, and we will flee through the gate unnoticed."

"The gate is guarded."

"I am counting on my friends to take care of that, and only that. I wish them no further involvement."

"It is full of risk. What if your friends choose not to help?"

"There is no one I trust more than Lysander and Gideon. They will help."

Armadeous nodded. "Then I will do as you ask." He frowned. "And if things should go awry?"

Alasdair sighed. "If I am not there at the appointed time, I ask that you take them to the Trenalyn gate. They just need to think of home upon walking through and they shall enter the human realm near to it. Also, to pass through, they must have a jewel."

"It is done."

Again Alasdair bowed. When Armadeous moved to object, Alasdair held up a staying hand. "Do not deny me the privilege of honoring you. It is all I have to give."

Armadeous snorted a burst of air and the torches went out, casting them in darkness.

Leisa took Sachi to the pool to wash. On their return, Armadeous sat alone in the cave. "Where's Alasdair?" she asked. She cast a quick glance over the room and stepped behind the boulder to the bedding she and Alasdair had shared. It was rumpled from earlier that day, but empty. She turned once more to Armadeous. "Armadeous? Where's Alasdair?" she repeated. Her brows lifted. Her throat grew suddenly tight.

Her chest ached as though someone close had died. She pulled a deep breath, cooling her fear.

"He is gone," Armadeous replied. He took a sharp claw and ran it between his teeth.

Leisa gasped. She stepped back, pulling Sachi with her. "Gone?" She stepped farther back.

Armadeous turned his sights on her. She grabbed Sachi and ducked behind the boulder.

Armadeous lifted a brow and laughed, a loud thunderous sound that rocked the cave. "Think you I ate him?"

"Well ..."

"Humans are such presumptuous beings. I took him across the river."

"To face Tazia?"

"Aye. To face his queen."

"No! I was to go with him."

"He did not wish it."

"I wish it!"

"You are not a part of this," Armadeous retorted.

Leisa stepped out from behind the boulder. She planted her hands firmly on her hips. "Who says? How do you know I'm not an integral part of this? How do you know that our meeting and my coming on this quest weren't predestined?"

"It is not so written."

"But it isn't written that I'm not part of it either, is it?"

Armadeous cocked his head in thought. "Nay." He shook his head. "But you must stay with Sachi. She is your daughter. You cannot further endanger her."

Sachi stepped out from behind the boulder, her eyes wide and fixed on Leisa. "Daughter? What means he?"

Leisa glared at Armadeous and then turned to Sachi. "Sachi." she said. She dropped to her knees before her little girl. This was not the way or the time she'd planned to tell her, but now she had no choice. She folded one of Sachi's hands in hers.

"Sachi," she said. "Four years ago, when you were just a tiny baby, you were stolen from me."

"S—stolen?"

"Yes."

"I remember this not."

Leisa sighed at the distress of four years past. "You were too young to remember."

"Who did steal me? Queen Tazia?"

Leisa nodded. "I'm afraid so."

"Why?"

"For the very reason you're here."

Sachi's chin quivered. "To give me to the trolls?"

Leisa nodded. "I'm sorry."

Tears filled Sachi's eyes. "She never loved me?" she asked.

"Alasdair loves you," Leisa replied. "Enough to steal you back from the trolls and return you to me." Leisa contemplated whether to speak her next words. "I love you," she whispered.

"But I want to be with Ali."

So do I, Leisa thought. She swallowed to keep from weeping. "I know." She turned to Armadeous. "What's his plan for *us*?" she asked with a sweeping gesture toward Sachi.

"To stay here two days, then meet him just north of the Galandorian Gate." Armadeous shook his head. "I do not like it. Tazia is shrewd. She will not concede easily, if at all."

"And if something goes wrong? Then what?"

"Then I take you to the Trenalyn Gate and send you through to your world."

Leisa stomped her foot. "Why the hell does he have to face Tazia? All for some stupid prophecy. He didn't even say goodbye. What if he's killed?" She sniffed, then murmured, "He didn't even say goodbye."

Armadeous snorted furiously and roared, blasting flame along the ceiling. "Do not judge him, *human*. To say goodbye would have stripped him of his courage. He does it for the child, and for all human children." Again he snorted.

Leisa spun around to face Armadeous, her expression steeled. "But we already saved ..." Her gaze darted to Sachi, then back to Armadeous. "For *the* child," she questioned.

"I did mean for all human children."

"No!" She stomped up to him. "You said that separately. You said *the child* first. We already saved *the* child." She leveled a look at him, her brows arched. "Or did we?"

Armadeous turned away.

"Don't turn your back on me, *dragon!* I want an explanation."

Armadeous looked over his shoulder at her, the glitter in his golden eyes now dull with regret. "You will not like it."

Chapter Twenty-Three

Faerie

"Lysander! Where have you been? Did you find him?" Gideon stood in the maze that led from the village market to the palace grounds. "What said he?" As Lysander drew close, Gideon balked. He pointed to Lysander's scratched face. "What happened?"

Lysander lifted a hand to his cheek, tracing the wound. It had been a rough landing in the forest, but it was the only safe place to leave him without the fae guard seeing them. "The dragon—"

"Sweet Creator! You crossed paths with the dragon and lived?"

"Barely. If not for Alasdair—"

"Then you did see him."

"Aye. He is well but ..." Lysander paused.

"But what?"

Lysander's eyes lowered in silence.

"But what?" Gideon demanded.

"Alasdair ..." Lysander looked up at Gideon. "He is human."

Gideon stumbled back. "Human!" His eyes grew wide. "But how?"

Lysander shrugged. "I know not."

Gideon began to pace. "Perhaps 'tis an illusion of the dust. Has he faerie dust upon him?"

"I know not," Lysander replied. "But yea or nay, 'tis no illusion. He is human."

"You are mistaken, I am sure. How could he turn from fae to human? I know of no fae who could perform such a feat with any amount of magic unless he be in the human world. And even then, the effects of the dust would last only until dusk. Not even Tazia has such power."

"Perhaps it was no fae who did it." Lysander's brows rose. "'Haps it was a deeper magic that transformed him. A magic of the ages before the fae."

Gideon stared numbly at his friend. "The dragon?"

"His name is Armadeous."

"He has a name?"

"Aye. And he speaks as well."

"A speaking dragon?" Gideon shook his head. "I think that 'haps you struck your head hard, my friend."

"I struck my head not at all," Lysander huffed.

Gideon paced. "But why? Why would the dragon change him?"

"I know not. 'Haps he wished that Leisa and Alasdair be the same."

"But why would he wish that? What purpose had it for the dragon?"

"None that I can perceive." Lysander clapped Gideon's shoulder as they headed back toward the palace.

Gideon's gaze lowered to Lysander's band. "Alasdair returned your band?"

"Aye. It cannot help him now."

Gideon shook his head. "He will never save the child now. Neither child! He has no magic of his own and none to protect him." He caught Lysander's gaze. "Did you tell him of Tazia's newest acquisition?"

"Aye." Lysander hung his head. "He will come. You know this."

Gideon groaned. "'Tis suicide if he comes for her as a human."

Lysander sighed. "What do we do now?"

Gideon's brows lifted. "Do?"

"Aye. You are the strategist, Gideon. We need a plan. We cannot allow Tazia to harm the child, a child who is not even a tithe. 'Tis against all moral code. 'Tis wrong, queen or nay."

Gideon nodded. "The air reeks of her anger. I fear for the youngling's life."

"Then we must steal the child away before Tazia can act. Should Alasdair come for her, the queen will surely order her slain. Or worse yet, cast into the dark swamp."

"And him."

Lysander nodded sadly. "Not in all my nine hundred years have I seen such infraction of the law. The tithe, aye. But not this. This is personal. As queen, Tazia must put it aside."

Gideon snorted. He slowed his steps. "Do you recall when we were younglings?"

"Aye. I remember. Alasdair was little more than a babe and us not much older when we became friends."

"Have you any recollection of his parents?"

"Nay. Always it was Tazia. Or at least always that I can remember."

Gideon clenched his jaw. "Something gnaws at Tazia. Something about Alasdair." His eyes widened. "By the stars, when she sees he is human, she will explode."

Lysander nodded. "She has no love for humans. This I know."

"Aye. But why? Not that I care much for them one way or another, but she carries a true hatred of them." Gideon sucked in a breath and released sharply. "We must warn Alasdair not to come."

"I did try."

"We must try again."

Lysander sighed and turned toward the river path. Gideon stopped him.

"'Tis my turn, friend," Gideon informed Lysander. "What you need do is steal back the child."

Lysander swallowed. "I think that 'haps I would rather warn Alasdair."

Gideon grinned. "Truly, the girl will respond more favorably to you than to me."

"Point well taken. Never were you popular amongst the younglings."

Gideon snorted. "They do not understand me is all."

"I am sure that is the reason." Lysander laughed, then quickly sobered. "Know you where the girl is being held?"

"Aye. The room next to the library." Gideon clapped Lysander's shoulder. "Be careful. I deem the door is well guarded."

"Deem? Do you not know for sure?"

"Tazia will not allow us close. She fears we will aid Alasdair."

"Then how know you where she is held?"

"Servants talk."

~*~

Sybil paced the small room. She listened at the closed door. It was large and heavy and bolted from the outside. When steps approached, she stumbled back. A click sounded and the door swung open.

Sybil caught her bottom lip in her teeth, her eyes wide. Before her stood a woman of such beauty, she had to be a queen. A fairy queen. Her dark hair shone under the lights, glistened as though tiny jewels had been crushed and sprinkled over it. Her gown dragged on the floor, purple and gold edged in silver gems. On her head she wore a golden crown of twisted vines that lifted in the front to a cluster of glistening jewels, jewels larger than any Sybil had seen in her book. On top of them a large red one sparkled.

A part of her wanted to embrace this fairy queen, but one look into her dark, callous stare sent Sybil stumbling back.

"So," Tazia said coolly. "You are the human's child."

"The human?"

"The one they call Leisa."

Sybil gasped. "I'm her niece," she replied softly. She lowered her eyes to her pajama top as she toyed nervously with its hem.

A slow grin lifted Tazia's lips. "Ah, of course, niece." She stepped forward. Sybil jumped.

"And do you know who I am?" Tazia asked, her hard gaze on the girl.

Sybil shook her head as she shuffled back.

Tazia swept the air with her hand as she spoke. "I am Tazia. Queen of the Fae." Glorious wings flashed behind her, their luminosity framing her dark beauty with dazzling light. Then they disappeared.

Sybil bit her lip. "Where's Aunt Leisa?" she asked. Her voice quivered, and she saw the queen smirk.

"Never mind about that. I deem she will be here soon enow. She and Alasdair."

"Alasdair is here?" Sybil smiled. "I knew he was a fairy."

Tazia lifted her hand as though to strike the girl. Then she lowered it to her side. "What else do you know about him?"

Sybil planted her hands on her small hips. "That he loves Aunt Leisa."

Tazia's eyes narrowed. Her mouth flattened to a hard line. "I forbid it!" she screamed.

Sybil scuttled back behind a settee.

"Guard!" Tazia bellowed. She spun toward the door, her long train sweeping the polished wood floor behind her.

The door opened and a large soldier entered. A shirt of metal rings covered his chest, topped by a vest of heavy leather. A long sword rested at his side, glinting in the light. "Aye, my Queen," he replied.

"Keep watch on this door and allow none but me to pass." She eyed him angrily. "None!" Without a backward glance at Sybil, she burst over the threshold. Then she turned to face him once more. "I shall have your head if you do." Turning away, she stormed down the hall.

The guard nodded. "Aye, my Queen. None shall pass," he called after her as he slammed the door shut, leaving Sybil all alone.

Sybil frowned. This fairy queen was nothing like what she had imagined from her book. This fairy queen was mean and cruel and scary. "Aunt Leisa," Sybil cried. She rubbed at her eyes and her tears flowed. Suddenly a beam of sunlight shone down on her. Looking up, she noted a small window high on the wall. Her gaze darted to the door, then back to the window. With all her weight, she pushed the settee until it rested against the wall below the window. Then she climbed on it. Still the window was too high. Climbing down, she looked around for something to put on top of the settee. Just a little higher and she could climb out the window and look for her aunt and Alasdair.

Across the room sat a tall stool covered in red velvet. It balanced on four wooden legs that ended in claws. She grabbed the stool and dragged it toward the settee. Heavy and awkward, it caused her to teeter and she fell, dropping it. The clatter echoed off the walls. She sucked in a breath.

"Quiet in there!" the guard yelled. He pounded on the door.

Sybil waited. When the door failed to open, she grabbed the stool and tried again. Balancing it on the settee, she was able to reach the window. The wide stone sill rested at chest level and she knew she could pull herself up. Quickly, she pushed the window open and, leaning forward balanced her chest on the sill. She looked down and caught her breath. It was a long way down. Too long to jump. Again her eyes filled with tears and she began to weep.

~*~

Lysander crept into the lower garden, the one he, Gideon, Alasdair, and Leisa had crossed in leaving the dark swamp. Vegetation had taken over the once popular site. It was thickly overgrown and deserted as usual. Lysander turned toward the back palace wall. If he was right, the room off the library was just above. He looked up and groaned.

Far above he could see the small window that led into the sitting room, too small for him to fit through. Even were he to fly to it, by the time he caught the girl's attention and got hold of her, he would be noticed and pursued. At that height, the window was in clear view of the main grounds, grounds guarded by archers. The window was also an impressive height up the wall on the inside. The girl would be too short to reach it.

Lysander lowered his head and rested his hand on the intricate hilt of his sword. He would have to go in through the palace. The thought unnerved him. It could very well lead to crossed blades.

Lysander pondered a plan. Perhaps he could come up with a diversion and avoid conflict. As he turned to leave, resigned to what he must do, he heard a sound. He shot a quick glance over the gardens, then realized it had come from overhead. He looked up. A small pale elbow rested on the sill of the window. How had he failed to see that? Again the sound—a soft weeping.

"Sybil," he whispered loudly. He looked around, hoping no one else heard him, then turned his attention back to the window. The elbow moved. "Sybil!" he called again.

Sybil peeked out the window. A small hand wiped at her eyes. Then her entire face appeared.

Lysander stared in amazement at the golden-haired child. How had she reached the window? "Sybil," he called, putting the 'how' on hold. "Do you remember me?"

Sybil nodded. "Uh-huh. You're Ly ... Ly ..."

"Lysander," he finished for her.

Again Sybil nodded.

"I am a friend to Alasdair." Lysander watched Sybil's face light up. Again she wiped at her eyes.

"Where is he?" she asked.

"He is close. But he cannot help you as soon as you need him to."

Sybil bit her lip.

"'Tis why I am here, to get you out."

At Lysander's assurance, Sybil released her lip. "How? It's too high."

Lysander smiled. "Will you trust me?" he asked. He had an idea that did not require him to reveal himself by flying.

Sybil paused, then nodded.

"Can you fit through that window?"

Again Sybil nodded.

Lysander sighed. "Good." He raised his hands and concentrated until his band glowed. "When I say jump, jump." He heard Sybil whimper and looked up at her. Her head was shaking.

"I can't. It's too far."

"I will catch you."

Again Sybil shook her head. "It's too far. I'll fall too fast."

Lysander drew breath. "Sybil, do you know that faeries have special magic?"

Sybil nodded.

"Then believe in this magic and jump. It will protect you."

Sybil hesitated briefly. Then she climbed onto the window sill.

"Fear not. I'll not let harm befall you." Again Lysander lifted his hands and concentrated until a cushion of air formed beneath the window. "Now!" he called. "Jump."

Sybil closed her eyes, caught her breath, and let herself fall. At first she plummeted quickly, but soon she met a thick cushion of air. Her descent slowed more and more until she felt Lysander's arms pluck her from the air. Quickly he lowered her to the ground.

"Come," he said, holding out his hand. "We must leave this place before Tazia finds you gone."

"But where's Alasdair? Where's Aunt Leisa?"

"We will find them, little one."

Sybil swallowed her fear. Trustingly, she placed her small hand in his and followed.

Faerie Dust / Linda Ciletti

Chapter Twenty-Four

Faerie

Alasdair worked his way up the river shoreline and passed through the wood that led to the palace maze. He stood for a moment outside the gate. How had it all come to this?

He released a long-held breath. It mattered not. The only way left to travel was forward. He reflected on the days of his youth, on Gideon and Lysander. How he wished they were with him now. Gideon, the strategist, always laid out the best plans.

Footsteps sounded on the dry ground cover. Quickly he slipped behind a towering oak. He was nothing now. He was human. He would mean no more to Tazia than Sybil or any other human. Tazia despised humans, and now he knew why. His human father had stolen her sister from her, and she had died because of it. Not by his father's hand, but Tazia blamed him all the same. It explained a lot. It explained that, though always she was civil to him, she never expressed love of any kind. He heaved a sigh. He was not so naive to believe that she would grant him a courteous audience—more likely it would be an angry one.

And if she caught word of his change, she would have him killed.

More footsteps. Closer.

Alasdair quietly slid his sword from its scabbard. He lifted it point up before his face and waited. Perspiration trickled down his back as the heavy leather mail protecting him absorbed the mid-day heat. His hands, slick with sweat, slipped on the hilt and he corrected his grip. Every nerve stood on edge as the sound of steps drew nearer until they were just on the other side of the tree.

Bracing his sword in his grasp, Alasdair lifted it high over his shoulder. When a shadow fell across him, he inhaled sharply and shot out from behind the tree. A battle cry thrust from his throat and his sword fell in a killing plunge, stopping just short of Gideon's shoulder.

Gideon jumped back, his hands raised.

"Sweet Mother Earth!" Alasdair cried. He lowered the sword and caught his breath. His heart raced. "What are you doing here?" he asked as he wiped the sweat from his brow.

"I could ask you the same," Gideon replied.

"I have come for Sybil and to confront Tazia."

An incredulous look crossed Gideon's face. "That is it? That is your plan?"

Alasdair's brows lifted. "I have not quite worked it through yet."

Gideon braced his hands on his hips. "Tell me then, what *have* you worked through?" He shrugged. "Thus far?"

"To get Sybil."

"A bit simplistic, think you not?" Gideon goaded. His mouth curved in a wicked grin.

Alasdair laughed. Stepping up to Gideon, he gave him a hug. "Ah, 'tis good to see you, friend." He stepped back. "Seen you Lysander? Did Armadeous keep his word?"

"Armadeous?" Gideon looked thoughtful for a moment. "Ah, the dragon. I daresay Lysander is quite pleased that he was not eaten." Gideon smiled. "He is well."

Alasdair released a breath and visibly relaxed. "And Sybil?"

"She was well the last I heard."

Alasdair sighed. "I must get her somewhere safe before I confront Tazia. If I do not, Tazia will use her against me." He slipped his sword back into its scabbard and made to storm the maze when Gideon held out his arm and stopped him.

"Be calm. Lysander already went for her."

"Nay," Alasdair cried. "I did not wish to involve you two so intimately. If Tazia finds out—"

"We will deal with Tazia when the time comes. Though I pray it does not."

Alasdair noted Gideon studying him. "What?"

"Where is Leisa? Did you find the other child?" Gideon asked.

Alasdair grinned. "Aye, we found her. I did have to fight a troll or two, but she is safe. As for Leisa, I forbade her to come. 'Tis too dangerous for her and Sachi."

"Ah, so you slipped away like a coward, did you?" Gideon cocked a brow and grinned.

"Nay!" Alasdair refuted. Then he nodded. "Aye." He smiled at Gideon. "I do not wish her or Sachi hurt. If Tazia got her hands on them ..." He paused. "I might not be able to protect them." Again a pause. "I am no coward."

Gideon clapped Alasdair's shoulder. "I know this," he said, dropping his hand. Again he studied Alasdair.

"Know you where is Sybil?" Alasdair asked.

"I know not. When Lysander departed to get her, I came directly here to warn you."

"Warn me? Of what?"

Gideon stared at Alasdair. "Lysander told me you are human now. I dared to hope he was wrong, but I see he was not."

Alasdair hung his head and nodded. "I am sorry. It was not my wish." He looked up at Gideon. "And I blame you not should you turn from me now. I but ask that you not stand in my way."

Gideon stepped up to Alasdair and set a hand on his shoulder. "Human or fae, it matters not. I will never turn away from you when you need me."

A warm smile crossed Alasdair's face. "Know you my years are numbered now."

"Aye," Gideon sadly replied. "But you will not be forgotten."

Again the smile. "Gideon?"

"Aye?"

"Should I not return, it has been agreed that Armadeous will take Leisa and Sachi to the Trenalyn Gate and send them through."

"Not Sybil?"

"Leisa does not know the fae have taken her. Had I told her, she would have been even more adamant to come this day."

Alasdair cast Gideon an imploring look. "Should I fall, I pray you, meet Armadeous at the wood to the north of the Galandorian Gate. That is where he will be waiting with Leisa and Sachi. Take Sybil as well if you can." He swallowed. "Tell Armadeous I have passed on and to do what we agreed."

"Can I safely do this?"

"Armadeous has vowed not to eat another fae. But tell this to no one other than Lysander. Fear of the dragons is what protects one realm from the other."

"By the stars, Alasdair. You have crossed lines no one else has."

Alasdair smiled. "Also, one thing more."

"Aye?"

"There is something I should have told Leisa ere I left, but I did not. Will you tell her for me?"

"Anything."

"Tell Leisa I love her."

~*~

"Where is she?" Tazia demanded. She shoved the perplexed guard into the wall.

"My Queen, I swear I did not leave my post. And no one passed."

The queen studied the settee and claw-footed stool stacked neatly against the wall. "Industrious child, I'll give her that. But still, the drop is too far for a human to survive. Surely she did not exit the window."

"Unless someone on the outside aided her," the guard suggested. "For certain she would fit through the opening."

Tazia huffed. "Find her!" Again she shoved him. "Find her now." Tazia stormed from the room, her train trailing behind her. "Wait!" She stopped suddenly and glared over her shoulder at the guard, her porcelain features hard. "And find the traitor who helped her."

"But where do I begin, my Queen? I know not—"

"Do not be an imbecile. Start with Gideon and Lysander." Tazia slammed the door and headed down the wide marble corridor toward the great hall.

"Mother?" Edeline stopped Tazia midway down the hall.

Tazia glared at her daughter. "What is it, Edeline?" she snapped. "I am busy at the moment."

Edeline stepped back at her mother's cold regard. "What is happening? The palace is in an uproar and double the guards are posted."

"Be not concerned."

"But I am."

Tazia turned to face her daughter, her visage contorted with anger. "Alasdair has committed treason. He is to be arrested the moment he sets foot near the palace."

Edeline gasped. "Alasdair?"

"I had always hoped that his other half would not come forward. That the fae in him was strong." She shook her head.

"Other half?"

Tazia waved her hand and turned to leave. "Be not concerned, Edeline."

Edeline crossed her arms. "Nay. Tell me, Mother," she commanded.

Tazia spun to face her daughter. Her voice rose to a bellow. "Alasdair is a half-blood."

Edeline gasped. "But how?"

"My sister fell in love with a human and brought him and their half-blood babe back with her from the unknown realm."

"And?"

"And I forbade that he stay!"

"I did never know your sister."

"She died many years ago."

"Died? The fae do not just die." Edeline's jaw dropped. She lowered her arms. "What did you, Mother?"

Tazia stood silent a moment, then released the truth in a sudden burst of rage. "I ordered her lover cast into the dark swamp."

Edeline caught her breath. "Few live who are thrown into the swamp. A human surely would not."

A slow grin crossed Tazia's face.

"Oh, Mother!" Edeline paused. "But that does not answer what became of your sister."

"The fool human caught word of my plan and escaped to the Sprite Wood. My sister and I argued and I banished her to the wood with her pitiful lover."

"And Alasdair?"

"I forbade her to take him. It was her punishment."

"By the stars, how could you!" Tears filled Edeline's eyes. "And then you had her killed?"

Tazia came alert. "Nay. I would not do so. 'Tis forbidden to kill royalty. You know this."

"But you wish to kill Alasdair."

"He has committed treason! But I will not kill him. He is half fae and therefore still of royal blood. I will have him cast into the swamp."

"'Tis the same!" Edeline screamed.

"Edeline, this is not your concern. I am still queen and I make the decisions."

Edeline gasped. "How did your sister die?"

"I tired of waiting for her to come to her senses and sent guards into the Sprite Wood to slay the human and bring her back. She was not at their dwelling. All that was found was her kirtle covered in blood." Tazia softened momentarily. Then her countenance turned cold once more. "The human killed her," she bellowed.

"You cannot know that."

"What else?"

"The sprites, a wolflych, an accident. Mother, how could you have condemned him for something that may not be true?"

"It matters not."

"What happened to Alasdair's father?"

He dared to come back. Dared to demand that Alasdair be returned to him."

"He was his son."

Tazia turned red. "How dare he ask for Alasdair after killing my sister!"

Edeline swallowed. "You slew him?"

"Nay. I would not dirty my hands so. I ordered it done. On the spot, in the courtyard, for all to see."

Edeline slumped to the floor, her gown billowing about her. "He merely wanted his son." Tears slid down her face. "Oh, Mother, how cruel."

"Be not a fool. There are laws to be upheld."

"I know the law, Mother." Edeline stood to confront Tazia. "I have been tutored on the law until I could scream, preparing for the time when I would become queen. There is no law against humans. This was personal."

Tazia slapped Edeline's face so hard that it knocked her to the floor. "Never speak to me thus again," she ordered. She turned away and stormed down the hall.

Edeline cupped her throbbing cheek as she watched her mother walk away. Hearing steps, she turned to see who approached.

"Edeline!" Lysander called. He half ran down the hall. Sliding to a stop before her, he grasped her arm and helped her to stand. Edeline leaned against him, her hand covering her cheek. "What has happened? I heard arguing and came as quickly as I could."

Edeline sniffed. "Mother has gone mad."

Lysander smiled. "She was always so."

"Nay, I mean truly and completely mad."

Lysander drew Edeline's hand away from her face, revealing a welt. "By the stars! Tazia did this?"

Edeline nodded. "She intends to kill Alasdair. She claims he has committed treason."

"She cannot kill him. She still believes him to be fae royalty. 'Tis forbidden."

"Still believes? What has changed?"

Lysander quieted. "Naught."

"Lysander," Edeline prompted. "What has changed?"

Lysander sighed. "Alasdair is human now."

Her jaw dropped. "How?"

"The dragon Armadeous transformed him."

"The dragon?"

Lysander nodded. "'Tis a long story."

"By the stars, she will not merely cast him in the swamp now. She will slay him where he stands. As a human, Alasdair will not be perceived to be of royal blood."

"She does not know."

288

"She will see it soon enow." Edeline sighed deeply. "She is mad, but not stupid."

Lysander stood quietly.

"You are helping him, aren't you?" Edeline asked.

"Tazia's crimes are mounting. I cannot let her kill him." A sadness fell over Lysander. "He will die soon enow as it is."

"Because he is human."

"Aye."

Edeline looked down, her gaze stopping at Lysander's wrist. "How is it that you have a band? I was told that mother confiscated it."

Lysander tugged his sleeve to cover it. 'Twas Gideon's band I wore when she demanded it returned to her."

"Gideon's?"

"Aye. I had loaned mine to Alasdair and we were sharing Gideon's until Ali's return. 'Twas Gideon's misfortune that I wore it at the time."

Edeline cocked her head in thought. "How did you get yours back?"

"Alasdair returned it to me. It holds no power for a human."

Edeline's expression saddened. "Lysander?"

"Aye?"

"I did hear Mother and the guard arguing down the hall. The human child has escaped." She eyed Lysander. "Know you something of this?"

Lysander swallowed.

"I will not speak of it, I vow. I wish that I had had the courage to do the same."

Lysander gripped Edeline's shoulders. "I do not wish harm upon Tazia, yet I love Alasdair, and those he loves I am bound to protect. But I know not what will pass this day. I fear much."

Edeline nodded.

"Stay clear of it, Edeline. You are born of your father, may he rest in peace, for there is none of your mother in you."

"Where hid you the girl?" Edeline asked.

Lysander pulled a breath. "I cannot say."

"Cannot? Or will not?"

"Edeline, what you know may well come against you. 'Tis best you know blessed little."

Edeline pressed her lips against a retort. "Stay safe, Lysander." When Lysander dropped his hold, Edeline slipped away down the hall.

Lysander sighed and continued out the front palace doors. He hoped Gideon had met Alasdair and warned him away. If not, all Hell would soon be upon them.

Chapter Twenty-Five

Faerie

Alasdair paused at the edge of the maze and surveyed the surroundings. It was slightly past the noon hour and the sun sat high in the sky, casting short shadows along the palace walls. The courtyard was exceptionally quiet.

"There." Gideon pointed to the right of the palace doors. Two guards stood at the ready, their eyes alert and their weapons in hand. He pointed to the left of the doors, where another one stood braced for battle.

"What of the side entrance?" Alasdair whispered.

Gideon motioned for silence and pushed Alasdair toward a shadowed corner of the hedgerow. Footsteps sounded on the far side of the hedge—heavy booted steps accompanied by the clang of metal armor.

When the steps subsided, Gideon replied, "Guarded as well."

Alasdair fell back against the jagged brush. "How shall I confront Tazia if I cannot get near her?"

Gideon grinned.

"The forgotten garden entrance," they said at once.

Alasdair straightened. "Think you it will not be guarded?"

"It has long been forgotten. Do you not recall using it the day we came through the dark swamp? Only you, I, and Lysander know of it now."

"Only for reason that we fell across it by accident as younglings running from Tazia."

"She did always have a temper. And never did she find us."

"Nay. Until the following morn, when we were punished."

Gideon quietly laughed. "'Twas well worth it."

"A stolen loaf of bread and jam was worth it?"

"Aye, it was."

Alasdair smiled at the memory. It truly had been. He clapped Gideon's shoulder and they headed back into the maze. Upon reaching the children's play area, they circled the back of the palace, concealing themselves in the surrounding flora. The vegetation of the garden was thick, and so tall that it nearly hid a dilapidated shed that sat off to one corner. A rustling sounded from within the shed and they stilled to listen. When no further sound came, they edged their way around the weathered wood outbuilding, crossed a small clearing and found the forgotten door.

"Go and do what you must," Gideon said. "I shall find Lysander and the child and meet you in the maze."

Alasdair nodded. When he turned to leave, Gideon pulled him back.

"Be forewarned," Gideon cautioned. "Tazia will not give in without a fight. You know this."

Again Alasdair nodded. "I have not a choice."

Gideon shook his head. "There are always choices."

"Not this time." Alasdair pulled on the door. It creaked with age as it slowly opened to a long, dark corridor.

"Blessings upon you, friend," Gideon said. He turned to leave through the garden. "May the Creator protect you," he called over his shoulder.

Alasdair watched his friend disappear into the tall grass, then slipped into the palace and shut the door. He made his way down the shadowed corridor and into the kitchen. The workers hushed and backed away. Alasdair looked at them, fae he had known all his life now frightened by his presence.

Nay, not of him, but of Tazia and what she would do if she thought they aided him. Alasdair motioned for silence and quickly slipped from the kitchen and up the stairwell. At the top of the stairs was the main corridor. It was wide and stately, a white marble floor rivered in gold that glimmered in the torchlight. Alasdair recalled the years he had played on it as a youngling, always believing it a safe place. Now it might well be the pathway to his death. He set the thought aside and glanced farther down the hall. He could see the dual doors of the great room, tall, pointed and gleaming of rich Galandorian oak. They sat slightly ajar. Golden sunlight spilled out from between them, setting a small section of the floor to glow. He scanned the hall. Seeing no guards, he stepped into the open. Instantly a hand grabbed his sleeve and pulled him back into a shadowed alcove.

Alasdair whipped his sword from its scabbard, swung it high, and spun to face Edeline. "By the stars!" he swore. He lowered the sword's tip to the floor. "What are you doing here?"

Edeline eyed the weapon's razored point until it struck the floor. "I live here." She looked up at Alasdair, her eyes filled with tears. "Do not go to her. She will kill you."

Alasdair gifted her with a warm but watery smile. "I must, Edeline. I have not a choice."

Edeline stared in silence. Her eyes widened. "You are the one!"

Alasdair knew she referred to the prophecy and nodded.

Edeline hung her head and toyed with the folds of her cerulean gown, then lifted her eyes to his. "I beg you, kill her not. She has lost her senses, to be sure, but she is my mother."

Alasdair inhaled deeply and released. "I do not wish harm upon her, Edeline. But I know not what shall come to pass this day. Truly, I wish only to take Sybil and convince Tazia to stop the tithes."

"Stop the tithes?" Edeline released a painful laugh. "Never will she do that. You fight a lost cause. What is a human life ever and anon in exchange for immortality?"

"Immortality for whom, Edeline?" Alasdair asked as he sheathed his sword. "Certainly, not for the human children."

"For the fae. For me, for you—" Edeline fell silent, then said, "I am sorry. I forgot that you are human now."

A mix of surprise and anger rose within him. "Who told you?"

"Lysander." She looked up at him.

Alasdair glared at the admission.

"Do not be angry with him. He did not mean to let it slip."

His expression softened and he shrugged. "It matters not. Tazia will know soon enow."

Edeline stepped back from Alasdair and studied him. "But how is it possible that you are now human? But for the illusion of the dust, there is no magic great enough to turn a fae fully human." She circled him and studied him further.

Alasdair watched her over his shoulders. "No fae in the faerie kingdom. But there is one who holds more magic than any fae."

"Who?"

"The white dragon, Armadeous."

Edeline gasped. "He did this to you?" She reached up and drew her hand across his cheek.

"Aye."

"But how?"

Alasdair forced a smile. "Edeline, cousin of my heart, I sorely wish I had time enough to explain all that has happened, but I do not. I am sorry. I must go."

Edeline nodded, sadness clouding her eyes. "Then go, Alasdair. Take the human child and leave," she begged.

"I cannot. I know not where she is."

"I do."

"Where?"

"In the back garden shed."

Alasdair groaned. "I did just pass there."

Edeline nodded. "Aye. I saw you. I have been watching the shed, fearful that someone would find her as did I."

"You found her?" Alasdair asked.

Edeline grinned. "Aye."

"How?"

"As a youngling, I spied upon you, Lysander, and Gideon. I knew all of your secret places." She smiled at the memory. "Or most. But never did I tell."

Alasdair stroked Edeline's golden hair. "I shall miss you terribly. You were always a sister to me."

Edeline took his hand in hers. "I pray you, take the child and leave. Granted your days are numbered, but you can live them out happily in the human realm. What happens here is no longer your concern."

"You are wrong, Edeline." Alasdair touched her cheek, felt the warmth of her caring. She carried the scent of lilies in spring, and he wished he did not have to cause her pain. "As long as Tazia continues to steal innocent babes, 'tis my worry and burden. I cannot abandon the prophecy I am to fulfill. I must confront Tazia." He lowered his hand. "I am sorry. I will do my best to convince her that the tithes have no purpose but to kill. That not one moment of life is gained by the death of another."

"The tithes do not grant immortality? Who told you such a lie?"

"'Tis no lie, Edeline. 'Twas told to me by a wise and knowledgeable source."

"Wiser than our queen?"

"Infinitely."

"The white dragon?"

Alasdair nodded. He rested his hands on her shoulders. "I vow Tazia will not be harmed by my hand." His brow lifted. "As far as her harming me, I doubt not that she will try." He watched Edeline's lips turn down and felt her pain.

Edeline wiped at her eyes and nodded. "Peace be upon you, Alasdair." She untied a large silk pouch from her gird strap and handed it to him. "After speaking with Lysander, I stole this from the strongroom. Please, take it."

"What is it?" Alasdair asked. He took the pouch and drew it open. "Faerie dust?" He pulled the drawstring closed and handed the pouch out to her. "I cannot accept this. It holds no magic for me now."

"Then take it as a gift," Edeline said, her words breaking with emotion. "As a remembrance of all here who care for you and wish you well." She caught his gaze with tear-filled eyes and kissed his cheek. Then, bunching her skirts in her fists, she hurried down the hall and up the winding marble staircase that led to Tazia's private solar.

Edeline's heart hammered in her breast as she inched inside the elaborate room to a tall, gilded mirror that rested against the wall in its far corner. She stood before the mirror, staring beyond her reflection to what lay on the other side. She had always known the purpose of the mirror, a mirror that allowed passage but one way. It was her inheritance. She reached out and touched the glass with the tips of her fingers. It immediately began to waver. Her throat tightened as she drew her hand back. A lie. It was all a lie.

She turned to Tazia's nightstand. On it stood an ornate golden candlestick as long as her arm, its tallow candle burning brightly. She blew out the candle and ripped it from its base. Grabbing the candlestick with both hands, she swung it fiercely and smashed the mirror. Shards of glass splattered across the room. Edeline spun away protecting her face with her arms. As she turned to leave, she saw a lone guard band sitting on the dresser. Gideon's. She picked up the band, stared at it for a moment, then hid it in the folds of her skirt as she made her way back to the main corridor.

~*~

Alasdair tied the pouch Edeline had given him to his belt. When he reached the great room, he slipped silently inside.

Tazia sat on her throne, engaged in conversation with two guards. Her dark chestnut hair was pulled high on her head and dusted with small, sparkling gems. Her gown of ivory jacquard glistened in the light and was embellished with a multitude of jewels. At her throat rested a golden clasp from which hung the finest woolen cloak in all the kingdom. Alasdair knew the deep-red cloth well. It was a color reserved for royalty.

"I have been expecting you," Tazia said coldly. She turned to face him.

The jewels winked at him. Foreboding crawled beneath his flesh. His hands felt damp as his heart pounded against the wall of his chest. He watched Tazia with the intensity and wariness of a wolflych's prey. Her bejeweled gown covered all but the head of the throne, and she sat with a smug confidence that angered him.

How dare she behave as though nothing was amiss. She had killed his parents and countless human children—and who knew who else. She had deceived her people into believing they were eternal as long as a tithe was paid to Hell. She had withheld the truth of his birth.

Alasdair felt his flesh grow hot with rage. Fear rose within him as well, fear that he would lose control. He caught his breath, held it a few seconds, then released it.

"Why did you not tell me?" he demanded when words finally came. He fixed a hard gaze on Tazia and strode toward her until the two guards crossed swords in his path, stopping him. The clang and slide of metal echoed off the stone walls and marble floor. He shifted his gaze to one guard, then the other. They were Tazia's personal bodyguards. He knew them well. Today, however, they felt like strangers to him. Their hard looks bore down on him and he knew, if he made a threatening move of any kind, they would slay him where he stood.

"Tell you what, Alasdair?" the queen asked. She eyed him sharply, then motioned to the guards to lower their swords and step back. Reluctantly, they obeyed.

Alasdair stepped closer to the throne, one hand braced on the hilt of his sword. "The truth of my birth. Of my parents," he said. He saw Tazia glance at his readied hand. He dropped it to his side.

Tazia leaned forward, the movement causing the jewels of her gown to catch the light and cast it back in riotous color. "What was there to tell? You were just a babe when they died."

Alasdair crossed his arms. Anger rose in his throat and he swallowed hard. "You mean, I was just a babe when they were cast out."

Tazia waved a flippant hand.

"Why were they cast out, Tazia? Tell me, for I would hear the truth from your own lips."

Tazia glared at Alasdair. "I need not explain myself to you."

"Aye. In this case, you do."

Tazia lifted her chin in regal haughtiness. "They broke the law. They should have thanked the Creator that I did not cast them into the dark swamp."

"Lie!" Alasdair shouted. He stepped forward. When the guards moved to stop him, he stilled.

"What know you of it?" Tazia flipped her gown to one side and the jewels began to glow.

Alasdair bristled at her arrogance. "I know there is no law forbidding fae and human relations. Therefore, they could not have broken it."

Tazia rose from her throne, her face flushed, her lips pulled tight. Like falling water, her cloak and gown spilled around her and rested in a billowy cloud at her feet. The two guards stepped closer to Alasdair. "So you know of your heritage," she said in a low, taunting tone. She eyed him warily. "Who told you?"

"What matters it? 'Tis the truth, is it not? You have caused the deaths of many innocents," Alasdair accused. "Who is the *true* criminal?"

Tazia snorted and turned from him. She began pacing the dais, dragging the long ivory train of her gown behind her. Finally she swung to face him. "*You,* Alasdair. You entered the unknown world without permission, you crossed into the other realms to get a changeling so you could steal back a child who was slated to be tithed—a child whose death is required to keep the fae immortal."

"Another lie." Alasdair leveled his eyes at Tazia. "There is no immortality."

Tazia quieted. "How know you this?" she said low and for his ears only.

"Then you admit there is no immortality?"

"I admit nothing," Tazia spat. She motioned for the guards to leave the room. "Close the doors, but stay near," she ordered them.

When they were out of earshot, she turned to Alasdair. "Aye," she said, keeping her voice low. "There is no immortality. *That* is the truth. But we need the jewels that the trolls mine for the making of faerie dust. Without the dust, our magic is limited. With the dust, we enhance our magic a hundredfold within the realm, and it allows us to carry magic into the outer realms. Faerie dust is where our greatest magic lies, and it is found in the jewels of the Trenalyn mines. Magic born of the earth."

"There are other sources of magic, Tazia. Air, water, fire."

"Magics of air, fire, and water are all well enough. But magic of the earth is the most beauteous and strongest magic of all. It is the foundation for all the others." She paced some more. "The trolls are too ignorant to realize the gemstones' true potential. To them, such jewels are merely pretty trinkets to hoard and look upon. But we, the fae, know their worth and use them wisely."

Alasdair thought of the mountain of jewels in the dragon's lair and understood his power. "At what cost, Tazia?"

"Cost? It costs us nothing. Hell has deceived the trolls into tithing a living soul every twenty years to replenish their mines. To spare their own children, they give us a hoard of jewels for that soul. In the beginning, we traded sickly faerie babes who would not last the year. But when we found that the dust had curing powers, we sent human children in their stead." Tazia snorted. "The trolls are too ignorant to realize the difference, since younglings gain not the ability to summon wings until adolesence." To speak it aloud caused Tazia to smile—cold, deliberate, heartless.

"Say not *we*, Tazia, but *you*. I venture few others know the truth of it—that this practice was not passed down from our ancestors, but began when you took the throne."

"It spares lives and keeps us strong in the magic of the earth."

"It spares faerie lives by stealing the lives of humans, who are promised a paltry seventy to eighty years as it is," Alasdair growled.

"Aye, if that is how you wish to see it. But with the healing powers of the dust, who knows how long the fae will live? None have died but by fatal injury. Before the dust, many were lost to sickness as well as accident."

"Then you did always know the trolls were deceived?"

"Of course. Hell cannot give what is not its to give. But the trolls do not know this, and we profit from their ignorance."

Again Tazia smiled, a cold smile that sent a chill up Alasdair's spine.

Anguish rose in his throat. His perfect world came crashing down. How had he ever believed that Faerie was superior to the human world? He raised a fist to his pounding head. "Tazia! Where is your conscience?" He dropped his fist to his side.

Tazia cocked her head in puzzlement. "Conscience?" She laughed. "'Tis a human weakness. I have no conscience."

"You are wrong. I know many a fae with a conscience. Having none, 'haps you are blind to it."

Tazia shrugged. "'Haps."

"But you are not blind to jewels, are you, Tazia?" He nodded at her gown. "So vainly and ostentatiously adorned in them. Such a shameful exhibition of—"

Alasdair fell quiet, his eyes widened.

Tazia grinned. "Why think you my powers are the greatest of all the fae? And what think you powers the bands of the guards? Locked within each band is a concentration of dust so strong that to cross them would be blinding."

"Sweet Mother Earth!" Again he thought of Armadeous and his hoard of jewels—and his power. Power enough, Alasdair thought, to make *him* human.

When Tazia glanced down at her embellished clothes, he pulled the talisman out from beneath his shirt and folded it in his cowl for easy reach. "And what of my parents?"

Tazia feigned boredom. "What of them? Your father was not worthy of my sister. Fae royalty coupling with an inferior human?" She snorted. "I cast *him* out, not her."

"You ordered him cast into the dark swamp, but he foiled your plan and escaped into the Sprite Wood instead. Then you cast out my mother."

"She followed the human of her own accord, choosing him over us. Over you!"

Alasdair clenched his fists. His jaw ground so hard it hurt. "Lie! You cast her out and forbade her to take me. *That* is the truth."

Tazia quieted then replied. "And I thank the Creator I kept you. The human killed your mother. He would have killed you, too."

"Nay!" Alasdair cried. "'Twas your own guards who killed my mother, or at the least caused her death. My father was not even there at the time."

"How can you know such a thing? You were just a babe."

"I know this because he was with Armadeous."

"Armadeous?" the queen whispered to herself. She stood in silence and Alasdair knew she recognized the name.

"You believe the lies of a dragon over me?"

"He has spoken more truth to me in one day than you have spoken in all my eight hundred years."

Tazia huffed. "Are you quite finished, Alasdair?"

"Nay. Today is the day for all truths. Upon my mother's death, my father came for me. He was not seen or heard from since. What became of him?" Alasdair caught his breath and waited for the answer he feared.

"Do you mean to say that Armadeous did not know this as well?" Tazia taunted.

Alasdair bristled at her haughtiness. "Answer me. Did you kill my father when he came for me?"

Tazia lifted her chin. "I did not."

"Did you *order* him slain?"

Tazia smirked. "I had not a choice. You are a prince of the fae."

"I was his son."

"He was not worthy of you."

"Worthy of me? He is a part of me."

Tazia stepped down from the dais and stood before Alasdair. Taller than most female fae, she faced him eye to eye. "What do you want of me, Alasdair? To forgive your crimes and spare your life?"

"*My* crimes!"

Tazia turned from him, ignoring his outburst. "I will grant you your life in exchange for your silence," she said facing him once more. "No one is to know the truth of the dust or the lie of immortality. For this, I will release the woman and one child back to the human realm. The other must be tithed. You choose which one."

A feral roar filled the room. Alasdair grabbed the collar of her cloak and twisted it until the knuckles of his fists bore into her throat. His gaze narrowed, his jaw tightened, every muscle in his face tensed. Tazia's face paled. Recalling his promise to Edeline, he released her with a shove. His breath came fast and heavy as he fought his rage.

Tazia gasped hoarsely. "Guards!" she shouted.

The two guards burst into the room, swords drawn. Alasdair spun to face them.

Tazia gasped.

Alasdair looked over his shoulder at Tazia. "You have just noticed?" he taunted.

"You are fully human!"

"Aye, as human as my father."

Tazia stepped back from him. "Fool! Who has done this to you?" She stilled in realization. "Armadeous," she whispered.

Alasdair scoffed, "Aye. Will you grant me clemency now?"

"You are not worthy of clemency." Tazia shouted over Alasdair's shoulder, "Kill him!"

Faerie Dust / Linda Ciletti

Chapter Twenty-Six

Faerie

"Alasdair has protection against the magic of the fae," Armadeous informed Leisa. "You do not. Should you find him, stay close to his side. The wall of protection surrounding him will shield you as well."

"And Sybil?"

"Aye. But you must be joined."

"Joined?"

"Touching."

"I understand." Leisa slipped into braies and a tunic from the trunk. She wound a gird strap about her waist, then turned to Armadeous. "Do you think he's there yet?" She pulled on a pair of soft leather boots and laced them to the knees.

"Aye." Armadeous looked out at the early afternoon sun. "Now is his time of reckoning."

"I have to get there," Leisa said as she slipped into a leather jerkin, then strapped a long dagger at her side. The smell of the leather reminded her of Alasdair, of the many times he'd held and protected her. Tears filled her eyes. She fought them back. "Just take me across the river to the woods. I'll find the rest of the way from there."

Armadeous shook his massive head. "He will not like it."

"I don't care. Sybil is in trouble, and I'm the only mother she has."

"But you are not her mother. You are Sachi's mother. Your place is here with her."

"Don't you dare tell me where my place is." Leisa tore a strip of cloth from her discarded gown and tied back her hair. "When my sister died, I became Sybil's mother."

"And now you choose between them?"

Leisa glared at Armadeous. "I choose to help the one in trouble. I trust that Sachi is safe with you."

Armadeous smirked. "Are you sure 'tis not for love of Alasdair that you risk your life?"

Leisa fell silent. "I would be lying if I said it had nothing to do with Ali," she finally replied. "I'm going for both of them."

Armadeous shook his head and snorted. "Humans." He nodded at Sachi as she slept on the bedding behind the boulder. "What is your plan for her? Your true child?"

Leisa looked at Sachi. Young, innocent, and sleeping peacefully. "She trusts you now. Stay with Alasdair's plan. Bring her north of the gate at the appointed time." Leisa knelt beside a slumbering Sachi and kissed her smooth forehead; she breathed in the innocent scent of childhood. After a last look at Sachi, she stood and walked toward Armadeous. "Take care of her."

"And should you two fail to survive?"

Leisa's throat tightened. "Take care of her," she repeated. She stepped toward the brightly lit cave entrance. The sun was high in the sky, it was slightly past the noon hour. "Hurry, before she wakes up. I don't want her to wake up alone."

Armadeous huffed. A spiral of smoke rose to the ceiling. It twisted and turned, then spread wide and dissipated. "Never before have I been reduced to a nursemaid," he mumbled to himself as he headed for the ledge.

Leisa walked beside him. She turned to hide her smile. "Armadeous," she said.

"Aye."

"What of Deliterous?"

"What of him?"

"What kind of dragon is he?"

"Young and impetuous, but not beyond reasoning. Why do you ask?"

"I just wondered. Is he anything like you? I mean, does he believe in the prophecy and would he help achieve it if he were needed?"

"Deliterous would do all that he must to bring back the old ways. When Tazia lost her mother to illness and became queen, the old ways changed. Tazia's lust for treasure, power, and immortality drove her mad. It fell upon Deliterous and me to protect the other realms from her mounting greed. 'Tis why we guard the rivers, to keep the fae at bay. Had they no fear of us, their growing numbers would spread throughout the other realms, creating a single world. A world ruled by Tazia."

"You said her mother died from illness. I thought the fae could die only from accidental death or murder."

"No fae has yet died of old age. But illness can strike any living creature. The fae are not exempt. Only the magic of the dust protects them, magic gained through the suffering of others."

"What if Tazia were no longer queen? Would that change?"

"'Twould depend upon her successor. Were her successor more concerned with the balance of the universe and fairness to all living creatures, much would change. Granted, some fae would fall to illness. It is the natural order of the cycle of life. Sacrifice is not." He turned to Leisa. "The prophecy dictates the coming of the defender of humankind. Alasdair. It does not guarantee an outcome. The futures of human and fae rest upon him."

Both fell silent, contemplating that future.

"Come," Armadeous said. He encircled Leisa with his talons and lifted her from the ground. "I hope you have made a wise choice in going."

Leisa caught her breath and clung tightly to a talon as Armadeous leapt from the cliff and spread his wings. Wind whistled through the gaps between his claws and ruffled her hair. *Me, too*, she thought. She watched as they passed over the cliffs and skimmed the border of the Sprite Wood. It smelled of forest greenery and moss. Then they crossed the River of Tears to the forest that bordered the city square and maze. When they touched down at a clearing in the trees, Armadeous released her.

"Can you find your way from here and through the maze?" he asked.

"I think so. We traveled this way to cross the river. And the night of the wedding, Ali and I went through the maze. It leads to the children's play area and probably behind the palace to the forgotten garden. I remember an old door back there. We slipped into the palace that way."

"Good. Then I shall return to Sachi so she awakens not alone. Remember, Alasdair has protection. Find him and you will have it, too." He lifted his wings for flight.

Leisa nodded. She started for the shelter of the trees, then stopped suddenly and turned to face the dragon. "Armadeous?" she called.

Armadeous lowered his wings and turned his glittery gold gaze on her. "Aye?"

"Thank you."

A slow smile crossed the dragon's pearlescent face. "May the Creator be with you and Alasdair this day," he replied. Then he spread his wings and headed for the mountain.

~*~

Alasdair spun away from the guards and drew his sword. He watched Tazia climb several steps to the dais, the train of her gem-studded gown dragging behind her. The jewels on her gown began to glow, and he knew she was drawing on their power. He sensed a presence behind him and ducked. The glint of a sword passed over his head, its breeze lifting his hair. He jumped out of sword reach and readied his own.

Tazia clapped her hands, slowly and deliberately. "Well done, Alasdair. I see, though human, you have not forgotten your training."

Alasdair's lips curled as he parried a thrust. He lunged forward and riposted. The clash of swords echoed off the walls, followed by the shrill of sliding metal. Again swords clashed and he stumbled back. He felt an unseen power pull at him. Quickly, he drew the talisman out from the folds of his cowl and clasped it in his free hand, forcing the magic back. From the corner of his vision he saw Tazia scowl.

The second guard circled behind him, and the vision of a sword felling him flashed before his eyes. Alasdair dropped and rolled, slicing the guard's ankle. The guard yelped, stumbled, and fell to the floor. Clamoring metal rang through the chamber as his sword bounced across pure marble before falling silent.

Alasdair heard the guard groan and felt a pang of guilt, but there was no time for regrets. His hand had fallen away from the talisman and he again felt the pull of Tazia. He grasped the talisman hard in his fist, felt its warmth seep deeply into his flesh. With his sword hand, he parried the second guard's blow, then swung low to block a thrust. Beyond the clash of swords, he heard Tazia cry out in anger. She grasped a pike from the wall and stormed at him. Alasdair leveled his eyes at her. "Tazia, nay!" He raised a hand and struck the air before him.

Suddenly she flew back off her feet and slammed against the wall. The guard turned at the spectacle and Alasdair struck him with the hilt of his sword. The guard crumpled unconscious to the floor.

Tazia stirred.

Alasdair swiftly slipped through the chamber's open doors and into the hall.

Edeline stood in the outer hall, trembling. "Have you killed her?" Her voice shook, and the fear in her eyes pained him.

"Nay, Edeline. I made a vow." He cupped her cheek with his hand. "She lives," he assured her.

Edeline sighed in relief.

"How long have you stood here?" he asked.

"Long enough." Sadness clouded Edeline's eyes. "Oh, Alasdair. I am so sorry." She handed the guard's band she had found in Tazia's chamber out to Alasdair. "Take this." She placed it in his outstretched hand. "Should you see Gideon, give it to him." Her eyes filled with regret. "He may have need of it."

Alasdair slipped the band over his wrist. Tazia's voice bellowed from the great hall chamber.

"Hurry! This way." Edeline grabbed Alasdair's arm and led him toward the kitchen and the secret door. "'Tis the only way out that is safe and 'tis closest to the girl."

Alasdair wondered how secret the door truly was.

When they pushed through the door to a small clearing in the weed-strewn garden, two guards waited. One grabbed Edeline and held her locked against him, a dagger at her throat. The other held onto Sybil by the scruff of her pajama top.

Alasdair froze.

"Ali!" Sybil cried. She struggled against the guard's brutal hold but could not break free.

Edeline tugged against the guard who held her. "Release me at once!" she ordered.

The guard's eyes widened. "Lady Edeline! I knew not that it was you." He lowered the blade but kept his hold.

Again Edeline struggled. "I said, release me."

"I cannot. You are directly aiding a criminal. Queen Tazia must decide your fate."

Alasdair readied his sword. He knew the guard holding Edeline would not harm her. Sybil was another matter.

"Surrender, Alasdair." The guard holding Sybil lifted his dagger to her face. "Or I shall cut her throat."

Alasdair glanced at his readied sword, then turned it flat before him. Crouching low to the ground, he set it on the grass.

"Now back away," the guard ordered.

Alasdair stood and took several steps back from his weapon. His head fell back and his eyes began to flutter.

The guard dragged Sybil with him as he approached Alasdair, his gaze watchful and wary. "What the—"

The door of the garden shed flung open. A shovel flew from its depths and struck the guard in the head. He fell still in the grass.

"Run, Sybil!" Alasdair yelled. He dove for his sword.

Sybil ducked behind the shed.

The second guard flung Edeline to the ground. Blade drawn, he jumped forward and slammed his boot onto Alasdair's weapon, resting his sword at Alasdair's throat.

Alasdair felt the cold point of the blade prick his flesh. Blood trickled down his neck. Slowly he rose, his eyes watchful of the guard's sword as it rose with him.

"And now?" Alasdair asked. "Would you kill me?" He raised his hands in surrender as he tried calling up something that would aid in his escape. But his thoughts would not leave the tip of the blade at his neck. He saw Edeline rise and run to comfort Sybil.

"The queen will not fault me for it. 'Twill save her the trouble," the guard replied. He tapped his sword against Alasdair's shoulder. "Turn around and kneel."

Alasdair turned and sank to his knees. He tried to focus, to fell the very trees if need be, but his thoughts ran rampant in one direction, then another. He thought of Leisa and Sachi safe with Armadeous and hoped the dragon would keep his promise to send them through the gate. He thought of Sybil, who would be tithed upon his death. And of his two friends. He wondered where they were now. Alasdair fought to cast his thoughts aside so that he could focus enough to move the very earth. He failed. Then the shadow of the sword fell over him. He pulled a final breath and, in that moment of calm, sensed a presence.

A painful groan sounded behind him. The shadow disappeared and he rolled to the side. When the guard stumbled forward and fell, Alasdair saw Leisa standing behind him, her hands covering her face. The sheath at her side was empty and he had no doubt where the blade could be found. He jumped to his feet and grabbed her in an embrace. "Leisa, why are you here?"

Leisa stepped back from him and cupped his face in her hands as though to confirm he lived. "I—I'm here to save you."

Alasdair smiled and gave her a fierce hug. He spun away and called out to Sybil.

"Aunt Leis!" Sybil cried. She ran toward Leisa, her arms spread wide.

"Sibby. Oh, God. Sibby." Leisa dropped to her knees, opened her arms, and caught Sybil as she crashed into her. "I was so worried."

Gideon hurried around the corner of the palace wall supporting Sachi with one hand, brandishing a sword in the other. Lysander followed close behind.

Alasdair swore. "Why is Sachi not with Armadeous? I asked but one request."

Gideon spoke. "Armadeous left her at the maze. He said there would be no time for you to come for her. He said that the love of four is the strongest magic of all."

"He has placed her in danger." Alasdair took Sachi in his arms and braced her on his hip. She grabbed his neck and clung tight. Bending forward, he picked up his sword from the ground. "I cannot fight like this."

"'Tis why we are here." Gideon clapped his back. "We will protect you."

Alasdair slid the guard band off his wrist and handed it to Gideon. "You may need this."

"By the fates, how did you come by this?" Gideon asked as he slid the band over his hand.

"Edeline."

Gideon glanced at Edeline and smiled, then turned back to his friend. "Come. We must go before the entire army is alerted to what has happened.

"How knew you where to find me?"

Lysander chuckled. "'We did not. When we saw Leisa heading for the forgotten garden, we followed her."

Edeline ran up to Alasdair. She kissed his cheek, hugged him as best she could with Sachi balanced on his side, and smiled regrettably. "Fare you well, cousin. Though you be human, may the magic of the fae keep you safe."

Alasdair returned her smile, stroked her cheek, and turned away. He held out his hand to Leisa. "Stay near to me. The talisman protects me from Tazia's magic. If we stay as one, I deem it will protect you as well."

Leisa nodded. "Armadeous said as much."

"Hurry," Lysander called. He led them into the trees and out of sight. When they reached the play area, he scanned it quickly, then led them through. "Once we reach the Galandorian Gate, pass through quickly. We will do our best to hold back the guards."

From the play area, they entered the maze. Alasdair's heart pounded at every turn. No guards came as they approached the exit to the market square, and he could see the Galandorian Gate in the distance. "Look," he said to Leisa. "We are almost there."

Leisa tightened her hold on Sybil while gripping the hem of Alasdair's shirt.

"I don't see any guards," Lysander said. "Let us make haste."

Alasdair pulled Lysander back. "Nay. Something is wrong."

They stopped short.

"He is right. There should be at the least two guards at the gate," Gideon said. He edged toward the exit, staying close to the tall hedge, and ran a quick perusal over the square. It was as wide and long as an open field, with various businesses strewn throughout the open market. People milled around, inspecting wares. It was a typical day but for the missing guards.

"'Haps they are merely changing shifts. 'Twas how I slipped through the first time," Alasdair said.

"Nay." Lysander tapped his chin. "Too much time has passed without a man on duty."

"'Tis what they want us to think," Gideon added. "That the guards change and the gate is unprotected."

Alasdair scanned the market square, then closed his eyes and concentrated. The square reeked of fearful anticipation. "I sense their presence," he said. He peeled Sachi's arms from his neck and lowered her to the ground. "Stay close with Leisa and Sybil," he said. Then he drew his sword.

"The magic of four," Lysander reminded him.

"I know not what that means," Alasdair replied. "Damn Armadeous and his cryptic advice." He looked at Leisa. "Know you what it means?"

Leisa shook her head. "I think it means that the more people who are joined through love, the more powerful their magic. But I don't know how we can use it for protection." She took Sybil's and Sachi's hands in hers and gave them a squeeze.

Alasdair swallowed hard and raised his sword before him.

"Go slowly," Gideon cautioned everyone. "And stay alert."

They stepped into the open market, with Alasdair, Leisa, and the girls in the center, Lysander and Gideon flanking them on either side. Townsfolk continued to mill about as usual. Now and again, someone's eyes would lift to them, then quickly fall.

Alasdair caught his breath. It was indeed a trap.

Chapter Twenty-Seven

Faerie

Guards, readied for battle, appeared from behind market buildings, trees, and carts. Alasdair spun for a quick count. Twenty in all circled the square. Ten gathered along the Galandorian Gate, and another ten in front of the maze. The guards surrounded them from both sides. Frantic villagers ran or flew from the market square out of the line of battle. Alasdair looked overtop the maze at the palace. He saw Tazia standing high on the ornate balcony outside her chamber, her jewel-studded gown weighing heavily on her. Her crimson cloak flapped in the wind. Though she stood far in the distance, the screech of her voice carried on the wind.

"You had your chance, Alasdair," she cried out. "Now you will *all* die."

Lysander and Gideon readied to fight. Alasdair stepped back toward the gate, his eyes fixed on Tazia. Leisa and the girls followed closely. As Tazia's power pulled at him, he felt his energy drain. He clutched the talisman. Again it warmed his hand, warding the magic back, but it was not enough. The jewels on Tazia's gown glowed brighter than before as she drew on the power of the stones. She combined the magic of the air with that of the earth.

"Ali?" Leisa worried her lip and touched him.

The talisman grew hot.

Alasdair dropped it in surprise, then picked it up.

"What is it?" Leisa asked.

"I know not." He clenched it in his fist. It was warm. "Touch me again, Leisa." When Leisa touched his arm, the talisman heated and began to glow. He could see Tazia throwing spells at him, but the shield of the talisman deflected them. Tazia grabbed a torch from the wall and held it high in the air. She was calling on the magic of fire.

Again Alasdair felt her power strike the shield. The shield weakened some. "Draw together," he said to Leisa and the girls.

Leisa pulled the girls close to her side. "Hold onto me," she instructed them. She wrapped one arm about Alasdair's waist.

The talisman grew hot in his hand. He covered it completely so as not to look at it. The heat intensified until he was sure it scorched his flesh; surprisingly he felt no pain.

It was an intensity of power he had never known existed. Tazia's magic bounced back and dissipated in the breeze.

Tazia let loose a fierce cry, and a dozen heads appeared over the battlement wall.

"Archers!" Gideon warned.

The hiss of arrows sliced the air. Alasdair shielded Leisa and the girls the best he could. *The talisman will protect you from faerie magic only, not physical danger*, he recalled Armadeous saying. He felt Gideon and Lysander move close to help shield the girls and readied for the arrows to strike. When none came, he looked up. Lysander's and Gideon's bands were raised high. They had deflected them.

Another volley of arrows sounded. Again the two held them off.

"Step closer to the guards," Gideon advised. His breath was labored. Alasdair knew his power was weakening.

"Closer?" Leisa gulped.

"Closer," Gideon repeated. "The archers will not shoot if they chance hitting their own."

"Aye," Alasdair replied. "But we will be engaged in battle."

Gideon grinned. "'Tis not a perfect plan, but a better choice, think you not? At least in combat, we stand a chance."

"Can't we just fly out of here?" Leisa asked.

"Have you forgotten? I am human now. The four of us would be too much for Lysander and Gideon."

"Pay heed!" Gideon admonished. He pointed to the battlement wall.

Alasdair looked up. A line of archers readied to shoot another volley. He turned to his two friends. "Cross your bands."

"Cross our bands?" Lysander scratched his head. "Why?"

The archers raised their bows.

"Just do it!"

Lysander and Gideon stepped close.

"Close your eyes when you do," Alasdair warned. He turned to Leisa. "You, also." Unsure the girls would shield their eyes, he grabbed Sachi and tucked her face against his shoulder. Leisa covered Sybil's eyes with her hands.

Lysander and Gideon raised their arms, closed their eyes, and crossed wrists so that their bands touched.

Blinding light speared over the palace and its grounds. Painful cries sounded all around them. Still they kept their eyes protected. When the cries fell away to groans, Lysander and Gideon uncrossed their bands and opened their eyes. Guards writhed on the ground, rubbing at their faces. The archers had fallen from sight. Only Tazia remained on the battlement, protected by her greater magic. The air about her glowed with vibrant energy as she called on the power of the stones.

More guards emerged from the maze with their swords drawn and readied to strike. The tall hedge had protected their eyes, and they came at the group with force.

"Now what?" Lysander asked.

"There are fewer on the gate side," Gideon called. "Make your way there. Quickly."

A huge shadow fell over them. They dropped to the ground.

"What was that?" Leisa asked. She heard the girls whimper and pulled them close.

Alasdair looked skyward. Armadeous soared over the market square, his head held high and drawn back, his throat glowing. Alasdair pushed Leisa down and threw himself over the girls.

A stream of fire fell from the heavens, laying a scorching path in front of the converging guards as the market carts burst into flame. Alasdair felt the heat of it on his back. He rose quickly. After pulling the girls to their feet, he and Leisa shuffled them toward the gate. Lysander and Gideon battled in front of it. Swords clashed and rang. An exalted royal guard broke free and came at Leisa.

Leisa reached for her dagger. It was gone. She pushed the girls behind her.

Alasdair stepped in front of her. He widened his stance and raised his sword. A stifling breeze ruffled his hair. Hot flames reflected in the ebony locks. The guard ran an assessing gaze over him.

"Surrender, Alasdair," the guard ordered.

"Nay!" Alasdair swung his sword in a wide arc. "Stand down and let us pass."

"Be not a fool. You cannot best me," the guard warned. His band glowed. Alasdair knew he drew on its magic, so he swung before it gained full power.

"Stand back!" Alasdair ordered. His blow was parried, and he retreated to gain his footing. When the guard advanced and thrust his blade, Alasdair lunged and parried it off to the side. Its razored tip caught his sleeve and ripped the length of it. Swords clashed until both men felt the weariness of battling an equal adversary. Again the guard lifted his sword. Alasdair raised his weapon, swung, and locked blades. He pressed against the strength of the guard until his arms ached at the strain. Still, he found himself stumbling back.

"Surrender!" the guard repeated.

"Never!" Alasdair reached deep and drew on inner strength. Again he pressed, this time forcing the guard back a step. Their swords fell to the side and slid apart. They both stumbled back. Alasdair caught his breath. Quickly he raised his sword to block a blow. When the guard pushed forward and knocked him down, Alasdair rolled to avoid being pierced, then jumped to his feet. He saw his sword lying on the ground and grabbed for it, but it was far out of reach. Again the guard swung. Alasdair jumped aside and stumbled back.

"You are done for, Alasdair," the guard taunted as he dogged Alasdair's steps. "You should have surrendered."

"For what reason? To die a dishonorable death later? Nay. I will not surrender to that."

The guard thrust his blade. Alasdair felt the sting of it on his arm. Blood trickled through his tunic.

"Give up, Alasdair. You have no weapon."

"But I do!" Leisa shouted over the guard's shoulder.

The guard spun with force and swung his blade. Leisa parried it with Alasdair's sword, the force of the hit causing her to fall.

"Nay!" Alasdair shouted. He tackled the guard, knocking him to the ground and the sword from his grasp. They wrestled and rolled. Pulling back his fist, Alasdair struck him hard in the face.

The guard's eyes rolled back, and he lay unmoving.

Alasdair jumped to his feet. After slipping the guard's dagger from its sheath, he rushed to Leisa. "Are you all right?" he asked. He took her hand and pulled her up from the ground.

Leisa nodded and dusted off her clothes. "I'm okay."

Alasdair looked frantically around. "Where are Sachi and Sybil?"

"They're okay."

Lysander approached. "Where are the girls?"

"Sachi! Sybil!" Leisa called. Sachi and Sybil crawled out from beneath a surviving market wagon and ran to them.

Gideon grinned, then quickly sobered. "More guards will be sent," he warned. "Go now, while it is clear."

Alasdair nodded and slipped the guard's dagger into the empty sheath at Leisa's side.

"Look!" Leisa cried, pointing to the sky. A massive red form soared through the clouds. It circled twice, then dove.

Lysander gasped. "By the stars! 'Tis the red dragon. And in full day."

Deliterous approached the palace and sprayed it with fire. Everyone took cover. All but Tazia.

Edeline raced into Tazia's chamber. "Mother, come inside," she cried.

Tazia laughed as she called on the magic of the elements for protection. Her bejeweled gown glowed brighter still.

"Mother, please."

"Earth magic is the strongest. No flame can touch me!" Again Tazia laughed, a high, maniacal laugh that made Edeline shiver. When Deliterous hovered before Tazia, she spread her wings fully, taunting him.

Deliterous narrowed his gaze, drew back his head, and shot a stream of flame. Fire wrapped about the shield protecting Tazia and struck the wall behind her, setting it to glow. The force of the strike sent Tazia stumbling backward. She heard the sizzle before feeling the red-hot stone at her back. Flames raced up her wings, scorching her aura. Tazia shrieked. Throwing herself away from the heat, she stumbled backward into the battlement wall.

"Nay!" Edeline screamed. She raced onto the balcony and grabbed for Tazia's outstretched hand, but her reach fell short and Tazia slipped between the crenellations and disappeared. Her cry was brief, silenced by a sickening thud.

"Mother!" Edeline cried.

~*~

"Go through now!" Gideon yelled.

A troop of palace guards approached from the forest. Wolflyches howled in the distance. Alasdair turned to Gideon. "What of you and Lysander?"

"Worry not of us. We can take care of ourselves." Lysander clapped Alasdair's back. "Go."

"Were our powers not so spent," Gideon said as he struggled to devise a plan, "we could create another blinding shield and escape unnoticed."

Alasdair smiled. This time, *he* was the strategist. "Link together," he said to Leisa and the girls. Drawing the pouch Edeline had given him from his side, he pulled it fully open. "Prepare to disappear," he called to his friends. He held the pouch up high. "Farewell, Lysander ... Gideon. You will not be forgotten."

"Nor you," Lysander replied

"Not in all the millennia of my life," Gideon added.

Alasdair whipped the open bag high into the air. "Shield your eyes!" he warned as it twisted and spun, casting faerie dust in all directions. A storm of particles lifted on the breeze and filled the air, then slowly floated down around them. Alasdair clutched the talisman in his hand and faced it into the falling dust. Soon the brilliant light of the talisman reflected off each tiny grain, creating a blinding rainbow of light. He wrapped his arms about Leisa and the girls. "Come," he said as he led them out of the light and through the Galandorian gate.

Human World

The dense, aged forest smelled strongly of moss and rain. Its brush, as tall as a man, spilled out onto the trail. Sunlight struggled through the foliage, stippling the path and setting the leaves to glow intermittently, while strands of twisted vines spiraled to the ground like masses of verdant hair.

Leisa ran a guarded gaze over the massive woodlands surrounding them. "Where are we?" she asked. She handed Alasdair his sword, then clasped Sachi's and Sybil's hands tightly in hers.

"In the deepest forest of Canada," Alasdair replied.

Sybil's eyes drooped. Alasdair picked her up, balanced her against his shoulder, and began walking swiftly.

"Why here?" Leisa asked, hurrying after him with Sachi close at her side.

"The wolflyches will follow. They do not relent."

"Then why the middle of nowhere? In the city we could have gotten protection." Leisa felt Sachi stumble and stopped.

Alasdair paused to look back at her. "From whom? The police? The police cannot protect you from the dark side of the known world. Humans are fragile creatures, even those in authority."

"*You* are human." Leisa reminded him.

Alasdair looked down at his new and declining body. Declining because he was equal to a third of the way through the years promised a human. But it was worth it to spend his short-lived eternity with Leisa.

Sybil sniffled. She held her arms out to Leisa. "Aunt Leis?" she whimpered.

Alasdair transferred Sybil to Leisa and picked up Sachi. "Come." He shifted Sachi in his arms. "We must hurry." He began pushing a trail through the brush.

"Hurry?" Leisa tightened her hold on Sybil and raced to keep up with his long strides. Sybil's sleepy head dropped to her shoulder. "Hurry where? There's nothing here but trees." She looked around. "And more trees."

A crash sounded behind them. Leisa jumped, waking Sybil.

Alasdair paused and listened. "They follow," he warned. He picked up speed.

"How do you know?"

"A wolflych cannot pass through the gate without setting off an alarm. They are the most dangerous of the queen's fae guard and can leave the realm only by her authority. If the alarm sounds and they were not dispatched by orders of the queen, they are hunted down and killed."

"Then why would they dare to cross it and set off the alarm?"

"The queen is dead. Until Edeline takes her place as queen, they are free to do what they will."

Leisa gasped. "And they *will* to kill us."

Alasdair glanced at her over his shoulder. "Stay close."

Leisa crushed the back of his shirt in her fist, needing to touch him. Her side ached as she fought to keep stride and she could barely catch her breath.

Rustling sounded in the brush, followed by a chorus of deep-throated growls. When they reached a clearing, Alasdair stopped and thrust Sachi into her arms as well, then drew his sword. He motioned her behind him. The clearing was small, but it allowed a full view of the treeline. If he had to make a stand, Leisa reasoned, it would be here where he could see danger approaching.

Leisa struggled to hold onto the weight of both girls. Finally, she set them down beside her and drew them close to her sides. "Hold onto me," she said.

"Aunt Leis," Sybil cried. Tears rolled down her soft cheeks as she clung to Leisa's leg. "Can we go home now? I don't think I like fairies very much."

Leisa's eyes watered. "Soon," she promised, her throat constricting at the lie. "Very soon."

Brutish, four-legged beasts slunk out from the tangled shrubbery, their wolfish bodies thick, muscular, and covered in heavy coats of dark, bristly fur. Their heads, broad between the ears, narrowed to gaping angular jaws and sharp protruding teeth. They were grotesquely mutated wolfish beasts with orange eyes that pierced the shadowy darkness of the woods. Leisa caught her breath at their ferocity, which far exceeded the illusion in the Sprite Wood.

The lead wolflych snarled and stepped forward, facing Alasdair. His voice was deep, raspy, and venomous. "What foolishness to think you could out run us," he said. "No one has ever escaped a wolflych. And no one ever shall." He padded several steps toward Alasdair.

"Hold!" Alasdair lowered his sword, setting its razored tip inches from the wolflych's face.

The creature spewed a guttural laugh. He nodded toward the other four beasts. "You cannot kill us all," he said in a thick raspy tone, a victorious grin twisting his snout.

"Nay. I cannot." Alasdair agreed. "So I shall kill only you."

"Whilst the others tear the woman and children apart?" the creature goaded.

"Is there another way?" Alasdair asked. "Is there a way to spare them?"

Again the creature laughed. "No. All must die."

Leisa gasped. She looked at Alasdair, who held his ground despite the futility.

"Then I will not lie down and accept my fate," Alasdair replied. "Nor that of those I love." He regripped the hilt of his sword. "If we must die, then so shall you."

"And the others?" Again the creature nodded to his companions.

"I care not of the others. It is you who will join us in death."

The creature snorted. "Then you shall watch the woman and children die first." He signaled to his four companions. "Kill them, but leave Alasdair to me."

Leisa hugged the girls close, kissed the tops of their heads, and readied her dagger to fight a battle she knew she could not win.

The creatures circled the four, snorting and snarling, their eyes sharp and focused on their prey. They nipped at their clothes, taunting them. Sachi began to sob, then Sybil.

"How could you?" Leisa screamed. "How could you kill innocent children?"

"'Tis an easy enough feat," one of the circling wolflyches replied.

"And humans are such a tasty repast," another chimed in. "Especially the small ones." Its tongue flicked out over its lips.

"End this amusement," the lead wolflych ordered. "Kill them now."

"Nay!" Alasdair shouted. He lunged forward but was thrown off balance by a sudden shaking of the ground.

Leisa grabbed onto Alasdair to keep from falling. "What's happening?" she cried. She loosed Alasdair and fell to her knees, pulling Sybil and Sachi close.

"I know not."

Losing the battle to stay afoot, Alasdair dropped to his knees beside them. Huddled together, they watched as two enormous beasts broke through the ground and rose in front of them.

Alasdair stared in wonderment. Ground Dragons. Nasty brutal creatures that burrowed beneath the earth and fed on anything that was not their own species. Alasdair had heard tales of such, but never had he seen one. Their bodies were long and thick and covered in metallic scales that would put the hardness of a diamond to shame. Their armored heads were elongated, rising from a narrow chin to a wide forehead that ended in protruding spikes on either side. They had several rows of blade-sharp teeth that could slice through rock as easily as flesh. He dropped his weapon and wrapped his arms around Leisa and the girls. A sword was of no use here. "I love you," he whispered. "All of you." Sybil wept and he cradled her against him.

Leisa clung to Sachi and squeezed Alasdair's arm in reply.

Thick drool dropped from above and landed inches away from them.

Alasdair dared to look up. The black scaled dragon loomed over them, its hard eyes scanning the clearing. He caught his breath.

Suddenly the dragon's head plunged to the ground. It snapped up the lead wolflych in its massive jaws. Blood sprayed the surrounding trees. In seconds the wolflych was gone. The white dragon grabbed another, biting it in two.

"Oh, God!" Leisa cried. She buried Sachi's face against her shoulder and her own face against Alasdair.

A howl of retreat rent the air, and the remaining three wolflyches fled for their lives. Moments later, the sound of the Galandorian Gate closing could be heard. The wolflyches had crossed back to Faerie.

The white dragon slid back beneath the earth. The black one remained. Drool dripped from the corners of its mouth as it stared down at them with glittering gold eyes.

Alasdair stood and faced the looming dragon. "Naois?" he said. His voice cracked with uncertainty. His heart raced. He hoped he was right.

The dragon twisted and shrank into a man with hair like night and golden wolfish eyes. "Once again we meet. Can you not stay out of trouble?" Naois sniffed the air, his expression bemused. "You are fully human now."

"Aye," Alasdair replied.

Naois shook his head. "You will die anon, you know."

"I know."

Naois nodded. "And these humans? Is this the child you wished to save?" He pointed to Sachi, recognizing her scent.

"Aye, she is the one."

Naois studied her. "Then I commend you. Well done. I had my doubts as to your success."

Alasdair grinned. "As did I."

Naois chuckled. "But you succeeded despite the odds. A true champion."

"Nay. Were it not for you, I would have failed."

"Had you not sought me out, you would have failed," Naois corrected. He smiled a wolfish grin. "Because you had the wisdom to seek me, you are victorious."

Alasdair nodded. "My thanks."

"Never did I think humans had such wisdom and sense. A bit of the fae must still remain in you." Naois's face suddenly saddened. "You know I cannot come to you again. We do not show ourselves to humans. They are frail but dangerous in their superstitious fears. What they do not understand, they destroy."

"*I* understand."

Naois howled, long and hollow. A white wolf with silver-tipped fur stepped out from the trees.

"In your frail human state, I cannot leave you in the midst of the deepest forest. Now that you are fully human, my thoughts cannot enter your head. So I will say my piece."

"Speak, my friend," Alasdair said.

"I shall take you to the nearest town. From there you must find your own way back home, wherever that may be." He looked at Leisa and grinned. "I deem I know where."

Alasdair smiled. "It is more than I dared hope."

"It is a last goodwill gesture to the faerie who was Alasdair. I would not show such kindness to a man."

"What about a woman and child?" Alasdair looked back at Leisa and the frightened girls. "Two children," he corrected. He took Leisa's arm and pulled her up beside him. The girls followed. "I would not go without them."

"This human form has made you soft." Naois chuckled. "But you were always half so and full of compassion, were you not?"

"You knew I was half human?"

"As I said, acute senses."

"And Leisa and the girls?" Alasdair asked.

Naois ran an assessing gaze over Leisa. "Is she your mate?"

Alasdair caught Leisa's gaze. He smiled warmly, then turned to Naois. "Aye. She is."

"Then she is worthy of our assistance."

The white wolf padded toward them. As she moved, she shifted into a white mare with a silver-tipped mane.

Alasdair motioned at her. "Is she *your* mate?" he asked.

Naois laughed, a laugh Alasdair recognized as coming from the heart. "You are quite observant for a human," he said. "She is Anona. And aye, she is my mate."

"Then you found what you were seeking?"

"Aye. As did you."

Alasdair grinned. "I found more than what I sought." He hung his head. "But I was unable to save Queen Tazia."

"She is dead?"

"Aye."

"Did you slay her?"

Alasdair shook his head. "I would not do so."

"Out of love?"

"Out of compassion."

Naois nodded. "Climb up and we shall begin our journey." He began his transformation. In seconds, a black stallion with golden eyes stood before them.

Alasdair aided Leisa and Sachi onto the snowy, silver-maned mare.

"What do I hold onto?" Leisa asked. "There are no reins or saddle."

The black stallion shook his head.

"Hold onto the mane," Alasdair said. "'Twill be enough. Travel will be slow for the girls' sake." He set Sybil on Naois's back, then swung up behind her. "We are ready," he said.

~*~

Night had fallen by the time they reached the outskirts of a small woodland town. Alasdair slid from Naois's back, then helped Sybil down. Anona lowered herself so that Leisa and Sachi could easily dismount. It had been a long ride and most of it had been spent in silence. Sachi and Sybil had slept part of the way, and more than once Alasdair had caught Leisa fighting to keep her eyes open. Exhaustion weighed on him as well. He shook the pouch Armadeous had given him and heard the clatter of jewels. They would pay for the trip back to Leisa's home.

Naois shifted back to a man, his golden eyes fixed on Alasdair, his face soft with regret. Though Alasdair had met Naois only once before, he would miss him. He would miss everyone from the known world.

"Alasdair," Naois said as though confirming the name and setting it to memory. He clapped Alasdair's shoulder. "Blessed travels." Naois turned then and morphed into a black wolf. His mate, Anona, again became a white wolf with silver-tipped fur.

Alasdair watched as the two wolves speed into the darkness. "For you as well, my friend," he whispered.

Leisa sighed. "I can't believe it's over." She wiped the dampness from her cheeks with her sleeve.

Sachi tugged at Leisa's shirt. "Do not cry, Mother. All is well now."

Leisa picked up Sachi in her arms. She stroked her daughter's fiery hair and kissed her cheek. "Yes, it is. She hugged Sachi tightly, then turned to Sybil and smiled. "You have a sister, sweetie."

"Do you not mean cousin?" Alasdair asked.

"No, a sister. I plan to adopt Sybil when we get back."

"But did you not say that would be difficult lest you be wed?" Alasdair looked at Leisa. Despite the dust and masculine raiment that she wore, despite her scent of smoke and fire, he had never seen anyone so beautiful. From beneath her vibrant and disheveled hair, deep green eyes looked to him with passion and hope.

"Will you marry me?" Leisa asked.

Alasdair laughed. "Do you propose to me?"

Leisa bit her lip. "Yes."

"I did think it the other way around." Alasdair reached inside his leather pouch. Drawing it open, he drew forth the jewel that Armadeous had given him specifically for Leisa—the Meridian Star of Wisdom and Light. "There is not another gem like it in any realm, human or faerie. Later we shall set it in a ring for you to wear upon your finger ... if you will have me."

Leisa smiled. "I already asked."

"But I did already think to ask you. Are you reading my thoughts? Have you already honed your human gifts?"

Leisa laughed. Then she turned to Sachi and Sybil. "Will we have him?" she asked.

Sachi nodded excitedly. Sybil screeched her approval.

Leisa accepted the stone and held it to the light. Her breath caught. "It's beautiful."

"Nay. *You* are beautiful." Alasdair cradled Leisa's face in his hands and kissed her soundly.

Sachi and Sybil covered their eyes.

When his chest burned for want of breath, he released her. His hand slid along her neck and his fingers caught on the gold chain he had gifted to her. He lifted the leaf lavalier pendant carefully tucked inside her top to look on the twisted vines that had once graced the neck of his mother.

Leisa cupped his cheek with her hand and he leaned into her touch. "I'll never take it off," she reminded him.

Alasdair smiled; then he turned to the two waiting girls. He set Sachi high onto his shoulders and took hold of Leisa's and Sybil's hands. Then he turned to face the welcoming lights of town.

As they neared civilization, his smile quickly faded as his thoughts fell to Lysander and Gideon—on the price they could pay for aiding him. Would they be banished to the dark swamp or would they be forgiven for their part in Tazia's death?

"Ali?"

He turned to see Leisa and the girls watching him. His frown lifted. "Come." He gave Leisa's hand a reassuring squeeze. "Let us find our way home."

&

If you enjoyed this story, please leave a review.
(Amazon, Goodreads, Barnes & Noble)

Sneak Peak
Hearts of Faerie Series, Book 2
FAERIE KNIGHTS

"Edeline!" Lysander called. He raced down the marbled hall, skidded to a stop before the tall arched doors that led to Tazia's chamber. One door remained closed, the other fully open. Lysander crossed the threshold and glanced frantically about the room. His gaze swept over the singed curtains that led to the balcony, stopping at a lone figure lying face down on the floor. The shimmery blonde hair splayed across the stone told him it was Edeline.

His heart pounded. *Please, don't be dead.* He pushed aside the curtains and fell to his knees next to her. Turning her on her side, he rested her head on his lap. She lay limp in his arms, her eyes softly closed. The cheek that had been pressed against the stone was mildly red but not scorched. Her golden hair, once neatly pinned, fell loosely over her shoulders.

He brushed it back, revealing a beautifully flawless face. "Edeline," he said softly. He stroked her cheek and a teary trail met his hand. "Edeline, 'tis Lysander."

Edeline moaned lightly. Her eyes, blue and bright with tears, lifted. "The red dragon," she cried. "Mother fell. I tried to save her, but I failed. I failed …" A choke cut off her words. She turned and, grasping him about the waist, buried her face against him and wept into his tabard.

At a loss for words, he held her in silence. "I am sorry," he finally replied.

Faerie Dust / Linda Ciletti

Reviews

Faerie Dust
Hearts of Faerie Series, Book One

"I selected this book as one from Amazon and am thrilled that I did. It is excellent …" *Amazon Review (5 stars)*

"…The characters are very well defined. I finished this book in two days and can't wait to see what else the author has coming up!" *Amazon Review (5 stars)*

"I don't usually read romance, but I like a good fantasy adventure and this delivers for readers of either."
Amazon Review (4 Stars)

Draegon's Lair
Epic Award Winner for Best Historical Romance

For lovers of historical romance, this is a book that should be on your shelf." *Coffeetime Romance Reviews*

"A powerful love story. It will leave you anxious for the turn of each page." *Scribesworld*

"I am in complete awe. Prepare to be swept away. Among the best medievals I've read." *MyShelf*

"Phenomenal. Gets harder and harder to put down."
Rogues and Romance Reviews

"One of the best medievals I've read. Well done, Ms. Ciletti, well done." *Ann B. Keller, Author of Briggen*

KnightStalker

"Kept me glued to the pages. Ms. Ciletti is a talented author, with a skill to bring her characters to life, and to create people that the reader will truly care about." *Catanetwork*

"This gripping tale from Linda Ciletti took my breath away and will take yours too. A superb tale that shouldn't be missed. B*etween the Lines Reviews*

"I enjoyed reading this book." *Amazon Review (5 Stars)*

"The love in this book is palpable and makes a wonderful read." *Amazon Review (5 Stars)*

"Truly a great read. Ms Ciletti writes in such a way that brings you into the story itself. A must read for fans of romance and time travel. You will not be disappointed." *Amazon Review (5 Stars)*

Dream of the Archer

"Exciting historical romance from the period of Robin Hood with many twists and turns along the way." *Amazon Review (4 Stars)*

"Original storyline that captures the imagination." *Amazon Review (5 Stars)*

"I thoroughly loved and so enjoyed this most wonder[ful] classic." *Amazon Review (5 Stars)*

Lady Quest
"What a delightful, rollicking good tale this is!" *Amazon Review (5 Stars)*

"This was a great read! I laughed almost from start to finish!" *Amazon Review (5 Stars)*

ABOUT THE AUTHOR

Linda Ciletti grew up in Pittsburgh, Pennsylvania, where she discovered her love for classic fairytales during her many childhood visits to the Carnegie Public Library in Hazelwood. She now resides in a quaint bungalow in the beautiful Western Pennsylvanian suburbs. She is a member of the Greensburg Writers Group, Ligonier Valley Writers, and a former member of Romance Writers of America.

A fan of "happily ever afters", Linda writes romantic adventures in the genres of medieval historical, time travel paranormal, contemporary, and fantasy. Her medieval historical, *Draegon's Lair*, won an Epic Award for best historical romance. Other published novels include *Lady Quest*, *KnightStalker*, and *Dream of the Archer*. Her poems and photos have been featured in literary magazines and her sole foray into horror, "The Hunger" has been both podcasted and published in the anthology, *The Wickeds*.

When not serving the writing muse, Linda immerses herself in illustration and graphics, doing photography, virtual world content creation, and book cover design.

Her favorite childhood fairytale? *Beauty and the Beast.*

Visit Linda at Facebook

Made in the USA
Middletown, DE
10 July 2024